Praise for
The Second Thirteen

ROBERT WERDEN - retired publicist of the Academy Awards, Los Angeles

"A complex, powerful story ... makes for terrific reading. Characters are image-rich and intense. You'll be swept away with this carefully crafted novel of deceit and murder."

———————

SAMELA HARRIS - Senior Issues and Opinion Writer, The Advertiser, Adelaide

"Gripping ... a confounding brain teaser that twists and turns!"

———————

HAMISH CAMERON - Mulray Productions, Sydney

"The book had me by the throat from page one ... bound to be a best seller."

———————

James HoustonTurner

About the Author

James Houston Turner was born in Baldwin, Kansas, in 1947. He was educated at Baker University and the University of Houston Clear Lake. His first writing assignment was for the Dr Pepper soft drink company in 1971, which was followed by numerous articles written for the Union Rescue Mission in Los Angeles. His previous books include *The Earth of Your Soul, The Spud Book,* and *The Search for the Sword of St Peter.* He currently lives in Adelaide, South Australia.

Visit James Houston Turner's web site at **www.JamesHoustonTurner.com.au**

THE SECOND THIRTEEN

JAMES HOUSTON TURNER

◆ Australia ◆ North America ◆

JB Books
is a trademark of
Life on Paper *Publishing*

JB Books
PO Box 115, Oak Flats, NSW 2529 Australia
Tel: 61 2 4256 4682   Fax: 61 2 4256 4680

PO Box 195, Semmes, AL 36575-0195, USA

E-mail: jabauer@ozemail.com.au
Web: http://www.ozemail.com.au/~jabauer

First published 1999 in Australia

ISBN 1-74028-000-8

Cover design and illustration by James-Mitchell White
Printed in Australia by Griffin Press on 65gsm Bulky Paperback

Acknowledgments

Deadlines and the lonely process of writing sometimes turns normally decent people into snarling beasts. For enduring that, as well as for her many hours of sacrifice and patience, I would like to express deep love and appreciation to my wife, Wendy. Without her, this book would not have become a reality. Thanks must also go to my son, Jeremiah, for his enthusiasm, prayers, and the best bookmarks in the world.

In addition, there are a number of others to whom I am indebted for their generous assistance. The information and timely encouragement given to me were of inestimable value.

Captain Andy Andrews, Charlie White, and John Lewis of Sea-Land Terminals Pty Ltd (Aust). John McArdle, Adelaide Airport Limited. Graeme Earl, Swiss Banking Corporation. Marke Lowen and Reece Discombe, Vanuatu. Graeme Elsby, South Australian Ambulance Service, and Roger Cook. Thanks also goes to Anita Cox, Ruth Oko, and Anne "Willsy" Wills for their critique of the manuscript, and to Philip Brunner and his gracious staff at the Parkhotel in Zug, Switzerland, and to Stephen Schibli. I am appreciative also for the help of Chief Superintendant Dave Eason, and Sergeants Charlie Tredrea and Rod Hill of the South Australian Police; and to Bob Werden, for advice on publicity. A special thanks also goes to John Doherty, Channel Nine television, in Adelaide, for his generous help.

Furthermore, it is a joy to mention the gratitude we feel for our dear friends Rob and Sarine Sieval in the Netherlands, and Bob and Georgy Carey in Switzerland. Thanks for opening your hearts and homes to us yet again. A special thanks also must go to Briony Hume and the staff at Channel Seven television in Adelaide for their eager assistance with research, and to Penelope Herbert, of Pepperpot Marketing and Media.

I want to acknowledge Nick Blair, Sally Kerr, Peter Ham, and the entire Wyndham Estate team for their generous sponsorship of wine for my United States tour. I am proud to endorse their range of quality wines. Furthermore, I could not have organized the launch without the wonderful help of Jerry and Melanie Rhodeback, and Dr Joe McCord and the University of Houston Clear Lake *Friends of the Library*. Thanks so much for your help.

Many thanks also go to Mick and George O'Rourke at Centari Systems, in Adelaide, for printing so many revisions of my manuscript, and for their wonderful help with computer issues, enchiladas, and those familiar accents on life.

And to Angelika Baumeister, I extend a hearty *thank you* for coming alongside at just the right moment.

Finally, where would I be without the sharp eyes and editorial insights of my publisher, Julie Bauer? My gratitude for your faith in me and my manuscript can only be summed up one way: I'm sure glad you like chocolate chip cookies!

For Janet and Scottie,
and for Karen

The characters in this novel are fictional but set against a backdrop of historical events. Department Thirteen, Balashikha, and Operation Ryan did exist.

1936 - Department Thirteen established by Nikolai Yezhov.
It's purpose: assassination and sabotage.

1967 - Yuri Andropov becomes Chairman of the KGB.

1980 - Ronald Reagan elected President of the United States.

1981 - 1981 - The Kremlin becomes alarmed by fears of a United States conspiracy for a nuclear first strike. Andropov's reaction is to initiate the largest worldwide Soviet intelligence operation in history - *Raketno Yadernoye Napadenie* - code-named, RYAN.

1982 - Andropov elected General Secretary of the Communist Party of the Soviet Union. The Balashikha sabotage and terrorism complex near Moscow in full operation.

1983 - Reagan announces plans for his Strategic Defense Initiative ("Star Wars") missile defense system in space.
- Pershing II missiles ordered deployed in West Germany.
- Andropov elected President of the Soviet Union.
- Korean Airliner KAL 007 shot down by Soviet Air Force; all crew and passengers killed. Andropov and much of the Soviet leadership were convinced that KAL 007 had actually been an American intelligence mission.
- Operation RYAN reaches its peak.

Prologue

Moscow: 26 September, 1983.

Tonight's secret conference would be the most vital ever coordinated by Colonel Aleksandr Talanov of the KGB. That morning he had driven from KGB headquarters - "the Center," it was called - with three units of men and cordoned off the street with an invisible net of eyes and ears. Without question the building was not bugged: it was an ordinary butcher shop closed for the night and it had been thoroughly scanned.

Arranging use of the shop had not been difficult. Talanov's KGB identification had easily convinced the owner to cooperate. As an added incentive for lips to remain silent, one of Talanov's more muscular agents escorted the owner back to his flat where he would stand posted until dawn, his pistol a visible bulge under the gray fabric of his jacket.

It was now two in the morning and the smell of hacked meat still permeated the back room of the shop. Talanov checked his watch; it was time for their final arrival.

He clicked off the lights and stood silently by the back door. In less than a minute a knock of two raps, then five, could be heard. Talanov opened the door to a shadowed figure who stepped quickly inside, the three armed guards outside giving quiet assurances that no one had followed. The door was then closed and locked before the lights were switched on again.

Talanov did not recognize the man in wire-rimmed glasses. His facial structure was definitely not Slavic - German, perhaps? - and his hair was blond and short. Without a word the man seated himself with the seven other men around a rectangular table. Three shaded bulbs over the table threw harsh circles of light on each man and cast overlapping shadows behind them on the floor. Talanov stationed himself against the front edge of a thick wooden cutting block with two cleavers hanging on one side.

In a chair at the far end of the table was an aging Yuri Andropov, the importance of tonight's meeting heightened by the fact that Andropov knew he was dying. Suddenly the Soviet leader began to cough, the extended seizure draining him of breath. Talanov approached the table and poured him a glass of mineral water. Andropov took a drink amid the thick swirls of cigarette smoke exhaled from several of the men. Finally he regained his breath. "Comrade Talanov is to be commended for selecting a location even I would not suspect," Andropov said, glancing up with a brief smile.

General Vladimir Timoshkin was not in uniform but sat forward as though he were. He was a large man with square shoulders and a broad face that had been lined by decades of harsh Russian climate. "Commended? For choosing a filthy butcher shop?" He looked around at the dreary features of the room and with a look of disgust crushed out his cigarette. "Not even the Americans with their satellites could know about this group."

Beneath his neatly-combed white hair, the gentle features of Yuri Andropov grew taut. "The Americans are not our concern."

"Then why must we meet in this stench?" demanded the general.

"Because I *ordered* it," replied Andropov, his tone one of unquestioned rebuke.

Timoshkin sat back, unwilling to challenge the authority of the president of the Soviet Union.

Andropov glanced up again at Talanov. "General Timoshkin does not appreciate your precautions, Aleksandr. Would you care to tell him why?"

The KGB officer looked directly at Vladimir Timoshkin. "Because, General, you have allowed your office to be penetrated."

"What?"

"Electronic intercepts have been discovered on your telephones thanks to a fondness your Colonel Gagarin has for a certain woman with a drug addiction - an addiction cultivated by Western agents."

Timoshkin exploded out of his chair. "That is *impossible!*"

"Sit down, General," ordered Andropov.

"Comrade President, there is *no way* these accusations can be true. I know Gagarin - know his *wife* - have known them for *years*."

Andropov slammed his palm on the table. "His wife *is* that woman! Now *sit down*."

Stunned, Vladimir Timoshkin obeyed.

"So you see," Andropov said, his eyes now including the others, "tonight's precautions are not without merit, just as this situation is not without parallel. The eyes of betrayal are everywhere."

"But *Gagarin*," Timoshkin said, his anger beginning to show. "I'll have him *sho*t."

"You'll do nothing of the kind."

Timoshkin looked disbelievingly at Andropov. "But why?"

"As I have said, we have other concerns."

"You refer to Operation RYAN?" asked another of the men at the table. Talanov recognized the short heavyset man in a suit as Nikolai Sofinsky, former ambassador to the United Nations and a man once feared as a tough, inflexible negotiator. He was now in his seventies.

"Operation RYAN is doomed," Andropov replied. The announcement was made simply and without emotion.

All eyes were now riveted on the Soviet president, the shock of his statement reverberating in the silence it produced.

"How can this be?" General Timoshkin finally asked. "Operation RYAN is the most successful intelligence effort in Soviet history. It has given us extensive inform-ation on American military expansion throughout the world."

A fleeting smile appeared on Andropov's tired face. "As well as data on research projects being conducted by the CIA regarding our currency reserves, our requirements for imported grain and produce, our needs for credit and investment, and foodstuff handling procedures at all ports. Yes, General, all of that has come from RYAN."

"Then why do you say it is doomed?"

Andropov reached for his mineral water. "The continuing struggle, General. We must not forget the struggle." He lifted the glass to his lips.

"The struggle?"

"My reforms... the future of the Soviet state."

"*Peristroika*," Timoshkin affirmed with an understanding nod. "I have heard you speak of this program. But why restructure what is already working... what is giving us the edge?"

"Because our vision must look beyond RYAN."

"I do not understand," Timoshkin said, lighting another cigarette.

"It is why we are here tonight," Andropov replied.

"We meet to look *beyond* RYAN? I thought we were here to *expand* it."

"Signal intelligence has its limitations, General, as does the monitoring of civilian installations and communications. Nothing takes the place of the spy: we know it... the West knows it. Which is why many of you are strangers to one another - an arrangement not by accident. It is for your protection and the protection of our purpose, which will be detailed to you shortly. Further, based on your specific fields of expertise, I have instructed each of you to fulfill certain assignments."

"Which I, for one, have completed, although not without complications," announced a thirty year-old man in a fitted Italian suit. Beneath thinning brown hair he wore an expression of confident detachment. "Seven million American dollars is not easily kept quiet, even for an experienced banker such as myself who knows Western procedures and the ways around them."

With the exception of the stranger, who eyed the banker coldly, those around the table stared at him with bewilderment before looking back at Andropov, hoping for some kind of explanation. Where did this banker - whoever he was - get seven million dollars? What was its purpose?

Andropov was observing the banker. "What kind of complications?"

The banker leaned back in his chair. "As instructed, I opened an account in Switzerland. Publicity has been difficult to avoid, however, for it seems the Swiss can smell a Soviet as easily as someone from NATO, regardless of what nationality we claim or the false documents which we produce." The banker then sat forward, his face now illuminated under the direct wash of the overhead lights. He glanced quickly at the others around the table, his attention then directed back to Andropov. "To be more specific, Comrade President, anticipation of our deposit appears to have preceded me. I determined as much from numerous subtle references, including use of my name prior to my having provided it. Likewise, deposit procedures were much too swift, particularly for the Swiss, especially for a double-alpha account. Without question, they were expecting me."

"You suspect someone alerted them?"

The banker shrugged, leaving the obvious deduction unspoken.

"Perhaps someone connected to one of us?" Andropov asked, scanning the others around the table.

Again the banker shrugged.

"If it was Gagarin I *will* have him shot," General Timoshkin growled.

The banker then slid a large brown envelope across the table toward Andropov. "What I have just told you, plus receipts and the signature code, are included in my report." He again leaned back.

The president watched the envelope come to a stop in front of him, then reached out and brought it closer. "You have done well, Comrade," he said. "Your completion of this assignment will enable us to survive."

"Survive?" asked General Timoshkin, surprised by Andropov's statement. "On seven million *dollars*? The border guards drink that in vodka. How can the restructuring of the Soviet Union be accomplished with such an absurd amount?"

The eyes of Yuri Andropov turned toward the stranger. "Perhaps our latest arrival would care to answer that. He is the man I have chosen to direct *Peristroika*."

The banker bolted forward, startled by what he had just heard. "But I thought..." he began, then hesitating.

"Thought another was to be chosen?" Andropov said, completing the banker's sentence.

"But what about Comrade Gorbachev?" asked the banker, glancing at the stranger then back at Andropov. "Naturally, I assumed a degree of truth to what we've been hearing."

"As had I," agreed General Timoshkin, leaning up to the table, again with military bearing.

"Restructuring has many dimensions," Andropov explained, "just as it has many enemies. The man I have chosen is someone whose qualifications and training are dedicated specifically and entirely to the fulfillment of our vision."

"What exactly *is* our vision?" inquired Timoshkin, extinguishing one cigarette and lighting another. "And who is this man you have chosen?"

Andropov looked over at the blond stranger. "Comrade?"

The man stood. He was not tall, but neither was he short, and behind his glasses were cold blue eyes which came eagerly to life as he pulled a pistol with silencer from under his coat. Three muffled spits sent the banker arching backward out of his chair before the stunned Talanov could withdraw his own weapon, his movement halted by a stern command from Yuri Andropov: "Put that away, Colonel."

Pistol in hand, Talanov looked at the Soviet president with incredulity.

"You heard me correctly," affirmed Andropov. "Put it away."

Reluctantly Talanov complied.

"To those in this room," the blond stranger began as though nothing had occurred, "*Peristroika* refers to a deeper, more comprehensive restructuring than has been presented even to the Presidium, and certainly not to the public." He walked over to the door and opened it. Two guards entered quickly and dragged the banker's body out of the room. The blond stranger then locked the door.

"Our vision is not merely one of reform," he continued as he began slowly circling the table, Talanov watching his every movement, his own hand still on the pistol holstered inside his jacket, "but of acquisition and control on a global scale. No longer will we be dominated by the West." He smiled briefly, coldly. "As one might expect with a project of this importance, any breach of security will *not* go unpunished!" He stopped beside General Timoshkin, whose cigarette fell from his mouth as he looked up at the killer, the implication about breaches in security now clear. The blond stranger laughed and walked on. "You have nothing to fear, General. You see, while our comrade's Swiss banking skills proved quite useful, his flirtations with becoming a rich double agent did not. It is of no consequence that each of you knows of our deposit in Switzerland. What matters is that our comrade was willing to tell - and, yes, *sell* - information about our plan." The stranger paused, his smile fading into an icy sneer, his inflection suddenly climbing like an excited dictator reprimanding his subordinates. "Such treason *will not be tolerated!*"

Talanov forced himself to ignore the sobering memory of the banker's corpse. *Who was this stranger? Why was he here? Had the banker succeeded in his betrayal?* Andropov had barely reacted to the killing, obviously because he knew what was to occur or because he had personally ordered it.

Yet something else definitely seemed odd, thought Talanov as he listened to the stranger addressing the group. He then realized what it was: although cultured and flawless, the stranger's Russian was spoken with an almost-indiscernible foreign accent. Had this man learned his Russian *abroad?*

The killer was not from any of the standard KGB directorates, that much Talanov knew. Where, then, had he received his training? How did Andropov know him? And why was the Soviet leader bypassing tested political figures in favor of this man?

Suddenly, Talanov realized the stranger was looking at him. Once again, he had been concentrating so hard on his analysis that he had missed what the stranger had said. Silence filled the room as the stranger stood poised as if waiting for a reply. All heads were now turning, *their attention focusing on him*! Talanov glanced at Andropov, then back at the killer. "Did I miss something, Comrade?" he asked.

"Your thoughts are elsewhere, Colonel Talanov?"

He must not reveal his suspicions. He stepped away from the cutting block, his hands relaxing to his side. "Indeed they are," he said. "If we are to achieve our goals, then problems must be anticipated - must be *solved* - before they appear."

The stranger approached, the pistol still in his hand. Soon he was facing Talanov, a maniacal energy in his eyes. "What problems do *you* envision?"

Talanov calmly maintained his position without flinching, ready in an instant to disable the assassin should the hand with the pistol be raised. "What I envision is unimportant," was Talanov's reply. "It's the *un*expected that can kill us."

"Such as our banking comrade?"

"So it appears. But then I'm not able to question him, am I?"

Suddenly, a broad smile appeared on the killer's face and he whirled toward the group. "Colonel Talanov's *excellent* reputation is deserved!" he exclaimed. He then continued circling the table, praising Talanov's insights with a sequence of supporting logic. He finally came to a stop at the opposite end of the table from Yuri Andropov. "If I am not mistaken, Comrade President, Colonel Talanov has been, *and is*, vitally important to you at the Center."

The Soviet leader nodded. "He is without fear and his loyalty to me is unquestioned."

"Without emotion, I believe you once said."

"A brilliant mind with excellent training," affirmed Andropov.

With his hands now folded behind him, the stranger smiled and again wandered casually around the room. "Colonel Talanov's training - which includes a number of commendations while at Balashikha - also includes outstanding achievements at the Surveillance College in Leningrad, followed by an appointment to the analysis section of Directorate Seven. Your contributions, Comrade, in the area of surveillance and security led to your promotion to Directorate Nine, where you were chosen by the great Dimitri Lazovic to coordinate the physical protection of important installations as well as the personal safety of Party leadership. It was in Directorate Nine that you came to the attention of Comrade Andropov, whose appreciation and influence rewarded you with entrance into the Moscow State Institute for International Relations, where you excelled. This, of course, resulted in your eventual selection to the First Chief Directorate, where you continue to provide analytical support to various sub-Directorates and Services, as well as invaluable service to Comrade Andropov on assignments of the most sensitive nature, such as our meeting tonight. Unmarried, you are fluent in both English and German, and have no addictions nor indiscretions worthy of mention." The stranger again smiled. "Did I forget anything?"

"The number of fillings in my teeth," Talanov replied icily.

The blond killer's smile remained firmly in place. "Which, of course, is on file."

The stranger was again standing at the end of the table beside Talanov. He turned now and spoke directly to Andropov. "Comrade President, should anything go wrong with tonight's plans - we recall how Colonel Talanov has already uncovered a breach in General Timoshkin's office security - his continued influence at the Center *must not* be compromised. As you yourself have said, the eyes of betrayal are everywhere."

"This is true," agreed Andropov.

"I therefore request Comrade Talanov be excused."

"*What?*" Talanov nearly shouted.

"For his own protection," the stranger hastened to add. "This in no way reflects mistrust. Should *Peristroika* prove successful, his invaluable services will again be required."

"*No!*" countered Talanov, his plea directed to the Soviet leader. "You yourself have chosen me for this task."

"And I alone will determine your part in it," Andropov declared. To the stranger, he said: "It is a strange request, Comrade, particularly in light of your statement that Colonel Talanov has provided me with exceptional service. He is indeed my eyes and ears, and, as I have said, his loyalty to me is unquestioned."

"Precisely my point. If opposition has been mounted against us, it would be coordinated through the Center, where Colonel Talanov would undoubtedly hear of it, an early warning then passed onto you. If, however, he is identified with our plans, then your eyes and ears would be lost."

"But I am identified *already*," Talanov broke in. "I am the *organizer* of this meeting!"

"Highly secret and known only to us," the stranger replied quickly and without losing eye contact with Andropov. "In the unlikely event that word of tonight's meeting *has* been leaked, no interrogation could endanger - indeed, no chemicals could extract - what is not known. Up to this point, Colonel Talanov has acted entirely within the boundary of his responsibilities as one of your most trusted agents, thereby preserving his ability at the Center to detect any threat to our purpose."

"Our comrade's arguments are sound," Andropov said, nodding thoughtfully and speaking slowly. "We must not lose your presence at the Center."

"But we speak only of dangers imagined," Talanov emphasized, his eyes locking briefly with General Timoshkin's.

"Imagined?" Andropov repeated with a thin smile, himself glancing at Vladimir Timoshkin before returning his attention to Talanov. "Are you so quick to forget?" He paused only for a moment before answering. "I think not. I have known you for many years, Aleksandr, and I know how loyal and dedicated you are. 'An idealist,' I think you are called. I know also how persuasive you can be, cleverly manipulating the truth, as you're obviously trying right now. Remember what happened tonight: Comrade Vaskin may have caused us much harm. In light of this, I find myself in agreement with Comrade Cheney. If we have been betrayed, word will be heard at the Center. As you can appreciate, Aleksandr, I must do everything within my power to prevent such an occurrence. Our vision *must* be preserved. For if we are stopped, the world will still see *Peristroika*, but not as we have designed it. And if we fail, the glory of Russia will vanish."

Recognizing what was about to happen, Talanov drew himself to attention, the soldier before his superior. "You have decided then, Comrade President?"

But while Andropov was voicing his reply, Talanov's mind had focused on something else: *his superior had made a mistake.* Andropov had inadvertently revealed the identities of two of the key figures in the room - Vaskin, the murdered traitor; and Cheney, the man who killed him.

The extended moment of silence caught Talanov's attention. He blinked and again focused on the Soviet president, who was scrutinizing him carefully, as were the others at the table.

"Colonel?" Andropov asked.

"Merely trying to formulate something which might alter your decision," Talanov replied quickly.

Andropov chuckled. "I thought as much. No, Aleksandr, your clever reasonings will not prevail. The dismissal stands. But I ask you not to judge this moment too harshly. My decision may well spare your life, just as your eyes and ears may spare ours."

Nearby, his head lowered slightly, the killer named Cheney smiled.

Chapter
1

Australian maritime waters: 18 December, 1996.
The burnished western sun was sinking below the horizon as the freighter *Coriander* made its way up the Gulf of St Vincent toward Adelaide. Beside the captain were three men he did not know, nor care to know, and ones he certainly would not remember to anyone asking questions. The captain, a French Canadian, was a burly man with a large belly and arms as strong as hoists. He had thrown his weight into many a brawl and seldom came out the loser. Yet these three drove chilling fear up the core of his spine.

He was grateful to know so little about them. Only one had ever spoken and all three wore dark clothing, beards, and woollen caps. They had boarded the ship at night in Hong Kong after the container freight had been loaded. Ling Soo, one of the vice-presidents of Spice Lines East, owners of the *Coriander*, had brought them aboard with orders to take them to South Australia, no questions asked. Soo was one of those three-piece corporate climbers who liked to throw his company weight around. The captain would long ago have fed him to the bilge rats had not Soo's personal signature appeared on each of his payroll checks.

As the three men and the captain looked out the windows of the bridge over the rippling gray waters of the gulf, the spokesman of the three spoke again, his cold but courteous English tinted with an indefinable accent: "Slow the ship, Captain. To which speed I leave up to you, so long as darkness reaches port before this vessel."

Nighttime had indeed settled over Outer Harbor before the *Coriander* had been secured to the concrete of the port's industrial peninsula. The captain kept a watchful eye on the ensuing activity: men were everywhere, cranes began operating, fork lifts scurried about. Yet something was wrong, not so much with what he was seeing, but with what he was not. The three strangers - where had they gone? How could they have disembarked without his having seen them?

"Captain, these are for you," a messenger said, handing over a sheaf of papers. The Canadian accepted the documents with a grunt. *Where had the three men gone?*

The small motorboat slowed its engine and surged gently on its own wake toward some moored sailboats bobbing in the darkness. The driver of the boat rotated the steering wheel to the left, directing the craft between the parallel arrangements of boats from the Port Adelaide Sailing Club. Damp sea air blew in gusts around the four silent figures, a brilliant canopy of stars piercing the dark sky above them. Expertly, the driver swung the steering wheel to the left again, moving a lever at his side to reverse the propeller. The motorboat slid up to a floating dock, the driver shifting into neutral before switching off the ignition.

It had been an easy task for the three strangers to rappel undetected down the side of the ship and into the boat, the looped rope then pulled from the railing. For this mission, secrecy was everything. Their entry into Australia must not be traceable in any computer.

"I have been waiting for you!" said a man named Percy as he stepped toward the motorboat in the darkness, his voice one of hushed anxiety.

The only reply was a metallic click.

Percy quickly realized his mistake, one that could cost him his life. "Tango-nine, *tango-nine!*" he said hurriedly. *How could he forget to identify himself, especially with these men?*

The pistol was put away. "*Tango-one,*" came the proper reply. "Do that again and you're dead."

"Of course, of *course!*" agreed Percy. "This way, there's no time to lose."

The three strangers followed Percy toward a Holden sedan as the driver of the motorboat started the engine and pulled away from the floating dock.

Within a few minutes, the sedan turned onto Lipson Street in Port Adelaide and sped toward the Britannia Tavern, established in 1850. The street was dark and deserted and beneath the tavern's balcony hung a West End beer sign, its illuminated red and black panels the most powerful beacon along this section of the street. Situated across from a waterfront warehouse known as Shed 2, the stone tavern was a haven for shipmates and wharfies in want of cheap food and grog.

Percy parked the Holden in a vacant spot by Shed 2. The four occupants got out, the three strangers then following Percy as he led them across a stretch of uneven pavement embedded with railroad tracks. Percy entered the Britannia first, followed by the other three, each of whom carried a black canvas bag. A wall of smoke and laughter greeted them harshly, the young blonde behind the enameled red bar smiling her usual welcome as she slid several beers to a group of wharfies telling crude jokes at the end of the counter.

Through the smoke a hand waved, catching Percy's eye. He led the others through the boisterous crowd to a pool table where an obese man in faded denims and a t-shirt was bent over the table in concentration, his cue stick lined up for a shot. "Expected you bloody hours ago," he said, glancing at Percy, then at the three strangers with him. He returned his attention to the nine ball. "Side pocket," he announced, taking aim. He snapped the stick forward, the white ball driving the nine into the designated hole. He straightened and motioned to the three strangers, who approached him. The fat man turned his back to the crowd at the bar. "One room, six hundred cash, nobody knows you're here," he said in a lowered voice. As the money was handed over, he grinned, showing two missing teeth surrounded by a round, stubbled face. Stuffing the currency into his pocket, he added: "Percy will show you the room. It ain't much but it's private, which is just what you blokes want." He stepped back over to the table and chalked the tip of his cue stick. "When you're ready, tell Beryl over at the bar that you're friends o' Mick and she'll pour all the beer that you want. Anything else is extra." Mick and several of his friends laughed coarsely before returning their attention to the game. Percy nodded for the three bearded strangers to follow.

"One moment," the spokesman said with a gesture of his hand. "We'll each want a shower, in a bathroom with a mirror."

Mick had already lined up another shot and with an impatient sigh stood and faced the stranger. "With a bloody rosewater massage, I suppose? This ain't the Hyatt, mate."

"It's been a long journey," the spokesman replied. He held out another hundred dollars. "For the extra trouble."

A quick eye was given to the cash but Mick did not take it. "Well bugger me now, won't you look at this? Maybe you three blokes have a bit more o' that down in one o' them fancy bags." Several of the locals began grouping around the strangers. Their movements did not go unnoticed by the three.

Smiling, the leader placed the money on top of two fives already laid down on the pool table earlier as a bet. "I see you are a man who likes to wager," he said. He set his canvas bag on the floor and took a cue stick from a rack hanging on the wall. "Now you can accept the money I am offering you-" he lined up a shot and drilled the white ball into the seven, sending it into a corner pocket "-or you can take a *very* big chance, you and your friends-" he lined up another shot and sent the three ball into a pocket like a bullet "-and risk, well, whatever you and your friends feel like wagering." The leader smiled his same polite smile, then banked the cue ball from behind the eight with a slight spin, sending it delicately into the four, which fell into a side pocket. The leader then straightened, cue stick in hand. "The choice is yours... *mate*."

Mick and the others had been staring transfixed at the shooting skill of the nameless man in dark clothing. There was something unnerving about his lack of fear, the polite smile, his strange accent and cold authority. Stepping up to the pool table, Mick sighted in on the eight ball and shot. The cue ball sent it into the cushion, missing the pocket.

There was a nervous silence around the table. All eyes were on Mick, whose eyes were now on the stranger. "Well bugger me dead!" Mick said, his spreading grin genuine to everyone in the room but himself. *Who were these men?* Lifting the hundred-dollar note placed on the railing, Mick handed it back with a hearty laugh and a slap on the stranger's arm. He then returned his cue stick to the rack. "My shout, Mates!" he called out. "A round o' beer for everyone." A cheer went up from the crowd as men began pushing their way up to the bar. "Will you join me, you and your mates?" Mick asked the leader.

"Another time, perhaps," the leader replied. "As I said, it's been a long journey.

A shower is what we prefer."

"In a bathroom with a mirror," Mick said agreeably. "Percy will fix you up."

"Come on, Mick, your beer's gettin' warm!" someone yelled.

"I'm on my way," Mick replied with a wave of his hand. He then turned back to the three. "You blokes go on. Like I told you, when you're ready, Beryl will pour all the beer you can drink."

"We'll need a car," the leader replied.

"Check the Yellow Pages," Mick said. "There's agencies all over town."

"We prefer to purchase."

"Purchase?"

"Private. No signatures."

Mick looked carefully at the man in dark clothing, trying to read his expression. "You mean one which no one can trace?"

The leader smiled, his eyes riveted on Mick.

"That'll take cash," Mick said. "Say, four, four-and-a-half thousand for a small one. And it won't be nothin' flash."

"Agreed."

"I'll need a couple of days."

"Six thousand, have it tonight."

"Bloody hell!"

Chapter 2

With his hands in the pockets of his linen slacks, Talanov stared past the mannequins in the fashion boutique's front window and watched the midday crowds outside. Downtown Sydney was normally brisk in the early afternoon, but today's gentle sun had cast a languid spell and people seemed content to be taking their time.

Talanov, in his early fifties and now retired, unbuttoned his blazer and loosened his tie. It was the type of day one should be on the deck of a sailboat rather than marching from store to store. But tomorrow night he and his wife, Andrea, were hosting an elegant dinner for more than two dozen diplomats, consular officials, retired KGB agents and spouses, and with a society columnist from the *Sydney Morning Herald* joining them at eight for photos, the right look was essential. At least that's what Andrea had been telling him for the last three days.

It was not that Talanov was not sympathetic. He was. But they had already been to six other boutiques today - or was it seven? - with his wife already in her ninth dress in this store: a blue summer evening number with iridescent gold shadows.

"Alex, what do you think?" Andrea asked while turning in front of the full-length angled mirrors.

Talanov glanced briefly at his wife. "It's nice," he replied.

His lack of enthusiasm annoyed her. "*Nice?* Is that all you can say?"

"What am I supposed to tell you?" he answered. "It's an exquisite color, a trendy style."

"I don't want an analysis of the material. How do I *look?*"

"What more can I say? You look nice."

Andrea shook her head in disgust. "'Great' I can take, even 'bloody awful'. But not 'nice'. Honestly, Alex, you can be so dreadfully indifferent at times."

Annoyed at the shallow insecurities of his wife, Talanov glanced at his watch. "I think I'll go buy a paper," he said. And with a polite nod to the young sales consultant, he walked out the door.

"Men," the consultant confided after Alex had departed: "You can't live with them and you can't shoot them."

Andrea tried to smile at the remark, the attempt fading as she again viewed her profile from various angles. "Alex can be generous, fun, and witty," she said, turning in front of the mirror, "yet a block of ice when it comes to intimacy. Sometimes I wonder why we got married."

"Doesn't that drive you mad?" asked the consultant.

"More than he'll ever know," replied Andrea, staring ruefully at herself .

Talanov paused on the sidewalk and turned his face toward the sun, closing his eyes, feeling the warmth. He liked Sydney, a city not just *by* the bay - as was frigid San Francisco - but a city whose soul was inextricably linked to warm water and sun.

Warm water and sun were what had drawn him to Sydney once the Soviet system had been dismantled under Gorbachev. His younger brother, Andrei, had remained in England to study while Alex opted for retirement in a climate with palm trees. The chill of that part of the world held no allure.

More importantly, however, he wanted distance: to be as far away from the old centers of operation as possible, including the memories. Several others had shared his sentiments, most notably General Timoshkin, who had settled in Adelaide and likewise had tried to forget. But the last he'd heard, the old warhorse was in a hospital with cancer, and by now could even be dead. Talanov wondered if the general had managed to find peace? He hoped so, wishing that he, too, could escape the residues of his past, not so much for what he himself had done, but for what the system had perpetrated... a system he once trusted and to which he had dedicated his life.

Until, that is, he began to see through communism's peeling veneer.

But not before his heart had been irreparably scarred in the corridors of Balashikha. Passion, intimacy, love - these were weaknesses, were *dangers*, against which he had repeatedly been vaccinated by his instructors. And he had fed upon their words like a carnivore chews on flesh, convinced they would keep him alive, be his nourishment, strength, and vitality.

Except they were now a curse, insulating him from the woman he wished he could love, and perhaps in his own way did love, but certainly not with passion.

And who could blame him? His own parents had divorced when he was young, his mother leaving him and his brother in the care of their father, who preferred his vodka. Within six months, they had been handed over to their elderly grandparents, who in turn couldn't cope. Before long, they were wards of the State.

So it was there, in the care of his State minders, that he first learned about happiness and how it came not from the fleeting illusion called love, but from achievement, discipline, and excellence.

Love. Sure, the desire was there. But how does one give what one does not feel... what one does not understand?

Talanov crossed the street with a thicket of pedestrians, his tie flapping lightly in the wind. On the other side, he quickly cut to his left and walked the half block to a small side street which he turned down, then angled across the pavement toward a small shop. Above him, the glass and concrete of high-rise buildings rose like canyon walls.

Through the cacophony of moving traffic, the smell of hot grease reached Talanov's nostrils as he approached Chang's Deli, a downtown delicatessen which sold hot chips and a large selection of fried foods, pies, pasties, groceries, newspapers, magazines, souvenirs, and cold drinks. Alex and Chang had been friends for many years, and never once during that time had Talanov known Chang's store not to be open during the day. It was therefore with surprise that he approached the delicatessen's closed door. Stationed in front of it, with folded arms, was a long-haired muscular man in sun glasses.

"We're not open today," the man stated as Talanov approached.

"Is anything wrong?" queried Talanov with a wrinkle of concern on his brow.

"Renovations," the man replied.

"So Chang's decided to modernize!" said Alex with an approving nod. "It's about time he spent a little of his money. Lord knows he makes enough of it."

The man did not reply.

"So what's he going to do?" Talanov asked, stepping toward the glass door in order to look inside. A 'closed' sign was hanging above an assortment of colored decals promoting ice cream, flavored milk, and candy.

The muscular man moved and blocked his view. "Sorry, mate," he said.

"Just a peek," insisted Alex.

"If I let you then I'll have to let everyone else. Come back tomorrow."

With a shrug, Talanov turned and walked away, then slowed as he once more noticed the familiar odor of hot grease. *Would Chang be cooking food during construction?* It was possible, of course, for work crews needed to eat and Chang was the type who would feed them. In fact, in many ways Chang behaved more like a doting grandparent than a proprietor. And his hot chips were the best in town.

With a chuckle, Alex resumed his pace, barely breaking stride to glance back when he heard the man brusquely tell two businesswomen in dark suits that the deli was closed for the day. But as the man stepped toward the women to direct them up the block, through the glass of the front door Talanov could see a second man holding a knife close to the face of a child while speaking angrily to someone behind the counter. Talanov's relaxed smile metamorphosed into a hardened stare as he looked quickly away. *The shop was being robbed*!

Involuntary reflexes - such as a hand recoiling suddenly from intense heat - occur in milliseconds and without cognitive thought. Talanov's reaction to the situation inside the deli was likewise immediate although by processes different from those of the central nervous system. His was a defensive tactic learned years ago at Balashikha. And because of that training, all natural fears and distractions about the safety of particular individuals were commanded out of his mind on behalf of the common good. Enemies allowed to go free were enemies who could strike again.

Wearing an embarrassed smile, Alex suddenly turned back toward the man at the door as if he had forgotten something. "Sorry to bother you again," said Talanov as he approached, "but I forgot to pay my account." He pulled out his wallet and stepped well to the side of the door. He then took out fifty dollars, the bright yellow of the money catching the man's attention. "Would you mind giving this to Chang on your next break? Tell him it's from Alex."

"I'll make sure that he gets it," the muscular man said, suppressing a grin and stepping over to take the money. *What a bloody sucker.*

Suddenly the yellow note slipped from Talanov's grasp and fluttered toward the sidewalk. Instinctively, the man grabbed for it.

An exploding front kick from Talanov's right leg caught the man squarely in the jaw, snapping his head to the side as his shocked eyes rolled back in his head. He crumpled to the sidewalk, unconscious.

Talanov frisked the man and found a large knife, which he withdrew from its sheath and slid toward the two shocked women. "Call the police," he said quietly. "There's a robbery occurring inside and a child has been taken hostage."

The two women could only stare.

"The *police!*" repeated Alex firmly. "And take that knife so no one gets hurt."

Startled into action, the two women nodded and ran up the street, one of them abruptly running back to pick up the knife.

Standing, Talanov approached Chang's front door, pushed it open, then walked inside.

"What the *hell* - you: get over there with the others!" shouted a wiry man in a brown balaclava as he looked angrily toward the door.

From behind a counter littered with postcard racks and novelties, Chang called out a warning which Talanov did not hear. His attention instead was fixed on the knife at the throat of a terrified nine-year-old girl, whose face was wet with tears, but who had been ordered into silence by the robber. The masked man again demanded that Talanov join the others. Beside a rack of potato chips, a frightened woman - obviously the girl's mother - was sobbing in the arms of an elderly man.

Talanov looked at the child, then at the man with the knife, and without a word removed his blazer and laid it across a stack of newspapers. The girl's mother looked at Alex, then at the man holding her daughter, then back at Alex. Surely this stranger was not going to try anything stupid.

The masked man looked at Chang and threatened to slash the girl's throat if he did not immediately empty his cash register. "And *you* - get over with the others like I told you!" he then screamed at Talanov.

"Please, do what he wants!" begged the mother.

"The *money!*" yelled the masked man.

"For God's sake, do it!" the elderly man shouted at Chang. "He said he'd let her go."

"He's lying," stated Alex to the old man. "The girl will be raped and killed."

"Shut up!" the masked man yelled at Talanov.

"Don't provoke him!" the elderly man told Alex.

Talanov looked at the thief. "Release the girl and you can walk out of here."

"I said, *shut up!*"

"You've got a minute, maybe two, before the police arrive," Talanov said in a calm voice, taking a step forward. "But once they get here, there will be no walking away. Let the girl go."

"The money or she *dies!*" the masked man shouted at Chang. He then looked

15

angrily at Talanov. "And *you* - asshole - get over there with the bitch. John-o, *get in here!*" he suddenly yelled, looking nervously toward the door.

Talanov shook his head. "I'm afraid your associate won't be joining us."

"*What?*"

"And you're in trouble if you don't clear out."

"Another word out of you and she's history!" screamed the masked man.

"I don't think so," replied Talanov evenly and without emotion. "Because to kill or harm that girl eliminates your shield, and we both know that without a shield, all you've got to protect you is that little zucchini slicer. Let her go and you can walk free. But like I said, your time's running out."

Frustrated, the man pulled the girl closer and held the knife up to her eye menacingly. "I'm leaving, but she goes with me."

"*Mummy!*" cried the little girl.

"For God's sake, let her *go!*" pleaded the sobbing mother.

"Shut *up!*" demanded the masked man, who then pointed his knife at Talanov. "Now get your bloody ass out of my way!"

"First let her go."

"Get out of his *way*, you idiot!" shouted the elderly man.

"*Now!*" screamed the masked man.

But Talanov remained immobile. "Release the girl, then I'll move."

"I'll kill her!"

"And I'll use that knife of yours to gut you like a Murray carp. Now, let her go, you bastard. I hear a siren."

"You son of a *bitch!*" shouted the man as he pushed the girl toward her mother and charged at Talanov, slashing the air viciously with his knife.

Holding his hands up in surrender, Alex stepped back into an aisle, creating a clear path. The masked man bolted toward the door.

Suddenly, Talanov sprang behind the man and pushed him, the force of the blow catapulting the thief into the metal frame of the door and smashing his face. The masked man spun clumsily and swung his knife. Alex blocked the arm in the direction of the swing, then angled his body and stepped quickly behind the man's lower back, creating a fulcrum with his hips. Jerking his blocking arm forward, Alex flipped the masked man backward over his hip and onto the floor, the knife bouncing away. He then leaped on the man's back, grabbed hold of the balaclava and smashed his head twice into the hardened linoleum, the second blow being unnecessary as the first had knocked him out cold.

"Alex, are you all right?" asked Chang, his face drained of color as he hurried from behind the counter. "They were going to kidnap the child!"

"He promised to let her go!" shouted the elderly man as he approached Talanov angrily.

"They were lying," Talanov replied, reaching for his jacket.

"Who do you think you are, walking in here and endangering lives? That lass could have been *killed* because of you."

"Please, sir," objected Chang, addressing the older man. "My friend is knowledgeable in these matters. If he says the girl would have been harmed, I believe him. I am certain he saved her life."

"Don't be a bloody fool!" the elderly man answered bitterly.

"Please," interrupted the mother, pushing past the old man with her daughter, who was clinging to her waist and crying. She stopped in front of Talanov. "You believe they would have killed her?"

"That's right," answered Talanov, standing. "To keep her from identifying either of them."

"Nonsense," the elderly man cut in. "He was wearing a bloody mask."

Talanov looked at the old man. "The one outside wasn't, and this pair fits the descriptions of two men who've been robbing deli's and taking children hostages, two of whom have been raped, one of whom has been killed, another missing and presumed dead. So don't lecture me about this girl's chances of being released."

Two police cars screeched to a stop outside. Within seconds, three officers, their guns drawn, burst through the door as a crowd was gathering. "What's going on, what happened?" one of them asked. Outside, a fourth patrolman attended to the unconscious thief on the sidewalk.

"This fool nearly got us killed!" shouted the elderly man, pointing at Talanov.

"He did *not!*" protested the mother, stepping forward. "This man saved my daughter's life."

"The lady speaks the truth," agreed Chang. "These men were going to rob me and had taken the child hostage. They both had knives."

"Is that true?" the first officer asked Talanov.

Talanov nodded.

"How did you disarm them?" the policeman inquired. "Did you employ the use of a weapon?"

Alex held up his empty hands.

"Bare-handed? Are you crazy?"

"That's what I've been trying to *tell* you," the elderly man broke in. "He's bloody *mad*. That thief was holding a knife not a centimeter from the girl's eye! Our *hero* here didn't give a *damn* about her safety."

The officer looked warily at Talanov.

Once again, Talanov held up his hands.

"Are you telling me you're some kind of martial arts expert?" asked the policeman.

Alex shook his head wearily. "I'm just a man who came in for a newspaper."

Chapter 3

The dinner guests were enjoying additional champagne now that the plates had been cleared. It was nearly ten o'clock and everyone was chatting happily to the strains of a classical medley being played by string quartet.

Talanov's multi-level home was situated in the suburb of Mosman among the other affluent houses built on the forested bluffs overlooking the winding arms of Sydney harbor. The pool-side terrace, where the guests were now seated, was surrounded by an ornate concrete railing with illumination provided by strands of tiny lights in the potted shrubs. Bordering the terrace was a thicket of shrubbery and trees which descended to an undulating stretch of well-tended grass, the course eventually ending at some rocks and sand at the edge of the water.

Sergei Zinyakin, an overweight official from the Russian consulate, joined Talanov at a balustrade. "Retirement has treated you well, Aleksandr," he said as some queen palms swayed above them in the warm breezes flowing up from Chinaman's Beach. The lights from the surrounding houses poked friendly holes in the night.

Alex looked at the diplomat. "A hint of disapproval, Sergei?"

Zinyakin shrugged. "Not really."

"I dedicated my life to our cause," Talanov said. "My uncle in Denmark did not. He loved Russia but hated the system, seeing things I refused to see. When he died, his estate gave my brother and me what communism could not."

"No one resents your good fortune."

"Why should they? I have kept my pledge of secrecy, although I will admit publishers still sometimes approach me."

"So, why do you not sell your story? Many of the old guard dream of having such an opportunity. You stood at the side of Andropov and coordinated KGB activities unknown even to this day."

Talanov looked down towards the harbor where the lights of a sailboat moved slowly by. "We became castoffs once Gorbachev's reforms turned against him - embarrassments to the new order because of what we represented, at least in the eyes of the public. I was lucky enough to have an inheritance open doors for me here in

Australia." Talanov returned his attention to Zinyakin. "I would tell my story if I thought it would make a difference. But it will not, and telling it would mean revealing the identity of many old friends in Moscow who are trying to forget the lies and live quietly for the remainder of their years. No, Sergei, I will not speak of it, not now... especially for money I do not need."

"Such nobility is admirable, my friend. There are many whom you could identify."

Talanov looked back toward Chinaman's Beach. The lights of the sailboat were gone. "I am not noble, Sergei, but merely attempting to live with my conscience. And please tell any of your worried comrades that I know far less than they think. Many coercive drugs were available even back then, and specific identities and activities within the network were unknown to me for that very reason."

Suddenly, a voice called out. Was there more champagne? Talanov laughed. Of course there was. He would be there in a moment. After again facing the diplomat, Talanov glanced at his guests, Zinyakin doing the same. "Look at them, Sergei, wearing their tuxedos and drinking champagne. It is life at its best, is it not?" The two men turned back toward one another. "But appearances can be deceiving, and you and I know the truth. We come from a system which purged Jews and dissidents and anyone else who got in our way. We created gulags, psychiatric hospitals, and Balashikha. It must never happen again."

Zinyakin chuckled bitterly. "And you think it is different here? That ASIO, or the CIA, behave like nuns in a convent?"

"We both know better, Sergei," Talanov answered with a patient smile. "Some, however, have more blood on their hands than the others."

"But we were a *superpower*."

"We were an upper Volta with missiles," countered Talanov, "with an empire built on oppression. Greatness is not determined by conquest, Sergei. Look at Switzerland." Talanov placed a hand on Zinyakin's shoulder. "Russia *is* great. But the old ways - never again."

"Your money allows you such dreams."

Talanov withdrew his hand. "It has nothing to do with money. The world is different... I am different. Let us learn from our mistakes, and not repeat them."

"The talk of one who forgets."

"Not at all, my friend; I remember only too well. But as I told you, there are many living in Moscow against whom revenge would be taken. It is why I *must* keep my silence, at least for the present."

"Alek*sandr*!" Andrea scolded as she crossed the terrace wearing her blue silk dress. "The cham*pagne*. The servers are waiting!"

"I'm coming!" Talanov replied. He turned again to Zinyakin, his smile sincere. "Let us not fight over the past. It *is* the past, you know, and the present is not so bad."

Sergei smiled. "You are right, of course. So hurry, refill our glasses."

Talanov nodded warmly to the diplomat as Andrea linked her arms in his and led him back toward the house, Talanov making a gesture of helplessness with his hands. Chuckling, Zinyakin lifted his empty glass in a toast.

At 11:15, the champagne was still flowing freely. Talanov and Andrea had been perfect hosts, stopping at each table several times to accept and return compliments on the beauty of the evening, youthful appearances, and other flatteries exaggerated by four hours of drinking. With the dinner guests chatting merrily, the couple then took a bottle for themselves and decided on a leisurely stroll.

Having slipped out the service entrance of the house undetected, they descended a path through the trees and crossed the grassy expanse beyond, walking hand in hand. At the beach they removed their shoes, Talanov pausing to roll up the legs of his tuxedo trousers while Andrea walked on to the edge of the water. She gazed at the reflections of light moving in fluid motions over the surface of the harbor.

Talanov had finished filling each of their glasses with champagne when he caught sight of Andrea's silhouette against the background of intermittent reflections, her long hair blowing softly, her silk dress clinging to a slim waist and willing curves.

He recalled how they became acquainted a year after his migration to Australia. Having purchased a house in Mosman, Alex had telephoned the number printed on a glossy brochure for a quote on catering for a party. A renovation crew would be arriving soon and he wanted to christen his new residence before construction began.

Andrea assured Mr Talanov that Elegant Cuisine was one of Sydney's most prestige gourmet catering businesses and that she would personally coordinate everything, from the mailing of invitations to valet parking. Satisfaction, of course, was guaranteed.

After the event, Talanov invited her to stay the night. Andrea refused.

"Scared?" he asked.

"Careful," she remarked at the front door.

"I'm impressed," he said. "A beautiful virgin who can cook."

Andrea smiled. "Sorry, Alex, but the first part of that solicitous query is none of your business; the second part, however, comes with a *very* expensive invoice, which I expect you to pay."

"Sorry, I didn't mean to get personal."

"Yes, you did," replied Andrea. "But never mind, I like a man who takes risks."

Talanov chuckled. "So what *is* this going to cost me?"

"More than you ever dreamed," was her answer. And with a smile that made Talanov ache, Andrea kissed him on the cheek, then crossed the darkened flagstone courtyard and started up the steep flight of steps. Half way up, she paused. "But it will be worth it," she said. "Good night, Alex." Within seconds she had disappeared into the tunnel of shrubbery which led to the street above, the noise of trickling water in a nearby fountain combining with the sounds of the evening.

She's leaving, you idiot - *do something!* Talanov told himself. "Wait!" he called out, hurrying up the steps after her.

Andrea had already started the engine of her car when he ran up to the door. "When will I see you again?" he asked, out of breath.

"You're not this slow at everything, are you?" she asked through a partially opened window. Then, without waiting for his reply, she shifted into gear and drove away.

Six weeks later they were married.

The ceremony, held on the terrace where their dinner guests were now seated, was but a formal confirmation of the relationship gossip columnists had been covering since the day they met. Almost immediately, their calendar became filled with social engagements, committee meetings and charity functions, and by the end of the year, the *Elegant Cuisine* employees rarely saw Andrea for more than a few hours a week. And while all of this was exciting, Andrea began to wonder if the incessant pace was her husband's way of avoiding deeper involvement. She began to see how, when alone with her, Alex managed to deflect her attempts at intimate communication onto impersonal topics such as upcoming events, trips, or decorating themes for the house. Try as she did, Andrea grew increasingly frustrated in her efforts to weave lives with her husband.

Her first and perhaps only real clue into the reasons for Talanov's insular behavior came when he confessed his involvement with the KGB, a fact quite shocking to Andrea because of all she had read and heard. Wasn't the KGB an organization of spies with square jaws, receding hairlines, and sagging permafrost eyes? On the surface, Alex was the exact opposite of this, and yet beneath his charm Andrea realized everything he had told her could be found in a public library. The only names ever mentioned were those of well-known figures, his stories recounted like espionage thrillers which one might hear in a pub. Tense moments were described at borders, along darkened streets, or in radio intercept rooms, with nefarious agents from the CIA presented like characters in a novel. In other words: lots of action but little of Alex.

Nevertheless, the relationship had an electric appeal and undeniably the sex was great.

Still, in those moments of honest reflection, Andrea could see that it was only sex... without closeness or depth. Erotic, however, it was, with their frenzied encounters maturing over the years into the practiced pleasure of satisfying one another in teasingly slow movements which lasted for hours. Exhaustion was followed by sleep and with each morning came the promise of more.

But more was never enough, and when Andrea gently sought deeper involvement, all she found was an impenetrable barrier.

"It's a magnificent evening," Talanov said as he approached her at the shore. He handed her some champagne while the water made gentle lapping noises near their feet.

"The stroganoff was not to my liking," she said curtly, "and the plates were not properly heated."

"Everyone thought it was perfect."

"I didn't hear one remark to that effect."

"Precisely my point," said Alex, taking a sip. "People were too busy eating. And such silence doth truly speak," he then added in a Elizabethan tone.

Andrea permitted herself a smile as he took a brief bow, then theatrically raised his hands toward the sky and quoted a few lines from Shakespeare's, *As You Like It*, the two of them oblivious to what was commencing back in their home.

Dressed formally, two of the men from the *Coriander* had entered the Talanovs' residence by the front door. Following a detailed floor plan, one of the men went immediately to the downstairs electrical master panel and extinguished all of the lights. Once this had been accomplished, each of them quickly fitted infrared night vision goggles over their eyes and pulled 9mm MP-5K machine pistols with attached silencers from under their tuxedo jackets. It took just under three minutes for the two assassins to fan out quickly and gun down every dinner guest in virtual silence, members of the orchestra included. Before an additional three minutes had passed, each room in the house had been searched.

"Talanov is *not here!*" the killer known simply as Number Three exclaimed in accented English as he joined his partner back in the kitchen.

"Are you certain of this?" Number Four asked.

"He is not here, nor is his wife."

"We could wait for him to return," Four suggested. "He may have gone for a walk."

"He may have gone for the night," countered Three. "We cannot wait. Someone may decide to investigate the sudden absence of light and music."

"Number One is not going to like this," Four said.

"Number One does not have a choice."

"Alex, it's twelve thirty!" Andrea said, holding Talanov's wrist up to her face and looking at the illuminated dial on his watch. "Your guests will consider you rude."

"My guests will consider me an idiot if I bring you back at this hour. I'm supposed to be ravaging your body."

"*Alex!*"

"All right, but I warn you - my reputation will be ruined."

Laughing, the two steadied one another against the effects of the champagne and started back toward the house. Within five minutes, however, Talanov's laughter abruptly ceased as they approached the trees which bordered the lower edge of their property. Andrea's chatter was then silenced by a halting grip on her arm.

"What is it?" she asked.

Talanov was scanning the darkness above them. "No lights, no music, no laughter."

"I said they would think you rude. They've probably all gone home."

But the former agent of the KGB was not satisfied. "Something's not right," he said, aware that for every light to have been extinguished, it could only have been accomplished at the master panel or by someone systematically going through the house and flipping dozens of switches. Whatever the case, the fact that it had occurred was a potential warning he could not ignore. "Stay here, I'm going to look," he said, starting off through the trees, his attention above on their darkened property.

"Alex, don't you *dare* leave me down here alone," Andrea called out, hurrying after him, shoving branches noisily out of her way and snapping twigs beneath her feet.

"Shhh!" he ordered.

"What is going *on?*" she demanded as she caught up with him.

Talanov suddenly whirled around and grabbed her by the arms. "I don't know," he said quietly, fighting to clear his mind of the alcohol. "But it's no game, whatever it is. We've got to be *quiet*... and be careful."

Frightened by the strength of his grip, Andrea agreed.

Reaching the base of the wrought iron spiral of steps which led to the lawn above, Alex began to climb carefully, attentive for signs of danger, Andrea following nervously behind. At the top he paused and listened. Everything was dark and peaceful, the only sound the wind in the leaves. Turning, Alex took his wife's hand and leaned his head next to hers. "If I'm overreacting, forgive me," he whispered. "But you're important to me. And this time I mean it - wait here. If nothing's wrong, I'll turn on the lights."

"Your behavior makes me afraid," Andrea whispered back, refusing to release his hand.

"Good," he replied. "Now, wait here, I *will* be back."

Leaving her by the top of the stairs, Talanov crossed a section of manicured lawn toward the brick patio which surrounded the pool. He carefully mounted the two steps and stopped, searching the darkness carefully. Nothing. Moving silently to his right, Talanov suddenly paused. Near the diving board were several dark shapes clumped together on the brick pavement. Had the orchestra discarded their instruments? He approached, the shadowed forms taking the shape of... *bodies!* "My God," he said to himself, rushing over and feeling quickly for signs of life. There were none. Instinctively, he examined their pockets. *Their wallets were undisturbed.*

Talanov stood, his mind racing: *mass murder without a sound* - which meant automatic weapons with silencers - and definitely not for robbery. Leaving things as he found them, Alex ran across the patio toward a grouping of tables that had been set up near a high lattice fence. More dark shapes were scattered over the bricks - corpses in twisted disarray, bodies on top of bodies. He felt the undisturbed wallets of the men again, then rushed toward the house where more bodies had been thrown from their chairs. There was no movement, no groans, no signs of life. Only darkness... and death.

Talanov fell to his knees, fear and anger filling his mind. Friends - some of whom he had known for over twenty years - all *dead!* Who had done this? *Why?*

Suddenly a scream pierced the sickening silence. Jumping to his feet, Talanov sprinted back to where Andrea was hysterically stumbling away from the deck of the pool and back toward the stairs, one hand pulling wildly at her hair, the other groping for the concrete railing. "Andrea, get *down!*" he called out, racing toward her, expecting any moment to feel the searing pain of bullets piercing his back.

"They're *dead!*" she cried out. "I *saw them!*" She turned and fell.

Talanov reached his wife and dragged her into the deeper shadow of the balustrade, alert for the sounds of attackers. But there were no shouts, no pounding of footsteps, no shots. Alex pulled her close and touched a finger to her lips. Sobbing, she buried her face against his chest, then just as quickly pushed away and jumped to her feet, screaming again.

"Andrea!" Talanov said sharply, leaping up and grabbing her.

"Why would someone *do* this?" she yelled, trying to wrench free. "It's because of you... *I know it!*"

He gripped her arm more firmly. "Stop it!"

"Let me *go!*" she cried out, lashing at him with her fists. "Who are you, what have you *done?*"

"I said, *stop it!*" he ordered, slapping her across the face.

Andrea collapsed to the ground and began weeping uncontrollably. Slowly, Alex knelt beside her, pulling her gently to his shoulder and letting her cry. Several minutes passed before Andrea's emotions subsided. "What is going *on?*" she asked.

"I wish to God I knew."

"But *why?* What are you not telling me?"

Helping Andrea to her feet, Talanov placed one hand on each of her shoulders and looked into her darkened face. "We'll talk, but not at this time. Right now we must get to the house."

"To call the police?" she asked.

"To do something else," Talanov replied as he took his wife by the hand and led her across the lawn and up onto the deck of the pool, then toward the large covered verandah which spanned the back of their home. His grip was strong, as much to keep her from running as to comfort her. He must not allow her to panic.

And he could not call the police.

They climbed the back steps and quietly approached the door into the kitchen. Alex opened it carefully and paused to listen. Hearing nothing, he led the way into the kitchen, gently closing the door behind them.

Alex tiptoed across the floor to a utensils drawer, which he pulled completely out and set on top of the polished granite counter top. He then reached in through the opening and up to where a pistol was secured to the underside of the counter top. Knowing the weapon to be loaded, he withdrew it from its holster and cocked it.

"Is that a *gun?*" Andrea asked upon seeing the silhouette of the pistol in his hand.

"Yes, and let's hope I don't have to use it," Alex whispered as he led her out of the kitchen, the weapon poised.

Near the front door was a curving flight of stairs which connected to the floor above. The front door, however, was standing open and a soft wind was flowing in off the flagstone courtyard outside. Although signs seemed to indicate the killers had gone - no gunfire had occurred earlier when Andrea had screamed - Alex proceeded cautiously with his wife to the first step and began climbing, pausing frequently to listen for intruders who might still be searching upstairs. They reached the top and paused, then slowly turned the corner, Andrea's hand in his. Staying close to the wall he guided her down the darkened hallway, advancing silently past several closed doors. They came to a large wall cabinet where towels and linens were kept.

Reaching into his pocket, Talanov withdrew a small pocketknife. Opening the door, he unfolded the blade and inserted it into a slot concealed on the inside of the casing. A latch was triggered which caused the entire linen cabinet to move back into the wall on hinges. Talanov then led the way into a small room his wife did not know existed. In the darkness to one side were two illuminated red dots.

"What *is* this place?" asked Andrea.

"A room for a man with a past," Alex replied as he closed the linen cabinet behind them and switched on an overhead light.

The room was no larger than a normal walk-in closet, with a narrow plywood counter running the length of the wall on the left. On this bench were several pieces of electronic equipment and a computer. On the far right was a desk and lamp and one small filing cabinet.

Alex sat in a chair in front of a multi-band radio and began flipping switches. Several red and yellow lights flashed on, as well as an illuminated green panel showing a number of frequency bands.

"Alex, *talk* to me! What is this place?"

"It was built by my renovators."

"But why?"

"We'll discuss it another time. Right now, we've got to listen."

"Listen to what? Aren't you going to call the police?"

He looked at her. "No, I'm not."

"But why?"

"Because they too, could be our enemies." He returned his attention to the radio.

"The *police?* You can't be serious."

Talanov did not reply but instead rotated a silver dial. Andrea's attention was soon drawn to the oscillating high-pitched sounds which erupted over a background of static. Alex continued turning the dial until a conversation could be heard.

"We copy the address," a patrolman's voice said. "But did you say multiple murders?"

"Several dozen," came the reply from a female dispatcher.

"Several *dozen?* Are you sure?"

"That's what the caller told us. The alleged killer's name is Talanov and all this supposedly took place in his home. If there's any evidence of violence, bring him in. But approach with caution; the informant said Talanov's KGB."

"KGB? In *Mosman?*"

"That's what the caller said," the dispatcher replied. "What's your time of arrival?"

"A few minutes. Are you sure this isn't a joke?"

"No, I'm not, but we'll find out when you get there."

"Who phoned it in?"

"Anonymous. He said he's a neighbor who witnessed the massacre and fears he'll be killed, too."

Andrea grabbed her husband on the arm. "Alex, you *couldn't* have," she whispered. "You were with *me.*"

"Shhh," urged Talanov, his head angled toward the radio.

"The informant called from a public telephone," the police dispatcher was saying, her voice crackling over the radio.

"A public phone? Isn't that a bit too convenient? Why wouldn't he identify himself?"

"Like I said, he claims he's a neighbor and that Talanov would kill him. He then told me he was going into hiding and accused me of being a bloody idiot when I said we could give him protection. He claimed the evidence would speak for itself."

"All right, we'll check it out," the patrolman said. "We'll be there in five, give-or-take."

"By the way," the dispatcher added, "Talanov is married and his wife's name's Andrea. If there's been a crime, put her in a separate car. We'll want her isolated for questioning, particularly if this story about the KGB turns out to be true. If it is, ASIO may need to be brought in. Incidentally, the Talanovs drive a black Jaguar sedan. Here's the registration number..."

The number followed, although Alex was already reaching for the phone book.

Andrea noticed him flipping pages. "Are you going to call and explain?"

"No."

"But I can verify you didn't *do* this."

"Somebody did, and until they have a better suspect, they'll want to hang it on me. And because I *am* former KGB, there will be questions I cannot answer."

"Cannot... or will not?" asked Andrea pointedly.

Talanov glanced at his wife. "Some things cannot be told."

"Such as?"

"Such as backgrounds on the murdered victims and why they were killed."

"Why *were* they killed?"

"Not for robbery," declared Talanov.

"How do you know that?"

"I checked their wallets. By ruling out robbery, the weight of probability shifts."

"Toward what?"

"Toward this being the work of assassins."

"*Assassins?*"

"Think about it: a very private gathering of former KGB agents all gunned down in virtual silence by killers firing weapons so rapidly no one had time to escape. My God, Andrea, members of the *orchestra* were cut down beside their instruments, nearly everyone else within a few meters of their tables. And we didn't hear a thing. Then, almost immediately the event was reported to the police by an anonymous informant claiming *I* did it."

"But you *didn't* do it."

"No, I didn't," he said punching the buttons on the phone. "Sure, you can corroborate my story, but that's not where it will end. Whoever did this wants me, for whatever reason. He knows about the murders, knows about my past, and is now setting me up with wild accusations that I'm out to kill him. One thing is certain: our caller is no frightened neighbor; he's a professional who's now using the police to try and reel us in. Because once we've been brought in for questioning - and we will be with all those dead bodies out back - it will be simple matter of waiting for our release... or *your* release, which will probably be first. When that occurs, they'll take you, knowing that once they have you they have me. Either way, both of us die."

"So what can we do?" she asked.

"Find out who's behind this and stop them, which I can't do from inside a police station." Talanov looked away as a voice was heard over the telephone. "Hello? Yes, I'd like to request a taxi; I'm afraid we've had too much to drink." A short pause. "No, we're phoning from the home of a friend. We can meet you at the corner of..."

Chapter 4

"Tango Blue," a voice said over the cellular telephone.

"Three, here," one of the assassins replied.

"Go ahead, Three," said Blue.

"All but one."

"Which one?"

"Talanov."

"You'll hear from me."

The line went dead.

Chapter 5

The Royal Adelaide Hospital is a sprawling assortment of aging brick buildings adjacent to downtown Adelaide. Yet in spite of its antiquated appearance, world-class miracles have taken place within its walls, especially in reconstructive surgery. Originally built near the close of the nineteenth century, the dreary complex kept expanding over the years until it now filled the space of several football fields.

Wearing blue jeans and a white lab coat over her blouse, Dr Emily Henderson was a physician on night duty in one of the hospital's cancer wards. She took a drink from a can of Coca Cola and looked at her watch. "Fifteen minutes and I can go for a smoke," she said to the male nurse beside her.

"Ever think about quitting?" Dave Jarrett asked, glancing up from the book he was reading in the sixth-floor nurses' station.

"Next you'll want me to start eating salad."

"Come on, Em, we work in a *cancer* ward." Dave looked out through the double panes of clear plexiglass into the darkened hospital room over which their lighted station presided. Ten beds, five on each side of the room, lined the walls. Some beds were occupied by patients requiring oxygen around the clock, while other individuals were connected to drip lines which fed chemicals into their deteriorating bodies. "Look at those poor buggers," said Dave. "Most are here because they smoked."

A slight shudder crawled up the doctor's back. "I know, I know... I've tried."

Dave laughed. "Right! About as hard as I've tried to quit eating meat pies."

Emily glanced sideways at Dave. "So you'll die suddenly of a heart attack and I'll waste away in here."

"It doesn't have to be that way," Dave replied. "Besides, you don't have to go outside to eat a meat pie. And I bet my breath smells better than yours."

"My tongue isn't coated with grease."

"Ah, but grease can smooth away that leathery skin on the back of your neck. Want me to show you?"

"Stuff a sock in it, Dave."

Dave grinned at his small victory, then asked, "By the way, how's General what's-his-name... the Russian?"

"Timoshkin? It doesn't look good. Now *there's* a person who *has* smoked himself into the grave. At least I've cut down." Dr Henderson reached for her clipboard. "The poor bloke is holding on by sheer stubbornness. I don't know how he does it."

"They're a tough lot, the Ruskies," Dave said. "Must be those bloody awful winters. Seems it's always snowing in Moscow."

After finishing the remainder of her soft drink, Emily glanced at the retired general's medical summary, a stethoscope slung casually around her neck. "His chart says he hardly sleeps and rarely eats." She looked up, squinting as she peered through the plexiglass window toward his bed. "He probably can't with all the drugs we have in him. At least he's not in agony." She shook her head reflectively, then added, "God, maybe it's time I *did* quit."

"A slight crack in the shell?"

Emily kept gazing into the darkened ward. "That shell is what keeps me from losing it." Without smiling, she looked down at Dave. "Just as it does for you... just as it does for all of us who work in this place." She stuck a pen in her pocket. "See you later. I'm going on my rounds."

Dave watched Emily disappear down the deserted hall, then found his place in the book again as a wheezing cough could be heard from one of the beds. He glanced toward an embankment of small rectangular white panels, each of which was connected to a corresponding button by the side of a patient. Dave waited a few moments but no light came on. Relieved, he returned to his story.

Not five minutes had passed before Dave heard footsteps. He turned toward the noise, expecting to see Emily. A man in a white nurse's uniform approached.

"Doctor Henderson needs you in 7-S," the arriving nurse said.

"What is it?" Dave asked.

"Beats me, mate. She pulled me from my station and sent me down here to get you. I'm to watch the desk until you get back."

"But there are nurses up there on duty."

"She wants you, mate. I guess she trusts your judgment more than mine."

"Sorry. I didn't mean to imply-" Dave began apologetically.

"Forget it," the nurse broke in casually with a wave of his hand. "Anyway, I'm on holiday as of tomorrow. Heading to the Flinders. Better hurry."

"Yes, of course," Dave said, jumping to his feet. "I'll be back as soon as I can."

"This your book?" the man asked, moving to take Dave's chair and picking up the novel which had been laid hastily upside down.

"Yes, but don't lose my place," Dave called out as he rushed down the hall toward the elevators, a faint odor of mineral spirits disinfectant floating in the recently scrubbed corridor.

"No worries," the nurse replied as he began to read.

Once Dave was out of sight, the leader of the three men from the *Coriander*, his beard now shaved off, tossed down the book and stepped quickly from the station and entered the darkened ward, his rubber-soled shoes barely making a sound. As he approached General Timoshkin's bed, he withdrew from his pocket an ampule and a disposable syringe. After removing the protective sheath from the needle, he inverted the tiny bottle, stuck the needle point through the top and filled the cylinder with poison.

The call from his two associates in Sydney had not been good: Talanov had escaped. Yet where could he run? He would eventually be caught by the police if he remained in Australia, and the longer his capture took, the stronger his guilt would appear. What the police needed was an incentive - say, the death of one of their men - to intensify their campaign to find him. Then, once Talanov and his wife were jailed, it would only be a matter of time.

All that remained now was Timoshkin's death.

A sudden, prolonged coughing spasm came from across the room. One of the patients had awakened in the process of clearing his lungs. "Nurse?" the patient called out in a weak voice upon seeing someone in a white uniform. The dark shadow of the patient's raised head was now visible against the beige wall. The assassin ignored the plea and continued toward the bed of General Timoshkin. "I need morphine," the patient called out. Again the assassin ignored the request as he came to the side of his target.

"Who are you?" the general suddenly asked in a deep, tired voice as the killer reached for his arm.

"It's time for your medication," the assassin said in a hushed tone, pulling back the syringe. "Doctor Henderson's orders."

"I know of no such orders," Timoshkin replied. "Bring me the doctor and I will discuss this medication I am to be given."

"She's upstairs on an emergency, mate," the killer said, trying to sound casual. "And if I don't give this to you, my job could be on the line."

"I take nothing until I have spoken with the doctor," the former officer in the Soviet army countered.

The assassin held up the vial, pretending to verify the label in the dim wash of light from the nurses' station. He then showed it to the general. "See, it's only morphine. Something to help you sleep."

"Sleep? Morphine has never helped me to sleep. I will summon this Doctor Henderson." He started to reach for the call button.

Without warning, the killer stabbed the needle into Timoshkin's leg. But the sharp pain caused the general to yank his leg away before the plunger could be depressed. With an angry curse, Timoshkin pulled out the syringe and threw it away, swinging his legs down onto the floor and turning to face his attacker, his breathing labored and shallow. Standing in his flimsy blue dressing gown, the general suddenly paused and looked carefully at the man facing him, the dim light from the nurses' station illuminating his face. "I *know* you," he said.

Without a reply, the assassin sprang forward and hammered his foot up into the general's groin. It dropped him immediately to the floor in paralyzing agony. The killer then rammed his knee into Timoshkin's face before throwing him to the floor. He would accomplish with his hands what he had intended with the poison.

Suddenly the lights of the ward came on. "Hey, what are you *doing?*" Dave yelled, rushing into the room.

The killer released the general and jumped to his feet. As Dave ran over to him, the assassin leaped into the air, his sudden movement surprising Dave for the split second needed for a high front kick to catch him squarely in the jaw, knocking him into a rack of drainage bottles connected by tubes to one of the patients. Jolted loose, the bottles shattered as they hit the floor, followed by Dave and the metal rack as they first wobbled then crashed noisily to the linoleum. Cries of alarm from other patients could now be heard.

Glancing at the motionless body of the nurse, then back at Timoshkin, the killer caught sight of the hypodermic near one of the beds. He hurried over and picked it up, only to see several of the patients struggling out of their beds.

"What is happening here?" one of them called out in a feeble voice.

"Who are you, what are you doing?" another patient demanded of the assassin.

The killer grabbed the syringe, then back-fisted a gray-haired patient onto his mattress.

"How *dare* you!" shouted a frail old man from a neighboring bed, pulling the monitoring wires from his chest and grabbing his cane as he struggled to find his balance. He stood proud and defiant.

The killer grinned maliciously and kicked away the cane, throwing the man off balance.

"I'll have you *reported* for this!" the elderly patient warned as he regained stability with the aid of the bed frame.

"I think not," the killer replied, tightening his fist as he prepared to pummel it into the old man's stomach.

Without warning a large hand grabbed the assassin from behind and threw him across the room and into the wall, smashing his nose into the concrete and again knocking the hypodermic from his hand. The killer spun around to see General Timoshkin, his face bloody, his mouth hanging open as he labored for each breath of air. "Now it is your turn," the general growled in Russian.

The assassin wiped the blood from his face, his eyes drilling angrily into his opponent's. "Try it," he replied, also in Russian, then realizing what he had done.

"So it *is* you," Timoshkin said. "*Peristroika*... the *Second Thirteen*."

"Your little trick may have worked," the killer answered, "but it will do you no good. You will not leave this room alive."

"But why? I helped *create* you."

"Dead," the assassin replied.

"What... what did you say?"

Yet Cheney, whom the general had not seen since their only meeting in a Moscow butcher shop in 1983, said no more as he picked up the syringe and started toward Vladimir Timoshkin, who was stooped and fighting for air.

Several other patients, however, were now rallying to the general's side. They were, for the most part, frail old men, one of whom swung his cane at the intruder, striking him on the shoulder. "Stand strong, lads!" the old man cried out, raising the crutch like a sabre.

Cheney quickly shoved the old man back into the other patients and all of them fell to the floor. He then faced Timoshkin again. He must hurry and complete this assignment!

At this time of night the job should have been quick and easy. How simple it had been to find out about Timoshkin's medical condition from his helpful neighbors. Several visits to the hospital were all that were required for Cheney to determine the general's location, where uniforms were kept, and which doctor was rostered on night duty. An easy impersonation was then used to manipulate the nurse out of the way once the physician had gone on her rounds. Except the general had been awake!

With resolve to finish this quickly, Cheney readied the syringe.

Unable to catch his breath, Timoshkin knew death was near. There was no way he could fight a man so much younger and stronger than he, especially a trained assassin from the Second Thirteen. If there was a Maker, he was about to meet him.

Suddenly, Doctor Emily Henderson shrieked from the doorway. Shocked by the unexpected noise, the fatigued general turned and lost his balance, tripping over the bed and falling onto the floor. Cheney lunged forward and drove the needle into Timoshkin's thigh, squeezing the plunger. The general cried out and swung his hand.

But the cylinder he knocked away was empty.

Cheney leaped to his feet and sprinted past the frantic doctor, who screamed again as she ran into the nurses' station where she began punching buttons on the telephone. "Hello... *hello?*" she shouted into the phone. "Is anyone there? This is an *emergency! Hello?*"

Without warning, Vladimir Timoshkin's sluggish hand ripped the receiver from her grip. He depressed the switch, then fell weakly against the wall, grabbing the lapel of her white lab coat and pulling her near. "Must... get outside line," he gasped.

"You need *help*, Mr Timoshkin, please lie down!"

"No *time!*" he said, struggling for breath. "Poisoned... get outside line."

There was a gray cast to the old Russian's face which had been deeply etched by many years of harsh climate and sun. And yet there was also a look of determined purpose in his eyes which she had never seen before. What was it he had said - *poisoned?* - and he was now demanding the phone. Against all her professional judgment, Dr Henderson felt she must obey. It was a strange request to be sure, but one of overwhelming importance, at least to him. With a nod she took the receiver and depressed the operating switch several times.

The general suddenly fell to the floor.

"Mr *Timoshkin!*" Dr Henderson screamed, dropping the phone and kneeling beside him. "Help me, *somebody help me!*" she shouted down the hall.

The general grabbed her. "Got... to have... *outside line.*"

Dr Henderson again saw that look in his eyes. "All right, I'll get it for you." She stood, listened to make sure there was a dial tone, then handed it to him.

"Dial... *quickly*," he said. Although his breathing was becoming erratic, the general managed to recite a number which Dr Henderson punched into the instrument. Within seconds a connection was made.

"Peristroika... Second Thirteen," he spoke into the phone, his voice barely a whisper. "Andropov created... sent deep. Killing has started... Royal Adelaide Hospital... poisoned me... to keep silent." Timoshkin's breathing was turning to gasps. "Must *stop* them! None... remaining... who *know*."

And with a final choking sound, Vladimir Timoshkin dropped the receiver and toppled dead on the floor.

13

Chapter 6

Talanov froze. "Mrs Taylor, how *nice* to see you!" Max, the hotel night manager, called out from across the foyer upon seeing Andrea, having been alerted by the desk clerk that the Taylors of Elegant Cuisine had just registered and paid with the company credit card.

A slender man with delicate features, Max was impeccably dressed in a dark suit with a small red boutonniere. He skirted an arrangement of couches and chairs on a plush Persian rug and hurried toward them. Nearby, a waterfall cascaded gently through some large volcanic rocks and palm trees into a goldfish pond. Classical music floated in the air like perfume.

Max was all smiles as he came to a stop in front of Andrea, his hands clasped excitedly in front of his chest. "How *wonderful* of you to join us again!" he exclaimed in an ebullient voice. "Your *Cinco de Mayo* banquet last May was simply *fabulous*. I still remember those enchiladas."

Recovering from the shock of being recognized, Andrea extended her hand. "Not from indigestion, I hope."

The manager feigned shock at the remark. "Good heavens, no!" he said, taking Andrea's hand and vocalizing a kiss in the direction of her cheek. "The evening was *magnificent*." Max then arched his eyebrows slightly. "Are you here on business at such a late hour?"

"Relaxing away from the telephones after a *very* long evening," Andrea replied casually. "My husband and I are taking some needed time to ourselves. I would appreciate it if people do not know we're here."

Max gave an assuring flip of his hand. "You needn't worry, Mrs Taylor," he said, lowering his voice. "I will make a special note on the computer that you are *not* to be disturbed, especially by the chef." His effusive smile then turned to surprise as he observed that they carried no luggage. "Have you no suitcases?"

Talanov reacted quickly. "I'm afraid *my* credit card will be taking care of that. Tomorrow our wardrobes expand."

"Wonderful! I know some exquisite boutiques-" Max began, then suddenly noticing the wearied looks on their faces. "Do forgive me, you must be *horribly* tired. I'll have someone escort you to your room."

"That's very sweet but we'll manage," Andrea said.

"As you wish. I will see to it that your stay is both pleasant and private."

"I'll remember your kindness when banquet facilities are again required."

Pleased, Max bowed and excused himself.

"He remembered you," Talanov whispered to his wife as they started arm-in-arm toward the elevator. The sound of water splashing politely into the pond could be heard as they walked toward the elevators.

"Thankfully, not that well," Andrea replied in a low voice. "He accepted the false registration."

"The name of Talanov will be in the hands of the media by morning. Cash and the company credit card should give us a few days of protection." Alex inserted their room key into the security switch by the elevators, and with a ding, the stainless steel doors parted.

Within five minutes of entering their room, Andrea was relaxing in a steaming hot shower. The pounding of the water was what she needed to help rid her mind of all that had happened. Dozens of people... murdered! *And someone was blaming her husband.*

Andrea had to admit she knew very little about their guests. As she reflected on it now, all of them seemed practiced at chatting for hours about nothing - at least in her presence - and not only tonight, but when they had socialized together in the past. Who were these people? Or, perhaps more accurately, who did they *used* to be? And what hidden truths had now made them targets?

"Hey, are you going to drain the tank?" came a shout from the bedroom.

"Five more minutes!" Andrea called back.

Twenty minutes later, her hair dried by the hand-held blower furnished by the hotel, Andrea was snuggled in bed with her husband. They were both naked, the lights out, the draperies parted enough to allow the reflective lights of the city to enter through the sliding glass doors.

"Alex, I'm frightened," Andrea said to the melancholy strains of a saxophone playing softly on the stereo.

"I am, too, but we have to fight it. Fear, anger, hate - they cripple our ability to think. And think is what we must do if we're to stay ahead of these killers. We must enter their minds, anticipate their moves, counter before they can strike. Together, we can do it, and we will."

Andrea drew near to her husband, entwining her legs with his, Talanov's arm pulling her close. She felt safe... safe with the man she had married, yet a man she was not sure she knew. How she wished their hearts could be entwined as closely as their bodies, that his love ran as deeply as hers.

Perhaps it did, and in a strange way the revelation had come because of tonight's dreadful tragedy. Andrea thought back to what he had said after they came back from Chinaman's Beach. Alarmed that the house was dark, Alex had led her quietly up the wrought iron stairs. And there, on the landing, he had whispered, "If I'm overreacting, forgive me, but you're important to me."

So he did care and had managed to express it. Still, who *was* this man with the secret room? And what was the past he was hiding?

Talanov seemed to read her thoughts. "You are much too intelligent," he remarked, "to have been fooled by my buccaneer stories. Many times I noticed it in your eyes, the questions you wanted to ask, and often tried to ask but I would not let you. I preferred my past to stay buried - and buried I thought it was - but now, of course, we know differently. So you must meet the man that I was... a man who no longer exists, but whom somebody wishes to kill."

Andrea's response was to turn her head slightly and kiss her husband tenderly on his shoulder, then pull herself closer still. It was a wordless message but a clear one: *I love you... I want to be near you.*

Talanov understood and placed his head against hers, his arm wrapped firmly about her. He held her in silence, wishing he could erase the years of covert strategies and violence... a world where actions and identities long since forgotten were reappearing with deadly consequence. Alex kissed his wife on the head, aware that for the first time he actually feared losing her. He ran his hand gently through her hair, wishing he could love her with the passion she'd always felt for him, a passion - he had to admit - now dying from virtual starvation.

How he wished she could understand! Coldness, isolation, an impervious heart - these were the means by which one stayed alive in the world of the KGB. Balashikha had taught him that. Couldn't Andrea see that love was a *weakness,* a vulnerability which enemies could exploit and with which they could *kill?*

Feeling the heartbeat of his wife as she lay next to him, Alex closed his eyes in anguish. *Couldn't he see how she was already dying, her emotional life-blood draining away?* Balashikha *hadn't* prepared him for that.

Thankfully, the agent in Alex knew that he could protect himself and anyone with him. The very training that was his curse was also a blessing, enabling him to calculate with computer speed what they must do to stay alive.

But if he were indeed so confident, why did he suddenly fear losing her so much? The truth was, no one had ever meant this much to him - a startling reality which had opened a whole new set of emotions... *emotions which made him vulnerable.*

And what really alarmed Talanov was not the fact that he had brought danger to himself, but to his wife, who was a victim merely because she had chosen to marry him. Andrea *was* important to him, and the sudden need to protect her made him willing to do anything - even sacrifice himself - in order to lead the hunters as far away as possible. *But* would these unseen enemies accept his diversion, or ignore it, or somehow miss it? Any miscalculation and she would die.

Or worse: be subjected to inhuman violations which Talanov dared not imagine.

No, he had to open his past to her and allow the combined strength of their minds to figure out a way of stopping them.

"Communism was my life," Alex began. "I studied it, lived it, breathed it."

For nearly half an hour he talked about the philosophy and structure of communism and the role of the KGB in maintaining absolute control over the people. Talanov was thankful to be hidden in darkness when he described assignments the KGB had carried out against suspected and accused enemies of the state. "The holocaust did not end in forty-five," he said, "and since that time, millions have been exterminated as real or imagined threats. Unfortunately, this obsession for control - it was a requirement if the system was to survive - continued until the first tastes of democracy allowed by Mikhail Gorbachev. That's when it began to unravel and unravel quickly it did. Workers became mobs, lathered into a frenzy over private ownership of property and the craving to rule themselves. *'Abolish the KGB!'* became one of their loudest cries. Which meant, of course, that numbers of sacrificial heads were needed on silver platters. I cannot say that I blame them. They were frightened about losing their freedoms, of forfeiting all they had gained. One does not easily forget the tactics used against them for seventy years."

Andrea leaned up on one elbow, being careful to maintain their intimate level of contact, her breasts still resting against him. "You said earlier that you started to change," she said. "What did you mean?"

"Communism on paper is what attracted my idealistic hopes: equality for all, freedom from oppression... that sort of thing. But during the closing months of Andropov's rule, I became increasingly aware of things I had *not* been taught: that communism outside the classroom was really state capitalism - the government's privileged elite taking from others what they wanted for themselves. That's always the way it is... the way *we* were. It's a situation ethic called greed and it's a condition of mankind. It's why communism can never work."

"You sound cynical."

"I am, of all the lies they taught at Balashikha. The trouble is, there are men out there with guns for whom these revelations don't matter one bit."

Andrea sat up. "It appears they matter a great deal. The question is - why?"

"I wish I knew," Alex replied somberly. He then finished with a summary of their dinner guests and a brief history of his association with them.

The looming question, of course, was why they had been murdered. Talanov posed the question, then admitted he didn't know where to begin looking because most of them had committed or observed more than enough covert activities to justify some kind of retaliation against them.

"What will our next move be?" she asked.

"We'll figure that out in the morning," said Talanov, looking at the darkened shape of his wife, the outline of her body visible in the faint light filtering into the room. Smiling affectionately, although he knew she could not see it, he reached over and touched her cheek. *Had they not taken that walk to the beach...*

The telephone rang.

"Who could be calling us *now?*" asked Andrea, startled at the intrusion.

It rang again and Talanov leaned across the bed and grabbed the receiver. "Yes?"

"Mr Taylor, this is Max, the night manager. I must explain that it is hotel policy for any and all credit card numbers to be automatically telephoned in for verification. This policy is completely non-discriminatory and without regard to personal acquaintance. I want you to know that."

Talanov sat forward with alarm. "You're calling us at this hour to convey your *credit policy?*"

"Well, I'm sure that it means nothing, but when the desk clerk called in the number from your wife's company card, we were told the Elegant Cuisine account has an *alert* placed on it by the authorization center. You will be relieved to know the card does not require confiscation. All they insisted upon was our address - they had us repeat it *twice*. Mr Taylor, you and Mrs Taylor *are* with Elegant Cuisine, aren't you? I mean, your wife *looks* familiar although the name of Talanov was mentioned, which caused the desk clerk some concern when she assured them our guests were the *Taylors*."

The anxiety of the night manager could be felt over the telephone. Alex forced himself to laugh. "Of course our name is Talanov. But do you think we can ever obtain privacy when we use it? Look what's happening now. This alert was actually issued by my wife in order to prevent unauthorized use of the card. That's why personal identification numbers - PINs - were created by banks and credit card companies. If your desk clerk forgot to ask for ours, then I suggest you wait until morning before correcting *your* mistake. Now, without wanting to sound rude..."

"I beg your forgiveness, Mr Tala... Mr *Taylor*. Good night... and sleep well. Naturally, a complimentary dinner for two will be-"

But Talanov had already slammed down the receiver. "Get dressed," he said, jumping out of bed. "They found us, we've got to leave."

After leaving by way of the back stairs, Talanov hailed a taxi with orders to be taken to another hotel across town. At that destination, after climbing out, Alex paid the driver and took Andrea inside, where they watched the cab drive away. Once the vehicle had gone, they went back outside and hailed a second cab, giving directions to a particular street in downtown Sydney.

In the back seat, Andrea was running a comb through her hair. "Do you realize I'm an absolute mess and that we're still in our party clothes?"

"Take off your bra," Talanov told his wife quietly.

"*What?*"

"Hurry. We're going to walk to a cheap hotel several blocks from where he's taking us. When we get there, I want the clerk's eyes on you, not me."

"And what if the night clerk's a woman?"

Talanov glanced over at her. "Where we're going, it won't really matter. Add some lipstick, and tease up your hair."

"You want me to look like a hooker."

"I'll pay cash," said Alex.

"*Bastard.*"

Talanov chuckled and looked at his wife. "Not for you, for the room."

Andrea was already slipping the bra from under her dress top. "Is this trick of yours going to work?"

"Unless we encounter another night manager who remembers you."

"You really *are* a bastard. He'd better not remember you, either."

He didn't.

The attendant was a undernourished man with long greasy hair and baggy clothes which smelled of cigarettes and beer. The hotel of choice was on a darkened side street and was an older brick building with a metal fire escape rising to the roof like obsolete scaffolding. On the sidewalk out front were some broken beer bottles, while on the window was painted an advertisement for adult movies. A red neon sign proclaimed its name, a locked door the kind of neighborhood.

Pausing his pornographic video, the night clerk finally responded to the bell being sounded repeatedly. Once assured they brought business, not trouble, he opened the door, Andrea's altered appearance having its desired effect. Ignoring Talanov, he took immediate notice of her full breasts which were plainly visible through the silk of her dress. A price for the night was quickly agreed, the reptilian eyes of the clerk grinning eagerly as he exchanged a room key for some of the cash from Talanov's wallet. After watching them enter the elevator, he opened a beer and returned to his movie.

"Did you see his eyes?" Andrea asked, squeezing her husband's arm more tightly. "I shudder to see the room."

"At least we can get some sleep. Tomorrow - *today* - we'll shop for some clothes."

The room was as they expected, the smell of several varieties of stale smoke greeting them as they entered. The frayed bedspread was a garish orange, while across the soiled blue patterned carpet was a dirty window framed with thick brown draperies through which strobed the pulsating reflections of red light from below. To the right, against the wall, was a long dressing cabinet covered with numerous burn marks, and above this a cracked mirror in a frame. A television set was bolted to one end of the dresser, which likewise was bolted to the wall. Andrea stopped and looked in the bathroom. "I've seen horse stalls cleaner than this," she said, recoiling at the stained porcelain and filth.

Alex walked to the sagging bed and pulled back the covers. The sheets had a brownish tint to them. He grimaced. "I think we should sleep in our clothes," he suggested gingerly. Andrea shuddered as she kicked off her shoes and wearily crawled into the bed. After placing his pistol on one of the night stands, Alex closed the drapes, removed his tuxedo jacket and shoes, then made sure the door was locked before joining his wife. Within minutes he was asleep.

Talanov was awakened by the sound of footsteps in the hall. He listened to them pass by their door then grow faint until they could no longer be heard. Unable to determine the hour because of the darkness maintained by the heavy drapes, Alex climbed slowly out of bed and walked quietly to the window. He peered around the edge of the curtains. Outside, the day was sunny.

"What time is it?" asked a sleepy voice.

Alex looked back toward the bed and smiled. "Probably afternoon. We were exhausted." He walked to the dresser and looked at his watch. "Not far off, it's nearly eleven."

Sitting up, Andrea stretched and rubbed her eyes.

Wanting to hear the news, Talanov selected the radio setting on the television control box and turned it on. Several beeps were heard which indicated the hourly report.

Their attention was gripped immediately by the opening headline about last night's murders. The gristly scene was detailed by the announcer, who concluded by saying that a search was now being conducted for a suspected former agent of the KGB - Aleksandr Talanov - in whose home the killings had taken place. Anyone possessing information on his whereabouts was asked to call the police.

Andrea stared across at her husband. "My *God*, Alex, what are we going to do?"

There was an imposed calm in Talanov's voice. "We need money, then some clothing and food. Then a place to stay."

"Can't we stay here?"

"Too expensive for long term and the place is a pit."

"Then I'll go to a teller machine for some money," said Andrea, sitting up and reaching for her shoes.

"No! I won't risk someone spotting you."

"Alex, the danger is less for me than for you. Judging by what we just heard on the news, you're the center of a man hunt. You stay here, I'll get what we need."

"I don't like it."

"Neither do I," agreed Andrea, "but we don't have a choice at the moment."

Reluctantly, Alex nodded. "All right, but please - be careful." He took out his wallet. "Here's some cash and my bank card. We'll need the room for another night."

"Another night?" asked Andrea. "I thought you said we can't stay here."

"We're only staying 'til dark. Then we make our next move."

"What is our next move?" she asked.

Talanov's expression was grim. "I haven't a clue."

Chapter 7

The cellular phone sounded in the pocket of the assassin. He looked over at his companion, each of them dreading this call. It sounded again just as he unfolded the mouthpiece. "Three here," he said.

"Tango Blue," a familiar voice declared. "This line is secure. What's the status on Talanov?"

"Negative," replied Three, glancing at Four.

"You'd better explain. I was advised that you were given the address of the hotel where he had registered. Your task should have been simple."

"It wasn't. His room was empty."

"This is twice you've missed your assignment."

"Someone must have alerted him because we arrived within minutes of the directive. The credit agency told me they verified the address *twice* with the night clerk, who let it slip that the people using that number had registered under the name of Taylor. If the credit agency was clumsy with their questioning, then the front desk may have become worried and called him."

"He can't be allowed to escape!"

"This was beyond our control. Are all of his cards now flagged?"

"Business and personal, for the both of them. Plus, we've frozen their funds. So when their pocket money runs out - and it will - they'll make a mistake and be seen. If you find them first, kill them. But if the police bring them in, we'll get word to you so that you can take his wife when she's released. Keep her alive until we have Talanov."

"He's the only one remaining?" asked Three.

"The only one," came the reply. "Tango Blue out."

Chapter
8

Talanov sat rigid before the television, his eyes fixed on a full-screen shot of himself. A voice was describing his height and weight and how he was being sought for questioning in regard to the brutal mass murders committed in his Mosman home. Anyone having information was to call the police.

After switching off the set, Alex strode impatiently to the window and looked down into the street for his wife. *Where was she?* Andrea's instincts had been right: her picture had not been shown, which meant the danger of her being noticed was indeed minimal. Still, he was worried and therefore walked back to the bed to unload and examine his pistol for the seventh time, thankful to have something to do. He sat on the dingy sheets, telling himself how unlikely it was that last night's desk clerk had watched the news. If he had, the authorities would have been here by now.

Nevertheless, recognition was still a threat and what they needed was some kind of strategy, initially for their own protection, then for proving their innocence. He snapped the loaded clip back into the handle and laid the weapon on the cheap wooden night stand. Restless, he stood and walked to the window again. *What was taking her so long?*

As he gazed out over the city, Talanov's mind began to focus on the problems they faced. Foremost, of course, was finding a safe place to stay. Relatives and friends were out, for they would be under surveillance, including taps on their phones. Another option was to rent a holiday cabin in the mountains although the problem of recognition was still a threat, perhaps even more so in a small community where strange faces attracted attention. By now, every newspaper and television station on the continent would be showing his photo. No place would be safe.

Complicating things even more were the unknown identities of the assassins. Any face in the crowd could belong to one of their killers. Which eyes would be watching and waiting? How many were there? Frustrated by so many unknowns, Alex walked back to the bed and once more unloaded and examined his pistol. What actual facts had he learned?

First, the killers were professionals... fast, efficient, and quiet.

Yet *who?* CIA... Mossad... common terrorists? As lethal as each of the first two could be, they were not normally involved in suburban mass killings. But what if a particular suburban gathering happened to be KGB? *Former* KGB, Talanov had to remind himself, which is something a sophisticated intelligence agency would know. Common terrorists, on the other hand - even well-trained ones - might not possess that information.

And what about motive? Had the assassinations been a horrible accident - innocent bystanders becoming statistics solely because they had been dining in the wrong place at the wrong time? Or had he, Talanov, been their primary target? Or had all of them been marked from the beginning? *Who was responsible? Why?*

A light knock sounded. "Alex," Andrea called out in a hushed voice.

Talanov raced to the door and opened it. "Where have you been... *what's wrong?*" he suddenly asked, reading her frightened expression.

"Our funds have been frozen," she said, stepping quickly inside, a white plastic shopping bag in her hand, "and the teller machine confiscated our card."

"My *God*," replied Talanov in a voice that was barely a whisper. After closing and locking the door, he walked to the center of the hotel room, one hand rubbing his forehead as he tried to assess this development. *In order to freeze funds, the assassins had to be part of something more vast and powerful than he had imagined.*

"How could they do that?" asked Andrea.

"Connections, that's how, either at the bank or in the world of credit. They alter our status to say we're delinquent, owing hundreds or thousands in back payments. An alert is then issued for our cards - including yours for the business - which is how they tracked us last night. I can't believe I miscalculated that badly."

While Alex paced to the window and back, Andrea explained how she had paid for another night and then gone for some food and a paper. She sat on the bed and waited anxiously for her husband's response, hoping she had done the right thing.

But Talanov was occupied with his own worries. How were they going to escape? And to where? Transportation, lodging, food - everything took money. By himself, of course, he could easily melt into the opaque world of the streets, using KGB strategies to survive like a rat until he had accumulated enough resources to take him abroad.

But he was not on his own, and it was because of his involvement with the KGB that Andrea was now in danger. Talanov was soberly aware of just how perilous their situation had become. Their options were disappearing as rapidly as their cash, and for the first time he began to feel a noose tightening about them. He leaned against the dresser and massaged a small ache in his forehead.

"Alex?" asked Andrea with concern.

Talanov looked at his wife, his tense expression softening into a weak smile when he saw her worried expression. He came and sat beside her. "Forgive my anxiety," he said, "but I've never been in this position before. During the Cold War, I played my government's covert games with nothing to lose. Life held no meaning and neither did death. Which meant each opponent I encountered was merely another piece in a senseless game. Those games, however, now involve you, and for the first time I'm frightened of losing. What we need a friend who will take us in... someone who can't be traced."

"But who?" asked Andrea. "Your friends are dead and mine are in Perth. And as for the ones we've made since our marriage - well, any columnist knows who they are."

Talanov did not respond immediately but looked down and away, his eyes squinted in thought. "All except one," he replied slowly.

"Who is it... do I know him, or her?"

"Him, and - no - you don't. I met Spiro and his wife when I first arrived in Sydney. They're an older couple who own a Greek restaurant across town."

"I've never heard you speak of them."

"I haven't," said Talanov. "The friendship ended before I met you."

"That doesn't sound encouraging."

"They're decent people - a bit too decent, in fact - and besides, they're all I can think of. Anyway, it's a long story and I'm hungry. What have we got?"

Andrea gave Alex a doubtful glance, then reached for the white plastic shopping bag and placed it on the bed. "Elegant Cuisine, at your service," she said, spreading out the contents. "Garden-fresh carrots and apples, some bread, a bit of cheese and some chocolate. It's hardly four-course but it's filling. Naturally, the bread is whole-meal."

"Naturally."

"And I figured we could use this," she said, taking out a bottle of wine.

Talanov nodded approvingly. "With a screw-off cap, I hope."

Her face fell. "I didn't think of an opener." Tears formed in her eyes.

Talanov smiled and hugged his wife. "Then we'll just have to push in the cork. But I'm afraid the cut crystal is out."

The remark made Andrea laugh and she wiped her face on his shoulder.

"You just used my jacket for a handkerchief," he said.

"It needed cleaning, anyway."

Talanov chuckled and began peeling away the protective wrapper from the top of the bottle. "By the way, I saw my face on the tellie. They've obviously searched the house and found a photo in one of the albums." Discarding the wrapper, he then pushed in the cork. "Anything in the paper?"

"Front page, above the fold," Andrea replied, placing some cheese between two slices of bread.

"Then we're going to have to change tactics," Talanov said, pouring each of them some wine.

"Are you having second thoughts about Spiro?" asked Andrea as she placed the sandwich on a facial tissue and handed it to her husband.

"No, I'm trying to anticipate what they're anticipating in order to construct a plan of action."

"I'm listening."

"Remember that secret room?" asked Talanov. Andrea nodded. "Well, if it hasn't been discovered, our chance for survival's in there."

"I don't understand."

"Specialists in clandestine activities - even former ones - always plan for the unexpected."

"Did you?"

"I did, although it requires us to return to the one place that's sure to be guarded, certainly by the police and probably by the killers."

"What do we gain from this?"

"Enough money to fight these bastards. You see, hidden in that room are several hundred thousand dollars' worth of investment certificates."

"My God, Alex, where did you get them?"

"From my uncle in Denmark. Prior to the war, he transferred his estate into Switzerland, and when he died, my brother and I were his only heirs. Later, when I migrated to Australia, I brought my portion with me. I cashed in most of them, but in that box are my remaining certificates, which we'll try and cash in. Interest has been accumulating for well over fifty years."

"Are you certain we can do that with our funds being frozen?"

"No, I'm not, but we'll find a way. We've got to."

Andrea hesitated, then asked, "Alex, has that money been stained?"

"Stained?"

"By the KGB. Is it dirty money?"

"Good Lord, no. My uncle *hated* anything communist." Suddenly Alex looked across the room, a vague memory coming into focus.

"What is it?" asked Andrea, noticing his strange expression.

"I wonder if it's still there."

"Wonder if what's still there?"

"Seven million American dollars, deposited in Switzerland back in eighty-three. The man who made the deposit was then murdered in front of my eyes."

"My God, why?"

"I'm not really sure. All I know is that Andropov had the money placed in Switzerland to fund *Peristroika*."

"I thought *Peristroika* belonged to Gorbachev."

"It was Andropov's originally. But he died and the concept was changed. But never mind all of that. Right now we've got a much bigger problem."

"Which is?"

"Getting back into our house."

13 Chapter 9

After darkness had fallen they left the hotel, Andrea hailing a taxi and giving directions while Alex kept his face angled away from the driver. During the trip, Andrea continued the distraction with an exaggerated preening in the back seat, the driver keeping a close eye on her tight-fitting dress rather than listening to her meaningless chatter. Talanov, by contrast, stared silently out the window, a shielding hand massaging his temples. It was carefully planned image: the bored husband, the fatuous wife.

Within twenty minutes, the driver had discharged them along one of the streets above Chinaman's Beach. The still night air was balmy and a few clouds drifted across the sky as the two followed a curving street down to a small parking lot near the sand. From there they angled across the grassy course toward some trees on the other side. Turning right, it was but a five-minute walk along the base of the bluff to the lower edge of their property.

Above them was their house. It stood noticeably dark amid the lights of the surrounding homes. Retracing the path through shrubbery they had taken the night before, they were soon standing at the base of the wrought iron stairs.

Talanov leaned toward his wife. "Remove your high-heels," he whispered as he pulled the pistol from his belt and cocked it. "Climbing will be easier and quieter. At the top, stay low and follow me. We're going to crawl through the opening, turn left, then make our way toward the house in the shadow of the balustrade. If anything happens, get back down these stairs. But if we make it all the way, I want you to hide behind the big oleander bush near the verandah while I enter our bedroom through the upstairs balcony doors. The trumpet vine should hold me."

Andrea removed her shoes, then asked, "Why not use the entrance at the far end of the house?"

"It's my guess a guard will be there."

"Couldn't there be one right above us?"

"A sentry out here is vulnerable and the terrace can be watched from the house. Besides, it's my hope they don't consider us stupid enough to come back here."

"Unless they figure we *have* to... that we're out of places to run."

"In that case-" Talanov began.

"Don't say it," interrupted Andrea. "I love you, come on, let's go."

They mounted the stairs slowly, Talanov leading the way, his pistol poised, his senses alert for the sound of voices or the whiff of a cigarette.

At the top, Alex paused to scan the darkness. When satisfied, he crawled through the opening and turned left. With Andrea close behind, they began circling the edge of the lawn in the deeper shadow of the concrete railing. The balustrade soon angled to the right and it was not long before they came to the tables near the high lattice fence. The bodies were now gone, although taped outlines of where they had fallen were visible on the grass and brick paving. They crept along silently in the darkness, eventually reaching the protective branches of the large oleander. The verandah was straight ahead.

Some movement to his right caught Talanov's attention. He quickly reached a hand back to Andrea, warning her to be still. Keeping well in the deeper shadows, very slowly Alex leaned back and placed his mouth to her ear. "On the far side of the porch, near the doors," he whispered. Suddenly there was the momentary flame of a lighter behind a cupped hand. The man had lit a cigarette, obviously relaxing with neither an expectation of trouble nor an awareness of their presence.

However, even with that in their favor, how could he manage to climb to the balcony? The least bit of noise would alert the guard in an instant. Some kind of diversion was needed. But what? The gardener kept the grounds so clean that finding even a small rock to throw would be difficult, especially in the dark. Still, he knew he must try and began feeling around with his hand.

"What's that?" the guard called out.

Talanov's heart leaped and he readied the pistol.

"Trevor, is that you at the front door?" the guard then asked.

When there was no reply, the guard dropped his cigarette and crushed it beneath his foot. He then turned and entered the living room through one of the open French doors.

"Now's my chance," Talanov whispered. "Stay here and you'll be safe. Even if you hear gunfire, stay put."

"Do you honestly think I could remain here knowing you've been shot?"

"The fact is, I may *not* be shot. It might just be a diversion."

"And how am I supposed to tell the difference?"

There was, of course, no way to tell and both of them knew it. Still, he did not have time to argue the point, and in the event he *did* get shot, there would be little that she could do. "Just stay here," he said.

And without waiting for her to protest, he stuck the pistol in his belt and sprinted to the nearest wrought iron column covered with thick growths of vine. Grabbing the thickest portion of trunk, Alex began climbing hand over hand, the vines crackling but holding his weight. Above him the branches fanned out and formed archways with the other columns.

Knowing he must hurry, Alex reached up toward the edge of the balcony but could not yet touch it. Without warning, some of the vines pulled loose and Alex grabbed another one to steady himself, all the while fearing that someone would hear him. Angling slightly to his right, Alex poked his foot into a dense section and pushed himself higher, again reaching for the edge of the balcony.

His hand touched the metal lip, and straining more, Alex climbed higher until he could grab the lower railing of the balustrade, then the upper. He pulled, swinging one leg up, then the other. Once over the top, he lay motionless on the deck, perspiring and winded, the pistol again in his hand.

Alex waited for well over a minute before crawling over to several palm trees planted in large terra cotta pots. He paused there, then slowly stood and quietly approached the double doors which led into their bedroom.

Peering through one of the panes, he surveyed the darkened room, the absence of any direct light making it difficult to see. He waited and watched but could see nothing. Cautiously he tried one of the handles. The door cracked open.

Talanov stiffened, his gun readied, his heart pounding. Could the sentries have been so careless? Or was the expectation of his return indeed so remote that caution had been abandoned? Certain this was not a trap, another thought then struck him: if the balcony was part of their rounds, which would account for the unlocked door, then a guard could return at any moment. He must get inside!

Alex pushed open the door and stepped quickly inside, then closed it carefully behind him. He then went to the door which led into the hallway, pausing to listen for voices. It was disturbingly quiet.

Move! an inner voice told him. *Patience*, another one said. Feeling the drumbeat of each second, Talanov slipped around the corner and ran silently down the hall, feeling in his pocket for the knife. Ahead was the linen cabinet.

But as he started to open the cabinet door, a series of muffled stoccado gunshots sounded downstairs. These were followed by frantic screams.

"Get out of my house!" shouted an angry voice.

Talanov hurried toward the stairs as more shots were fired.

From the top of the staircase, Alex saw the darkened form of a man run out through the open front door. A second man raced to the door after him, firing several shots in their air - *purposely missing*, it seemed to Talanov - then shouting that he would kill *all* the bloody police rather than let them take him alive. The man then raced back through the house.

Alex listened carefully to the sound of running footsteps - the killer was now on the verandah! - the noise then fading as the man ran down the steps and across the patio.

After quickly descending the stairs, Alex crouched by the railing at the bottom and looked around the darkened living room. In the lighter shades of the night beyond, Alex could see that the French doors were still open. Keeping low, he sprinted across the carpet and out through the doors, searching for the gunman.

Alex realized he had heard no scream from his wife. Moving silently, he ran toward the steps, pausing near one of the wrought iron posts covered with trumpet vine. Once again he searched the surrounding darkness, and once again, there was nothing.

Crossing the patio, he approached the oleander bush. "Andrea!" he called out in a harsh whisper.

"Alex?" came her reply as she climbed to her feet.

"Come on, we've got to hurry. The police will be on their way."

Holding hands, they ran into the darkened house and up the stairs, Talanov recounting what had happened. He explained how the whole scenario was made to look as though he, Alex, had come back and killed one of the officers guarding the premises. And by allowing the other policeman to escape, the killers created a witness to verify the murder of a fellow officer. The resulting manhunt would be relentless.

Alex stopped in front of the linen cabinet and pulled out his knife. Unfolding it, he opened the cabinet door, located the slot and inserted the blade. The cabinet swung back on its hinges, the two illuminated red dots becoming visible in the darkness. "They didn't find it!" he exclaimed, closing the cabinet behind them once they had entered. He then turned on the lights and went immediately to the desk where he dropped to his knees and rolled back a section of carpet. Mounted in the floor was a small safe. He spun the dial back and forth several times, then took hold of the handle and lifted. The heavy steel panel swung open.

Talanov reached inside and pulled out several brown envelopes which he gave to his wife. "Don't lose these," he said, closing the safe and spinning the dial. He then replaced the carpet. "Now, go to the dresser and grab us some clothes. And don't forget our passports. Meet me back here in two minutes."

"I'm on my way," Andrea replied as Talanov went to the radio. Pulling back the latch, she let herself out and ran down the hall.

Talanov was fine-tuning the dial when the hysterical voice of the patrolman erupted over the speaker. "It was *Talanov*, I tell you, and he killed *Trevor*."

"Killed *Trevor?*"

"Yes! Get someone *down here*. I'm up the street from his house."

"We're on our way."

Talanov switched off the radio and sat there, hearing what he had expected to hear but stunned by it nonetheless. *Again* he was being set up, this time for the death of a policeman. *Who was doing this... why?*

Alex was startled by the linen cabinet opening.

"What's wrong?" asked Andrea, seeing the look on his face as she closed the door. She was dressed in blue jeans and a dark shirt and carried a small suitcase.

"As expected, the policeman who got away is accusing me of murdering his partner."

"This is beginning to sound familiar."

Talanov stood. "Come on, let's go."

But before Alex had opened the cabinet door, he noticed a tiny red light flashing at the end of the counter. His unlisted, private telephone had recorded an incoming message. "My answering machine," he said, touching his wife on the arm, "and virtually all of the people who had access to this number are dead." He tapped the replay button and the two of them listened to the sound of a cassette tape being rewound. Within seconds the voice of General Vladimir Timoshkin spoke to them from the unit's small speaker.

Talanov listened in shock to the general's message and the difficulty with which it was spoken. The drama escalated with each labored breath, the dying soldier's final words being recorded as clearly as his moment of death.

"My God, he's *dead*, he's been *poisoned!*" a woman screamed in the background as the phone was dropped to the floor. The woman then grabbed the instrument and yelled into it, demanding to know who this was. After repeating the demand twice more with murmured curses about the lack of reply, the line suddenly went dead.

"Who was *that?*"

Talanov did not have time to reply before a high-pitched beep was heard, signaling a second message.

"Alex, this is Sergei. What's *happening*, my friend, where are you? Fiona and I couldn't locate you at the party to tell you we had to leave. My God, all those *murders!* And now, accusations and lies. You *couldn't* have done it, Alex; I've known you for too many years. Just remember, you're a Russian as far as the consulate is concerned and I'm working on diplomatic immunity for both you and Andrea. Believe me, we'll sort this out. You've probably left the country by now, but in case you haven't, *call me!* We have a shack near the beach north of Sydney and you can stay there as long as you need. Keep safe, my friend."

"Alex, Sergei's *alive!*" said Andrea excitedly.

"Thank *God*," replied Talanov, breathing a sigh of relief.

The two of them instinctively embraced, Talanov closing his eyes, the embrace lingering as they held one another tightly. Admittedly, the fear of losing Andrea had kindled emotions he had never before felt. As a lad in the Komsomol, he had been taught to suspect all personal relationships - especially family members and friends who confessed values based on religion. Commitment to the State was supreme, with emotional attachments but crutches for the weak.

And yet other lessons from Balashikha were proving uncomfortably true. This new surge of passion for his wife was indeed proving to be a danger and nowhere was this more glaring than with what happened in the hotel after the massacre. Were he to try and fool himself he could argue that retirement had made him careless. But in truth it was the distraction caused by his emotions which had caused him to miscalculate on safety. Had the night manager not called and inadvertently alerted them, they most certainly would have been killed. The whole episode pointed unmistakably to the fact that he needed to focus, to detach himself from those emotions in order out-think his opponents.

For as much as he treasured his wife, he needed to keep her alive.

"Tomorrow, I'll call Sergei and let him know we received his message," said Alex, relaxing his embrace. "What I'm hoping is that the consulate's computers can dig up some information on the Second Thirteen."

But Andrea did not let go, instead holding Talanov tighter. "I don't understand any of this, Alex, and I probably never will. I'm just glad we have each other." Talanov's response was to wrap his arms around his wife again. Andrea looked up.

"I love you, Alex," she said.

The words filled Talanov with warmth. "I love you, too," he replied.

With a contented smile, Andrea laid her head against Talanov's chest. "How I've longed to hear you say that and mean it."

"I know, and I'm sorry... for everything." He pulled away. "And I hate to say this - especially right now - but we need to leave."

"That's right, the police - I forgot," said Andrea, reaching for the suitcase.

"I'm just glad he believes in our innocence," stated Talanov. "Maybe now we can begin to figure out who they are, how to stop them, and why they want me killed."

But as Talanov reached for the latch, he heard the sound of muffled voices in the hallway. An immediate finger to his lips told Andrea the obvious before he switched off the light.

Footsteps could now be heard running up and down the corridor as doors were opened and rooms were searched. Next came numerous shouts and the sound of furniture being overturned. Someone was looting their house!

Or worse - *conducting a search.*

Andrea gripped her husband's arm at the sound of a loud thump. Someone had opened the linen cabinet! Alex aimed his pistol as they listened to hands pulling towels and sheets from the shelves. A voice then called out: "Nothing in here. What did you find?"

The reply was too distant to be understood. The linen cabinet door was then slammed shut and the intruder ran down the hall.

An unnerving period of silence followed. What was going *on?* The darkness of the tiny enclosure only amplified their emotions which were already wrung to the limit. An occasional, indistinct sound reached their ears, but from exactly where neither of them could tell. The aching minutes passed.

What was that sound? It was faint, like the snapping of twigs or crunching of dry leaves beneath a boot. Alex listened carefully to the sound growing louder and louder. What was it?

Then came the smell of smoke. *Fire!*

Talanov quickly opened the linen cabinet door and looked down the hall toward the front stairs. Flames were climbing the walls of the corridor while overhead a ravenous sheet of yellow hugged the ceiling and moved steadily toward them.

"The back stairs, *hurry!*" said Alex, grabbing the suitcase and his wife by the hand. He led her the short distance to a doorway at the end of the hall.

Suddenly an explosion rocked the house from below and sent a violent blast of flame billowing up the stairwell. Alex lunged back on top of his wife, knocking her to the carpet as the flaming tornado thundered over them, scorching the ceiling and shattering windows. Down the corridor behind them the inferno had become a solid wall of fire, with the back staircase now the same.

Alex rolled to the side. "I'll be back, stay here," he told his wife before crawling hurriedly toward some bed linens and towels which had been scattered over the floor. He grabbed several sheets and flapped them free of their folds, then tied the ends together. He then dragged the makeshift rope back to his wife, along with an antique chair from the bedroom. Securing one end of the rope around the chair, Alex threw the loose end out the window, followed by their suitcase.

"Quickly!" he said, assisting Andrea to her feet. With the chair, he knocked the remaining shards of broken glass out of the frame before bracing the chair across the window. Alex then boosted his wife onto the sill, the sheet-rope now in her hands. "Turn around, back out of the window and lower yourself to the ground."

"I *can't!*" cried Andrea.

"You've *got* to, and the ground isn't far. Let it slide through your hands."

"But-"

"*Hurry!*"

Another explosion sounded, this one down in the foyer. Glass and debris flew up the front stairs and pushed a tremor of fire down the corridor toward them. Andrea screamed and lost her balance. Talanov grabbed her under the arms as she slipped from the window, her feet scraping the side of the house.

"I've got you, take the rope," he told her, straining to keep her from falling.

"I can't!"

"You *can!* Let go of my neck."

Reluctantly, Andrea took the sheet with one hand, then the other. Alex gave her a nod of encouragement, soot and ash covering his face. "Now, slide down the rope, you can make it." Slowly he released her and, hand over hand, she lowered herself to the ground.

Another flaming blast detonated below and flew up the stairs beside Talanov. He quickly leaped onto the sill and backed out of the window as a ball of fire pushed through the stairwell doorway, igniting the chair and the rope. With only moments remaining before the rope would burn through, Talanov rappelled down the outside of the house, reaching the earth as the cloth gave way.

Talanov ran to his wife. "We've got to hurry," he said, grabbing their suitcase. Sirens and the horn blasts of several fire engines could now be heard in the distance. With his wife's hand in his, he led the way down through the trees to the edge of their property.

They paused by the fence to look back.

"Our house is *destroyed*," Andrea said, wiping tears from her eyes. Through several of the upstairs windows, frenzied tongues of yellow were spreading up the walls and devouring the eaves. Smoke and cinders were billowing into the night sky.

The flashing lights of a police car were now visible up the slope as it screeched to a halt. "Come on, before they see us," said Alex bitterly.

And after a final glimpse at their burning house, Alex and Andrea fled into the night.

Chapter 10

The taxi stopped two blocks from a restaurant known as Spiro's. Andrea paid the driver while Alex climbed out of the vehicle with the suitcase, a hat pulled down to obscure any clear view of his face. He stood waiting in the shadows until his wife joined him before leading the way down the block.

They had cleaned up as best they could with a handkerchief soaked in a sprinkler. Ironically, the converging of police cars and fire trucks provided more than enough distraction for Alex and Andrea to slip unseen from the neighborhood. Coupled with the exploding columns of flame, the entire scene was like a narcotic for the curious and excited, their insatiable appetite stimulated by the approaching wails of more sirens.

It was not until they had climbed into the relative safety of a cab that the impact of their ordeal burst into Talanov's mind like a tormenting demon: *why had their house been destroyed?* Was it merely an act of vengeance, a gesture to intimidate and frighten? Or was there some deeper reason? What had been gained by doing it?

"You said Spiro's a friend?" Andrea inquired as they angled across the street and proceeded toward a door of heavy planks. Over the arched doorway was an illuminated sign advertising the owner's name, while along both sides of the darkened street were dozens of cars, some parked so close that passage between them was impossible. Lively Greek music could be heard as they neared the restaurant.

"A very old and untraceable one," Talanov replied.

"What happened?"

"I found Spiro to be an unreasoning, narrow-minded dictator."

"Then why are we here?"

Alex looked at his wife. "Because he's a man you can trust with your life."

"After all that's been in the news, are you sure the dictator will be as merciful as you hope?"

Talanov knocked on the door, knowing that he had not considered the full effect of the media. He had merely *assumed* Spiro would welcome them, based largely on intuition. *What if he were wrong?* What if the man's orthodox religious views impelled him to call the police? Those rigid principles had divided them once before and Talanov had angrily ended the friendship, over which issue he could not recall. But with Andrea's safety now his concern, Alex knew they must find shelter, at least until Sergei could arrange diplomatic protection. He again pounded on the door and waited impatiently, anxious about Spiro's reaction. What was taking him so long to answer?

He was about to knock once more when a man's voice shouted through a small window in the door: "We're closed tonight for a wedding." Laughter from a large crowd of people could now be heard with the music.

"We're here to see Spiro," answered Talanov, scanning the street to avoid showing his face to the man asking questions.

"Spiro is busy. Who are you?"

"Alexi... a friend of the family."

"Alexi, is that *you?*" The door suddenly swung open, revealing a short, older, heavy-set Greek man dressed in a tight-fitting suit. "It *is* you!" he cried out joyfully.

Talanov recognized the man. "Vasilios!" he replied with a smile as the short Greek embraced him.

"It has been too long," Vasilios declared, stepping back to gaze into the face of his friend. "Spiro will *weep* with happiness." His smile widened as he looked at Andrea. "This is your daughter, of course?"

Talanov chuckled and shook his head. "You still haven't lost your touch. Andrea, meet Spiro's extremely charming brother. Vasilios, this is my wife."

"The pleasure is mine!" Vasilios said with a broad smile, shaking Andrea's hand vigorously. "Come in, come *in*," he said, ushering them into the brick courtyard and again bolting the door. To their left, thick vines of wisteria had spiralled up painted white wooden posts and across an arbor.

Vasilios led the way into the foyer of the restaurant. Through some arches ahead, Talanov could see dozens of tables surrounded by laughing guests, all eating and drinking. Further back was a rotating circle of other people dancing to the spirited accompaniment of a trio of musicians.

"Who's getting married?" asked Alex.

Surprised, Vasilios stopped. "Has it been that long, Alexi? Tonight is the marriage of Helena, the youngest daughter of Spiro."

"Little Helena?"

"Not so little, Alexi. She is now twenty one, and very much with a mind like her father. The two of them are like wild horses. Last year, she wanted to move into her own flat." Vasilios shook his head at the memory. "Well, you know Spiro and can imagine what happened when he refused. Oh, how she screamed, but Spiro would not change his mind. Helena was so angry she smashed dozens of plates and glasses! In the end, of course, she stayed. And tonight - look, all is forgotten." He offered an approving smile at the wedding and then motioned for them to follow.

"I understand now what you meant," Andrea whispered to her husband as they passed beneath an arched doorway, its white plaster trimmed in blue.

Alex smiled at his wife. "And yet it is why we are here."

Vasilios led them into the main dining area. Suddenly there came a booming command in Greek from the other side of the room. The musicians ceased playing and all laughter immediately grew silent. As if sliced by a knife, the crowd parted for a powerful, barrel-chested man striding to the center of the floor, his mouth open in astonishment. The disbelief then turned into joy, tears forming in his eyes. "Blessed *God* of my fathers!" Spiro thundered, his deep voice resonating across the whitewashed hall. "*Alexi!*" He hurried over to Talanov and encircled him with thick, brawny arms.

"Greetings, old friend," Talanov replied, returning the Greek's embrace.

Finally Spiro stood back, the tears now streaking his cheeks. "Tonight you make my joy complete!" He then turned to Andrea. "And who is this?"

"My wife," answered Alex. "Andrea, meet Saint Francis, the dictator."

With a bellowing laugh, Spiro shook Andrea's hand. "So he has been talking about me!" Suddenly, he became serious. "Alexi, I never thought I would see you. And with this nonsense now in the news... it is good you are here."

"You've heard, then?"

The Greek nodded, then looked straight into Talanov's eyes, carefully searching their depths. A confident smile then appeared. "Good... *good*. I know now they are all lies." Spiro suddenly whirled around and held up his hands for silence. When all was quiet, he spoke in Greek to the crowd, making several obvious references to the man beside him, his arms gesturing for emphasis. He then stepped back beside Talanov and embraced him, then ordered wine to be poured. Vasilios and several of the men began filling glasses for every person, with brimming ones brought to Spiro and the Talanovs. As soon as everyone had been served, Spiro held up his hand. The room grew quiet again as the owner of the restaurant looked carefully around the room to make sure everyone held a filled glass. When satisfied, he lifted his goblet in the air. "*Isihia!*" he called out. "Our pledge of silence and loyalty for my brother and his wife." The entire wedding party solemnly repeated the word and then drank, completely emptying their glasses. When finished, everyone held their empty containers high overhead, and at Spiro's command, began hurling them into the empty rock fireplace. The smashing lasted for nearly a minute until Spiro was satisfied. The crowd then broke into a cheer, applause erupting simultaneously as Spiro once more embraced Talanov, this time including Andrea.

"More glasses... *start the music!*" Spiro shouted. To Talanov: "Come, you will join us."

The brisk, amplified sounds of bouzouki and mandolin broke out as Vasilios began sweeping up broken glass.

"We need to talk," Alex said privately to Spiro as they crossed the floor toward a round table occupied by immediate members of the family.

"Later," Spiro replied as he waved to some guests.

"Spiro-" tried Alex.

Spiro held up a hand. "I explain to them concerning the lies," he said. "We all drank and now you are safe."

"I don't want to put you in danger," Talanov protested firmly.

The Greek smiled at his friend. "Which is why I know you are innocent. A guilty man thinks of himself. Come and have something to eat."

"*Eat? Spiro, assassins* are stalking us!"

"We will speak of it later." Approaching the family table, Spiro gestured first toward his daughter. "You remember my little Helena?" Dressed in an elaborate white wedding gown, Helena stood and smiled.

"Of course," said Alex, forcing a smile. "How could I forget?" He stepped forward and gave her a kiss.

And the introductions began.

There was still plenty of revelry when the clock struck three, the circular chain of dancers all hopping and side-stepping to the delightful rhythms of music, their hands on one another's shoulders. Over the last several hours they had been fueled by a steady flow of liquor and bitter black coffee. Soon there would be more food.

Encouraged by Spiro, all family members at the table had joined in the dancing. "We talk now, Alexi," said Spiro, pouring each of them more red wine. "Tell me, who are these killers?"

Talanov told Spiro what he knew, beginning with the slaughter in their home while he and Andrea were down on the beach. He related how neither of them had heard any gunfire - which meant silencers - nor had any of the guests been robbed. This combination of facts led him to the conclusion that assassins had been responsible. Talanov then told Spiro about the police conversation he had monitored and how an anonymous informant - supposedly a neighbor - had called in claiming that he, Talanov, was responsible! Alex knew then if they were taken into custody, he would lose any chance of proving his innocence. Their only choice was to run.

Which they did, to an airport hotel. But that nearly became a trap because of a trace on their credit cards, which meant the killers had connections into the financial computers. The next day their problems intensified, for not only had Talanov's photo had been given to the media but their assets in the bank had been frozen. Their one choice was to return to their house for some investment certificates, which they hoped to cash in.

However, as expected, the house was guarded, although Alex was able to gain entry by climbing up to the balcony. "But once I was inside the shooting started," he said. "A police officer was killed by someone posing as me."

"But why all this trouble to blame you?" asked Spiro.

That, of course, was the mystery. Alex then told Spiro about the two messages recorded on his unpublished telephone line. The first was from General Vladimir Timoshkin, a former officer in the Soviet army. The history of their association dated back to Talanov's KGB days, which culminated in a 1983 secret conference with Yuri Andropov. According to the general, a second Department Thirteen was created during that meeting.

"Department Thirteen?" asked Spiro.

"The original Department Thirteen was a covert KGB assassination and sabotage unit," explained Talanov. "They were so despised and feared that even Balashikha had to deny their existence while continuing to train them in secret. Officially, they never existed and unofficially they were thought to have been disbanded during the reign of Stalin. But if what I've been told is true, Andropov sent a second group of them into the West as part of his restructuring program. From what I remember, they were to have been funded by an investment account in Switzerland. But because Andropov died soon thereafter, they seem to have disappeared and I never heard anything more. What their intended purpose was - or is - I've no idea because I was ordered out of that meeting before any of this took place."

"But you think they exist and are here in Australia?" asked Spiro.

"General Timoshkin was killed by them - poisoned, actually - but not before warning me about their existence. Based on what he said, I'm convinced it was the Second Thirteen who killed our guests although I can't tell you for what reason, why they're in Australia, or why they're after me."

"Perhaps they think you could identify them?"

"If they do, they're badly mistaken."

Andrea touched the hand of her husband. "But didn't the general say something like, 'you must stop them, there are none remaining who know'? If General Timoshkin thinks you know, isn't it possible the killers do, too?"

"But know *what?*" asked Talanov, his frustration evident.

"That's what we have to find out," said Andrea gently.

Smiling at the reassuring touch of his wife's hand, Alex took a couple of calming breaths, then recounted his second message from a Russian diplomat named Sergei Zinyakin. Alex explained how he had met Sergei at nearly the same time he'd met Spiro, and that over the years, Sergei and his wife had become friends. "Apparently, they were the only two guests to have escaped the massacre. As luck would have it, they left early and Sergei's now trying to arrange diplomatic protection for us through the Russian Consulate." Alex then related how intruders set fire to their house.

"Which is why we're on your doorstep," Alex told Spiro. "We need a little food and some rest, and you're a friend who can't be traced. We'll leave in a day or two."

Spiro was about to take a drink of his wine when he suddenly lowered the glass. "Leave?"

"We have to, Spiro. If we're to survive we need to vanish, which we can do once we've cashed in my certificates."

"*If* you can cash them in," replied Spiro, "which may be impossible if your funds have been frozen."

"Regardless, we can't stay here. Both the killers and the police are combing the city for us and in the hands of either we're dead. For us to remain here would endanger you and your family. Anyway, Sergei has a beach shack north of Sydney where we can stay until he gets us out of the country under diplomatic veil."

Spiro shook his head. "You should stay here."

Talanov ran a hand wearily through his hair. "I thought I made myself clear."

After downing the remainder of his wine, Spiro turned to watch his daughter dancing in a circle with some friends, the spectators from surrounding tables clapping to the beat, the music filling the restaurant. She looked his way and he raised his glass. "Family is important," Spiro declared while watching Helena. "We work together, laugh together, fight together." He looked back at Talanov. "No, Alexi, you will stay."

"We *can't*," replied Alex firmly. "Spiro, these killers aren't local thugs. The risk is simply too great."

"And you think there is less risk by hiding in the house of one of your known friends? Why are you so stubborn, Alexi? If you leave here they will find you - one of you, anyway - and what if it is Andrea? You cannot spend each moment together, and here with us you are safe."

"But for how long? If just one of tonight's guests lets it slip that I'm here, then all of you become targets. And the danger of that is real, Spiro. Very, very real."

Spiro leaned up to the table. "Listen carefully, Alexi. You are my family, for I love you as a brother. This must be hard to understand for you are not Greek. But the bond of family is strong. None of these people will talk."

"We're not staying, Spiro."

The Greek placed a hand on the arm of his friend. "You must, for you cannot outrun them. They will find you wherever you go."

"Darling," Andrea said, "I believe Spiro is right. I know Sergei is working on some kind of diplomatic protection, but we don't know who might be watching him. I really think we should stay, at least for now."

"To stay may cost Spiro his life," stated Talanov.

The Greek was the one to reply. "To stay may help us save yours."

13 Chapter 11

Next door to the restaurant, in one of the upstairs bedrooms of Spiro's home, Alex and Andrea had fallen asleep shortly before dawn. They had eaten again with the others, Spiro and Demetria then joining the circle of celebrants for another two hours of dancing before telling the cooks to start breakfast.

A gentle hand on his shoulder awakened Alex, who jerked open his eyes to see Spiro with a finger to his mouth. He then motioned for Alex to follow, slipping silently out of the bedroom. Once Alex had tiptoed into the hall, Spiro led the way downstairs. "Come," he said in a lowered voice when they were halfway down. "You must see what is happening."

"What is it?"

"You will see."

The lounge room of Spiro and Demetria's house, where the television was located, was an example of how not to decorate. The seating area was an odd collection of sofas and chairs, with no two pieces the same color or style. These, in turn, were adorned with pillows featuring scenes from the Sistine Chapel and Star Wars beside others in floral, paisley, and brilliant geometric patterns. Draperies of thick orange velvet competed with crimson carpet and throw rugs of synthetic zebra, giraffe, and tiger. Floor space around the perimeter was congested with bookshelves, large porcelain statues, and arrangements of bright plastic flowers. The Greek flag was prominently displayed on one wall, with pictures of the Grecian countryside filling the others. To say the room was crowded was an understatement; it was more of a suburban cockpit.

Yet this concentration of color and texture was not at all unpleasant. In fact, it was restful and secure, the clutter giving it warmth, the chaos creating order.

But Talanov's attention was not on furnishings when he and Spiro entered the room. Instead, it was immediately drawn to the television screen where a blonde female announcer was speaking, her accent American. "For the latest report from Australia, we switch to Alf Epson, in Sydney."

"Thanks, Marnie," the red-haired Epson said, a microphone in his hand. The journalist was wearing a tan trench-coat and behind him were the charred, smoking ruins of a house. "I'm in front of what remains of Aleksandr Talanov's home, the accused KGB spy in whose garden terrace over two dozen people were deliberately gunned down, an act which authorities are calling the worst terrorist attack in Australian history. Last night, the million-dollar residence was destroyed by explosions and fire, with experts confirming the use of plastic explosives to set the blaze."

The camera then pulled back to include a man whose face had been purposely blurred. Epson adjusted his posture toward the man. "With me right now is a man whose identity has been obscured to protect his very life. He identifies himself only as Sergei and he says he was in Talanov's home the night of the massacre. Sergei, is it true the dinner you attended was for members of the KGB?" Epson held the microphone in front of the blurred face.

"*Retired* KGB," Sergei corrected. "My wife and I had been invited by the Talanovs even though I was never personally involved with the KGB."

"So Mr Talanov is, or *was*, KGB? You're confirming that?"

"Yes, but he's retired, happily married, and living a quiet life here in Sydney. Look, I've known Aleksandr for many years and I want to make it perfectly clear that I cannot believe he is responsible for *any* of the things for which he's been accused."

"Then tell us why you insist on having your identity protected."

"Because the ones responsible for these acts of terrorism are still out there, and letting them know who I am will not only jeopardize me and my wife, but the lives of Aleksandr and his wife."

"How can you be sure Mr Talanov did *not* commit these murders? Were you with him the entire evening?"

"No, I wasn't, but I know the kind of man he is."

Epson leaned forward. "Are you saying you cannot vouch for his whereabouts that night?"

"We were with them most of the evening, but he and Andrea disappeared after serving champagne - probably to take a walk - and later my wife and I left. But as I said-"

"Why did you leave early?" interrupted Epson.

"It was late and we took a taxi home because we had been drinking. But as I started to say-"

"What time was that?"

Annoyed at Epson's rapid-fire tactics, the blurred face inhaled deeply to suppress his frustration, and when he spoke he spoke slowly. "Dinner was at eight, with champagne being served for another three or four hours. Our taxi driver came to the door just before midnight and that's when we left."

"Forensics experts say the murders occurred around midnight," Epson said. "Having admitted your inability to verify Talanov's whereabouts for that part of the evening, how can you be certain of his innocence? After all, he's been accused and you were not there."

"My God, man, each person there was a *friend*. The Talanovs have entertained us on *numerous* occasions and have never - I say *never* - demonstrated any hostility whatsoever. Plus, if he were guilty, why would he not have killed us earlier? No, I don't know why he and his wife disappeared or where they went, but that doesn't make them *killers*. There's no motive, and many in that group have known one another for well over twenty years!"

"Might there be KGB secrets a former agent would want kept quiet?" inquired Epson. "Might that be a possible motive?"

"All agents have secrets."

"But serious enough to kill for? That's what the police have to be asking."

"I'm working with the authorities right now to try and sort this out. Alex, if you're listening, *please* call the police. They can give you protection."

"One last question, Sergei. There's been considerable speculation about the identities of those present in the Talanovs' home that evening. Witnesses such as yourself say the guests were merely retired Russian government employees. Other sources speculate that the assassins may have actually been dining there and that the evening was a trap engineered by Talanov. Some analysts suggest the group was a collection of agents from Operation RYAN, an intelligence network created by Yuri Andropov in the eighties, and that espionage activities are still being conducted in Australia for sale to the highest bidder. Could you elaborate on any of this?"

"No, I could not."

"But you were there, and had yourself received an invitation."

"Your theories are offensive and ridiculous."

The trench-coated Epson looked back into the camera. "We have been speaking with a man identifying himself only as Sergei, who claims to have been in the home of Aleksandr Talanov the night of the massacre. While giving us few details on what actually happened, he is convinced of Talanov's innocence and has issued a plea for Talanov to surrender himself to the police. Sergei, however, refused to confirm or deny any truth to the rumors relating to the identities of those dining in Talanov's home the night they were killed, an occasion to which Sergei himself had received an invitation, although he and his wife admit to having left early. For *World Network News*, I'm Alf Epson in Sydney."

Rendered speechless by what he just heard, Alex lowered himself slowly into one of the stuffed chairs as the camera switched back to the blonde. Using the remote control, Spiro clicked off the set although Alex continued to stare at the darkened screen. He finally looked over at Spiro, whose eyes were directed back toward the doorway.

Talanov glanced over his shoulder and noticed his wife. Dressed in a terry cloth robe, she had been watching quietly. "You saw?" he inquired as Andrea walked to the couch and sat, drawing her legs up beneath her.

She looked at her husband and nodded. "The news is spreading. Maybe you were right: call Sergei, I think we should leave."

Talanov did not reply.

Andrea noticed his silence. "What is it?" she asked.

"I'm bothered by what Sergei said," Alex replied. "He urged me to call the police, and - in fact - admitted that he was now working with them."

"What's wrong with that?"

"Because Sergei would know that once I'm in police custody, I'm right where the killers can find me. All they need to do then is simply wait for my release or hire someone inside to finish the job. In other words, calling the police is like calling the killers."

"Maybe he was pressured to say that," reasoned Andrea.

"We're talking life and death, not a traffic violation," countered Talanov. "And I'd think Sergei would want us to be absolutely clear about where he stands and what's at stake."

Andrea silently contemplated what she was hearing. Alex was right: there *was* a glaring inconsistency.

"Who is this Sergei?" inquired Spiro.

Talanov sat back and explained Sergei's current administrative position in the Russian Consulate. As far as Alex knew, Sergei had no association with the KGB although he had to admit he knew nothing about the diplomat's background other than what Sergei had told him. In other words - he could verify nothing. Even so, at least until now, there had never been any reason *not* to believe what Sergei had told him.

"Do you think it's because he's unsure of your innocence?" asked Andrea.

"Perhaps it's something more sinister," answered Talanov.

"Surely you don't think he's one of the bad guys!" protested Andrea. "That implies he was in on the killings from the very *beginning*."

"New identities for agents are constructed all the time. Proper backgrounds get entered into the computers which then generate birth certificates, drivers licenses, passports, tax numbers, and employment histories."

"You're talking government *conspiracy*."

"The consulate need not be part of this if Sergei or a friend has gained access to the right computer. It doesn't have to be vast, only well-planned and clever."

Andrea stood and strode impatiently to the center of the carpet. "But he offered us diplomatic *immunity*. I just can't believe a man we've known and trusted all these years could carry out such an agenda. Sergei has never given us the slightest inkling of anything but loyal friendship."

"I'm not saying he's guilty," countered Alex from his stuffed chair. "All I'm saying is that I find it odd for him to be announcing on television that he's working with the police and that I should surrender myself to them. Yes, he may be saying that under pressure. On the other hand, we shouldn't automatically dismiss the possibility that darker motives exist."

"Is there some way to find out?" asked Spiro. "Because if Sergei *is* telling the truth, then he can get you safely out of the country."

"That brings up another problem," Talanov said. "Sergei's possible involvement aside, I'm not so sure I want to accept diplomatic protection."

"Good heavens, Alex, why not?" asked Andrea, returning to the couch.

"It's certainly an appealing carrot. But I'm beginning to wonder if that offer might also be nails in our coffins... assuming, of course, the Russian Consulate would grant it to us, which I'm not sure they would since I'm an Australian citizen now. The fact is, once we surrender ourselves into anyone's care, the killers will know where to find us. Put simply: we become sitting ducks. Which brings us back to Sergei and his loyalties."

"I'm all for asking the question," said Andrea, "but how on earth can you find out?"

"We prove it by fabricating a scenario to see how Sergei responds."

"You mean by setting a trap," Andrea stated, rather than asked. "Doesn't it seem a bit odd, using deceit to look for the truth?"

"Not when our lives are at stake," Talanov replied simply and without apology. "I'll use a public telephone and ring Sergei at the consulate. Sounding weary and frantic, I'll plead for his help. The type of help that he renders will let me know whether or not he's in league with the killers. If he is, then some very nasty men with guns will appear."

Andrea nodded and stood. "All right, when do we leave?"

"Right away but you're staying here."

"No, I'm not and quit trying to play the hero. I'm not some piece of useless baggage."

"I'm not saying you are," Talanov said as he approached his wife and took her hands in his. "But if Sergei's part of the conspiracy, then we're dealing with assassins again. So like it or not, you're staying here." He squeezed her hands affectionately but emphatically and turned. "Spiro, I'd like you to come along and rent us a room in a particular hotel, then another room across the street. From there we can watch what occurs. By the end of the day we should know whether Sergei can be trusted or not."

Standing, Spiro nodded and started for the door.

"Alex," said Andrea. Talanov paused. She walked over and took his hands. "Be careful... okay?" She gave him a kiss.

"I will," he said, squeezing her hands. And with a parting smile, Alex followed Spiro out of the room.

Chapter

Spiro's old Kingswood station wagon betrayed the success his restaurant had brought him. Yet in spite of its rusting green paint, the vehicle's powerful V-8 was kept in perfect operating condition by one of Spiro's four sons, who was a mechanic.

It did not take long to reach their destination. Spiro parked the Kingswood on the street and the two men walked slowly down the sidewalk toward the shabby brick hotel where Alex and Andrea had stayed two nights before. Across the street was another cheap hotel similar in appearance to the first. Both stood beside the squalid street like two derelicts in a community of derelicts.

Talanov stopped in front of a telephone booth, his hat pulled low over his brow. He was fully aware that with his face now being shown all over the city, it took but an accidental glance from a passerby for him to be recognized.

Yet it was vital to know whether or not Sergei could be trusted. For if he could, then the consulate might well provide him access to their extensive computer files. Perhaps then he could identify the Second Thirteen and why they had marked him for death.

While Spiro rented a room in each hotel, Talanov dropped the required coins into the telephone. Within moments Sergei had answered.

"Sergei, it's Alex," said Talanov.

"Thank God, you got my message!" Sergei virtually shouted over the phone. "Alex, they're combing the *city* for you. Are you all right?"

"Sergei, I'm being set up... I didn't do *any* of this!" Talanov replied, wanting to sound frantic.

"I believe you, my friend. Where are you?"

"In one of those rent-by-the-hour hotels. Sergei, you've got to *help* us. We went back to the house last night and I saw someone *shoot* a policeman. Now word is out that *I* did it. But I didn't, I *swear* I didn't!"

"Calm down, Alex."

"We need rest and need it badly. Our money is gone and we barely had enough for our room. Andrea's sleeping and-"

"You're in a room?" interrupted Sergei. "But I hear traffic noise."

Talanov's heart leaped. "I'm not phoning from our room because there *are* no phones in the rooms," he said, thinking quickly. "Like I said, this place rents by the hour. And I didn't want to phone from the lobby - if you can call it that - because of the man at the counter. He watches everything. You've got to help us... but *no police.*"

"No police? They can protect you."

"I don't trust them... don't trust *anyone* but you."

"Alex-"

"*No police.*"

"All right, no police. Now, tell me where you are."

"We've got to have time to rest... to think... to plan what we're going to *do*. Sergei, this is so crazy, so *monstrous*."

"Calm *down*, Alex and let me come and get you."

"Later today... tonight. No, it can't be tonight, we're leaving."

"*Leaving?* Alex, don't be absurd! The consulate has promised to help. They've offered diplomatic protection."

"For both of us, are you sure?"

"It's been confirmed at the highest levels. Now, tell me where I can find you. I'll dispatch my driver."

"Your driver?"

"He can be trusted."

"Only you, Sergei!"

Sergei lowered his voice. "I can't, I'm being watched."

"I don't care!" insisted Talanov, feigning desperation and fear. "You and nobody else."

"The risks are too great."

"You, Sergei, or we're calling this whole thing off!"

Sergei responded with an exasperated sigh. "All right, I'll manage it. You have my word."

"Andrea's on the verge of collapse," Talanov said, diverting the conversation. "I've got to let her sleep. I'll phone you once she's awake - yes, I'll phone you - and when you come, you must be careful... you've *got* to be, someone might *see!*"

"*Calm down*, Alex!" Sergei said sharply.

"You'll wait for my call?"

"Yes, I'll wait for your call," Sergei replied impatiently. "Now, *tell me where you are.*"

"Okay, we're in..."

Once the directions had been given, Talanov hung up the telephone and hurried across the street to meet Spiro near the other hotel. With the room charges having been paid, the desk clerk barely looked up from his magazine when he saw Spiro entering again. Within minutes they were inside a room and Alex was peering between the slats of a louvered blind. Spiro brought two chairs to the window.

Talanov sat. "We should know within the hour."

"What do we look for?" asked Spiro, sitting next to Alex.

"I wish I could tell you," answered Talanov. "I made Sergei promise to come alone, and if he does, I'll assume he's clean. But if he's got company, then at the very least he's an informant; at worst, he's in with the killers." Talanov shook his head. "If that's the case, he may not come at all, but send hired guns in his place."

"Why do you say that?" asked Spiro.

"Sergei's a desk man... soft and nervous. Not the type to carry a gun."

"Then I must repeat myself - what do we look for?"

Talanov exhaled. "If we're talking someone other than Sergei, then my guess would be two men in a hurry. If we're lucky, we'll spot the bulges of pistols in their jackets."

"And if they are women? Much can be hidden in a large purse or bag."

Alex glanced at Spiro with a grim expression before looking silently back out of the window.

As the minutes passed, both men continued to watch the street, each fearful of missing what he needed to see. How simple things would be if Sergei came alone. Unless, of course, he was followed, or - and Talanov did not want to consider this possibility - he was involved but chose to come alone, preferring a more timely moment for betrayal.

If Sergei did choose to send killers in his place, whom would he send? What if they *were* female, or a delivery man, or a couple? What if they strolled casually rather than hurried, conversing merrily to disguise their purpose? What if they used a rear door?

So many variables... so little time. More minutes passed.

Admittedly, the trap was an amateur attempt. For if Sergei were a traitor, and if confirmation of that fact were to be discovered within the next hour, Sergei needed, above all, to be careless. Talanov knew the success of this gambit depended on two things: trust and haste. "Trust" in that Sergei must completely believe what Alex had told him in apparent desperation; "haste" in that Sergei must then act quickly to intercept his targets and therefore disregard caution, figuring Alex would never suspect. Would the plan work?

Restless, Talanov stood, his eyes never straying from the scene across the street. "If killers have a potential weakness," he stated, "it is in the blind spot created by their weapons. One can easily become careless when heavily armed or with a feeling of advantage. It's one of the basic principles I learned at Balashikha."

The comment brought a smile to Spiro's weathered face. "It is far older than Balashikha," he remarked. "One mustn't forget Goliath."

Spiro's reply made Talanov chuckle. "You and your fables. Forgive me for saying so, Spiro, but your faith in those stories seems foolish. People today want proof."

"No apology is necessary, my friend, although I think you misunderstand the nature of faith. Faith gives one insight into truths unseen by others. Let me give you an example. As you know, I had faith in your innocence in spite of everything being said in the media, including many reports issued by the police. Now tell me, why would I do that?"

Talanov could not answer. He did not know.

Spiro smiled. "Well, I will tell you. I believed in your innocence because I knew you personally and, therefore, could see you through eyes which others did not have.

The truth about your innocence was not altered by the fact that no one else saw what I saw. It was still the truth."

There was a long moment of silence.

"I used to hate you for your religion," Alex finally admitted.

"And yet now you seek me because of it."

Talanov glanced down at his friend. "Are you always so bloody smart?"

The Greek laughed. "That depends on whether or not you are asking my wife."

Alex smiled and again turned his attention back onto the hotel. "Speaking of Demetria, I've never forgotten that wonderful lamb stew she used to make."

"You would order it each time you came in," Spiro recalled. "I hear you have mentioned it twice already."

"Three times to be precise."

Both men chuckled and continued their surveillance, the slats of the blind throwing alternating strips of light and shadow across the face of each man.

"Look," Talanov said a short while later. "Two men, long coats, their hands in oversized pockets. They got out of that white sedan."

"I see them," the Greek replied. "They look everywhere as they walk."

"And with urgency in their step. I don't want to believe what I'm seeing."

"I, too, find it hard to believe," Spiro said. "Sergei was proclaiming your innocence."

"All lies! Everything was concocted just to get me to call him, which I never would have done if I thought he was involved."

In less than a minute, the two men ran out of the hotel and back to the waiting car, which sped away.

Once they were gone, Alex and Spiro ran across the street to the other hotel, up the stairs, and down the hall to the room which Spiro had rented. Several bullets had been fired into the lock, doubtless from pistols with silencers, after which the door had been kicked open.

"I'll kill the bastard," said Alex, his eyes hardening.

A gentle hand on his shoulder drew Talanov's attention. "Don't you want to question him first?"

"What's there to question? I've got my answer."

"Put aside your anger, Alexi. We have learned something important here."

"Which is?"

"Until now, your killers were invisible. Not so, any more."

The revelation hit Talanov like a thunderbolt. "My God, you're *right!* Sergei's my door to the killers!"

"Which you must approach with care. Don't become, in your haste, like Goliath."

"Come on," Talanov replied, leading the way back down the hall. "We're going to start looking for stones."

The two men were soon back in Spiro's living room, Talanov sitting beside Andrea on one of the colored sofas, a fake zebra throw rug under his feet. He recounted his telephone conversation with Sergei and how the diplomat had repeatedly assured him of his promise to help. Then, once the address and room number had been given, from a neighboring hotel he and Spiro sat watching. Within thirty minutes, two gunmen had entered the hotel and shot open the door. Finding no one they raced away.

"I never dreamed it would turn out this way!" exclaimed Andrea. "He was our *friend.*"

"Nor did I," replied Talanov. "And personally, I'd like nothing better than to run him through a mincer. Spiro, however, has offered a more level-headed plan, reminding me that this is our first identifiable connection to the assassins. Through him we can get to them."

"How do you plan to do that?" asked Andrea.

Talanov stood and pulled some change from his pocket. "By placing another call as the desperate, trusting fool. My goal is to get him alone and make him talk. Spiro, is there a public telephone nearby? In case of a trace, I don't want him to suspect that someone's been helping me."

"In front of the cafe, near the gum tree."

"I'll return in a few minutes."

Talanov left Spiro's house and walked to the corner. To his left was a large eucalyptus tree under which was the metal booth. He deposited the coins and made the connection.

"Zinyakin here," answered Sergei.

"The manager must have called the *police!*" Talanov shouted into the phone. "I *knew* he was watching me strangely."

"Thank God you're safe, Alex! What happened?"

"When I came back from calling you, Andrea was awake and complaining of hunger. She was feeling weak and said she needed food. So we slipped out the side door and went to get something to eat. That's when I *saw* them, Sergei... two policemen, plain clothes, a white car. They've also put a freeze on our funds. We've got to get out of town!"

"Where are you now?"

"In front of some cafe. I can't *think*... we've got to keep *moving!*"

"Let me come and get you."

"No, Sergei, I won't endanger you. You've already done too much."

"Alex, you're my *friend.*"

Liar! Talanov wanted to scream. But he forced control over his emotions and commanded his mind to take charge. "We've got to get out of the country, which is why we're heading north. We'll spend the night in Port Macquarie, then drive to Darwin or the Cape. I'll steal a car if I have to."

"Don't be stupid, I'll come and get you."

"It's too risky. But this evening, I'll call you at home. I'll know then what our plans will be. We may need you to sell our house and transfer the money to Europe."

"Of course, but-"

"Someone's coming, I've got to *go!* I'll phone you tonight with details."

Talanov slammed down the phone and stepped away from the booth, his heart pounding rapidly. He took a deep breath to calm himself. The trap was set!

Chapter 13

"We'll leave as soon as it's dark," Talanov said as a white bowl was placed in front of him by Spiro's wife. He looked up at the plump, smiling woman with surprise. "What's this?" he asked.

"Lamb stew, what else?"

"You shouldn't have."

Demetria arched her eyebrows slightly. "After all the hints you have been dropping? Alexi, you are a terrible liar."

Everyone laughed as other bowls of the thick stew were given to Spiro and Andrea. A basket of warm pita bread was placed on the table along with an even larger bowl of sliced tomatoes, olives, cucumbers, red onions, and fetta cheese, all tossed in an olive oil dressing.

Alex gave Demetria an appreciative smile. "I'm glad we're here, but for more reasons than your wonderful stew."

Spiro's wife patted Talanov on the shoulder. "Your smooth tongue will take you far, Alexi. Watch out for him, Andrea."

"I do," laughed Andrea, who had already taken a bite. "But this time he's not exaggerating. This really is the best."

"Enough, both of you," Spiro broke in. "Any more and my wife will demand a raise."

"That is not such a bad idea," Demetria answered back, shaking a finger at her husband. "Who cooked you all of these?" She patted him on the stomach.

"Better quit while you're ahead," advised Talanov with a grin.

Spiro held up his hands in surrender. "All right, all *right*," he laughed. "I am outnumbered. You shall have your raise."

Demetria encircled Spiro's neck with her arms. "I do not want such a thing," she said, giving him a kiss. "But it was nice to hear you say it."

The Greek smiled affectionately and watched his wife return to a large blackened skillet of sizzling onions. Beside her two assistant cooks were busy arranging ingredients in casserole pans. Spiro directed his attention back to his friends. "I would be lost without her," he confessed, glancing again at his wife. "We were children together and fell in love when we were thirteen."

Talanov grew serious. "I don't want that to change, Spiro. Like I said, my being here puts you in danger."

"And like I said," responded the Greek, "we will fight these killers together."

A somber but appreciative nod was Talanov's reply.

"Now, what do we do first?" asked Spiro as he reached for the bread.

While they ate, Alex outlined his plan. The first step, of course, had been the diversion of Sergei's killers, who - if his calculations were correct - were now on their way to Port Macquarie.

"What if Sergei goes with them?" asked Andrea.

"He won't. I told him I'd call him at home tonight, so he'll stay near the phone to take my call. He figures I'll tell him where we are, after which he'll relay the information to the assassins."

"Given that Sergei's involved," said Andrea, "do you think it's in an official capacity?"

"I can't see the Russian government committing such a crime. Three people from the consulate were killed the other night, which to me rules out official involvement. It's my guess the Second Thirteen is part of Andropov's old *Peristroika* program which has remained dormant for all of these years. What baffles me is why they've surfaced now."

"Could The Second Thirteen be part of a movement within the Russian government which hopes to overthrow the existing regime in order to restore military rule?"

Alex paused with his fork over his bowl. "That's pretty far-fetched but not out of the question. The night of our party, I remember Sergei complaining about how Russia was no longer a superpower. I corrected him by saying that Russia's greatness is not in missiles."

"Whoever's behind the Second Thirteen may not agree with that definition," Andrea replied to the clanging of pans in the kitchen. "Those lusting for power will do anything to get it."

"I know, and what we need to do is figure out who's lusting and why they want me dead. What is it they think I know?"

"From what you've told me," reasoned Andrea, "it has to be linked to that meeting in the butcher shop. What do you remember about it?"

Alex thought for a moment, then recalled how Andropov had telephoned him one morning to ask that he join him for a stroll. It was there, in the garden, that Talanov was directed to personally coordinate security for a veiled, high-level conference. He was instructed to pick a location which no one could trace and make sure that it stayed that way. He chose a butcher shop near the Moscow Ring highway.

The meeting, Talanov remembered, convened at two in the morning, and of the eight or nine people in attendance, only three were men whom he knew. "Andropov was there, of course - he was quite sick by then - along with former UN ambassador Nikolai Sofinsky - he, too, was in poor health and is now dead - and General Vladimir Timoshkin... who, as we know, is now dead." Talanov then smiled. "The general was certainly surprised when I confronted him about a security breach in his office. One of his adjutants was found to have a wife with a narcotics dependency, itself not so unusual except the addiction was being funded by the CIA in exchange for classified reports. We turned it around, however, and began feeding them false information."

"Keep talking!" Andrea said eagerly. "Visualize... expand!"

Talanov looked up, remembering. "That meeting was also where I learned about the seven million dollars deposited in a Swiss bank. The banker who handled it was then murdered by the man chosen to direct *Peristroika*. I don't recall his name but I remember he wanted Andropov to excuse me from the meeting, allegedly because of my importance at the Center - our name for KGB headquarters. Andropov agreed and I was dismissed. But because Andropov died the next Spring, *Peristroika* was adopted by Gorbachev, who made the word famous. As for Cheney - that's right, the killer's name was *Cheney!* - well, he never resurfaced."

"What was the money in Switzerland to be used for?" asked Andrea.

"To fund Peristroika. But like I say, I was dismissed before learning anything specific - including any information about the Second Thirteen. That's why I can't figure out why I've been targeted. I was completely excluded from the loop, and am as ignorant now about what's going on as the clerk at the petrol station."

"Not in the eyes of the Second Thirteen," replied Andrea. "They consider you very relevant. I just wish we knew why."

Chapter 14

By ten o'clock that night, Spiro had parked the Kingswood away from the wash of the streetlights a block from Sergei's house. It was a quiet evening and the sidewalks were lined with flowering jacaranda trees, their lavender clusters hanging motionless in the nighttime shadows. From inside the car, Talanov studied the view in both directions until he was satisfied no one had noticed them. He then gave the nod and the two men climbed out of the vehicle.

They made their way along the darkened pavement, Talanov leading the way. At the corner they turned left and crossed toward the darker side of the street, Talanov stooping to pick up a loose brick from beside the sidewalk. Midway down the block Alex stopped. "It's that one," he said, pointing to a small brick bungalow.

"The house with the brush fence?"

"That's it. We'll watch from here for a few minutes. I want to make sure it's safe."

"You watch; I'll patrol the street," Spiro whispered.

"All right, but take care. If there's a guard, he's sure to be armed."

Spiro returned in ten minutes. "The street is clear," he reported. "How does it look inside?"

"Normal movements," Talanov whispered back, "and no one's patrolling the grounds. It appears we're not expected."

"Are we are ready to go in?"

Talanov turned and faced the Greek. "I'm going in, Spiro, but I need you to observe what happens."

"Keeping an old man out of the way?"

"Quite the contrary," answered Talanov. "I need a witness to what occurs while I'm questioning Sergei. Plus, in case things turn against me, I'll want you to heave this brick through the window. The shock of that moment might just save my life." He handed the brick to Spiro. "While I circle around back, position yourself behind one of the bushes. Remember, you mustn't be seen. I need not remind you what can happen if that occurs."

"It has been said enough already," Spiro replied as he placed a calloused hand on

Talanov's shoulder. "And I need not remind you to be on *your* guard, especially for the unexpected. It can kill you... or it can save you."

"You always have the last word, don't you?"

Smiling, Spiro clasped Talanov's shoulder but did not reply.

Talanov led the way to the corner of the driveway occupied by a large tangle of jasmine. It spilled over the top of the brush fence and cascaded down the other side, scenting the balmy night air with its fragrance. Behind the fence stood several large oleander bushes, and beyond these was the bungalow with its wide verandah.

Alex directed Spiro into the deep shadows behind one of the oleanders. "No matter what happens," Alex whispered, "unless you actually *see* me in danger, *stay put*. I may have to bluff my way through this, so don't react to what you think might be happening. And if I give you a signal, go with it."

The Greek agreed.

Withdrawing his pistol, Alex crept down the driveway toward the carport. From previous visits to Sergei's house, he knew there were no exterior lights connected to motion sensors.

And yet while the darkness provided him with protection, it also veiled any danger. He could not be seen, but neither could he see. Each step must be taken with care.

But more important than not making noise was the extraction of information. Could he impose on himself the required calm to carry it off? *He had to*, for this would be his only chance to question Sergei.

Which meant there was no room for error.

With a steadying breath, Alex moved silently down the driveway toward the first of two parked cars, his darkened form melting into deeper shadows beneath the roof of the carport. Proceeding carefully, he crept along next to the house, avoiding any contact with the automobiles, their activated alarms indicated by small red lights flashing on their dashboards.

He paused at the corner of the house. A few steps ahead was a large metal shed, to his left a concrete patio over which was a covered pergola. He turned the corner and walked forward slowly.

Suddenly, off to his right was a shadowed movement! His finger gripped the trigger as he stood motionless, ready to fire. Carefully he turned his head and saw the shape of a large dog move from under a bush, the clinking of metal tags on its collar now audible as the animal paused to scratch its underside. When finished, it entered the metal shed through a small hanging door in the wall. The lapping of water could soon be faintly heard.

When had Sergei acquired a dog? It must have been recently, for there had not been one here last month. Squinting, Alex saw the outline of a chain link fence. He was protected, but the dog could still make noise... *noise that would draw Sergei's attention*.

Alex was no more than half a dozen steps from the mesh security door which led into the house. The dog had not yet reappeared so he stepped toward the door quietly, his hand almost touching the handle. Another step... the door was *locked!* He tried it again, a metallic squeak sounding as he gently shook the handle. Alex quickly released it and listened for the dog, his breath suspended, his gun readied. Several seconds passed but there was no reaction. He exhaled slowly and stepped closer to the door, wondering if it could be forced. Most doors like this could be, but even then there was no guarantee that the inside door wouldn't be locked. What to do?

Looking up, Alex saw the round darkened form of a light globe mounted to the brick exterior of the house. Suddenly the sound of dog tags could be heard. *The unexpected can kill or save*. He slowly reached for the globe.

From the deep shadows behind the oleander bush, Spiro knelt on one knee and watched Sergei and his wife discussing something vehemently in the front room, the occasional sound of a raised voice escaping into the night. The overweight diplomat was defensive and impatient, pacing frequently around the room while his wife, an attractive woman with short dark hair, sat angrily on the couch with folded arms. If only the window were open, thought Spiro, then I could know why they argued.

Without warning, the barking of a dog sounded from the rear of the house. It was the deep, powerful bark of a large animal. Spiro stood and looked nervously in the direction of the carport. A large dog... the rear of the house... *Alexi!*

A bolt of fear shot through Spiro and his impulse was to rush to the rear of the house. He would kill the dog if he had to in order to rescue his friend. But the Greek forced himself to remain in position as he recalled Talanov's words about not reacting to what he *though*t might be happening. The raging of the animal grew in intensity, yet there was no cry for help, no cracks from the pistol which Spiro knew Talanov carried. From his hiding place, Spiro watched Sergei and his wife look at one another and exchange comments. The woman finally stood and accompanied her husband to the back door. There he repeatedly flipped a switch by the door and looked out through the small window into the darkness. The exterior light was not working. Sergei flipped the switch several more times, then yelled something at his wife, obviously for her unwanted advice while the dog continued to bark. He then looked out through the window again.

After another heated exchange with his wife, Sergei finally unlocked the door and peered out through the mesh of the security door. He called out to the animal and attempted to calm it. Spiro, however, could still hear it barking. *What was going on?*

Unable to pacify the dog, Sergei unlatched the screen door and opened it.

Talanov suddenly burst through the opening and shoved Sergei back into the kitchen, quickly shutting the door behind him.

"Alex, what are you *doing here*?" asked the stunned diplomat as he and his wife were ordered into the front room and told to sit on the couch, the sight of the pistol commanding obedience.

"I'm here to ask a few questions," Talanov replied once they were back in the lounge room.

"What do you mean?"

"Who sent the killers downtown, Sergei? And who sent them the night of our dinner party? Who tracked us to our hotel, fire-bombed our house, then killed an officer who guarding our home? Who, Sergei, and why? And don't bother lying, I know it's you."

"This is preposterous!" declared Sergei as he started to rise.

Talanov cocked the pistol menacingly and pushed Sergei back onto the couch. "You killed General Timoshkin, you want to kill me, *and I want to know why.*"

Sergei stiffened his posture. "I've had enough of your threats. Fiona, call the police."

"If you don't start talking - *now!* - I'll begin with your kneecaps and start working upward," said Talanov, his face lined with anger. He aimed the gun at Sergei's leg.

"Alex, *don't!*" cried Sergei.

"He's not going to shoot and he knows it," Fiona declared in an acrid tone. "His gun has no silencer and the first shot, not to mention your blubbering screams, would bring the whole neighborhood running. And that *would* bring the police."

Fiona's defiance startled Alex. Unlike Sergei, she was not frightened or nervous, and she had noticed that his pistol had no silencer. *Professionals noticed such things.*

"So you're in on it, too," Talanov stated rather than asked.

"I have nothing to say to a killer," Fiona replied contemptuously.

"Don't provoke him, he's got a *gun*," Sergei said worriedly.

"Shut up!" Fiona snapped.

"But he knows, you heard him say so."

"Shut *up*, he knows *nothing*."

Alex was startled by the exchange in that he had quite naturally assumed Sergei to be the one in charge. But Fiona was the one issuing orders, and she was worried that Sergei might talk.

It was a valid worry, for Sergei was convinced that Talanov knew all about them. But knew *what* about them? The sight of the pistol had nearly frightened Sergei into talking, and yet Fiona was right: *he couldn't shoot.* He must do something or all would be lost.

Talanov suddenly laughed and walked to the front door. Momentarily stunned, Sergei and Fiona watched in silence as he opened the door.

"Have you got the photos?" he called out while keeping an eye on the couple. "Answer me, quickly!"

"I've got them," Spiro replied from his concealed position, accepting Talanov's lead.

"Good... now, get them out of here. Hurry, *run.*"

Stunned by what was occurring, Sergei and Fiona saw the darkened form of a man run from the shrubbery just as Talanov closed the front door and walked back to face them. "I have enough to confirm your guilt," he said.

"Photos?" asked Sergei. "Alex, what are have you *done?*"

"We're onto you, Sergei, and those photos of us together will prove it. I'll make sure everyone knows that you talked and by tomorrow your life will mean nothing."

"You know nothing... you can't prove *anything!*"

Talanov smiled. "I know more than you think and I've known *longer* than you think. Why else would I have told you we were in the wrong hotel other than to film your assassins and their car? Registration numbers can be traced. And why do you think I had you send them to Port Macquarie tonight?"

Sergei clenched his fists angrily. "You can't *do* this! I've worked too long and hard to allow Andropov's double-cross to succeed."

"Double-cross? What double-cross?" pressed Talanov, stepping closer with the gun.

"*Shut up*, you fool!" yelled Fiona.

"I told him *nothing... you* shut up!"

Suddenly the discreet trill of a cellular phone could be heard from the other room. It rang again to the alarmed glances of Sergei and his wife. Fiona tried to jump up but Talanov pushed her back down with the barrel of the pistol. The ringing continued as Talanov hurried to the formal dining room table adorned with crystal and silver. He picked it up and switched it on. "Yes?" he answered into the phone.

"Tango Blue here. Are we secure?"

"Go ahead," Alex replied.

"Don't *talk* to him!" Fiona shouted from the couch, leaping to her feet.

"Is Talanov dead yet... what was that?"

"Nothing... the television, that's all."

"It's Talanov!" Fiona screamed. "Don't say anything, it's *Talanov!*"

"Who is this?" the voice demanded. "Identify yourself."

"I said we're clear, go ahead."

The line went dead.

"*No!*" Fiona shrieked as she grabbed a fireplace poker from the hearth. She turned just as Alex leveled his gun.

But Fiona was not after Talanov. Instead, she drew back the long iron rod and swung it at Sergei with all her might. It caught the stunned diplomat in the temple, the deadly spike crushing its way into his brain. Sergei's head snapped to the side as Fiona withdrew it and struck him again... then a brutal third time. "Shoot me, shoot me!" she screamed at Alex, who was momentarily shocked by what he had witnessed. Then, in Talanov's few seconds of hesitation, Fiona sprinted to the door and fled, the poker still in her hand.

Alex started to follow but instead ran to the couch and checked Sergei's neck for a pulse. There was none. Shaking his head, Talanov stepped away from the body, a look of regret on his face. Sergei was indeed a traitor, and for that Talanov despised him. But not enough to have killed him.

So why had Fiona done it? What was her role in all of this? Was Fiona really his wife?

Knowing there was no time now for questions, Alex stuck the cellular phone in his pocket and looked quickly around the room. Against the paneled wall near the fireplace stood a roll-top desk. He hurried over to it, lifted the top, and began sifting through papers, hoping to see something which might give meaning to all the madness. Seeing nothing, instinctively Alex scooped the desktop papers plus the contents of all the drawers into a trash basket lined with a white plastic bag, then threw in Sergei's private telephone directory, bank records, and business card file. As he lifted the grocery bag out of the basket, Alex realized his one link to the assassins was now dead. He had accomplished nothing, but instead was facing even more questions. Who was Tango Blue? What was Fiona's role in things and why had she killed her husband? What was Andropov's double-cross?

Moving swiftly to the front door, Alex took a last look at the corpse of Sergei Zinyakin. Another senseless murder, and by morning he would be blamed for it.

After closing the front door, Alex turned to leave just as a shadow moved toward him. He raised the pistol and sprang to his left.

"*Don't shoot!*" Spiro said, his hands held high.

"Spiro, I could have *killed* you!"

The Greek came up to him. "I saw what happened. That woman actually *murdered* her husband!"

Talanov stuck the gun in his belt. "I may need you to testify to that fact," he said. "You can bet she'll be blaming me."

"I will gladly tell what I saw," Spiro replied as they hurried up the driveway and along the darkened sidewalk.

While they walked, Alex told Spiro what had transpired inside, including the mysterious phone call by Tango Blue asking whether he, Talanov, was dead yet. Even more puzzling, however, was Sergei's outburst about Andropov's double-cross.

Spiro looked over at Alex. "Andropov's double-cross?"

"I know, it baffles me, too," replied Alex. "Obviously, Andropov pulled something because Sergei shouted that he had worked too long and hard for Andropov's double-cross to succeed." Talanov shook his head in frustration. "What do they think I *know?*"

"Or who?" added Spiro as they turned the corner. "What troubles me is this under-lying sense of urgency. General Timoshkin was a dying man and yet they considered it necessary to kill him. Why? And why the urgency to kill you? Whatever Andropov did, there seems to be a time clock attached to it."

"Which stops ticking the moment I'm killed."

"So it appears," replied Spiro as they reached the car. "And the one person who might have told you what it is has just been murdered by his wife." Spiro stuck his key in the lock. "Beware of that woman, Alexi. She will kill you if she gets the chance."

"We both had better beware," Talanov told the Greek. "You and I are tonight's only witnesses."

Chapter 15

Back in Spiro's living room, Demetria served mugs of hot coffee while Talanov recounted his experience.

"Does this mean the Russian Consulate will not help you?" asked Demetria.

"It's my guess Sergei was lying," Alex replied.

Having already downed his coffee, Spiro jumped angrily to his feet. "There must be *something* we can do to fight these killers!"

"I think there is," stated Talanov. "Based on the probability that Sergei was using his position in the consulate as a cover, I believe I've found a way to find what's beneath that cover."

"How will you do that?" asked Andrea from a curled-up position on the sofa.

"There's a young diplomat in the consulate named Ivan Lazovic. Admittedly, I don't know him all that well, but his father was a mentor of mine back in my days with Directorate Nine. While I'm certain Ivan would never knowingly cooperate with the Second Thirteen, by the same token, because of his honesty, he may refuse to help me at all."

"At this point, I wouldn't assume anyone in the consulate is that honest," objected Andrea.

Talanov agreed but reaffirmed his basic trust in Ivan due to the character of his father. It was conceivable, of course, that the son was much different from the father, and that anyone - including Ivan - could be lured away. Alex confessed that his one reservation about Ivan came from the fact that Ivan was not able to attend their dinner party because he said he was sick. All things considered, Talanov felt that if he could get through to Ivan by phone, he could determine whether or not he was on the level. If he was, then the real challenge would be in trying to convince him to use the consulate's computers to investigate Sergei. The obvious objection, of course, would be that Talanov, not Sergei, was the wanted criminal.

At half past ten the next morning, wearing sunglasses and a hat, Alex drove Spiro's Kingswood to a public telephone where he placed his call.

"Russian Consulate, good morning," a pleasant female voice answered in English.

"Ivan Lazovic, please," Talanov replied, speaking in Russian.

"One moment, please," the receptionist said before transferring the call to the proper extension.

Within seconds another female voice came onto the line. "Mr Lazovic's office, may I help you?" the woman asked.

"Yes, thank you," Talanov said in Russian. "I would like very much to speak with Ivan."

"Who may I say is calling?"

"My name is Yuri Lazovic and I am a cousin of Ivan's father, Dimitri. I have not seen Ivan in nearly ten years and I am now visiting in Sydney and wish to surprise Ivan. If possible, I would like to speak with him, but please do not tell him who is calling as I will enjoy hearing the shock in his voice. How does Ivan look? Has he gained any weight? Has he found himself a good woman?"

The secretary laughed. "He continues his running with great discipline and remains single, much to the displeasure of several of my friends. One moment and I will connect you."

Talanov waited impatiently. Finally, the crisp, hurried voice of a man interrupted from his duties came onto the line. "Ivan Lazovic here."

"Ivan, don't hang up. This is Aleksandr Talanov and we go back to the years of your father. I need you to recall those years and for his sake, hear me out." Alex held his breath. This was a critical moment.

There was a lengthy pause. "All right, but I haven't much time," Ivan replied curtly. "I'm certain you're aware of the reason."

"That's what I need to explain. I realize, however, that your first obligation is to the consulate and I will not jeopardize your position."

"Am I to be grateful? What do you want?"

The first hurdle was cleared, thought Talanov. He then continued: "During the last few days, my wife and I have been the target of assassins. They killed our dinner guests and they nearly killed us. With the help of a friend - and he will testify to everything I'm saying - I've now linked those murders to someone we both know, which is why I need your help, either to verify his guilt or disprove it." Alex paused. "That man is Sergei Zinyakin."

"*Sergei?*" Ivan exploded. "Such an accusation is so offensive that I won't hear another word of it! The man's proclaiming your *innocence*."

"It was an act," said Talanov.

"And you're *lying!*"

Alex hesitated only for a moment. "It's no lie, Ivan, and neither is this: Sergei was killed last night by Fiona."

There was a long pause of silence. "*What did you say?*" hissed Ivan.

"It's true. Yesterday, I telephoned Sergei and told him my wife and I were staying in a downtown hotel. I even gave him the room number. What he didn't know was that instead of being where I told him I was, my anonymous friend and I were actually watching from across the street. Within twenty minutes two killers entered the hotel, shot open the door to the room they thought we were in, then fled when we weren't there. They drove off in a white sedan."

"I don't believe you."

"If I had any lingering doubts, they were fully erased last night when I went to his home to confront him. While I was there, his cellular phone started ringing. He and Fiona were quite nervous about it, and when I answered it, I heard someone ask if Talanov was dead yet. At that point Fiona screamed, grabbed a fireplace poker and smashed his skull. I'm convinced they were in on the massacres in my home, Ivan, and I have to find out why."

Ivan's lips curled into a sneer. "You're insane and you're a *killer!*"

"I've been set *up*," stressed Talanov from the phone booth, one hand cupped around the mouthpiece. "*Sergei* was the killer!"

"This call is terminated. I've listened to your rubbish and I'm sick of it. The police can take it from here." Ivan reached for the disconnect button.

"*Tango Blue!*" Talanov shouted in desperation.

There was silence on the line but Ivan Lazovic did not hang up.

"My God, you're one of them," Alex stated. "I should have known that's why you missed our party."

"Where did you hear that name?"

Talanov's anger was starting to burn. "Why, Ivan? What are you people *after?*"

"I said, where did you hear that name?"

"I know what you said," Talanov replied coldly. "Now you listen to what *I* say: whatever you're plotting, I will expose you and stop you whatever the cost. You monsters killed two dozen people, damn you, *two dozen people*. You're a disgrace to your father's name, and if it's the last thing I do I'll bring you down."

Ivan sat forward in his chair at the mention of his father. Talanov had once earned his respect, and his father, before his death, considered Talanov to be one of the few honest men ever to pass through Directorate Nine. "What am I supposed to think?" replied Ivan, relenting slightly. "You're wanted everywhere."

"You *bastard*. Your father trained me - trained *you* - and you turn against him and Russia and everything that's decent."

There was now worry in Ivan's voice. Talanov was accusing *him*. "Alex, listen to me: I'm not part of whatever this is."

"Damage control, Ivan? Worried that I found out the truth? Well, you can bet I'll be telling the truth. By the time I'm through advertizing your name, you'll be of no further use. You'll become a liability to them, a sudden threat to their cause. Start looking over your shoulder, Ivan, because soon they'll be coming for you."

"Alex, *listen* to me!" Ivan shouted.

Talanov remained calm. "Save it, I've heard enough. I'll make you pay for what you've done."

"I heard a voice mention the name, that's all," Ivan said quickly. "I must have picked up the phone at the same moment as someone else in the consulate. The caller said, 'Five, this is Tango Blue.' It's all I heard because I punched another button. Alex, I'm telling the *truth!*"

There was silence again on the phone, this time from Aleksandr Talanov.

"*Please*," Ivan pleaded.

"All right," Talanov said at last. "The son of Dimitri Lazovic deserves a chance to explain."

"I had nothing to do with those murders, or with Tango Blue, or whatever happened downtown. Like I said, all I heard was a man identify himself by that name to someone here in the consulate."

"But you're not sure to whom? There wasn't a name or a voice that you recognized?"

"No, I punched another line before anyone had time to respond."

"Then it may or may not have been Sergei." A statement more than a question.

"I'm unable to confirm either way. At the time there was no reason for me to suspect anything. You know as well as I do that we still use codenames and tags. Tango Blue was merely one more."

"Could it have been Sergei?" inquired Alex.

"His office is nearby, so it's possible we would have used the same line. Plus, because the call came in during lunch, when his secretary's away, Sergei - if that's who it was - would have answered the phone himself."

"How long ago was this?"

"A couple of days."

"But why would Tango Blue risk being overheard on an office phone, even at lunch time, when Sergei carried a mobile phone specifically for those calls?"

Ivan lowered his voice even though his office door was closed. "For reasons you can appreciate, Alex, certain rooms in the consulate were designed to prevent the intrusion of unwanted signals, including mobile telephone frequencies. A land line was the only option for a call that just couldn't wait."

"So we're left without confirmation."

"I don't know what else I can tell you."

"You can tell me what's in his file," replied Alex. "There's got to be something there."

"Now hang on," objected Ivan. "While I may be sympathetic to your claims, I still have an oath to uphold, which I won't violate even for you."

Talanov smiled in the phone booth. Perhaps Ivan could be trusted. "Fair enough," he said. "Have a look, that's all I ask. If anything stands out, you let me know. I'll call you back in an hour."

"And if Sergei's background is clean?"

"Then I'll disappear from your life and you can report me to your superiors. But make no mistake: if you're discovered to be doing this, you'll be killed, no questions asked."

"It's that serious?" asked Ivan.

"It's that serious. General Timoshkin was assassinated for what he knew."

"*Timoshkin?* Over in *Adelaide?*"

"Poisoned. He died on the telephone while warning me about a second Department Thirteen, created in a *Peristroika* meeting we both attended with Yuri Andropov. He said they had come for him and his dying words were for me to stop them, that there were none remaining who knew. I have his message on tape although I don't know what he's talking about because I was asked to leave that meeting before anything took place."

"A *second* Department Thirteen? Alex, you and I both know Department Thirteen never existed."

"I'm aware of the text-book position. Believe me, Ivan, they existed, although why a second one was created I've no idea. That makes it vital that you have a look into Sergei's file. He's my only link and I've got to find the connection - something which identifies who they are and what they're doing."

"Surely you don't expect an official dossier to contain such information?"

"Not directly, no. The clues I'm after will be in amongst those details one normally overlooks: career history, phone records, travel patterns, banking portfolio, names of relatives, friends, and associates. And don't forget Fiona: where she comes from, the date of their marriage, how they met. You may have to go deep on this one, Ivan, but for God's sake, *be careful*."

"And you want all of this in an hour?"

"Yes."

"Anything else?" asked Ivan with an exasperated sigh.

"Watch your back. I'll call in an hour."

Chapter 16

Alf Epson, red-haired reporter for World Network News, stood in front of the camera with Fiona Zinyakin, her dark hair and clothing dishevelled, her eyes bloodshot from crying. "Aleksandr Talanov *murdered* my husband!" she cried out angrily before burying her face in the shoulder of the well-dressed female attorney standing beside her. While Fiona sobbed, the attorney patted her consolingly, her tailored gray business suit and erect posture advertizing her professional status.

Epson spoke directly into the camera, his expression somber. "It is a tragic day in Sydney with yet another murder in a long line of murders for accused killer, Aleksandr Talanov. I am with Fiona Zinyakin, widow of murdered Russian diplomat, Sergei Zinyakin. According to a statement issued earlier by Mrs Zinyakin through her lawyer, Talanov is said to have broken into their home making threats and wild accusations. She claims Talanov was carrying a gun, which her husband managed to wrestle free in a struggle. Mrs Zinyakin says Talanov then grabbed a fireplace poker and brutally killed her husband before running away. Fearing for her life, Mrs Zinyakin is now going into hiding, and has offered a five-thousand-dollar reward to the person who delivers Talanov into the hands of the police."

The attorney shifted toward the microphone. "When are the police going to start taking Talanov seriously? When is this going to *stop?*" She continued to pat Fiona, who was wiping her eyes with tissues.

"You're her attorney?" Epson asked, holding the microphone in front of her.

"I'm her solicitor, yes. My name is Lee Baker - that's Lee with a double-e - and it's absolutely *appalling* that an innocent woman be treated in this way."

"To say nothing of her dead husband," replied Epson.

"Well, yes, of course, that goes without saying," the attorney added just as her mobile phone sounded. She whipped it to her ear. "Lee Baker, solicitor," she said loudly before the camera was able to cut away to Epson.

"As I said, yet another victim has been added to the growing list of victims for accused murderer, Aleksandr Talanov. Back to you, Marnie."

While the horror-stricken Andrea sat with Spiro and Demetria and watched the unfolding story on the living room television, a split image appeared on the screen, with Epson on the right and the blonde Marnie on the left. Marnie spoke first. "Alf, what's the mood there in Sydney? Is there a feeling of panic with an accused mass murderer on the loose?"

"There's certainly a degree of that, Marnie - although I'd call it worry rather than panic - because while the number of murdered victims is indeed staggering, there's not a pattern of indiscriminate, random killing. Rather than threatening the general public, everything about this bizarre case has to do with KGB, espionage, and clandestine operations. The police, of course, are working overtime, but they just don't have any leads. All of Talanov's known friends have been interviewed, as have leading officials in the Russian consulate, as well as the business associates of Mrs Talanov, who operates a successful catering company. The Talanovs have simply disappeared, although the reward may produce some results."

"Is there any doubt about Talanov's guilt?" asked Marnie from the left-hand side of the screen.

"The initial scene in Talanov's home, where over two dozen people were gunned down, was reported by an anonymous informant claiming to be a neighbor who witnessed the carnage. That individual has never come forward to identify himself, however, which means there's no proof that Talanov did it. Another troubling issue is how one man could manage to shoot so many people without anybody getting away. In fact, none of the victims were more than a few steps from their table, suggesting several killers rather than one. Plus, the question of motive - why Talanov would murder his own friends - has yet to be answered as well. Amazingly, no one has even *seen* Talanov or his wife since that night with the exception of a hotel night manager, who reported their checking into his hotel but later disappearing. The next killing, of course, was in the Talanov's home the night it was fire-bombed, where a policeman was gunned down, *supposedly* by Talanov, although the officer who escaped was forced to admit that he did not actually see Talanov, but only heard a series of wild threats made by a shadowed figure *claiming* to be Talanov. Again, there was no positive identification."

"But all that has changed?" asked Marnie.

"As unbelievable as it sounds, until now the accusations could have been a malicious fabrication. But a credible eye-witness - Fiona Zinyakin - has just come forward claiming she *saw* Talanov kill her husband, and her testimony is indeed damning. For World Network News, this is Alf Epson, in Sydney."

"And, once again, here is a photo of accused killer, Aleksandr Talanov," said Marnie's voice while a full screen shot of Talanov was shown. "Anyone having information on his whereabouts should call the police."

Spiro pushed a button on the remote control and switched off the set. Beside him on the couch sat Andrea, her expression one of shock. She looked over at Spiro, tears filling her eyes. "How can Fiona stand there and tell such lies? We've eaten with them, had them in our home, even been away once on a holiday together."

"That woman thinks she can offer her blood money and just disappear," said Spiro bitterly. "But I saw her kill her husband and I will *testify* to that fact!"

"Not yet, you won't," announced Talanov as he walked into the room carrying the plastic sack from Sergei's house.

Surprised as much by the unexpected entry of his friend as by what he said, Spiro jumped to his feet. "But *why?* I will oppose those lies!"

Andrea jumped up and ran to her husband, Talanov dropping the sack and holding her tightly while looking at Spiro. "Because to do so requires you to step forward and admit to having given me shelter as well as being with me last night *as an accomplice.* And that's the least of your worries. Like I told you, once you've been identified, every friend and relative you have becomes a target. Make no mistake, Spiro, they will torture and kill anyone in order to find me."

Andrea looked up at Alex. "Did you see the news?"

"No, but I can imagine. Is it Fiona?"

Andrea nodded. "World Network News is covering the story. Fiona said you broke in and threatened them with a gun, which Sergei wrestled away, after which you killed him with the fireplace poker. She's offering five thousand dollars to anyone who turns you over to the police."

"Then we'd better work fast," Talanov said, kissing Andrea and releasing her. He grabbed the sack and took it to the kitchen table, spreading the contents over the speckled laminate surface while he briefed Spiro and Andrea on his conversation with Ivan. "With luck, he'll spot something in Sergei's file," said Alex, "and I'll call him back in an hour. In the meantime, I want to go through this stuff with a microscope. Maybe we'll find something which links Sergei to the killers."

Very little conversation occurred during the next half hour as concentration was intense. Receipts were scrutinized, as were bank statements, letters, business cards, and each number in Sergei's personal telephone directory. Nothing of importance was found.

Alex looked at his watch, discouraged. "I was certain we'd find a clue."

"Call Ivan and we'll keep looking," said Andrea, leaning back in her chair and rubbing her eyes.

With a sigh, Alex nodded and stood, asking himself where he would conceal an important name or number. For a final time he looked over the collection of papers, his eyes coming to rest on the telephone directory. It was an expensive book made of leather, with both covers padded and Sergei's initials embossed on the front. Alex picked it up and looked carefully at the spine, then inside the front cover, inspecting the patterned silk lining and running his finger along the seams. Nothing.

However, upon examining inside the back cover, Alex noticed a slight difference in thickness along the seam nearest the spine, where the silk overlapped the leather. Using his fingernails, he pried at panel. A harsh ripping sound was heard as some embedded Velcro separated from a strip of fabric, revealing a pocket in the lining. While the others stood watching, Alex withdrew a tiny book from the pocket.

"It's from a bank," Alex said, opening it.

At the top of the front page was printed: *Reishi Pacific Banking Group, Vanuatu,* and below this: *Public Service Fund.* On the line below this was written, in blue ink, a seven-digit account number composed of five numerals and two letters.

With the others now gathered around, Alex turned to the first page of printed columns and saw but a single entry, made almost exactly one year ago, for an amount of one hundred dollars. Alex knew Vanuatu was a tax haven for corporations and investors. The question was: why had Sergei opened an account on Vanuatu with only one hundred dollars? Even more puzzling was why there had been no activity since it was opened.

"It makes no sense for Sergei to have such an account," said Spiro. "One *million* I could understand."

"I agree," said Alex, closing the book. "And I intend to find out why." He stuck the book in his shirt pocket. "I'll be back in an hour or so."

"Why not use the phone in front of the cafe?" asked Andrea.

"Because if I'm recognized and caught, I want to be as far away from here as possible."

"I don't like you talking that way," said Andrea worriedly.

Alex took his wife's hands in his. "I've got to be careful, for all our sakes," he said. "I'll be all right," he then assured her, forcing a smile. "In case of a chase, I'm certain Spiro's Kingswood can outrun a Stinger missile. For added protection, I used a black marker to alter the numbers on the plates. I'm no artist, but it's adequate, even from a short distance."

"I hope so. What we don't need is for the police to be pulling you over."

Talanov kissed his wife, hoping his eyes were not broadcasting his worry. She was right: an officer might spot the alteration. But he could not risk being tracked through Spiro's number plates.

"I'll be all right," he said unconvincingly as he squeezed Andrea's hands a final time.

But as Talanov walked out the door, he was aware of other problems. First, even if Ivan managed to locate something on Sergei, in the end it might not be of much use. With a desperate lack of money still crippling their movements, and with renewed efforts by the police to find him, every bank would be on the lookout. Which meant it would be virtually impossible to cash his certificates. Plus, with public carriers sure to be on the alert, their chances of escape were indeed poor. The obvious alternative - departing Australia by night in a boat off the northern coast - looked appealing until one realized the abundance of people in that dubious trade who would quite happily sell him for five thousand dollars. But this may well be their only option, for each passing day only placed Spiro and his family in greater peril.

Talanov drove the Kingswood to the end of the block and turned, eventually reaching a main intersection, where he turned again. But as he sped toward the stoplight, he was unaware of a red Mitsubishi turning onto the street from which he'd just come. In the car were assassins Three and Four.

Chapter 17

"Ivan, this is Yuri."

"I've been instructed not to speak to you - Yuri - and promptly notify the Vice-consul should you try to make contact. You've seen the news, I presume?"

"I have and we're wasting time. You know why I'm calling and what I told you: if there's nothing in his file, go ahead and report me. To do otherwise might cost you your life."

There was a pause. "What I found isn't much, but it's sufficiently odd to warrant scrutiny."

"I *knew* it!" exclaimed Talanov, making an excited fist. "Let's have it."

"First, Sergei and Fiona were married only two days before Sergei accepted his position with the Australian consulate. That was on a Saturday and he showed up for work on Monday. I suppose that's not so unusual if you've been living together, but these two had hardly seen each other since meeting in London the year before. Me, I'd be romping in a Gold Coast hot tub, not turning up for work."

"*Ivan!*"

"Sorry. Now there wasn't much on Fiona other than a notation about her having graduated from the University of London."

"Any family history?"

"No."

"Any protest movements or extremist affiliations while in school?"

"I couldn't find anything," Ivan replied.

"Hmmph. That fits with what she's told me - or *hasn't* told me - since I've known her: a painful adolescence, which she refused to talk about, and a degree in classical studies."

"As for Sergei," continued Ivan, "well, you probably know he was transferred from a post in Finland. He's a career diplomat from a working-class background whose skills are what mortar is to bricks. Stated simply - he's a trusted gopher, holding things quietly together for the ranking egos, never attracting attention and certainly not possessing any outstanding abilities. Vanilla, through and through."

"Then why was he sent here?"

"Bingo, Yuri. We both know that Australia's a diplomatic plum. I'm here because of my father, although - yes - you're correct when you say I'm a brilliant economic analyst."

"Get to the point, Ivan."

"The point is - Sergei has no such father or mother. In other words - to paraphrase what you just said - how did he land this job? Why was he not left in Finland?"

"And?" asked Talanov impatiently.

"You're not going to believe this, but it was because of Ambassador Kharkov, by special request. It wasn't difficult to run down the paperwork, complete with signature and seal."

"*Kharkov?* My God, this goes deeper than I imagined." Alex ran a hand across his chin and shifted the receiver to the other ear, glancing around to see if anyone was watching him while he talked. Seeing no one, he turned and again faced the wall of the gray metal box. "Might Kharkov be Tango Blue?"

"It's possible," replied Ivan. "As I remember, the Tango Blue call came on an outside line."

"Was Kharkov in the consulate that day?"

"No, he was in Canberra. But if Kharkov *is* involved - and I find it hard to believe he would be tied up with a group of assassins - then we're talking politics at the highest level."

"What's his expertise?" asked Talanov.

"Economics, like me. He lectures in universities here and abroad and sits on a dozen government committees, not all of them ours. The guy is big time, and I don't want to think what it implies should he be involved with the Second Thirteen. By the way, your story about General Timoshkin checks out and his murder hasn't been linked to you."

"I'm surprised they let one slip by," replied Talanov without enthusiasm. "Listen, I need you to run The Reishi Pacific Banking Group, of Vanuatu, through your computer."

"Vanuatu? As in sheltered investments?"

"The same. Sergei has a one-hundred-dollar savings account with their Public Service Fund. Can you give me a rundown on anything you can find: who the directors are, where they're located, amount of assets, phone number, computer links, that sort of thing?"

"I'll do what I can. Give me a couple of hours."

"Thanks. By the way, did Sergei make any trips to Vanuatu a year ago?"

"I've got his itinerary here." There was a pause while Ivan looked over the list. "Nope, and I've cross-referenced each official trip he's made during the last four years with time gone from the office. Sergei made no trips at all a year ago, meaning that if he did fly to Vanuatu, it had to have been on a weekend. Not only would the banks be closed, but I can't see him spending the money to fly all the way out there just to open a savings account for one hundred dollars. Unless, of course, he's a lousy investor."

"Neither can I," agreed Talanov. "Anyway, check it out and tell me what you find. I'll call you back in two hours."

"One more thing," said Ivan.

"What's that?" asked Talanov.

"This runs deep, so watch *your* back."

Talanov smiled. "I will."

A short while later, Alex paused the Kingswood at a stoplight several blocks from Spiro's cafe, his mind replaying the shocking news: *Ambassador Kharkov had recruited Sergei.*

Kharkov's involvement indeed meant politics at the highest level. And yet if he had been acting as a representative of the Russian government, warning bells would have sounded in every intelligence agency on the earth. For whom, then, was he working? The discovery that he could be linked through Sergei to the Second Thirteen indicated a much deeper threat than he had imagined. It was, of course, unlikely that the entire Kremlin leadership was involved. But the fact that their diplomatic corps had been infiltrated to such a degree was an indication of global conspiracy. The question was: how far had it spread?

The stoplight changed to green and both lanes of vehicles started forward. Although he felt sufficiently disguised, Alex was still nervous about being in traffic.

At the first opportunity Alex turned right into a side street. It was lined with trees and modest houses, with older cars parked sporadically on both sides of the patchy pavement. He directed the Kingswood toward an intersection, where he would be turning again, a corner delicatessen of brightly colored advertisements standing on the left like a synthetic additive.

But as he approached the corner, Alex was startled by two ambulances which sped by, their emergency sirens screaming. Turning in the same direction, Talanov watched them race on ahead, his curiosity turning to alarm within minutes. *They were stopping in front of Spiro's!*

Talanov rammed the accelerator to the floor and the Kingswood shot forward. Screeching to a halt in front of the restaurant moments later, Talanov saw a crowd of onlookers gathered around the front door. They parted for the medics, who rushed inside with their stretchers. After shoving the gear stick into Park, Alex jumped out and ran toward the door.

The inside of the cafe was in pandemonium. Numerous tables had been overturned and urgent instructions were being shouted back and forth by paramedics trying to disperse the crowd while attending to a downed victim. Nearby, another medic spoke into a mobile telephone for the police to be summoned. Alex pushed by a man who tried to halt him and froze at what he saw. On the floor was Spiro, attended by two medics attempting to revive him, his chest a mass of blood. Nearby on the floor, being comforted by a friend, Demetria was sobbing uncontrollably. Alex threw off the hat and glasses and rushed to her side.

"My *God*, what *happened?*" he asked, kneeling beside her and placing an arm around her shoulder.

Demetria looked up, her face swollen and red with anguish. "Oh *Alexi*," she cried. "Spiro... is he... ?"

"They came with guns, two of them, wearing masks," Demetria said, wiping her eyes. "We were seated at a table, waiting for you."

"Where's Andrea?" asked Alex.

"Spiro, he jump up and demand the men to leave. The first man laugh and *shoot* Spiro, who fall back against the table as the man laugh and shoot him again. Alexi, I think Spiro *is dying!*"

"He can't breathe, get him *up!*" one of the paramedics suddenly shouted.

Alex and Demetria turned to see Spiro being elevated into a sitting position by the two uniformed medics, who then leaned him against an overturned table. Spiro's shirt had already been cut off and an oxygen mask had been positioned over his nose and mouth. The sterile dressings which had just been taped over his wounds were already saturated with blood.

"What's the sound in his chest, Ann?" the first paramedic asked while yanking an alcohol swab out of the kit. Ann placed the stethoscope against Spiro's chest while her teammate, Kevin, cleaned a patch of skin on the inside of Spiro's forearm.

"Good entry on the left side, diminished breathing on the right," Ann replied quickly. "The bandages have plugged the bullet holes but I'm worried about that lung. It's filling fast, and he's got a shattered clavicle."

"Get the dots on him," said Kevin as he stuck a cannula into Spiro's forearm. He then withdrew the needle to leave the exterior teflon sheeth inserted into the vein. Kevin pulled a neighboring table closer and laid a plastic bag of saline solution on top of it, then connected a plastic hose from the bag to Spiro's arm. Turning the stopcock, he started the drip.

"You've lost a lot of blood," Kevin told Spiro in a calm, clear voice, "so we've got to increase your fluid levels, which will help raise your blood pressure. Ann is going to connect you to a heart monitor and we'll get you to the hospital shortly."

Spiro nodded weakly.

Ann made sure the five self-adhesive electrodes were all in place and the wires connected to the monitor. She then turned on a switch and a high-pitched beep occurred which then kept pace with each of Spiro's heartbeats. "H-R, 120," Ann told Kevin while wrapping an inflatable black band around Spiro's upper arm and pumping it up.

"Saturation?" asked Kevin.

"Eighty-seven percent and dropping," Ann replied after a quick look at the monitor, her eyes telling Kevin the seriousness of the low percentage of oxygen in Spiro's blood. With her stethoscope, she determined Spiro's blood pressure while slowly deflating the black band. "B-P is eighty," she announced, "and his resps are shallow and thirty-six."

Kevin looked down at Spiro. His skin was turning pale and his eyes were unfocused. Suddenly Spiro's head started tipping to the side as he drifted in and out of consciousness. Struggling for breath, a surge of panic then swept over him and he stiffened before uttering several short cries as he jerked back and forth.

"His B-P's low and falling!" Ann said with quiet urgency. "I can't get him stabilized."

"If we lay him down, he'll choke," replied Kevin while the monitor beeped fsater and faster. "He needs to sit up in order to keep that blood in the bottom of his lung."

"His heart's working overtime, Kevin! Even with the saline, his pressure's too low to get any blood to his brain. You've got to decompress his chest so he can lie down."

"All right, grab me a needle," Kevin replied as he leaned down and told Spiro what he was going to do. The needle would sting for a moment, but ultimately allow him to breathe.

Suddenly, from the entry into the restaurant, where the crowd of spectators was growing, a tall man in an Akubra hat saw Alex. "Hey, isn't that the Russian?" he shouted. "He's worth five thousand *dollars!*"

Followed by several of his mates, the man rushed toward Talanov, shoving chairs and tables from his path. Demetria screamed just as one of the paramedics ran to intercept them. "Stop it!" he yelled. "There's been enough violence here!"

"Get outa my way!"

The driver held up his hands. "For God's sake, we're trying to save a man's *life.*"

"And that bloke's wanted by the *police!*" the man in the Akubra yelled back, pointing at Talanov.

"The police are on their way. Now, wait outside!"

"You're not cheatin' *me* outa my reward!" the man in the Akubra shouted back. Cheered on by his mates, the man pushed by the medic and charged toward Talanov.

Alex jumped to his feet and stepped clear of Demetria just as the man in the Akubra swung wildly. Talanov's arm shot up, deflecting the blow while his left fist pounded into the man's solar plexus, doubling him over.

Two other men grabbed Talanov from behind. Alex ducked forward and twisted, throwing them off balance. One fell onto a table before crashing onto the linoleum with the table's cutlery and glasses. Spinning, Talanov stepped quickly behind the other man, his hand rigid as it delivered a disabling chop to the neck. The man fell limp to the floor.

"Mattie's down!" the man in the Akubra called out as he staggered to his feet. "I'll tear your bloody *arse* apart!"

"Get him, Ian!" the crowd began shouting. Others began surrounding Alex to cut off his escape.

But a sudden piercing scream stopped everyone where they stood. As one, all eyes turned toward Demetria as she rushed to the side of Spiro, who was trying to lift his head. Talanov broke through the crowd and joined Demetria at the side of the Greek, who was on a stretcher with an intravenous drip feeding into his blood-matted arm.

Spiro slowly reached up and pulled the oxygen mask away from his mouth. "Listen to me!" he called out in a hoarse whisper. Stunned into silent obedience, the crowd gathered around Spiro's stretcher while Ann attempted to place the mask back on his face. "No!" Spiro said, pushing it away. Then, with barely the strength to lift his arm, he took the hand of his wife.

"We *must* get him to the hospital!" Kevin shouted, his hands up as he tried in vain to move back the crowd.

"Wait!" said Spiro weakly, releasing Demetria's hand and reaching for Talanov. He then looked at the man in the Akubra. "Ian, come near to me."

Ian removed his Akubra reverently and knelt beside Spiro. "Yeah, mate, I'm here."

Spiro pointed to Talanov. "This man - Alexi - is my friend," he told Ian, his voice still a weak whisper. "And he is innocent. I was with Alexi the night the diplomat was killed, and I tell you he did not do it. With my own eyes I saw the man's wife murder her husband."

"You saw his *wife* do it?"

"With my own eyes," replied Spiro, "and you know that I do not lie. So you must help Alexi, Ian. Give me your word."

Ian looked suspiciously at Talanov, then back at Spiro. "Whatever you say, Spiro. When no one else thought I was anything more than a loser on the dole, you found me a job... gave me back my life. You've got my word."

Spiro nodded and tried to smile, but his eyes began to flutter and close.

"Hang in there, Spiro!" a woman called out as the oxygen mask was replaced over his mouth.

"The Big Man's watchin' over ya!" someone else exclaimed.

Weeping, Demetria kissed her husband on the forehead and tenderly stroked his cheek. Spiro opened his eyes and responded by squeezing her hand as the medics then wheeled his stretcher toward the waiting ambulance.

"Come on, you can ride with us," one of the other paramedics told Demetria.

"One moment," she replied, turning to Alex. "Come, Alexi, we must talk."

Reading her expression, Talanov halted her by the arm. "They took her, didn't they? The bastards took *her*!"

Demetria nodded. "They broke in, shouting for you. That's when Spiro jump up and tell Andrea to run. One man run and catch her while the other man shoot my Spiro. When they leave, the man with gun pull me away from my Spiro and push phone in my face... tell me to give it to you." Demetria fought back her tears. "I use it to call an ambulance for my Spiro. But here - now it is for you." She handed the phone to Alex.

"When are they going to call?" asked Talanov frantically.

"I do not know. But they say I am to tell you this: if you ever want to see your wife again, then you must give them what they want."

"For God's sake, what do they *want*? The bloody *bank book*?"

Demetria was sobbing as she shook her head. "No, Alexi. I think what they want is you."

Chapter 18

Fiona Zinyakin punched the buttons on her cellular telephone, dialing a number committed to memory.

"Tango Blue," came the reply.

"Fiona here. We have Talanov's wife."

"Excellent! How did you track her?"

"I followed Talanov and his accomplice to their car the night they came to the house. This morning I obtained an address using the number off the rear plate. It was registered to the owner of a Greek restaurant. Three left his mobile phone with the Greek's wife with instructions to give it to Talanov when he returned. We will call him later and order him to an isolated location, ostensibly to trade for his wife."

"Perfect. But once you have him, I want no clever speeches. Just shoot him, then dispose of his wife."

"Should we make it look like an accident?" asked Fiona.

"Don't bother. Just put a bullet through his head."

Chapter 19

Ambassador Andrei Kharkov stood behind the golden oak lectern positioned to one side of the stage in a darkened theater in Walnut Creek, California. Students from Stanford University, the University of California at Berkeley, and San Jose State University had filled the theater to standing-room-only capacity.

Behind the lectern was a massive curved screen which dwarfed the five-foot-five figure of the Russian Ambassador. Overpowering the diplomat even more was the rapid, action-packed sequence of film clips advertising fast food hamburgers, soft drinks, men's and women's fragrances, athletic shoes, and more. Actors of all races, young and old, male and female, were seen bicycling, sky surfing, abseiling, horseback riding, dunking basketballs, and gardening. Most would pause to endorse a particular product, while others were seen enjoying life to the fullest, the assoc-iation of product to lifestyle both intended and obvious. The action was heightened by a dozen huge speakers pumping voice-overs and pulsating quadraphonic disco music into the theater. It was stimulation to the extreme. The presentation lasted a full twenty minutes, with the completion of the frenzied finale coming as a relief to the exhausted crowd.

As the lights were turned up, the Ambassador raised his hands and yelled, "Now doesn't that beat war any day?"

The responding applause was thunderous.

Finally, as the clapping died down, the Ambassador wandered into the center of the stage with his hands clasped behind him and a warm smile on his aristocratic face. His fitted suit and neatly combed gray hair were themselves advertisements: today's Russian - in particular this one - was contemporary, cordial, intelligent. "So, my learned colleagues," he said in Oxford English, "I hope you can see how economies can be stimulated by what I call the Elective Spending Industry, which not only furnishes a population with basic goods and services, leisure time, and disposable income, but ultimately strips away the enticement of using armed conflict for production and employment."

Suddenly a hand shot up in the front row.

"Yes?" said Kharkov.

"With due respect, Mr Ambassador," said a young woman, standing, "weren't you yourself part of one of those military systems? Where were you when Soviet troops were killing Afghans and rolling tanks through Eastern Europe?"

Several disapproving jeers were directed at the woman as she sat.

The Ambassador held up his hands. "Please, my friends, she raises an extremely valid issue - an issue which many of you were probably thinking but were afraid to ask. I commend her for voicing her concerns, for we in government *must* be account-able to the people."

A round of applause spontaneously erupted, with Kharkov again holding up his hands for silence.

"I have served a very broad spectrum of political leaders," he began once the clapping had died down, "in what used to be the Soviet Union. Within that system, as well as throughout the new independent states and in nearly every political framework around the world, there are abuses which range from minor infractions to the blatantly tyrannical. Now, depending on one's battle of choice, one can elect to fight those abuses either by direct confrontation or through relational influence. For those of us who have chosen the latter, accusations may be levied that we are but trying to preserve our standard of living - and rightly so, in some instances, for I do not deny that I prefer your fine California wine over the crude libations found elsewhere in the world." A brief outpouring of applause rippled through the theater. "But I have fought for, and helped achieve, an emancipation of my country thought impossible a short while ago. So you ask: where was I during those awful years? I was pleading, influencing, at times sacrificing for the cause of freedom. Politicians come and go, and a great many have done so in my nation as well as in yours. And while the changes have not come overnight, they have come, and they will continue to occur long after I am gone. I can only hope that history will deal kindly with what I have accomplished and the means which I have employed."

As Kharkov graciously bowed, nearly the entire student population stood and began cheering and clapping.

Smiling appreciatively, the ambassador politely held up his hands and the noise eventually subsided. "Thank you, my dear friends, for your kind support. Therefore, in conclusion, it is through bitter experience that I have discovered how the Elective Spending Industry achieves prosperity for a nation more than military spending ever could. For it is only when individual preferences increase that economies must expand in order to satisfy those demands. And what happens next? Revenues are generated because jobs are created, not only in large industry - which, as you know, is necessary for economic stability - but also in the small-business sector, which includes entrepreneurs such as the skydiver we saw in the film clip who changed clothes in mid-flight so that he could drop into a cocktail party wearing the right brand of jeans." A brief wave of laughter occurred and Kharkov approached the front edge of the stage. "Like Australia, California enjoys an advantageous position on the Asia-Pacific Rim. But take care not to ignore your South American neighbors. That continent is a vast untapped market, as are Russia and Africa. The future is yours, my friends, and the world is waiting. Feed them, entertain them, *dazzle them*."

A standing ovation greeted Kharkov as he moved back several steps to center stage, where he bowed half a dozen times to reverberating cheers and applause, which climbed to even higher crescendos when he attempted to leave. Students whistled and shouted until the smiling Ambassador reluctantly waved his farewell and departed through one of the side exits and into a waiting limousine. The black Cadillac, its windows tinted nearly the color of its paint, pulled quickly away from the rear of the theater and out of the parking lot. Soon they were on the freeway heading toward San Francisco, Kharkov with a glass of scotch in his hand, his aide-de-camp across from him removing a silver tray of canapes from the small refrigerator.

"Another excellent presentation, Mr Ambassador," the uniformed major, Pyotr Marshak, told him in Russian.

"Thank you, Pyotr."

"There is no need to thank me for observing the truth, sir," Pyotr replied in English.

"Major, if you don't watch that charming tongue of yours, you'll be drafted into politics and I'll be the aide-de-camp."

Pyotr responded with a brief disciplined smile. "Then please don't tell anyone what I said, sir. Politics are much too dangerous for a military man."

Within seconds, a discreet warbling could be heard from the limousine's telephone. The major answered it and promptly handed it to Kharkov.

"Yes?" answered the Ambassador.

"Greetings, my friend," a voice said in American English. "Did your final lecture produce the usual standing ovation?"

"The Americans are such an enthusiastic people," Kharkov replied. "It exhilarates me to address them, especially their students."

"Enthusiastic people can overturn cars while they're looting and burning."

"The Americans hold no title there, Bob. One needs only to travel the world or watch the news to see mobs of angry citizens degenerating into barbarians."

"Can't argue with you there."

"So to what do I owe the pleasure of this call? Surely it's not to inquire about my lecture."

There was a short pause. "As usual, you're extremely perceptive."

Kharkov took another drink of his whisky. "Don't flatter me, Bob. What is it?"

"There's been a death in the family."

The Ambassador sat forward in the plush velour seat and pushed a button which closed the window into the driver's compartment. "Who?" asked Kharkov once the glass partition was closed.

"Sergei Zinyakin."

"*Sergei?* When, where?"

"Yesterday, in Sydney, not counting differences in time. It's been on World Network News. Haven't you heard?"

"You know what I'm like before a speech," Kharkov explained. "I spend all my time meeting people and touring the city. How did it happen?"

"Aleksandr Talanov broke into his house and crushed his head with a fireplace poker. He's still on the loose."

"I'll see him locked behind bars if it's the last thing I do. My *God*, I brought Sergei into the circle myself. He was a valuable man. How's Fiona, the dear woman?"

"Distraught and going into hiding. She's given the police her sworn testimony about how Talanov broke into their house making threats and waving a gun. Sergei made a heroic attempt to disarm him and almost succeeded. Before he could act, Talanov crushed his head with the poker. It was brutal and cowardly."

"The bastard won't get away with this. I'll also order full and immediate diplomatic protection for Fiona. After all, it was her charm and persistence back in London which brought Sergei to my attention."

"I knew you'd act decisively. It's why you should run for President."

"Now you *are* flattering me. Where are you, Bob? Conducting another appeal?"

"Philadelphia. I just helped a women-and-children's hospital raise six million. I'll be guiding them with their investments."

"Russian ingenuity!"

"I'm an American now, you know that."

"You even *sound* like one, which is even more alarming than your new name and citizenship. To me, you're still a Russian."

"I'll take that as a compliment, my Oxford-tongued pal."

" 'Pal'? Now you annoy me," chided Kharkov, taking another sip of his whisky.

A short laugh could be heard over the phone. "You'll phone Sydney, then?" asked Bob.

"As well as Canberra. Fiona shall have protection until Talanov is brought to justice. Is there progress being made toward his capture?"

"There's a drag-net out for him now. But he's slippery; after all, he came through Balashikha. Even so, the police are now saying it looks as though someone may be giving him help. Does Talanov have any friends in the consulate... any ties from the old days?"

"I'll give it some thought," answered Kharkov.

"Back to Fiona," said Bob. "Andrei, we may want to keep her on. She's intelligent and capable in her own right... no offense to her late husband."

Kharkov smiled. "*We?* You're an American now, Bob, remember?"

"If I may be permitted, Mr Ambassador, to remind you of your gracious words about my always being a Russian?"

"Always a step ahead of me!" laughed Kharkov. "But first things first. I'll arrange Fiona's diplomatic protection and then turn up the pressure to find Talanov."

"I knew you'd act decisively."

"Good-bye, Bob. Go charm the Yanks out of another six million."

13 Chapter 20

The cellular telephone rang in Talanov's hand and he almost dropped it. His every thought - his obsession, at the moment - concerned his wife and her safety.

He knew too well the tactics of terrorism from his training at Balashikha. Every part of a hostage's body was merely a tool for the extraction of information, the necessity of such torture contributing to the greater good.

At least that's what he had been taught... and what he had come to despise.

The phone rang again and Talanov took a deep breath. He stepped away from the curtained window and brought the instrument to his ear. "Talanov here," he said.

"It had better be," replied a voice in accented English. "We have your wife and she lives so long as you do what we say. Here, speak."

"Alex, I *love you!*" Andrea called out.

"How sweet," the voice said mockingly. "Now, listen and obey what I command you. Do you remember the old hotel where you said you were staying?"

"I remember," said Talanov while Andrea's words echoed in his mind.

"Thirty minutes. Be out in front."

"I'm at least an hour away, more likely an hour-fifteen," lied Talanov, not telling them he was but fifteen minutes. Yet he knew he needed time to plan some kind of a counter-offensive. "I'm on the run, remember, and your little act in the restaurant brought every police car within miles."

There was a brief pause. "All right, I give you one hour. You and the woman can live, but only if you give us what we want. Refuse and your wife will die."

"What is it that you want?" asked Talanov, noting the man's lack of English conversational idiom. *Were these men strangers from overseas?*

"You can take us to it once we meet," said the man. "We will be in a red Mitsubishi automobile. When we stop, you must get in."

"How do I know you won't kill us, anyway?"

"You do not. But you can be certain I will kill your wife if you refuse. She will be in the back seat with a gun pointed at her. One hour."

The call was disconnected and Talanov switched off the phone. He then walked to the window and again looked down at the activity in the street. Police cars and spectators were visible in front of the cafe.

In a chair across the room was Ian, his Akubra hat tipped back on his head, a clump of brown hair hanging down over his forehead. "How can you be so calm?" he asked, staring at Talanov with disgust. "They've got your bloody *wife!*"

Talanov turned from the window and looked coldly at the Australian. "If I start screaming at those bastards - which every molecule in me wants to do - then their egos will demand they do something to put me in my place." Talanov walked over to Ian, his anger visible but controlled. "So I'm not going to say *anything* which might jeopardize her life."

"If they had my wife, I'd be doing a bloody sight more than talking, I can tell you that."

"Well, if you don't like the way I do things, then maybe you better run along back to the pub and let me do things the way I choose."

"I don't like your *attitude*," said Ian, rising.

"I don't really *care*," said Talanov, standing firm. "And I don't have time right now to fight you and your macho ego. But if I get out of this alive and you still want to have a go, just name the time and place. Until then, *clear out.* They damned near killed Spiro and I don't need your short fuse getting my wife or me killed, which could very well happen anyway."

The two men locked eyes momentarily, with Ian then lowering his eyes and sitting back down. "I see your point about not pissing them off."

"I'm glad you do. Get out."

"I reckon I can't do that," replied Ian.

"Why not?"

"I promised Spiro."

"I don't care what you promised Spiro," said Talanov. "My wife's life is at stake and I don't need a Mallee bull charging through the minefield I'm in."

Ian nodded. "I guess you do have feelings behind that fossilized front of yours. I don't mind sayin' it, Lex, but you're all right."

"Lex?"

"It's a damn sight better than Alexee. Now, what do you want me to do?"

"I want you to *clear out.*"

Ian smiled. "And like I said, I promised Spiro and I don't go back on my word. So you're stuck with me, Lex, and we're wasting time. Now, what do we do?"

Alex threw up his hands and walked angrily to the window. He paused there to massage away the throb of a sudden headache.

"Look, I'm sorry I read you the wrong way," said Ian. "I give you my word - it won't happen again."

Talanov turned, then nodded his acceptance of the apology. He then came back and sat near Ian and gave him an assessment of recent events. Probability: the Second Thirteen wished only to lure him into the open in order to kill him. Probability: they would keep Andrea alive until that happened. Probability: this time, they would bypass using the police because of the risk involved to their plans.

Ian listened carefully to all that was said and then asked, much to Talanov's surprise, several penetrating questions which betrayed his slovenly, beer-guzzling look: was Talanov absolutely sure there was no item or document which the killers wanted, such as the bank book from Sergei's desk? Did Alex think they would shoot him in front of the hotel - either from a car or a neighboring rooftop - or after transporting him to some remote spot? Did Alex believe the man on the phone when he said that Andrea would be in the car? And did Alex think there was any way the killers could be lured from the car?

When Talanov expressed his surprise at Ian's line of questioning, to Talanov's even greater surprise Ian confessed that he was a security guard - midnight shift - who normally was in bed at this hour. "Which is why I look a bit rough," he said, referring to his stubbled face and old clothes.

With renewed hope, Talanov quickly discussed Ian's questions with an eye on the time. No, he did not think the killers wanted the bank book, but were merely trying to bring him into the open for a clean shot. Ian countered by pointing out that since Talanov's house had been fire-bombed, the killers might well be trying to destroy some document which they assumed he possessed. Alex disagreed, stating that since Sergei knew that he had a secret telephone line, which General Timoshkin also knew, the destruction of his house was merely an attempt to destroy the dying general's recorded warning to Alex about the Second Thirteen. Ian was forced to admit that Talanov's reasoning made sense although Alex may want to keep open the possibility that there was indeed something which the killers desperately wanted, assuming that even if Alex did not possess this hypothetical something, the Second Thirteen *thought* that he did.

It was also agreed there seemed to be no way to determine whether the killers planned to shoot Alex on the spot or drive him to an isolated location. A rooftop sniper was certainly a possibility although the problem of witnesses and escape posed risks they would seek to avoid.

More difficult to assess was whether or not Andrea would be in the car. From the perspective of the killers, Talanov could see the logic in either choice. To have her in the car with a gun to her head prevented any attempt by Talanov to try and capture the driver, either to extract information or to hold as a bargaining chip. In fact, the sight of Andrea under such circumstances might easily immobilize Talanov into compliance. On the other hand, having her in the car could result in her rescue should they be stopped by the police. The simple solution would be to hold her in a separate location. In the mind of the killers, the risk here was that if Alex did not see her as promised, he might assume she was dead, not cooperate, and either run or try to disarm the driver and force him to talk.

"So what do you think will happen?" asked Ian.

"It's my guess they'll have her in the car with a gun jammed into her ribs. One of the killers will then command me into the open, and when I step forward, he'll open fire. They know that with my wife being held as a hostage, there's no way I'm going to shoot first."

"And you're convinced there'll be no police?"

"Counter-productive. They won't want any cops around if they're planning to gun me down. Plus, based on the way they speak, I think the killers may have been hired overseas, which - if I'm right - means they'll be unfamiliar with the city. If that's the case, I'll gamble this will extend to other things, too."

"What are you gettin' at, Lex?"

Talanov told him. "So, what do you say?" he asked. "Think we can carry it off?

"I reckon. But we better nick outa here now. I don't mind sayin' you've got one hell of an imagination."

"Only if it works. Come on, let's go."

Suddenly there was a knock and Demetria entered the room.

"What's wrong?" asked Talanov upon seeing her reddened eyes. "Bad news about Spiro?" As Demetria started to cry again, Alex walked over and gave her a hug. "Don't lose heart, Spiro is tough."

Still wearing a restaurant apron over her patterned cotton dress, Demetria stepped back and wiped her eyes on a handkerchief. "I do not cry for Spiro," she replied. "The doctor, he call and say the bullets, they miss Spiro's heart and he will live. No, Alexi, I cry for Andrea. Those killers have her!" She looked over at Ian. "You must help them, Ian, I beg you!"

"I gave my word and I'll keep it," Ian stated. He looked over at Talanov. "I don't mind sayin' we need to move."

Alex stepped away from Demetria and forced a smile. "Give Spiro my best," he said, walking over to the door. He then turned, the smile replaced by a look of regret. "I'm so sorry I brought this upon you."

Demetria walked over to Alex and took his hands in hers. "We are family and you know what that means."

"But I nearly got Spiro *killed*."

"No, Alexi, it was not you. But the ones who did these terrible things are still out there. My prayers are that you will stop them."

Alex gave Demetria an appreciative smile. "Thanks, that means a lot. I don't know how to repay you for all you've done."

"There is a way," she said.

"Name it."

"Bring back your little Andrea."

Chapter
21

Ian made two stops on the way to the hotel: the first to his home for a quick shave and a change of clothes; the last to Anvil Security - a solid, unadorned building of gray concrete with bars on the windows and a black-and-silver shield painted on the door. Now in uniform, Ian strode into the office like MacArthur taking the Philippines. "Anyone interested in breaking the law?" he asked.

The off-duty uniformed guards - three men and two women - plus the receptionist and the uniformed supervisor, all laughed heartily at Ian's remark. But Ian was not showing the least bit of humor as he went immediately to a heavy steel gun cabinet and pulled open the doors.

"You been drinking red cordial again?" Barry, the supervisor, asked as he walked over to Ian with a concerned look on his face. The concern then turned to alarm when Ian pulled out a holstered 9mm pistol and belt. "You're bloody *serious!*" He grabbed Ian by the arm. "You can't walk out of here with that."

"I *am* going to walk out of here with it and I'll tell you why," said Ian as he removed Barry's hand from his arm before pulling a box each of real and blank cartridges from a drawer. He then closed the cabinet and turned toward the others. "Does the name 'Talanov' ring any bells?"

"That KGB killer who gunned down all those people?" asked one of the male guards.

"And murdered that Ruskie diplomat with a fireplace poker?" asked a petite female guard.

"That's the one," replied Ian as he strapped the pistol around his waist.

"You're going after *him?*" one of the male guards asked. "Count me in. I could do with a bit o' that reward."

"Don't bother, he's in the car."

"*What?*"

"And he's innocent," announced Ian, his expression resolute, unwavering. "I have a reliable witness who will testify to that fact."

"Then what's this heap o' shit about breaking the law?" asked Gail, the taller of the two female guards as she pushed herself away from the desk top where she had been leaning. Her long brown hair was pulled back into a loose bun and her arms swung loosely at her sides as she strode confidently over to Ian. "And why the bloody hell do you need that?" Her quick glance indicated that she meant the pistol.

"I'll say this once, Gail - say it to all of you - and I don't have time to argue." Ian then told them about the shooting in Spiro's restaurant and how Talanov's wife had been taken by the killers. He concluded with their demand for Talanov to wait in front of a cheap downtown hotel for a red Mitsubishi to drive by, supposedly with Talanov's wife in the back seat. "The killers claim they'll hand her over in exchange for something they say he has. Obviously, it's a set-up and someone is going to try and shoot him when he approaches the car. Our job is to prevent that from happening."

"At the risk of sounding *logical*, why not call the police?" asked Barry sarcastically.

"The police can't be brought into this because Talanov's a wanted man and his wife would be killed at the first sign of trouble. I've agreed to help, which is why I'm walking out of here with this 9mm."

"You know I can take it away from you," Gail told Ian matter-of-factly.

With his lip pursed thoughtfully, Ian nodded. "Yeah, Gail, I know you can try using that kung fu shit o' yours and land us both in the hospital. But I'd rather you throw your lot in with me and help save a couple of lives."

"Have you got a plan?"

"Talanov's got one and I think it'll work. We're out of time, though, and I need a vest - anyone else coming along had better grab one, too - plus your cooperation by not phoning the cops. I don't need them showing up with screaming sirens and flashing lights. That will only spook the killers and get someone killed. Now, who's in? We've got to go."

After looking pointedly at Gail, Ian stepped around her and walked over to another large cabinet where he removed a thin bullet-proof vest.

"Grab one for me," said Gail. "Do I need a piece?"

"Yes, and one for Talanov. I've got enough blanks."

"We're using *blanks*?" asked Gail as she opened the gun cabinet and grabbed two pistols.

"It's an act and I don't want any bystanders getting hurt," answered Ian. "But we'll have some real ammo with us in case the bad guys get out of hand."

"And who says *they'll* be shooting blanks?" argued Barry vehemently. "Can you guarantee no one will get hurt by one of *their* bullets?"

"Life's not always porky pie," Ian replied. "I didn't start this stinking mess, but I'm sure as hell going to try and stop it."

Barry jabbed an angry finger toward Ian's face. "I may not be able to stop you because you're Spiro's bloody charity case and the boss thinks Spiro's *God*. But I can sure as hell call the police. You're harboring a wanted criminal!"

Ian looked hard at his supervisor. "Do that and you murder his wife." He stepped around Barry and walked toward the door. "Anyone else?"

"I'm in," said Jenny, hurrying to grab a gun and a vest.

Ian glanced at the men. "I can tell who has the balls."

"Eat shit," snarled one of the male guards.

Ian chuckled. "Wouldn't want to steal your lunch."

Satisfied with having the final insult, Ian strode out the door followed by the two women.

"He's going to get someone *killed*," Barry shouted as he grabbed the phone and began dialing the police.

"But you heard what he said about Talanov's wife," one of the younger guards replied.

"I don't give a rat's arse about some Russian crim's wife. And if you don't keep your trap shut, I'll be wondering if I hired the wrong man."

While speeding toward downtown in one of the Anvil Security cars, Ian made the introductions while Gail and Jenny removed their uniform shirts, put on the vests, then dressed themselves again.

"Based on their accents," Ian said to the two women while keeping his eyes on the street, "Lex here believes the assassins are from outside Australia. Which is why he thinks they'll be fooled into thinking we're cops."

"Our uniforms are definitely similar," observed Jenny.

Gail looked over at Jenny. "They're a damn sight better, if you ask me, and certainly more flattering."

"It's hard to flatter a broom handle," said Jenny as she glanced out the window with a sigh, then back at her shapely partner. "At least you've got boobs."

"Will you two *shut up?*" ordered Ian with an annoyed glance in the rear view mirror. "Now, pay attention. All yours, Lex."

Still wearing sunglasses and a hat, Talanov outlined his plan. As instructed by the killers, he - Talanov - would wait in front of the hotel, casually using whatever parked cars there were for protection. Based on the assumption that Andrea would be in the red Mitsubishi when it finally came - probably in the back seat with a gun trained on her - the object was to separate the killers by luring the driver from the car. This would be accomplished by what would appear to be Talanov getting wounded in the leg during an exchange of gunfire with a policeman - Ian - who had recognized him and opened fire. The spaghetti sauce from Ian's kitchen should provide enough authenticity to fool the killers. With Ian appearing to have been killed, the plan is for the wounded Talanov to drop his gun and limp around the corner and down the street a short ways before collapsing to the sidewalk, creating an irresistible lure. When the driver leaps out to finish off his defenseless target, and with the attention of the others sure to be focused on what's happening, with a loaded weapon Jenny will approach the vehicle from across the street along the angle of the blind spot, while Gail waits crouched between two cars for the driver to appear, at which time she'll use her loaded pistol to disarm him. Ian, meanwhile, will spring miraculously back to life and provide back-up support. Were there any questions? Shakes of the head indicated that there were not.

"Good," said Talanov, looking at his watch. Seven minutes to go.

Ian turned onto a street lined with monotonous storefronts, their tired exteriors a reflection of the same hopelessness worn by the prostitutes who worked this section of the city. In numerous places, streaks of rust had discolored the oxidized paint of awnings which overlooked cracked sidewalks and rubbish. This was not a postcard section of Sydney.

In less than two minutes Ian had driven past the hotel and turned onto a side street, where he parked. Everyone climbed out, with Talanov still wearing his sunglasses.

At the corner, Talanov pointed to where he would be standing. He figured the assassins would approach the hotel from the same direction as had they, thus allowing their car to be close to the curb without interference from oncoming traffic. The others concurred and Ian pointed to a recessed doorway several buildings away. He would hide there. Assisted by Jenny, Ian then saturated his back with spaghetti sauce which, when he turned and fell, should give the illusion of his having been killed. Gail, meanwhile, chose two parked cars around the corner where she could hide, with Jenny taking up a concealed position across the street.

After sticking his own loaded gun in the back of his trousers, and with Ian's pistol with the blanks in front, Alex pulled out his shirt to conceal both weapons, then smeared spaghetti sauce to the back of one leg. The salivating odor of sugar and vinegar wafted around him as he rubbed the condiment into his trousers. Would this amateur trick deceive a team of trained assassins? He glanced again at his watch: it was time.

Talanov looked down the street and saw a red sedan turn the corner and speed toward him. He watched it draw nearer, instinctively holding his breath as it approached. Alex looked carefully... *it was driven by a woman with two children.*

Disappointed and yet relieved, he looked back down the street and waited, each second reverberating as it passed. *Where were they?* While he anxiously waited, Alex became aware of his hands forming and unforming fists. Attempting to relax, he shoved his hands in his pockets, then took them out again, all the while taking care not to stroll back and forth and reveal the sticky red blotch on the back of his leg.

Suddenly, down the street, Alex noticed another red sedan creeping slowly toward him. Impatient drivers sped past the vehicle, which contained - Alex squinted and tried to focus - three, yes *three*, individuals! The car drew nearer... it was passing the doorway where Ian was hiding... it was nearly in front of him now and the driver - a man - was looking pointedly at him! In the back seat was another man, and beside him an upright figure covered with a blanket. *Andrea!*

Alex stepped toward the street, his hands at his side, several parked cars lining this section of the curb. The red Mitsubishi stopped and the driver leaned across the seat, his eyes meeting Talanov's through the gap between two of the parked cars. "Lie down!" he commanded, "face down, hands spread. You will be searched."

"Not until I see my wife!"

"You do not give me orders!"

Alex knew he could not provoke the killer without risking harm to Andrea... *if indeed the blanketed figure was Andrea.* But even if it were a mannequin, his wife was still their prisoner. Lowering himself to one knee, from the corner of his eye, Talanov saw Ian step from the doorway. *Now!*

"Halt right there!" Ian shouted. He fired his gun once into the air.

Pulling his gun, Talanov spun toward Ian and fired twice, then freezing in horror at what he saw as Ian fell to the sidewalk. For his eyes were not on Ian, but on the two police cars at the far end of the street racing toward them with their red and blue lights flashing.

But as Alex started to shout a warning to Ian, he saw some movement from the corner of his other eye. Talanov dove to his right just as a fusillade of bullets blasted into the wall of the hotel, shattering windows and sending shards of brick flying into the air.

"*Andrea!*" he yelled as he rolled to one side.

There was no reply as Alex quickly scrambled to his feet and tried to peer through the windows of one of the parked cars. *Why hadn't she answered? Who was under that blanket?*

Seeing the shape of Talanov's head, the killer sent another spray of bullets exploding through the car's windshield just as Alex dropped to the concrete. He lay still as tiny chunks of tempered safety glass showered down upon him.

Suddenly hearing sirens, Alex knew that he had to flee. He must not be captured by the police! Climbing to his knees, Alex again peered up over the parked car at the blanketed figure. *It had not moved!*

Without warning, an ear-shattering blast shook the block as the hood of the first police car flew up into the air in a thunderous burst of flame. The car skidded into several parked cars, flipped and exploded into a ball of fire. Behind it, the other squad car screeched to a stop.

"Who called the *police?*" yelled Number Four from behind the wheel of the Mitsubishi as he instinctively ducked at the sound of the explosion.

Number Three leaned back in the window with his M-79 grenade launcher and reloaded it just as he saw Talanov run with a limp toward the corner. "I do not know, but Talanov has been hit," he replied as he exchanged the M-79 for his smaller MP-5K machine pistol. He watched Talanov disappear around the corner with blood showing on the back of his leg. "He has been hit!" he shouted.

Four jammed his foot on the accelerator and the Mitsubishi squealed around the corner before coming to an abrupt stop beside a parked car. There, lying against the painted white brick of the building, was Talanov, panting heavily. He was attempting to crawl toward a doorway. "There he *is!*" shouted Four as he grabbed his weapon and jumped out of the car.

"Stay behind the wheel!" yelled Three from the back seat.

"He is disabled... an easy mark!" Four shouted back as he rounded the front of the sedan and sidled between the parked cars. Grinning, he ran over to Talanov and took aim.

"Where... where's my wife?" asked Talanov weakly while holding the back of his leg, a look of pain on his face.

Number Four laughed. "Did you think we would bring her with us? You are indeed a fool and I shall have her before she dies." He made several thrusting motions with his pelvis and then laughed.

"Drop that weapon!" a woman's voice shouted.

Startled, Four whirled to see a uniformed female walking toward him, her gun drawn and aimed. Jumping toward the space between two of the parked cars, the assassin lifted his machine pistol and fired just as Gail also leaped toward a similar space two cars back. The assassin made it; Gail did not.

Three 9mm bullets struck Gail in the chest, the impact flinging her back onto the hood of a car, her pistol clattering across the top of it just as her knees buckled. With a choking groan she slid face-down onto the pavement.

Jenny screamed when she saw Gail fall. With her gun drawn, she sprinted to the protection of a parked car near the corner. In the street behind her, traffic had jammed to a halt and screaming people were running in all directions just as the police vehicle's fuel tank blew apart.

Leaping from the back seat, Number Three pulled out the grenade launcher and aimed it at the car where Jenny was hiding. He pulled the trigger and the weapon detonated, kicking against his shoulder. The result was another deafening explosion which ripped the automobile in half with a billowing cloud of flame. Throwing the discharged weapon into the car, the killer then jumped into the driver's seat and closed the door.

Number Four was stunned momentarily by the explosion, then turned back to finish Talanov. But as he turned, he felt the cold barrel of a pistol press hard against his temple.

Talanov grabbed him by the collar and pushed him behind a parked van, smashing his face against the sliding door. "Drop your weapon... *now!*" The assassin did as he was told, Talanov then spinning him around. "Now, you low-life bastard, *I want my wife!*"

"You were *shot*, you dropped your *gun*."

"Tell me where she is." Talanov thrust the barrel of his pistol up under the man's chin, making sure it brought pain to his throat.

"All *right*," the killer said. "Give me some *air*."

Talanov kneed the man in the groin. "*Talk, damn you!*"

Without warning the silencer on the end of Number Three's MP-5K pressed hard against Talanov's skull. "I believe it is *your* turn," the killer said, having crept around the front of the van undetected. "Drop your gun!"

Closing his eyes in anguish, Talanov dropped his pistol. It bounced off of the curb and under the van.

"Get in the car," Three ordered Four.

"I *want this bastard!*" yelled Four, still in pain.

"There is no time. *Get in the car*."

Reluctantly, Four obeyed, picking up his weapon and limping to the sedan.

Number Three yanked Talanov around and pushed the silenced MP-5K into his forehead. Then, without warning, he kneed Talanov in the groin. Alex cried out and crumpled to the concrete. "That is for my associate," he said calmly. He then curled his finger around the trigger and pointed the gun at Talanov's head. "And this is for all the trouble you and Andropov have caused."

Chapter 22

The shot rang out and at first it was not known what had occurred. The killer's hand flew back and the MP-5K catapulted into the air.

"Step back and put your hands on your head!" announced a voice over an amplified hand-held speaker. "If you don't, I'll shoot again!" Number Three turned to his right to see two police officers advancing toward him, one with a loud-speaker to his mouth, both with pistols drawn.

On the sidewalk, Talanov groaned and rolled onto his side, attempting to get up.

"Stay where you are!" shouted the officer.

Holding his groin, Alex remained curled up on the concrete.

Stepping away from Talanov, Number Three placed his hands on his head although his eyes were on Number Four, who was now crouching between two of the parked cars, his MP-5K in his hand. Suddenly he sprang to his feet and aimed the gun. The two officers dove to the sidewalk as the assassin's bullets cut into the building behind them. Seizing the opportunity, Three leaped into the sedan behind the wheel just as Four let go another burst of gunfire before jumping in beside him. "*Go!*" he shouted.

"Shoot Talanov, he's right there!" Three shouted at Four.

Hearing the order, Alex rolled under the parked van to where his gun lay.

Four jumped out with his weapon just as the two officers climbed to their feet. They both fired, sending Four ducking back into the sedan. "*Get out of here!*" he screamed. Three rammed the accelerator to the floor and the car careered up the street and out of sight.

The two officers ran up to Talanov, their guns trained on him. "Get up, you terrorist bastard!" one of them ordered. "And slide that pistol out here where I can see it."

"I'm not one of them," Alex replied, scooting the pistol out onto the sidewalk.

The officer stepped over and kicked it and the assassin's MP-5K out of reach. "No, but you're that KGB killer we've been looking for. Face down, on the pavement."

Talanov crawled onto the sidewalk and laid face down. "They've got *my wife*."

"I'm touched. Hands behind your back."

Footsteps sounded from up the walk. Craning his neck, Talanov saw Ian and Gail running toward them, Gail breathing with difficulty from the bruising caused by the bullets hitting her protective vest. "Bloody hell, you *got him!*" Ian called out.

"Who are you?" one of the officers called back, holding up his hand for them to stop.

"The two security guards who tried to stop all of this from happening," Ian said, approaching at a full gallop. Suddenly, Ian appeared to trip and flew headlong into the two officers, knocking them to the pavement, their guns flying out of their hands.

As the three men tumbled to the pavement, Talanov looked up at Gail, whose eyes and quick head nods were telling him to run. Ignoring the pain in his groin, Alex jumped up and bolted through a doorway into a store.

"He's getting *away!*" one of the officers shouted.

"Get off me!" the other officer yelled at Ian as he attempted to push him off. But Ian stumbled and clumsily fell into the policeman, knocking him onto his back.

"Go after him!" Ian shouted at Gail. "Don't let him escape!"

"Right!" yelled Gail, sprinting after Talanov just as Ian stumbled again, once more knocking the two officers to the concrete.

"Your *arse* is *history!*" the other officer shouted just before Ian's elbow accidentally caught him in the chin.

The sounds of three ambulances and a dozen police cars were distant wails as Talanov hurried with Gail across a small asphalt parking lot two blocks away. Losing the two officers had not been difficult thanks to the head start provided by Ian.

"He'll face serious charges for this," remarked Talanov.

Gail waved away the possibility. "Don't worry about that old bugger," she said. "We were coming to render assistance and he tripped. He'll repeat that story so many times they'll want to scream. In the end, it will be his word against theirs."

"But you brought me here and everyone in your office knows that."

"Hearsay, because none of them actually saw you, other than Jenny and me, and as far as we know, you were planning to give yourself up. Ian will simply plead a misinterpretation of what he meant to say."

"Misinterpretation of what he *meant* to say? Can he get away with that?"

"He'll mag 'em until they don't know which way the wind's blowing. They'll give him a good chewing, but then let him off, although I wouldn't want to be the nose on his supervisor should Ian find out he called the cops."

"How's Jenny?"

"Damn lucky to have moved behind a second car when that grenade blew the first one apart. Still, you can bet bickies I'm going to put that assassin's balls in a vice once I catch him."

"Stand in line... they've got my wife."

"She's lucky to have you," Gail said as she pointed them toward an open door beside which were two large wooden crates full of cabbages and squash.

Talanov looked at Gail. "That's very kind, but don't forget I'm a wanted man."

"Rubbish. Any man willing to fight for his wife the way you do ... hell, I'd give anything to have that. So far, I've had three husbands and none of them lasted very long."

"What's wrong, do you wear them out?"

Gail snapped her head glaringly toward Talanov, then laughed when she saw the gleam in his eye. "See what I mean?" she said. "You're no killer. And I'll do my damnest to help you find her."

"I'm not sure how to thank you."

Gail glanced over at Talanov. "Have you got an available twin brother?"

Talanov chuckled and shook his head. "I'm afraid not. My kid brother's still in school and lives in England."

"Great," said Gail without enthusiasm. "A school boy - just my type."

With a smile, Talanov followed her into the rear of a fruit and vegetable shop, Gail grabbing an apple off a display counter as they entered.

The shop was plain and narrow, with three tiers of angled shelves along each wall and a number of wooden tables positioned in the center. But as artless as these utilitarian furnishings were, each section was lined with tiny wood shavings on which had been carefully placed a vast array of quality produce, the colors of which were accentuated by freshly-cut flowers in bright plastic buckets. The owner, a gray-haired Frenchman, was wearing a plastic apron and dark blue beret. At the sound of footsteps he looked up from a tub full of carrots. His face brightened into a wrinkled smile. "*Mignon!*" he exclaimed upon recognizing Gail. Shorter than Gail and much thinner, his eyes sparkled as he rushed to greet her with a kiss on each cheek. He then stepped back. "And still pilfering when you think I am not looking!"

Gail took a bite of her apple. "And a happy *vichyssoise* to you, Henri. Have these apples been in cold storage?"

The Frenchman laughed. "Ahh, my Gail... ever so unique, and still insulting my produce." He leaned back against the edge of a table. "Explosions and sirens... so much excitement. It is why you are here, *oui?*"

"It's why both of us are here," Gail replied, nodding toward Talanov while taking another bite of her apple.

The old Frenchman's eyes narrowed. "I have seen your face, *Monsieur.*"

"You have," answered Gail, stepping over to Henri and lowering her voice. "In the news. His name is Talanov and he's wanted for murder."

"*Merde*, I knew it!"

"He's also innocent, Henri, so don't get your cholesterol worked up. It's why we need your help."

My help? thought Henri, a wrinkle now creasing his brow. By all accounts this man was an accused *killer*, and to consent to such a request could bring trouble from the police. Still, Gail was quite passionate about his innocence. And yet...

Unsure about what to say, the Frenchman brought a worried finger to his lips, looking quickly at Talanov then back at Gail.

"Henri, I don't have time to *argue*," said Gail. "I mean it - my friend is innocent. Now, will you help us?"

Noting the conviction in Gail's eyes, Henri nodded. "Of course, *Mignon*, but what can I do?"

"Keep quiet and lend me your car."

"My car? It is as arthritic as I, but yours if you need it."
Gail nodded. "We need it."
"I never saw you... I'll fetch my keys."

13 Chapter 23

The cellular phone sounded in the front seat of the red Mitsubishi. Number Three answered it.

"Tango Blue," a familiar voice announced. "Why is Talanov still alive?"

"The police arrived and we barely escaped. However, I'm certain Talanov was captured."

"He wasn't," declared Tango Blue curtly. "Fiona has been monitoring police communications and he's reported to have escaped. I need not remind you what it means if Talanov is not captured and killed. *Everything* will be lost."

"Perhaps we should change our tactics," offered Three.

"Is this another excuse for failure?"

"Obviously, people have been helping Talanov even though he has no money and is wanted by the police. We did, of course, manage to hunt down the Greek, but others will take his place and it will be impossible to locate them all. My suggestion is to use Talanov's wife to force him out of Sydney and away from those who keep assisting him. Since we must return to Adelaide for our scheduled departure aboard the *Coriander*, why not trap him there, away from the protection of his friends? If he is captured along the way, we will have achieved our goal and simply wait for his release. Or, if he is sent to prison, we hire someone inside to kill him. But if not, we use his wife as our bait. Either way, he is ours."

"You redeem yourself, Number Three."

"I am in this for the same reason as you."

"I'll contact Number One and he'll set things up. Tango Blue out."

Chapter 24

Gail's flat was a ground-level unit in a block of six. It was surrounded by gum trees and oleanders and exuded a pleasant feeling of wooded isolation even though it was in the midst of suburban sprawl.

While the spaghetti sauce was being laundered out of his clothes, Alex took a quick shower. After toweling himself dry, he put on one of Gail's terry cloth robes and went to the kitchen to make some calls.

The first was to the hospital to check on Spiro's condition, which - thank God - was stable. Demetria, who was in Spiro's room with several of their children, was glad to hear from Talanov. For obvious reasons, Alex told her that he could not return to their house and so arranged for Gail to pick up his and Andrea's belongings which had been stored in the upstairs closet. To authenticate any third-party messages in the future, the password "Lamb Stew" would be used. Talanov's choice of terms made each of them smile, the smiles then fading as they remembered Andrea.

The second call was to an overseas operator in Vanuatu for the number of the *Reishi Pacific Banking Group*, spelled R-e-i-s-h-i. After a full minute of waiting, the operator informed him that no such listing could be found. Talanov asked if she was absolutely sure, and with a tone of irritation, the operator repeated her statement and terminated the connection.

The final call was to Ivan Lazovic, who still found it difficult to believe that Kharkov was in any way involved. "I dug through every electronic and paper file and could find nothing," reported Ivan. "Other than having a flamboyant ego, he's a saint as far as his records are concerned. There's nothing whatsoever to suggest an allegiance to anything far-right or anti-Western. In fact, Andropov refused to promote him because of his moderate stands. It wasn't until Gorbachev came into power that Kharkov began to be heard, and his influence on the Soviet president was so enormous that he is credited with having motivated Gorbachev to liberate Russia from the strain of Eastern Europe."

"Come on, Ivan," countered Talanov. "You know as well as I do that Russia's abandonment of Eastern Europe created an economic nightmare for the rest of the continent. I think a very strong anti-Western case could be argued against him for that."

"I disagree," said Ivan. "Aside from the hard truth that we were an occupation force in Eastern Europe, the fact that he helped free Russia from that economic burden - and it was a burden - does not necessitate anti-Western feelings. On many occasions Kharkov has openly declared his desire to introduce marketplace economics into Russia once our industrial sector has been renovated. Plus, he's courting more business investment on the solid premise that everyone will profit. For him to be anti-Western would be the same as cutting his own throat. It simply doesn't make sense."

"And yet if Kharkov is Tango Blue, he would *have* to have such a cover."

"I agree," said Ivan. "It's just that I can't find any indications that such a cover exists."

"Keep looking."

"There's nowhere else to look. If something exists, it's not in our files."

Talanov sat silent for a moment. "Other than those high profile government committees reported in the media, what directorships does he hold?"

"I've got a summary right here," said Ivan as he quickly sorted through the papers scattered across his desk, the phone lodged between his chin and shoulder. Finally he saw it. "Okay, here we are. You know about his university lectures in the United States, and I'll skip the well-publicized industrial boards. That leaves the rather inconspicuous International Development Council, where he serves as one of the directors. The IDC is working in Russia, South America, Africa, India, the Far East, and on a number of island nations."

"My God, the *IDC!* That means he's got influence literally around the *world*."

"But to what end? Serving on the IDC doesn't make him a criminal."

"That's what we need to find out. Did you run a search on Tango Blue?"

"I did and nothing turned up."

"What about in the mainframe?"

"I'm one step ahead of you, Alex. I ran a search and came up empty. With this kind of luck, it's no wonder I don't win at pokies."

Talanov, however, was not smiling as his eyes narrowed at a thought now coming into focus. "But did you try Tango Blue as a password?" he asked.

"A password?"

"Maybe it's more than just a code name," said Talanov, his thoughts racing. "Maybe Tango Blue is a project - a mission. Admittedly, the leader may be using it to identify himself over the phone. But what he's really referring to is the name of their mission. If that's the case, then it might well be a password which allows us to access their highway."

"I hate to remind you of this, but it's not possible for there to be a covert communications highway within our diplomatic loop. There's no external access, which means there's no chance of outside penetration. Besides, it's nestled in shielded concrete. And before you say it: yes, I know the departmental systems are linked to the mainframe, but with the security measures we have in place, there's virtually no way anyone, no matter how deep - inside or out - could be operating undetected."

"Ivan, I'll wager sheep stations there's an underground link you don't know about... a link which no one knows about except for those in Kharkov's fold."

"Impossible."

There was demanding, heavy silence on the line.

"All *right*, I'll give it a try," snapped Ivan irritably. "But no grizzling when I'm saying, 'I told you so.'"

Talanov smiled. "I'll be waiting. Now, what did you find out about the Reishi Pacific Banking Group?"

"This you're not going to believe," said Ivan, brightening. "Ownership of that company has been veiled in a circular blind. Get this: the Reishi Pacific Banking Group of Vanuatu is owned by Pekoe Trading Investments, Limited, of the Cayman Islands, with ownership of *that* company listed as the Reishi Pacific Banking Group, Vanuatu. Simply put, it's a circular ownership, on two island tax havens, with the directors of each corporation a collection of fictitious names in care of the other, with residence addresses - not surprisingly - on empty lots. And their corporate assets are definitely not Gibraltar: one thousand dollars each."

"One lousy *thousand?*"

"That's it. Even less surprising is the fact that there are no listed phone numbers and no known computer links like the ones our banks have with teller machines around the world. Even the filing was handled by a law firm which no longer exists."

"So *they* don't exist!"

"I didn't say that," corrected Ivan. "I merely said that ownership was veiled in a circular blind. In other words, they exist, but in such a way that no one can trace who they are. However, I did locate the name of the solicitor - or lawyer, or whatever they call them over there - who filed the paperwork. His name is Maxwell Ferguson."

"Someone's gone deep on this, Ivan," declared Talanov while writing down Ferguson's name. "We have two corporate shells possessing minimal assets - one named after a mushroom, the other after a tea - with each owning the other and, therefore, protecting the other. But for what reason? And why would Sergei possess a bank book which represents nothing but a token account in a token corporation? It's as if they've been put in place to *dis*lead any pursuers, if I can use that word in the same sense as constructed disinformation."

"That brings up a good point," said Ivan. "How do you know the Second Thirteen really exists? Now before you jump down my throat with the obvious - that there are killers on the loose - let me ask how it is you know for sure they're Andropov's assassination unit other than from what General Timoshkin told you? Isn't it possible he might have been programmed?"

"I've thought about that," replied Talanov, nodding affirmatively at Gail's holding up a box of Twining's tea, "and it's inconceivable to me that he could have been programmed about something he helped create."

"You would know better than I about that; it was just a thought. In any case, I'll try using Tango Blue as a password and see where it leads. Call me in a couple of hours. Anything else?"

Talanov took a deep breath and swallowed a surge of emotion that burned like bile. "They've kidnapped Andrea," he stated quietly.

"*What?*"

"Fiona must have followed us the other night and tracked my friend's address using his vehicle's number plate. This morning while I was out phoning you, they broke in, shot my friend, and kidnapped Andrea. Then, an hour ago, using Andrea as bait, they tried ambushing me near downtown. I'm lucky to be alive."

"My *God*, Alex."

"So I'll say it again - take care. The stakes are extremely high. I'll phone you back in two hours."

After hanging up the receiver, Talanov accepted a mug of tea from Gail and followed her into the living room, the two of them sitting across from one another on separate couches. Having changed out of her uniform, Gail now wore a simple dress, its scooped neck and snug waist emphasizing each curve. She drew her feet up under her and leaned against a cushion with her fingers curled round the mug.

"I can't imagine the pain you're feeling," Gail remarked. "Your plan to trap the killers and free your wife - it was all for nothing."

"The bastards who took her ripped out my heart," answered Talanov, still in the terry cloth robe, his hairy legs and black socks a sharp contrast to the soft pink of the fabric. "There's so much I never told her... so much I wish I had said."

"She must be very special."

"She is," answered Talanov with a sad smile.

"What's she like?" asked Gail.

"Your size, same color hair, and like you, full of life. Some years back, using her own savings and initiative, Andrea started her own catering business which, arguably, is now the finest in Sydney. She's a quick thinker who can find something good in most people, including me. Trouble is, I didn't realize how special she was until this madness with the killers. Like so many men, I lived in my own world, occupied with things far less important than lavishing the most important person in my life with what she wanted most: time and love. I remember when she received her first award for women in business. The night of the presentation, I was in Canberra in the Russian Embassy, and I never did tell her how proud I was of her accomplishment. Right now, it's not those embassy meetings that I miss, and I sure as hell don't want to come to the end of my life - which may be sooner than later - and be filled with regret." But Talanov's face suddenly grew hard. "And yet I must force away all those feelings and function as though she were a stranger."

"For God's sake, why?" asked Gail.

"It's the same challenge a surgeon faces each time he picks up a scalpal."

"Some might call that heartless."

"It's called survival, and I must do it because Andrea's life depends on my doing it. It's not easy to disassociate myself from the love and passion she's kindled within me. God knows, I want her back."

"Don't get clucky," said Gail, rising and taking her mug to the kitchen.

Talanov moved from the couch to the counter and handed his mug to Gail, who placed it in the sink. "Clucky?" asked Talanov. "Is that what you call it?"

She ran some water into the mugs. "I just don't like soft men."

"Soft-hearted doesn't mean soft."

"Says who? My last husband was clucky, and not only could I drink him under the table, but I was a better cook and a better lover. And the gutless bastard walked out on me."

"Maybe he didn't like the competition."

Gail yanked a dish towel off the stove handle. "What are you, some kind of amateur psychologist?" Her voice was edged.

"Come on, Gail, quit trying to pistol-whip everyone. Who cares if you're better at this or that? Be a partner, not an opponent. I've had plenty of opponents and I have my share of them now, but my wife is sure as hell not among them. Of course we're different, but we're a team... or could have been if I'd allowed it." Talanov gave a discouraged sigh. "I just hope I can find her." Placing his elbows on the counter, he rested his head in his hands.

"Alex, I'm sorry," said Gail. "I didn't mean to stick my foot in it."

Talanov lifted his head. "You didn't. I just hope you can find what you're looking for. I lived far too much of my life pushing people away, and then, when I finally wake up, the one who means the most has been taken away. Don't make the same mistake. Now, enough waffling from an old fool. Mind if I lie down?"

"You're no fool but you do look worn," said Gail, noting Talanov's tired eyes. "Come on, my bedroom's this way.

Gail led Alex down a small hallway and into a darkened room, switching on the light as she entered. Much to Talanov's surprise, Gail's bedroom was a cozy feminine retreat, with a polished brass bed and lots of ruffles and pillows. Two of the walls were painted a sunny yellow, the others being covered in a patterned paper. A brass baker's rack with glass shelves held a collection of books and collectables, while along one wall was an oak dresser beneath a framed Renoir print.

So this hard-drinking security guard's not as tough as she wants me to think, thought Talanov. "I'm impressed," he said.

Gail walked over and pulled back the covers. "Glad you like it. And since this is probably the only time I'll ever get you into my bed, hop in, pink robe and all. While you sleep, I'll go fetch your things."

"Be sure to say 'Lamb Stew.' That way Demetria will know you're a friend."

"Lamb stew," repeated Gail.

"And hers is the best," replied Talanov. "Wake me when you get back."

When Gail returned, the laundry was finished, and after ironing Talanov's clothes, she brought them quietly down the hall on hangers and stood in the doorway watching him sleep. Although muscular from her workouts at the gym, Gail's arms and legs were not at all disproportionate with her physique. Her brown hair now hanging loose, Gail folded her arms and leaned against the door frame, her desires unexpectedly kindled for a man she knew she could not have.

Alex, of course, loved his wife, and in a strange way Gail felt stimulated by that fact. She liked the way he brightened when speaking about her, unlike so many men who were too weak to speak lovingly of their wives, especially in public. Alex, on the other hand, was secure and confident and those qualities ignited her desire.

Talanov stirred and rolled onto his side, curling his arms in front of his chest. Gail walked over and carefully brought the comforter up over him. How she longed to kiss him, if only on the cheek, as much for admiration as for passion. Drawing the quilt around him, Talanov then shifted onto his back. Standing over him, Gail paused, then took a small step closer. She knelt on the floor beside him.

Leaning toward Alex, Gail kissed him lightly on the cheek, then impulsively moved her lips over to meet his. Suddenly awakened, Talanov reacted but did not push her away. Pulling back the covers, Gail ran her hand inside the terry cloth robe and across the dark hair on his chest, the robe opening wider as she nibbled on the side of his neck. Soon she had crawled on top of him, her kisses becoming wild and fierce. She felt Talanov's hands begin to explore her body, then lift her dress, his own passions exploding as he pulled her furiously to him.

Breathing heavily, Gail blinked twice, her daydream evaporating as quickly as it had appeared. She looked down at his sleeping body, tears forming in her eyes as she drew one hand across her mouth. She knew Talanov was not a man who would betray his wife, and as much as she wanted to, she would not tempt him.

Wiping away her tears, Gail took a last longing look, then hung Talanov's clothes on the door knob and turned quietly away.

Chapter
13
25

Ivan Lazovic sat before the mainframe monitor in a low plastic cubicle along one side of the communications center, a modular concrete bunker installed in the dreary Russian Consulate on Fullarton Street in Sydney's inner suburb of Woollahra. The center handled all scrambled diplomatic transmissions in and out of Sydney, including encoded military messages sent by satellite, as well as the various high-security computer links with Russian embassies and consulates around the world. In addition to the mainframe, the center possessed a highly-trained staff of three who operated an array of cryptographic computers and specialised electronic equipment.

Like its much larger counterpart at the Russian Embassy in Canberra, the center had its own independent power supply and circuitry, and its radio frequency shield included a transparent metallic film over the door and all walls, including the large double-pane, argon-filled plate glass window separating the room from the corridor. In addition, there was a filtered air supply which always remained at a constant nineteen degrees Celsius.

Ivan nodded to one of the operators who greeted him as she passed by. He watched her stroll over to a slowly rotating reel of magnetic tape on a floor-to-ceiling recording unit. In one of the sound-proof booths across the room sat Katcha, a stern woman in her early forties who was the assistant to the Vice Consul. Through the window, Ivan could see she was deep in conversation on one of the scrambler phones.

Returning his attention to the keyboard, Ivan typed his password, then answered a series of additional security questions capable of shutting down the entire system if not satisfied within forty-five seconds. Once these had been cleared, Ivan found himself standing - electronically speaking - at the mainframe's "elevator shaft," a digital thoroughfare whereby one could gain access to any of the numerous "floors" of data, each of which in itself was a labyrinth of storage rooms, directories, and individual files.

To avoid arousing suspicion, Ivan knew that he must appear as though he were calmly going about his normal consular duties. But tiny droplets of perspiration had already formed on his forehead as he sat before the darkened screen. There was no menu, just a blinking cursor. Ivan adjusted his glasses - more from nervousness than for sake of vision - and after a deep breath, typed the name Tango Blue. He then tapped the key marked Enter.

The huge computer accepted the command. Like a key inserted into a lock, the coded impulses were recognized by pre-programmed receptors and channeled at the speed of light across highly restricted electronic neurons and along otherwise inaccessible paths. Several seconds passed. Suddenly, four words began flashing on the darkened screen: *International Access, Omega Level.*

Talanov had been right! Tango Blue was indeed a password into a hidden network. But there was no telling where the primary database was located with the availability of instantaneous worldwide connections. A normal telephone call to Moscow took but four seconds, thus enabling anyone to access these files in the time it took for a phone call.

Ivan had never been this deep before, and his heart nearly imploded when the blinking cursor advanced three lines, then issued its own command: *Special Clearance Required. Enter Your Name.*

My name? thought Ivan, a momentary surge of panic sweeping over him. He had to remain anonymous! But a thought then occurred to him as Ivan Lazovic he was not cleared for the Omega Level. *But Kharkov and Sergei were!*

After rubbing the stiffness out of his fingers, Ivan carefully typed in Sergei's last name, first name, then Enter.

Incorrect Entry, the computer replied.

Ivan licked his dry lips and adjusted his glasses, then squinted in thought as he looked to one side thoughtfully. What was it he had overheard that day when the call had come in? Someone had said, 'Five, this is Tango Blue.' Was Sergei's code name 'Five'? That had to be it, and after rubbing his hands together, Ivan typed the number 5, followed by a colon, then Zinyakin, Sergei. Holding his breath, he tapped Enter.

A shiver of panic swept over him: *Incorrect Entry*, the computer responded. He had but one more try, and if this failed, the entire system would be shut down!

Which would result in more questions than he'd care to answer, especially after Talanov's warnings.

After taking several steadying breaths, Ivan began to wonder if he was making this too complicated. The simplest entry - Sergei's first and last names in that order - he had not yet tried. It was worth a try. And so, after another steadying breath, he typed Sergei Zinyakin, then Enter.

The screen suddenly lit up with row upon row of alpha-numerically-coded entries scrolling down across the screen, one after the other, the reflection in Ivan's glasses a pulsating strobe of blue, white, and green. Ivan watched the rapid sequence in petrified shock, his mouth agape, his transfixed eyes hardly blinking.

What in God's name were these? Ivan's heart pounded as he watched hundreds of entries roll down across the screen. Then, just as suddenly, the screen went dark. Closing his eyes momentarily, Ivan took a deep breath, opened his eyes and typed in Andrei Kharkov, then Enter. Again the screen lit up with hundreds of coded entries, although this time with a difference: *Kharkov's list was categorized under headings of member nations of the International Development Council!*

For an entire minute the screen flashed the coded listings before suddenly going dark, the only evidence of remaining life the blinking cursor.

Ivan could not move. What had he *found?* Were these the numerical identities of Second Thirteen agents around the world? How extensive was the conspiracy? Were there others in the consulate? Was Kharkov in charge, or was someone higher?

Realizing that he had been nervously holding his breath, Ivan gasped, then jumped, as he looked up to see Katcha observing him over the top of the cubicle.

"You do not look well, Ivan," she said, "and your complexion is pale. Are you all right?"

Ivan wiped his forehead and managed a smile. "Just a little tired from all the long hours," he explained.

"You should take care of yourself or you will become ill. I will mention your condition to the Vice-consul."

"No need," Ivan replied hastily. "I'm going to bed early tonight."

"Perhaps you should see a doctor?"

Ivan smiled. "Really, I'm fine. But thanks for your concern."

Katcha raised a doubtful eyebrow before leaving. "As you wish," she said.

After Katcha had disappeared down the corridor, Ivan once more typed in Sergei's name, and as the list rolled down across the screen again, he hastily wrote some of the coded listings on a pad of paper. Then, once the scrolling was completed, he tried accessing them only to have another password required. He entered Tango Blue.

Access denied.

Ivan escaped that command and entered a request to print. Again, a different password was required. "They've really protected themselves," he said to himself as he made a few more notes before returning to the main level. He stood and looked at his watch. Talanov would soon be calling.

Speaking in Russian on the airline telephone in First Class, Ambassador Kharkov was put through immediately to the office of the Vice-consul.

"Where is Ivan Lazovic?" he asked Katcha, who had just returned to her desk. "He's not answering his telephone and I was told he's in the building."

"He is, Mr Ambassador," answered Katcha. "I saw him using the mainframe in the communications room."

"I see. Is the Vice-consul in?"

"No, sir. I do not expect him until tomorrow."

"Then I must ask an important favor of you, Katcha."

"Yes, sir?"

"Put me on hold and call Ivan Lazovic's secretary on one of the intercom lines. Ask her on my behalf if Ivan has had any contact from Aleksandr Talanov. If my recollection is correct, Ivan's father, Dimitri, was one of Talanov's instructors in Moscow. Naturally, neither of you should say anything to Ivan about this."

"Of course, Mr Ambassador," said Katcha, placing Kharkov on hold.

The wait was not long before Katcha came back on the line. There had been no recorded calls from Aleksandr Talanov.

"It's possible Talanov would use an assumed name," Kharkov replied while a steak dinner was placed in front of him by the airline attendant. "Ask her if there have been any unusual calls, or any calls from the same individual."

Again Kharkov was put on hold while the questions were asked. Again, the wait was not long.

"The only instance she remembers was from Mr Lazovic's cousin, Yuri, who is visiting in Australia."

"Yuri Lazovic?"

"Yes, sir," replied Katcha.

"Run a complete family history on Ivan Lazovic. Maintain the blackout and find out whether or not he has a cousin named Yuri. I'll stop by the consulate tomorrow morning and come directly to you."

"Yes, sir, Mr Ambassador."

"One more thing, Katcha: order immediate diplomatic protection for Fiona Zinyakin. Give her whatever she needs, including travel privileges. We're going to help that dear woman all we can. Whatever it takes, I'll see that Talanov pays and pays dearly for the murder of her husband."

Chapter

13

26

Rested and dressed in his freshly-laundered clothes, Talanov washed down the last of a fried egg sandwich with a gulp of black coffee. "I didn't realize I was so hungry," he said, wiping a smear of mustard off the plate with his finger.

"I reckon you need another," Gail remarked. "That plate's so clean I could put it back on the shelf."

"You twisted my arm," replied Talanov with a grin.

Gail placed the skillet back on the stove. "What are your plans?" she asked as she walked to the refrigerator and took out an egg.

Alex glanced at the mobile phone on the table. "Wait for that bloody thing to ring," he said.

"And then?" asked Gail.

"I'm working on it. Right now, all I've got is the name of a lawyer in Vanuatu. Even if this lawyer might be of some help, my first priority is finding my wife before the killers find me. It doesn't take a diploma to realize how desperate things are: I can't call them but they can call me... and they're holding Andrea. I'm at their mercy."

"Do you think your friend in the consulate may find something else?"

Talanov glanced at the kitchen clock. "I sure hope so."

Using Gail's phone, Talanov then called the Russian Consulate, Ivan answering the phone himself.

Although the consulate was now closed for the day, Ivan still lowered his voice as he described the mainframe's Omega Level. Ambassador Kharkov - *unbelievable!* - and linked at the deepest level with what looked to be hundreds of agents around the world. And while he was not able to access any of the individual files, he stressed to Alex how many numerically coded entries had scrolled past his eyes. And from dozens of IDC nations!

Not pausing long enough for Talanov to comment, Ivan then told Alex about something else: although he did not know for sure why, there seemed to be a strange tension in the consulate, particularly with his own secretary, whose relaxed nature had been suddenly replaced with a chilled obedience.

"Kharkov may be onto you," stated Alex.

"No way," Ivan answered. "The only notice *anyone* has taken of me was while I was using the mainframe. The vice-consul's secretary had been using one of the scrambler phones and stopped to inquire about my health. She thought I looked pale. I handled the situation and told her not to worry, although I'm still not feeling up to par. Must be a cold."

"Could she have witnessed what you saw?" asked Talanov with concern.

"No, and I'm certain no suspicions were aroused."

"Yet you feel someone suspects we've been talking?"

"Not especially. There's just an intangibly strange tension around the building, either because Kharkov is due here tomorrow, or because *I'm* nervous about our talking. All I can say is that it's a good thing you picked the name Yuri. I have two cousins by that name, one of whom lives in New York and will cover for me. By the way, was that luck or brilliant foresight on your part?"

"A little of both," answered Talanov, trying not to sound worried. He ran a hand across his forehead. "To be on the safe side, we'd better not talk any more."

"What about Kharkov and his files? This may be an opening."

"It is but I'll pursue them through other channels. What's imperative now is that you shut down your investigation."

"But-"

"No buts, Ivan, just do it."

"All right, whatever you say."

"And Ivan..."

"Yes?"

"Thanks. You've been an enormous help."

Ivan smiled. "Don't mention it. Take care."

"I will. The same to you."

After hanging up the phone, Talanov ate his second sandwich and drank another mug of coffee. Once he was finished, Gail handed him an envelope from Demetria. Inside was three thousand dollars. Alex closed his eyes, once again aware of the sacrifices people were making. And all because Spiro had believed in his innocence. Now others like Ivan and Gail were risking their lives.

Suddenly the mobile telephone rang, startling Talanov out of his reflections. Gail came quickly to his side as it rang again. He brought it to his ear. "Talanov here," he said.

"It had better be," the voice of Number Three said. "Your wife is alive... a situation which can easily change if you do not do as I tell you."

"Let me speak to her," replied Talanov.

"You are not giving orders! I will give them to *you*, and this is what I tell you: be in Adelaide tomorrow at noon. I will contact you there on this telephone and we will meet at a place I will designate."

"You said I had something which you wanted and that I was to take you to it."

A tense silence occurred at each end of the conversation, from Talanov because he suddenly regretted exposing the flimsy excuse invented by the killers to lure him into the open, from the assassin because they had indeed been exposed and he did not know how to reply. "You will be given new orders tomorrow," he said curtly, then hanging up.

Clicking off the telephone, Talanov quickly dialed the number of Spiro's restaurant. "Demetria... Alex here. How's Spiro? Good, good. Listen, I've been ordered to Adelaide by the killers and I'm to meet them tomorrow at noon. Do you have any friends living over there who might be able to lend me a hand?" Grabbing a pencil and paper, Talanov wrote down a name and number. Demetria then told him that she would arrange for a private airplane to pick him up at the Bankstown airport at ten o'clock tonight and take him to Adelaide. When finished, Alex thanked Demetria for the envelope... for everything.

"Things are beginning to move," Alex said after switching off the phone. "The killers are retreating to Adelaide, probably because they haven't been able to catch me here. I'm guessing it's an attempt to isolate me from my support network by forcing me to deal with them in a strange city. Thankfully, Demetria gave me the name and number of a friend of hers who lives there."

"What's his name?" asked Gail.

"Con Kanellopoulos. Demetria says he has lots of contacts."

Gail pursed her lips skeptically.

"In any case," added Talanov, ignoring the response, "might I trouble you for a ride to the Bankstown airport? Demetria's arranged for a pilot and plane and we're scheduled to leave at ten."

"I guess I can do that," said Gail. "But on one condition."

"What's that?"

"That I go with you."

Talanov shook his head. "Forget it, Gail, I'll go this alone. You've risked too much already."

"Cut the protective horseshit, Alex. You're not Superman, and the sooner you realize that, the better. I'm from Adelaide, I know that city, and you're liable to get killed attempting this by yourself."

"I won't hear of it," stated Talanov with a definite shake of his head.

"Then you don't get to the airport, unless you enjoy the thrill of some taxi driver recognizing you and phoning the police."

"That's blackmail!"

"Furthermore, Demetria may trust this Con-what's-his-name and the bloke who's flying the plane, but I trust nobody until I know them. And if I don't like the pilot's looks, you can bet your clacker I'll be flying the bloody thing myself, which I'm fully qualified to do. Now, while I change into some jeans, make me a sandwich and some coffee. There's a thermos under the sink."

"Sandwich and coffee?"

"You heard me. Every clucky spook that I know is a veritable whiz in the kitchen. Especially the ones in pink. Two eggs, tomato relish."

"Anything else?" asked Talanov, annoyed.

"Think you can operate a toaster?"

"You're a rotten bloody nuisance," Talanov mumbled as he headed for the kitchen and started banging pans and cupboard doors.

Darkness had fallen by the time they left for the airport, Gail deciding to drive Henri's car, which he could collect from the parking lot. Within sight of the terminal, she pulled up to a telephone booth and called the Frenchman in order to tell him about their plans. "One more thing," Gail said once she had given Henri the information: "Get a wheel alignment. Your old bucket pulls to the right."

But Henri was not amused. "This man - is he worth the risks you are taking?"

"It's for him and his wife, not me," replied Gail.

"*Merde*, now I worry! Is he aware of this love you feel for him?"

Gail turned her back to the car and lowered her voice. "Don't be an idiot, Henri! He's married and I'm helping him find his wife."

"What greater love is there, *Mignon?* You risk your life, knowing you will get nothing in return. *Mignon*, you are in love!"

"I don't need this, Henri, not from you and certainly not now. We have a lot of work ahead of us."

"*Mignon*, listen to yourself. Talanov is a former agent of the *KGB!* He has been trained to kill and survive under the harshest of conditions. He does not require your help."

"He's not a killer, Henri, but a kind and devoted husband."

"I did not say he was not. I merely point to his training."

"He could be a white pointer and still get caught out of the water," argued Gail. "The fact is, he needs help and I can give it to him. And for once I feel needed by a man who's not trying to get into my pants, not that I wouldn't mind him showing a little interest."

"Be careful, *Mignon*. One places oneself in the greatest of danger in these kinds of situations. Besides, I will have no one to insult me if something happens to you."

"Nothing's going to happen," Gail reassured the Frenchman. "Just get some decent fruit on your shelves. That apple was bloody awful."

"*Au revoir*, my little one... take care."

"I will, Henri... and thanks. I'll leave the key on top of the left rear tire."

After hanging up the phone, Gail climbed back into the Renault and was about to start it when Talanov gripped her arm. "Look!" he said, pointing to a rush of headlights down the street.

Slouched in the front seat of the darkened Renault, they watched five New South Wales police cars roar up the street and turn into the airport parking lot. Two sped over to a gate in the chain link fence, which was swung open by an airport official to admit them onto the apron. The other three screeched to a halt in a blockade formation across the entrance. All four doors of each vehicle were thrown open and several squadrons of officers climbed out, the uniformed men and women quickly fanning out across the pavement with flashlights to inspect registration plates and the occupants in each car.

"How could I have been so *careless?*" exclaimed Talanov. "They must have tapped Demetria's phone."

Gail glanced quickly at Talanov then back at the police cars. "Let's try the Schofields airport. It's a lot smaller, and with luck there'll be a plane for hire and I can have us airborne within the hour."

Talanov shook his head. "If you thought of it, they will, too."

"Then what do you suggest? All the commercial flights out of Sydney will be covered, and Adelaide's too far to drive and be there by noon."

"We need to find out what arrangements Demetria made. Doesn't Ian live down the street from Spiro?"

"Only a few houses away and he should be home. But what good will Demetria's arrangements do with cops all over the place?"

"First things first. Get on the horn and tell Ian to run and get Demetria. Have him bring her back to his house so she can call us using his phone."

Gail telephoned Ian and within ten minutes Demetria had returned the call. Alex told her about the police at the Bankstown airport, most certainly because her phone lines had been tapped. He then proposed an alternative plan, and after hanging up, darted back to the car where he waited five minutes before again stepping over to the telephone booth. Alex deposited the required coins, dialed the number of the restaurant, and soon had Demetria on the line.

Sounding winded, Alex informed her that his car had broken down and would it be possible to have the Cessna pick him up at the Schofields airport, which was near where they were at the moment. Demetria said that she would contact the pilot on his mobile, and that the plane should arrive there soon. Alex then advised Demetria that he was planning to have the pilot take him only as far as western Victoria - exactly to which town, he wasn't yet sure. There he would hire a car and drive the rest of the way to Adelaide, thus avoiding the risk of being recognized in any of the airports. With best wishes for a safe trip, Demetria said goodbye.

Alex and Gail's wait in the Renault was not long. In less than a minute, four of the five police cars screeched away from the airport with their lights flashing and roared past them, the final car waiting until the single-engine Cessna had lifted off into the darkened sky before squealing out of the parking lot and up the street.

Once they were gone, Gail started Henri's car, shifted into first, and drove quietly down the street and into the parking lot.

"Go do your stuff," Alex said after Gail had placed the key on top of the left rear tire. "I'll climb the fence the meet you at the far end of the taxiway. Hold there until I jump in."

"Aren't you a bit old to be climbing fences?"

"You're *definitely* a nuisance, you know that?"

Gail laughed and started toward the terminal.

After producing her log book, license, credit card, and pilot's kit full of maps, a fully-fueled Cessna was chartered and Gail strode out the door carrying two duffle bags and her thermos of coffee. She walked casually across the open concrete past a variety of single and twin-engine planes illuminated by tall apron floodlights. Looking toward the unlit holding point at the far end of the taxiway where she would pause to rev the Cessna's engine before taking off, Gail tried to locate the silhouette of Alex moving through the darkness. He was nowhere to be seen, a fact that both worried and relieved her.

She had purposely taken her time inside the terminal with paperwork and conversation in order to allow him opportunity to scale the fence and get into place. Although she had tried to make light of the situation, *what if Alex couldn't negotiate the fence?* What if he were injured while trying? Any unusual delays in taking off would attract the binoculars of officials in the tower. And if Alex was indeed seen and reported, the authorities would be on hand when they landed.

Gail made her own safety check of the plane with a flashlight - again, taking her time - and once satisfied, climbed in, started the engine, and within minutes had the Cessna rolling along the tarmac.

"Tower, this is Charlie Echo Oscar, preparing to hold short," Gail said into the microphone as the Cessna reached the far end of the darkened taxiway and made a half pivot toward the main runway.

"You are cleared to hold, Charlie Echo Oscar," the tower replied.

With the Cessna's passenger door now facing an open ditch running alongside the fence, Gail depressed both brake pedals while she pulled the throttle knob out half way to rev the engine. The propeller accelerated against the straining force of the brakes, rocking the aircraft back and forth while Gail peered anxiously out the window. *Where are you, Alex?*

In the darkened cockpit, Gail looked at her illuminated gauges. The hydraulics were fully pressurized and she could not wait much longer. Soon the tower would take notice.

Gail scanned the outside darkness again. *Where was he?*

Suddenly the passenger door swung open, admitting a blast of balmy night air while Alex jumped into the seat. "Let's go!" he yelled over the sound of the engine.

Gail yanked the microphone from its hook. "Tower, this is Charlie Echo Oscar requesting clearance for takeoff."

A torturous few seconds ticked by. "You are cleared for takeoff, Charlie Echo Oscar," the tower finally said. "Have a good flight."

"Will do, tower. Charlie Echo Oscar, out."

Releasing the right brake pedal, the Cessna pivoted onto Bankstown airport's main runway. Ahead on each side of them stretched two parallel strands of white lights which marked the edge of the landing strip. After a quick glance at her gauges, Gail removed her foot from the other pedal and pulled the throttle knob all the way out. As if suddenly set free, the Cessna bolted forward, pressing its two passengers back into their seats. Enveloped by the engine's vibrations, and with the runway lights speeding by faster and faster, the small airplane raced toward the darkened void at the end of the runway where the lights abruptly stopped. Before reaching that point, however, Gail pulled back on the stick and the craft lifted gently into the sky.

Talanov peered out the window at the quilt of suburban lights sinking quickly away. In the distance, downtown Sydney appeared as a deceptive concentration of vertical black columns dotted with tiny rectangles of light. To one side was the illuminated outline of the Sydney Harbor Bridge. Climbing higher, the Cessna then banked slowly toward the Blue Mountains, and soon the lights of the city disappeared behind them.

"We'll be cruising at about ten thousand feet," Gail said over the muffled roar of the engine. "I'll need to set her down in Mildura for some fuel, but while we're there, I'll call an old friend and tell her to meet us at Parafield, a small airport north of Adelaide. She's like a sister and will give us whatever we need."

"Why are you doing this, Gail? You're putting a lot on the line."

Gail kept her eyes on the darkened expanse ahead of them, the dim light from the gauges softly highlighting her face while Henri's words kept echoing through her mind. She *was* in love and she knew it. But she must never reveal this to Alex, for Alex was in love with his wife.

And one day, the fantasy would end.

But end how? With Alex and his wife reunited? Or by a terrorist's bullet?

She glanced quickly at Talanov. "I have my reasons," she said. "Now, why don't you get some sleep? I have the feeling you're going to need it."

13 Chapter 27

The corporate jet chartered by the Russian consulate landed at Adelaide's domestic airport just before dawn. Aboard was Fiona Zinyakin and three guests: assassins Three and Four, and - handcuffed to her seat - Andrea Talanov.

For the trip to Adelaide, the pair of assassins had gladly abandoned two days of hard driving in favor of a diplomatic jet, a seafood buffet, and all the whisky they could drink. Back in Sydney, a private limousine had chauffeured the four passengers to a special hangar by means of a top-level clearance arranged by Ambassador Kharkov of the Russian Embassy.

As the engines whined down, the jet taxied to a stop in front of a secured hangar and the four passengers stepped immediately into a waiting limousine, which then sped away through a private gate, again with diplomatic clearance. Once they had turned onto Burbridge Road, the darkened window separating the passengers from the driver was lowered. Behind the wheel was Number One: Cheney.

"I trust you had a nice flight?" Cheney asked with a thin smile.

"Thanks to my new diplomatic status," Fiona replied as she sat back and crossed her legs. She was dressed in a tailored business suit the color of ivory. It accented her short dark hair and red lips.

Cheney's smile broadened. "We'll talk in depth once Mrs Talanov has been lodged safely aboard ship."

"Is our access secure?" asked Fiona.

"We'll be driving on board. No one will notice."

While they sped along, Andrea made sure that she appeared to be in a hopeless state of defeat as she stared aimlessly out the tinted window at the occasional storefront decorated with Christmas lights. In actuality she was very much aware that her captors had provided her with some useful information: first, they would be hiding aboard a ship; and, second, there was concern about not being noticed, which could well mean the ship's crew was not part of their operation.

And that increased her possibilities for escape!

The time passed quickly and soon the limousine was driving along beside a high chain link fence topped with spirals of razor wire. They pulled up to a gate and Cheney opened his window. "Tango Blue, for the *Coriander*," he said to the guard.

"You're that diplomatic mob I was told would be coming in late," the guard remarked while flipping through pages on his clipboard. Finally he located the proper sheet. "Here it is, Tango Blue. How many passengers?"

"This car has special clearance."

"And I need a head count," the guard explained. "I don't care about names."

"There's four besides me," Cheney replied.

"I need to see 'em, mate."

"Is that necessary?"

"If you want in, it is."

Andrea readied herself to scream.

A pistol with silencer was pushed into Andrea's ribs by Number Three. "Remain quiet or you will die," he said quietly as Cheney pushed a button which lowered the rear window. The guard looked inside and made a quick count, then stepped back.

"All right, you're clear," the guard said, opening the gate.

The limo sped through, its tires squealing.

After making several turns, the limousine slowed as it entered the brightly-lit asphalt apron where hundreds of semi-trailer-size ribbed steel containers of various colors were stacked, sometimes three and four high. To their right, a yellow straddle carrier maneuvered into position over a stack of three blue containers and lowered a fourth on top. Cheney proceeded slowly down a wide traffic lane between the stacks of containers.

Directly ahead of them now was the massive hulk of the *Coriander*. It was being unloaded by two towering gantry cranes mounted on tracks, each similar in appearance to a giant "H," but with an extended cross bar - the boom - to which were attached thick cables and a spreader capable of lifting many thousands of pounds. Mounted to the steel girder frame of each crane were numerous powerful flood lights, making the huge structures appear as though they had been ornamented for Christmas.

Cheney swung the limousine left toward the angled stern of the ship, where a wide steel ramp extended onto the wharf from a brilliantly-lit opening. Several cars drove into the opening, while above this and covering nearly one third of the freighter's deck was a self-contained city - the ship's accommodation - which appeared as though it had been constructed out of giant, smooth white building blocks.

The limousine drove up the ramp into "the cathedral" - a cavernous interior deck where hundreds of vehicles had been loaded. By special orders from Ling Soo in Hong Kong, a reserved parking space had been allocated for the limousine near one of the elevators, and into this space Cheney maneuvered the long black sedan.

He quickly opened his door and stood, scanning the interior deck around them and seeing no one. "We're clear," he said, "let's go."

The others climbed out, Number Three grabbing Andrea by the arm and pulling her from the car. Once she was on her feet, he pushed her toward the elevator where Cheney was now standing. The doors opened and they stepped inside.

Andrea did not resist, and by all appearances, she was indeed a woman without hope. Her long brown hair fell tangled about a face that was drawn and depressed. In truth, the brutal shooting of Spiro had nearly broken her, and this - coupled with the pounding agony of not knowing if she would ever see Alex again - had brought her to the edge of collapse.

But then something had happened.

In Sydney earlier that day, sitting blindfolded and handcuffed in the killer's flat, Andrea heard the two assassins burst through the door cursing Talanov and the luck which seemed to surround him. At that moment a glimmer of hope appeared, and for the first time she realized these killers of the Second Thirteen were not as omnipotent as they had seemed. It was then that Andrea started hardening her emotions into a determination to remain passive but alert until just the right moment when she could escape. Assuming they planned to kill her once they had Alex, she resolved to exploit whatever weaknesses she could find. What was it Alex had said? That if killers have a weakness it is in the blind spot created by their weapons or with a feeling of unquestioned advantage. Therefore, the first step was in not giving them any reason to be on guard.

Andrea was led out of the elevator and down a narrow corridor with pipes running along the ceiling. The walls on each side were constructed of girders and riveted steel plate, all painted gray. After making a turn, Cheney led the way up a flight of metal stairs to another corridor deep in the interior of the ship's accommodation. They followed this for a short distance, and after stepping through a large hatch, proceeded to a cabin door, which Cheney opened. Without a word, Andrea was pushed into a small room and the door was locked behind her.

Across the room was a single bed and dresser, and beside these, a small sink, toilet, and mirror. Nearby stood a narrow metal wardrobe which could hold no more than half a dozen garments on hangers. Along another wall was a small desk with a fluorescent lamp. Andrea looked carefully around the cabin. There were no portholes to the outside although a ventilation duct provided the room with a flow of fresh air.

Sitting on the bed, Andrea was well aware that she was being held for the sole purpose of trapping her husband. Yet in the perverted logic of the assassins' obsession with killing Alex, what *didn't* make sense was the fire-bombing of their house, particularly when no one knew they had been hiding there. After murdering a policeman in their home, why had the assassins taken both the time and risk to then search the house, knowing that other officers would be on their way? What had they been seeking? And why had they burned the house?

Was it possible their goal included something Alex possessed? Then, because he had escaped their initial massacre, and because he continued to slip through their fingers, emergency measures had been taken to destroy that "something". Whatever it might be - and if it really existed - Alex genuinely did not know what it was. Accepting for the moment the possibility that something *might* exist, it could easily be inconsequential, at least by all appearances. A photo, perhaps, or a letter? A receipt, an old deed, a signed document?

Andrea laid down on the bed, her mind once again reflecting on the driver's remark to Fiona that no one would see them. If this was an indication that the crew was not involved, then she may well have indeed discovered a weakness.

She allowed her eyes to roam across the ceiling to the air vent. Was that voices she could hear? If so, *then perhaps they could hear her!*

Suddenly the door into her room swung open and Cheney stepped inside. He raised a gun and fired a narcotized dart into Andrea's thigh. Andrea screamed and pulled the tiny point from her flesh.

"We don't want you calling out before we spread the word that you're delirious with fever," he said. "Fever from a contagious, deadly disease."

"You *bastard!*" Andrea yelled, starting to jump up but falling back on the bed, the drug now taking effect.

"Night, night," said Cheney with a smile as he stepped out of the room and locked the steel door behind him.

13 Chapter 28

A beautiful, clear dawn was illuminating the South Australian sky as the Cessna circled over Adelaide in preparation for landing at Parafield airport. Drinking coffee from Gail's thermos, Talanov had watched the vineyards and farmlands of the Adelaide Hills give way to suburban sprawl, the congestion of concrete and bricks abruptly ending at a ribbon of sand. As Gail banked the Cessna in a wide circle back toward the north, the buildings of downtown Adelaide began to glow in the morning sun.

Talanov had managed to sleep all the way to Mildura, where Gail brought the Cessna to refuel the plane and recaffeinate her system. From Mildura to Adelaide they drank coffee and talked, Alex briefing Gail about everything that had happened. Now, as they made their final approach, Alex expressed the desire to question those staff members at the Royal Adelaide Hospital who knew General Timoshkin. Gail raised the obvious objection about an accused mass murderer wandering around a public hospital asking questions about an assassination, but said she would ask her friend, Liz Langdon, about what could be done about finding out what information on the general was available.

"Liz said she would meet us near the office of Southland Air," said Gail as she brought the Cessna gently down onto the runway. "After we've parked this bird, you can go with Liz to the car while I hand back the plane."

"Tell me more about Liz," said Talanov.

"Such as whether or not she can be trusted?" asked Gail with a sharp glance at Talanov.

"Not just that, but - yes - I want to know if Liz Langdon will give quarter to an accused mass murderer on the strength of your word."

Feeling the sting of a mild rebuke, Gail glanced over at Talanov then lowered her eyes momentarily before returning them to the taxiway. "Sorry, Alex."

"Don't worry about it," Alex replied. "It's just that I can't forget to consider the range of reactions which others might have."

"How can you manage that with every person you meet?"

"If I don't, my wife and I will never see each other again. It's a question of motive."

"You really love her, don't you?" Gail asked, a film of moisture glossing her eyes.

"Of course I do," replied Talanov. "Haven't you ever been in love? Not the white water of summer romance, but the deep water of commitment that enables you to endure the deserts in life. Then, no matter how perilous things become, the bonding strength of that love keeps you going... keeps both of you going." Talanov looked over at Gail. Tears were visible in her eyes. "What's wrong?" he asked.

"Nothing," she said, wiping her eyes. "And to answer your original question, Liz is definitely a person who can be trusted. I've known her since childhood and she works in the news department of one of the local television stations. Don't worry, her lips can be tight as a fish's bum and she knows this is one of those times."

"Might not the temptation of a story be too much?"

"Not Liz and not when lives are at stake. Trust me."

Talanov had no choice, for in less than a minute the Cessna had rolled to a halt near the office of Southland Air, the rapidly decelerating propeller finally coughing to a stop.

"That's Liz over there," said Gail, "the shortie with the copper-colored hair."

Wearing black tights and a loose green silk top, Liz Langdon stood by a chain link fence smiling enthusiastically as she waved, her pixie-cut hair blowing in the hot north wind.

"I won't be long," said Gail and she waved back at Liz before climbing out of the airplane.

While Gail hurried toward the office, Talanov stepped out of his side of the plane and grabbed the duffel bags and thermos. Slipping on his sunglasses, he started toward Liz.

"So you're Australia's most wanted," said Liz as Talanov approached. She offered her hand. "Mr Talanov, I'm Liz Langdon."

"Call me Alex," replied Talanov, shaking hands. "I see Gail has filled you in."

"More than you realize," explained Liz, pointing the way to her car. "If I may be direct, Alex, I don't mind saying that Gail's version differs considerably from what we've been getting over the wires."

"I'm not surprised," answered Talanov, perceiving an edge to Liz's voice. "And - no - I don't mind your being direct... nor avoiding the triviality of meaningless small talk."

"Touche," answered Liz, "and, believe it or not, I'm not normally this rude. It's just that I'm concerned about Gail's welfare and, therefore, suspicious of her association with someone of your reputation. So allow me to persist by asking what you've been telling her. Because unless you really can walk on water, I have a number of serious questions. Don't get me wrong: I gave my word to Gail that I'd keep silent and I won't go back on it. Still, I can't help wondering what magic spell you've cast over her. I've never seen her this protective of a man she's known for what - twenty four hours? Plus, you're married... 'happily,' she says. Something doesn't add up."

Talanov smiled briefly. "She's right, I'm happily married. But I'd better set the record straight about walking on water; I'd sink faster than a lead ingot. However, as far as any magic is concerned, all I can say to you is what I've been saying all along: I'm being hunted by a group of assassins known as the Second Thirteen, for what reason I've no idea. Plus, yesterday they kidnapped my wife and now they're using her to trap me, which is why I've been ordered to Adelaide. I'm being set up for a kill. Believe me, I've tried to keep Gail out of this because she can get killed as well. But Gail has a mind of her own."

Liz laughed as she took out her keys. "That's Gail, all right! Still I can't help wondering what spell she's under. I've never seen her this way."

With hot December gusts swirling around them, they approached the car and Liz pushed a button on her key ring. The parking lights flashed and the door locks were released automatically. Alex walked around the vehicle and opened the rear passenger door, but paused before getting in. He looked at Liz over the top of the car. "Gail has already faced those bastards once and nearly been killed. Now, why she would want to persist in helping me, I can't tell you. The risks are still there, but so is the truth. And the truth is this: I'm an innocent man who's being blamed for murders I didn't commit. The actual killers have now kidnapped my wife, and the reason is because they want to kill me, for what reason I wish I knew. Now whatever Gail's reasons are for helping me, I'm grateful because I couldn't have made it without her. So maybe you should allow her to believe the truth and forget this nonsense about magic."

Liz smiled. "My apologies, Alex. Actually, I do believe you and I can see why Gail does, too. But don't underestimate the magic. Truth often casts such a spell."

On their way to Liz's home in Hyde Park - one of a number of high-priced inner suburbs of shaded streets, Victorian houses, and boutique shops and cafes - Gail asked Liz if she could stop by the Royal Adelaide Hospital. Alex had some lingering questions about the death of a Russian general, and since he could not risk showing his face in public to ask the questions himself, maybe they could ask them for him.

"Are you referring to General Timoshkin?" asked Liz.

"You've heard of him?" asked Talanov, surprised.

"I hear most of what's going on in this city," answered Liz. "Including the rumors and gossip people wish would stay buried. What do you want to know?"

Talanov told her.

"It's a little early yet, but I know just the person I can lean on," said Liz as she steered her sedan down O'Connell Street, one of North Adelaide's trendy boulevards of cafes and shops. The street soon made a gentle descent past the imposing St. Peter's Cathedral, whose towering twin steeples pierced the clear blue of the morning sky.

They had soon turned onto North Terrace, one of the main thoroughfares separating downtown Adelaide from the parklands which enclosed it. The city possessed a conservative skyline which rose dramatically from a flatland between a range of hills and the Gulf of St Vincent. The traffic was light as they sped beneath overhanging trees and the shadows of department stores. Finally they turned right onto East Terrace, where Liz found a parking space across from the old East End Market, an ornamented brick facade of arches and windowed shop fronts. Built just after the turn of the century as a site for local growers to sell their fruit and vegetables, the four-acre market's original interior of wooden stands and stalls had now been gutted to make room for expensive high-rise apartments.

While Talanov waited in the car, Liz and Gail hurried down the block and across North Terrace to the hospital, where she went immediately to the office of Brandon Huxley, Media Liaison Officer. Upon seeing the familiar face of Liz Langdon, Brandon shot out of his chair and ushered the popular newswoman and her companion to comfortable chairs.

Preferring to stand assertively at the front edge of Brandon's desk, Liz declined Brandon's offer of cafeteria coffee as the pressing business of General Timoshkin's murder by poisoning was now being investigated by the network. Not wanting information about a terrorist strike to irreparably damage the hospital's reputation, Liz wanted to shut down the investigation but needed the complete story from Brandon's own lips before she could act.

Brandon had already turned pale as he unsteadily lowered himself into his chair. "You *know* about the poisoning? *How?*"

Liz glanced around the office with an aloof sigh. "Brandon, Brandon," she said in measured tone which told Brandon he should know better than to ask such a stupid question. "You know I can't tell you that."

"I thought we'd managed to keep a lid on this," Brandon said in a despairing voice. "If you know, why haven't you run it?"

The drilling stare of Liz Langdon was accentuated by the planting of both her hands on the front edge of Brandon's desk. "Because I'm no cut-throat, as you well know. So, to contain this I need you to tell me everything: names of the attending physicians and nurses, comments made by patients and staff, descriptions of the killer. If I'm to stop this nightmare-in-the-making before it gets out of hand, I need your help. By the way, that's *your* hand and *your* nightmare."

"This sounds like a police investigation!"

Liz lowered one eyebrow menacingly. "Talk to me, Brandon, or this story gets run in every major capital around the world, your name included."

"All right, all *right*, but you've got to keep this quiet!"

"There's a good chance I can shut it down *providing* you cooperate."

After a groan of resignation, Brandon Huxley withdrew a thick folder from a locked drawer and spent the next thirty minutes going over everything he had managed to withhold from the media. Dr Emily Henderson was the attending physician, Dave Jarrett the station nurse, both of whom said the male assassin looked to be in his mid-forties, with blond hair and a medium build. Two patients were reported to have recalled General Timoshkin telling the killer that he knew him, with two others remembering that the killer spoke a strange language which the general understood - meaning it was probably Russian - with one patient also recalling how General Timoshkin protested being threatened by something he helped create. Two patients also remembered the general saying, "*Peristroika... the Second Thirteen,*" with the killer then reported to have said something about the Second Thirteen being dead, deadly, or something to do with death. Dave Jarrett also filed a statement that the killer obviously had the assassination well planned because he wore a nurse's uniform, knew Dr Henderson's rounds, and knew exactly where to send Dave to get him out of the way. Dr Henderson affirmed that after the general had been poisoned, he staggered to the nurses' station pleading for an outside telephone line. He then recited a Sydney telephone number he'd committed to memory, which Dr Henderson dialed for him although she could not recall the number when she filed her report. General Timoshkin had no belongings to speak of, nor were there any known relatives.

Liz had taken a number of notes and gave every assurance to Brandon that she felt confident she could contain things. She and Gail then said their farewells and left the liaison manager slouched in his chair and blotting his forehead. Once they were back in the car, Liz and Gail briefed Talanov on what they had uncovered.

"What strikes me is how well planned the assassination was," said Talanov ten minutes later as they drove down a brick-paved section of King William Road lined with quaint shops and covered sidewalks trimmed with grape vines. "Proper planning and execution take time, which means they may have a center of operations here. The question is: where? And is that where they're holding Andrea?"

"Maybe Demetria's friend can help," offered Gail. "What did you say his name was?"

"Con Kanellopoulos," said Alex.

Liz looked at Talanov in the rear view mirror with surprise. "Do you know Con Kanellopoulos?"

"No, but some friends in Sydney gave me his name. Who is he?"

"One of the richest Greeks in South Australia. Aside from operating the Kanellopoulos Brothers market gardening farms and produce stand at the Central Market, he owns some vineyards, a real estate company, two used car lots, and a large number of downtown office buildings. Beneath that legitimate exterior, though, Con has been known to smuggle everything from Levi jeans to Pontiac Firebirds. He's dead set against drugs, though, so he's okay by me."

"But will he know where terrorists might be holding a hostage?" asked Talanov.

"If anyone knows, it will be Con," answered Liz as she turned down a quiet street where fences and shrubbery obscured all but the briefest of glimpses of attractive homes of cut stone, shady verandahs, gabled roofs, and decorated wrought iron trim.

But Talanov's mind was reflecting on how he had almost been captured at the Bankstown airport. "The trouble is, when Demetria gave me his name, her phone had been tapped by the police. That means he's sure to be watched."

"Leave Con to me," replied Liz.

"Thanks," said Talanov from the back seat. He then leaned forward. "But I'd like to return to something you said earlier, Liz. You remarked that one of the patients remembered the killer telling General Timoshkin that the Second Thirteen was dead, deadly, or something to do with death."

"That's what Brandon said," replied Liz. "I'm presuming he or one of his administrators interviewed the patients and recorded their comments."

"I realize that statement might very well be an inaccurate paraphrase," said Alex, "but if we assume a general fidelity to what was recorded, for the killer to tell General Timoshkin that the Second Thirteen was *deadly* borders on the ridiculous. That fact is so obvious I doubt a trained assassin would bother with such an inane threat to an experienced military general. This rendering becomes even more absurd when we remember General Timoshkin helped *create* the Second Thirteen."

Gail looked back at Talanov. "So what are you trying to say?"

"That the assassin might have let it slip that the Second Thirteen is *dead* - no longer in existence," replied Talanov. "In other words, it's possible an *image* of the Second Thirteen is being used as a decoy."

"But a decoy for what, and by whom?" asked Gail. "Everything points to the Second Thirteen being very much alive and well. I needn't remind you how one of them poisoned General Timoshkin - who helped create them - and witnesses say the general recognized the man who killed him. Add that to the assassinations in your home and all that's happened since. And if this isn't enough, we now learn the Russian ambassador is involved and that your friend Ivan has discovered a secret computer network in the Russian Consulate. How can you say they're a decoy?"

Alex shook his head. "I wish I knew, Gail. Whatever it is, they have every appearance of being a powerful black operation with political objectives."

"Which is just what the original Department Thirteen was. Correct?"

"Yes," agreed Talanov.

"Then why not a *second* Department Thirteen, as seems to be verified by one of their creators?"

"Because a simple comment got me thinking that while General Timoshkin may have helped create them, they have become something else."

"Such as?" asked Gail.

"I wish I knew."

13 Chapter 29

At ten o'clock sharp, Ambassador Kharkov entered the Russian Consulate at a full gallop. Beside him was Major Marshak, his aide-de-camp, in dress uniform but without a sidearm. The ambassador went immediately to Katcha.

"Good morning, Mr Ambassador," Katcha said upon seeing him enter.

"Good morning, what did you find?" he replied.

Impatience and expectation were visible in Kharkov's hazel eyes as he watched Katcha reach into a bottom desk drawer and take out a large brown envelope, which she handed to him. He grabbed the envelope and tore it open, withdrawing a single sheet of paper. With a growing frown he read it over. "Damn, there's nothing here." He looked at the secretary. "Did you handle this matter personally?"

"Yes, sir. We maintain complete family profiles on all employees. It was not difficult to retrieve."

Kharkov looked at the report again. "Two cousins by the name of Yuri - one in Moscow, the other in New York." Frustrated, he made a fist. "I've *got* to find out if Talanov has been calling Ivan." He folded the paper, stuffed it into his suit jacket pocket, then paced to the door and back, a hand held over his mouth thoughtfully. He suddenly brightened and looked at his watch. "It's early evening on the East Coast of the United States," he told Katcha. "Ring Ivan's cousin in New York and tell him that Ivan received a telephone call several days ago from someone named Yuri although his secretary lost the message slip and cannot remember any details. Say Ivan was most distressed about the error and that you are now trying to locate the correct person. Be sure to confirm whether or not this Yuri has telephoned Ivan within the last seventy-two hours. If he did not, then do the same thing with the other one."

"But it is the middle of the night in Moscow."

"Apologize for the inconvenience but tell him it's urgent. I've got to find out whether or not Talanov's been using Ivan to penetrate our system. While you do that, the major and I will be in the communications room. We are not to be disturbed."

"Yes, sir," replied Katcha, picking up the telephone.

With Marshak stationed outside the door into the communications center, Ambassador Kharkov sat down at the mainframe's keyboard and entered a series of commands which admitted him to the Omega Level. He then opened a concealed utility file and went to the entry log which automatically recorded the names of all individuals accessing the Tango Blue files. Kharkov scanned the list. No unusual names were recorded.

But the ambassador looked again. According to the entries for yesterday, *both he and Sergei had accessed the files!* Not only was Sergei *dead*, but he himself was in a commercial flight over the Pacific. *It had to be Ivan Lazovic!* But how did he discover the password? Ivan was not in the loop.

"We have a problem, Major," the ambassador said in a lowered voice on the way back to see Katcha.

"Sir?"

"Tango Blue has been penetrated."

Alarmed, Marshak looked at the ambassador. "Penetrated? By whom?"

"I'll tell you in a moment."

Kharkov entered the vice consul's office just as Katcha was hanging up the phone. She made a few brief notes and looked up. "Your intuition regarding the falsified use of Yuri's name appears to be accurate, Mr Ambassador. Neither cousin has called Ivan within the last seventy-two hours. When I asked if he was certain of this, the New York cousin suddenly remembered Ivan had telephoned him. He then became extremely vague and digressive, adding that it was possible he may have called Ivan but had forgotten."

"He's covering for him. Come, Major, it's time we asked Mr Lazovic some very direct questions."

"I'm afraid that will not be possible," said Katcha. "Ivan Lazovic called in sick."

Ambassador Kharkov's small stature became rigid as he whirled around and looked hard at Katcha. "*Sick?*" He hurried to the edge of her desk where he planted his hands authoritatively. "Ivan Lazovic called in *sick?*"

Katcha withdrew slightly under the ambassador's stare. "Yes, sir, I took the call myself. He did not specify his illness although he was not looking well yesterday when I saw him at the mainframe."

"What's his address?" demanded Kharkov.

A flurry of typing on the computer keyboard brought Ivan's address onto the screen. Katcha wrote it on a small slip of paper and handed it to the ambassador.

Kharkov snapped up the paper. "Let's go, Major, you drive," he said as he led the way out of the office. "Ivan Lazovic's going to talk."

Using a white consulate sedan, Marshak drove the ambassador to Ivan's flat some twenty minutes away. There were a number of shaded parking spaces in front of the three-story brick building and Marshak pulled into one of them. The uplifted branches of three handsome red gums swayed in the morning breezes, their dappled red and gray trunks contrasting majestically with the light green of their leaves and the blue of the sky.

"Shall I fetch him, sir?" asked Marshak as he switched off the engine.

"Good idea," said Kharkov from the back seat as he removed a mobile telephone from his suit jacket pocket. "Unit Four. Bring Mr Lazovic to the car while I make a call. Accept no excuses. If he's there, I want to see him."

"Yes, sir," said Marshak, getting out of the car and walking toward the cream-colored units.

Kharkov punched a series of numbers and put the instrument to his ear. Before long, a man's voice answered. "Bob? Andrei here. Disturbing news, I'm afraid. It looks as though an employee named Ivan Lazovic has penetrated Tango Blue. I don't know how he got the password or what he knows."

The two men talked for several minutes, Kharkov explaining how Ivan had come to mind because of his father's link to Talanov in Directorate Nine. Suspicions were aroused even further when of a number of calls had been placed to Ivan by someone identifying himself as a cousin named Yuri. A search of the computer records revealed two cousins by that name although neither of them had telephoned Ivan recently, but that the New York cousin became evasive as if trying to cover for him. Kharkov then told Bob that he was in front of Ivan's block of flats now and that Major Marshak would be bringing Ivan down for questioning. One way or another, he would get to the bottom of this. If Ivan *had* been accessing classified documents for Talanov, then his career as a diplomat was finished.

Kharkov looked up to see Marshak approaching the car. Ivan Lazovic was not with him.

"Just a moment, Bob," Kharkov said as he laid aside his phone and rolled down the window. "What's wrong, Major?" he asked.

"You'd better come with me, sir," Marshak answered, his composure visibly shaken.

"What is it? I'm on an important call."

"The door to Ivan Lazovic's flat was closed but not locked," explained the aide-de-camp. "So, after knocking several times and ringing the bell, I tried the handle." Marshak paused, his lips nervously moving as if the words would not come out.

"Dammit, man, what *is* it?" asked Kharkov impatiently.

The major looked away briefly, then back at the ambassador. "I'm afraid Ivan Lazovic is dead, sir. Two bullets, in the head."

13 Chapter 30

Cheney unlocked the door into Andrea's cabin to see her still on the bed where she had fallen. With his loaded dart gun poised, he stepped into the room, followed by assassins Three and Four.

Andrea was on her back, her head to one side, her mouth open, both arms hanging loose across the bed. Assassin Three stepped over and slapped her lightly in the face. She did not move.

Noticing the top several buttons on her blouse were unbuttoned, Three lifted the cloth and peered in. Grinning, he unbuttoned the garment further.

"Stop it," Cheney ordered. "We have other things to do."

Three straightened and looked disagreeably at Number One. "We have plenty of time before we phone Talanov," he growled. He reached down and ripped the blouse open, revealing the swell of Andrea's breasts in a soft thin bra which fastened in the front. He unclipped the bra and began running his hands across her flesh.

"We don't have time!" snapped Cheney, himself feeling stimulated.

"And I say we *do!*" argued Three, turning angrily to face Number One. "You want only to assign me to some insignificant task and return to have her yourself!"

"Do with her as you wish," countered Cheney, "but not until Talanov is dead. I don't want him being driven over the edge by learning that she's been raped. You know as well as I do that we must be on board this ship when it sails tomorrow morning. Until then, keep your pants zipped."

Three jabbed his finger at One. "Do not betray me on this!"

Cheney looked down at the unconscious woman lying half undressed on the bed. Admittedly, he wanted her, too - and have her he would - but not before they had killed Talanov. Then he would kill Three as well.

Raising his eyes to meet Three's, Cheney smiled. "When this assignment is over, we can have all the women we wish." His smile then faded. "But not before."

His lips forming a sneer, Three stormed out of the cabin and waited in the corridor. Four was next, followed by Cheney. But before he shut the door, Cheney paused and looked back at Andrea. She groaned and started to move. Raising the gun, he fired another dart into her leg. And with a slight jerk and a moan, she once more went limp.

"That should keep her," said Cheney, handing Three the dart gun and locking the door. He then handed the key to Three. "Check on her at noon and leave some food," he said, leading the way down the corridor. "Four and I are going out to locate an ambush site. We'll be back no later than four." Cheney paused at the top of the stairwell, his hand on the heavy pipe railing. "Come morning she'll be yours."

Appearing mollified, Three nodded and followed Cheney down the gray metal stairs.

"What if Talanov's mobile runs out of charge?" asked Four as they reached the bottom.

Cheney stopped abruptly and looked at Four. "I hadn't thought of that." Cursing, he took several slow steps, his eyes squinted in thought. Suddenly he stopped. "I can do nothing about it now. We'll see what happens at noon when we call."

Once the corridor was quiet, Andrea tiptoed to the door and listened. She stood there for several minutes, attentive for the slightest sound which might indicate the presence of a guard. She heard nothing.

Fastening her bra, Andrea went back to the bed and removed the dart, placing it near her feet on the floor. She then pulled the hand towel out of her jeans. The folded cloth had been enough insulation to keep the dart from penetrating her skin.

It had been almost more than she could endure to remain motionless on the bed while the assassin ran his hands over her body. But Alex's words kept coming back to her, giving her strength: *If killers have a potential weakness, it is in the blind spot created by their weapons. One can easily become careless when heavily armed or with a feeling of unquestioned advantage.*

Andrea thought about the words spoken by her husband. Right now, deception was her only weapon and she had used it to gain information. They had, of course, assumed she was unconscious and talked carelessly in her presence. As expected, their purpose was to kill Alex.

But there appeared to be fractures in their unity, for a brief quarrel had broken out between two of them. *A* weakness? Plus, the leader had said that when this assignment was over, they could have all the women they wished. Assignment? Such was more the talk of mercenaries than a group of political extremists, who tended to justify actions by their ideals. There had been no talk of ideals. Also, she heard them say that they needed to sail with the ship tomorrow morning in order to get out of the country, which appeared to indicate some kind of timetable. *Another weakness?*

The clock in the room indicated that she had well over an hour until one of the killers returned with some food. Although she was beyond hunger, Andrea knew that she needed to eat. She had a constant headache and felt unusually tired.

Andrea walked to the sink and quietly filled a glass with water. But she had barely tipped it to her lips when she heard footsteps in the corridor. Almost dropping the glass in her panic, she set it on the sink and hurried back to lay on the bed, pulling open her bra as the killer had left it.

But then she remembered the glass! Andrea started to get up when she heard the sound of a key being inserted in the lock. Her head reached the pillow just as the door swung open.

Who it was Andrea could not tell. And whoever it was stood in the doorway for what seemed like an eternity. With extreme effort she forced herself to breathe deeply and slowly as a sedated person would do. *How long would this go on? How long would the intruder stare?*

What was that sound? *He was coming toward her!*

Andrea could now sense someone standing over her and soon detected the sound of heavy breathing. Suddenly Number Three sat on the bed beside her and began running his hands over her breasts, massaging them passionately, his breathing becoming excited. It took all the discipline Andrea could muster to endure this violation. Revulsion churned in her stomach.

Without warning the hands moved down to her jeans and started to unbutton them. *O God, he's going to rape me.*

"Hey, what are you *doing?*" a man's voice called out from the corridor. "She's got a contagious *disease!*"

Number Three jumped to his feet and whirled around to see one of the ship's crew standing in the doorway with a look of horror on his face. Three walked over and pushed the man out of the door. He stumbled back against the corridor wall and nearly fell. "Mind your own business!" Three snarled as he stepped out of the cabin and locked the door.

"Easy, mate, I'm just telling you what I heard," the man said, his hands held up in surrender.

But Three had already turned angrily away and was walking back toward the stairs.

Andrea lay on the bed weeping silently. *Where are you, Alex, where are you?*

Chapter 31

For the sixth time in ten minutes Talanov looked at his watch. It was nearly noon and his increased worries were making him tense, unable to think. *Where are you, Andrea?* He felt so close and yet so far!

No one spoke in Liz Langdon's spacious kitchen as the minute hand crept toward twelve. Gail sat at the cooking island on a bar stool, a mug of tea in her hands, her eyes fixed on Talanov who was beside her. Above them a collection of saucepans and skillets hung from a large stainless steel rectangle suspended from the ceiling. Nearby, Liz wiped the kitchen counter again for the third time, cleaning under the toaster and electric kettle as she had done the previous two times.

Having grown weary of coffee and tea, Talanov drank from a glass of water. Earlier, Liz had made him a late breakfast of crumpets and eggs, which he initially refused but finally ate once Gail reminded him that she didn't want her life - not to mention Andrea's - dependent on a man who didn't have sense enough to eat.

The mobile telephone was laying on the counter near where Liz was cleaning. Talanov looked at his watch again. It was twelve o'clock. Liz and Gail both glanced at one another, their eyes then focusing on Talanov, who sat drinking his water, his attention riveted on the phone.

One minute ticked by, then another... then several.

"Where the bloody hell *are* they?" he asked angrily. "Why don't they *call?*"

"Did they say *at* noon or *around* noon?" asked Gail.

"I don't remember!" snapped Talanov.

Gail looked away and did not reply.

Talanov ran a hand across his forehead. "Gail, I'm sorry. I had no right to snap at you."

Gail looked back at him with a forced smile. "Don't worry about it."

"I just wish they'd *call,*" said Alex, standing and walking into the connected dining area where a large window overlooked a manicured back lawn encircled by thickets of shrubs. At the far end of the yard, planted along a high brush fence covered with ivy, were several white "ghost gum" eucalyptus trees casting filtered shadows across the lawn.

Liz walked over to the window beside Talanov, her short plump figure a contrast to Talanov's athletic build. She looked up at him. "I need to ask you a question."

Alex looked down at her. "Go ahead."

After glancing back at Gail, she looked up at Talanov again. "This thought just came to me: have you checked that mobile's battery? If it's depleted, they may have tried to call but couldn't get through."

"Oh *no!*" cried Alex, rushing into the kitchen and picking up the instrument. He turned it on and put it to his ear. There was no sound. "It's fucking *dead!*" he shouted, hurling the phone at a brick wall where it shattered into pieces. With his hands curled into fists, he covered his eyes in anguish, then dropped to his knees and began to weep.

The two women came over and knelt beside him on the hardwood floor, their arms encircling him as he cried. For several minutes the emotion poured out of Alex like burst artery. "What am I going to *do?*" he finally asked.

Gail was the one to answer. "Allow that bottled-up shit to come out, then regroup and fight these bastards."

In less than a minute, Talanov had shifted into a sitting position on the floor, his forehead resting in his hands. After several deep breaths, he wiped his eyes. "Having a good cry was something we were never taught at Balashikha," he finally said.

"Maybe that's why you lost the Cold War," Gail replied.

A welcome laugh was Talanov's reply.

Gail stood and offered Alex her hand. "Come on, get up and put that sexy mind of yours to work."

Accepting it, Talanov stood. He then offered his hand to Liz, who grunted as she climbed to her feet.

"Maybe someone at the station can fix that mobile," Liz said, walking over and picking up the pieces.

Talanov was already at the sink pouring himself more water. "Let's leave it as it is," he replied, then taking a drink.

"For God's sake, *why?*" asked Gail.

"That dead phone has given us an opportunity. Since these killers are using mobile phones themselves, they'll have to assume my battery has gone dead and give me time to recharge it. Which means they'll keep Andrea alive, at least for the present. Our task is to find out where they are."

"What's your back-up in case we *don't* find them?" asked Gail, who had strolled to the sink and poured the last of her tea down the drain. "That mobile phone is history, and sooner or later they'll know something's up." She turned and looked at Alex. "I don't mean to sound cruel, but once that happens, your wife could get killed."

"I know," answered Talanov, sitting on a bar stool. "Thankfully, we still have a link to the killers."

"Demetria!" exclaimed Gail. "That's right - they'll call her thinking she'll be able to get a message to you."

"That's true, but I was thinking of Ambassador Kharkov," stated Talanov as Gail sat beside him. "Because if we allow them to get messages to us by way of Demetria,

147

we endanger her, lose control, and again become their puppets. But if I start pushing on Kharkov, we take the offensive. I'm not sure how long this window will last, but we may find out some information which will enable us to determine where they're holding Andrea. In the meantime, phone Ian and ask him to warn Demetria. If they call her, she's to tell them she doesn't know where I am or how to reach me. It's imperative she not let them frighten her with threats about killing Andrea. Tell her to stand by her story. That's critical."

"I'll take care of it," said Gail. "What's your strategy with Kharkov?"

"This is one I'll play as I go, although something about this whole scenario keeps bothering me."

"What's that?"

"By all appearances, the Second Thirteen is an assassination unit created by Yuri Andropov for the ultimate purpose of resurrecting his hardline political system. Their initial actions, then, would be to get rid of all those who might expose them before they've achieved their aims - hence, the assassinations in our home, the poisoning of General Timoshkin, and the continued emphasis on killing me. Even more disturbing is the link we've discovered between the Second Thirteen and Ambassador Kharkov which, if true, means the conspiracy has tentacles both in the Russian government and the International Development Council!"

"You're not alone, Alex, and it concerns me, too," said Gail. "I don't think any sane person would *not* be alarmed by such a destabilizing threat to the West."

"But that's not what bothers me," replied Alex.

"Then what does?" asked Gail.

"It's Kharkov himself. In looking at him, we find not a political extremist, but a man of integrity who lectures throughout Australia, the United States, and Europe on market economics and cooperation with the West. In fact, he was even held back from political advancement by Andropov because of his progressive ideas. On the other hand, my contact in the consulate recently discovered a secret computer network linked to Kharkov through the same mysterious codename used by the assassins - Tango Blue. However, this covert network could not be accessed. In the end, all my friend could say he saw were hundreds of numbers - which, if we're honest, mean little apart from creating the impression of something vast. Now it's certainly possible that Kharkov is part of some massive conspiracy. But if he's not, then his apparent involvement - including those secret numerical files - might be a cleverly-constructed ruse to give the *appearance* of a conspiracy."

"But isn't this just a theory?" asked Gail. "You don't have any evidence, do you?"

"No, I don't," answered Talanov. "But let's say for the sake of argument that Kharkov has been told Tango Blue is something different from what it is. And let's say the Tango Blue files are actually a listing of odometer readings made to look like something sinister."

"In other words, you're proposing that Kharkov has been led to *think* Tango Blue is a church social when actually it's a narcotics ring?"

"In essence, yes," stated Talanov.

"Assuming, for the moment, that he's been taken in, this would mean the highly intelligent Russian Ambassador to Australia has been fooled by a group of assassins in such a way as to enlist his support while keeping him blindfolded to what's really going on. And, of course, he doesn't think to ask questions."

"You have a certain way with words," said Talanov.

"Do you realize how ridiculous that sounds?" argued Gail as she stood and walked to the sink. She turned and leaned against the edge of the counter, her arms folded. "I'd sooner believe I could win Cross-Lotto."

"Which, of course, does occur," Talanov pointed out.

A long moment of silence passed.

"All right, dammit, it's possible," admitted Gail with a scowl. "But I sure as hell wouldn't bet on it."

"I'll know more once I talk to Kharkov," replied Alex. "So, after you ring Ian, I'd like you to drop me off at a public phone while you two make a visit to the Central Market. When I'm finished, I'll walk back to the house."

"I'll ring Con first," said Liz, "and have him call me back on someone else's mobile, in case his number's being monitored. I'll tell him what we need, and by the time we get there he'll have things in motion."

Ten minutes later, Liz pulled into a parking space on King William Road near a telephone booth. Wearing his sunglasses and hat, Talanov got out and shut the car door. He then looked back in through the open car door window. "You two be careful," he said. "And this isn't protective horseshit, Gail."

Gail looked hard into Talanov's eyes. "Then what is it?" she asked.

Talanov paused. "I guess maybe it is," he finally admitted. "Just remember, it's likely the police and the killers have a description of you by now."

"Noted. Is that all?"

Exasperated, Alex shook his head and straightened. "I guess so," he said. "See you later."

After giving Gail a look of disapproval, Liz leaned across the seat. "Alex?"

He looked back through the window. "Yeah?"

She smiled. "Be careful yourself. We don't want to lose you, either."

13 Chapter 32

Holding two sandwiches wrapped in plastic, Number Three inserted his key in the cabin door. Pushing it open, he saw Andrea still lying on the bed. He stepped inside and closed the door, not wanting any of the ship's crew to interfere with him again.

He tossed the sandwiches on a chair and walked over to the bed, his eyes on Andrea's exposed breasts gently rising and falling with each breath. Already he was stimulated at the sight of her lying helpless on the bed.

Her jeans would be easy enough to remove. How long it had been since he had forced himself on someone so beautiful. Usually his women were street tarts who required a knife to the throat. But this time it would be different. This time he would do everything he desired. And while she slept!

The thought of such an easy rape aroused him, and with a grin Three approached the bed and took hold of the button on her jeans.

Without warning, a rigid hand knifed out, stabbing him in the eyes and temporarily blinding him. He cried out and staggered back, his hands covering his eyes just as a foot kicked him in the groin, doubling him over. Andrea then grabbed the assassin's hair and yanked him toward the metal railing of the bed, slamming his head into the tubular steel with all of her strength. Unconscious, the killer collapsed to the floor.

Panting, Andrea fastened her bra and buttoned her blouse. She then knelt beside the killer and quickly felt through his pockets, hoping to find a weapon. There was none. Grabbing the key, she stood and moved to the door, opening it a crack and peering up and down the corridor. It was clear.

Emerging into the hall, she closed the door and locked it, looking both ways as she tried to remember which direction they had come in. Looking again to her right, she saw a large open hatch. *They had stepped through a hatch.* Hoping this was the way out, she ran toward it.

She stepped through it and soon came to an ascending flight of stairs. Which way should she go: up the stairs, or further along the corridor to another flight which led down? She couldn't think, wishing now she had grabbed one of the sandwiches.

Andrea closed her eyes and rubbed the dull pain in her temples. Which way?

Then she remembered. They had driven up a ramp... yes, they had come aboard *in a car*, driving onto the ship and then up a ramp - or was it down? - to an elevator which took them up - yes, it must have been up, for the lower levels were filled with vehicles and freight. She needed to get back to those lower decks, which meant she must go *down*, not up!

Bypassing the ascending stairs, she ran toward the other flight of stairs which led down. Suddenly, from behind her came muffled shouts and a pounding sound. Looking back, she saw her cabin door fly open off its hinges and assassin Three stagger out holding his head. Andrea grabbed the gray metal handrail and hurried down the stairs, hoping she had not been noticed.

But she *had* been seen and the killer shouted after her. As she reached the bottom of the stairs, she could hear the sound of running footsteps in the corridor above.

She paused and looked each way. Was she above the main deck or below it? Had her room been high in the ship's accommodation or somewhere deep in the hull? *Where was she?* She ran around a corner - *the elevator!* Andrea pushed the button several times but the doors did not open. She could not wait and so sprinted along the passageway to a junction. Which way now?

To her right were voices - *men talking!* - and she carefully approached an open door and looked around the corner. Three men in blue overalls were sitting in a small room. But on the other side of that room was a door - an *open* door - and through that door was daylight.

Andrea burst through the group of surprised men and out onto the main deck of the freighter, the bright sunlight momentarily blinding her with its brilliance. Shielding her face with a hand, Andrea squinted for the gangway. *There it was, just ten feet away!*

She ran over and grabbed the handrail and started down the steep metal stairs, only to halt when she saw two men climbing up toward her. They saw her and started shouting.

Andrea ran back to the top. What to *do?* To her right were dozens of huge steel containers positioned on the freighter's rusty steel deck by the giant gantry cranes. They were an impenetrable wall and blocked escape in that direction. To her left was the stern of the ship where she saw several large winches wound with thick rope. *Mooring lines!* But she had not eaten and wondered if she would have the strength to keep from falling.

A horn blast sounded from the harbor. *Another ship!* Running to the opposite side of the freighter, Andrea stepped around a domed exhaust vent and saw a small orange pilot boat motoring past. She waved her hands and screamed for help.

No one took any notice.

Stepping over a pile of chains, Andrea ran to the stern of the ship and began shouting and waving. One of the men on the pilot boat saw her and waved back. *They thought she was just being friendly!*

She peered over the railing to the greenish water far below. She would jump! The height was frightening, but not as frightening as again being captured.

Behind her came shouts and Andrea glanced to see the angry assassin and two men running toward her. She looked over the side again. The man in the pilot boat waved. He was looking... *now was the time!*

Suddenly, she felt a sting in her shoulder. Arching her back, Andrea turned and saw Fiona Zinyakin holding the dart gun. Andrea frantically tried to reach the dart and pull it out. Her fingers touched it... it was out! She looked back over the side. The pilot boat was nearly gone. She had to *jump!*

Andrea tried to step over the railing, but something was wrong. A strange sensation was rushing over her... she was feeling dizzy. Suddenly clumsy, Andrea lost her footing and slipped back just as assassin Three grabbed her and yanked her away from the railing. Spinning her around, he slapped her across the face, knocking her into the white exterior of the ship's accommodation and down onto the dirty deck.

With blood running from her mouth, Andrea groaned and tried to get up but could not. Number Three pulled her to her feet and slapped her again. Andrea's knees buckled and she collapsed.

With a loud curse, the killer grabbed Andrea by the hair and lifted her head, drawing back to hit her again.

"That's enough!" shouted Fiona.

The assassin looked angrily at Number Two.

"She will not feel it," Fiona told him.

Number Three looked down at Andrea, who was unconscious.

And with another loud curse the assassin released her, Andrea's head smashing onto the dirty steel of the deck.

13 Chapter 33

While Gail and Liz drove to the Central Market for their meeting with Con Kanellopoulos, Alex telephoned the Russian Consulate in Sydney and asked for Ambassador Kharkov. The call was put through to the office of the vice-consul.

"Vice-consul's office, may I help you?"

"Ambassador Kharkov, please," said Talanov with implied urgency.

"I'm afraid the ambassador is not receiving any calls right now due to the death of one of our staff."

Talanov was suddenly worried. "Then may I speak with Ivan Lazovic?" he instinctively asked.

A nervous silence followed. "Who is this, please?"

"Ivan's dead, isn't he?"

"Who *is* this?" pressed Katcha.

"*Tell me!*"

"I... I cannot say."

"You just did. Tell Kharkov it's Aleksandr Talanov."

A gasp was all Talanov heard and he was instantly put on hold.

Talanov was stunned. Ivan was *dead*! This was no mere coincidence and there *had* to be a connection to what Ivan had discovered. The question was - how had he died? Was Kharkov responsible?

"Mr Talanov, this is Ambassador Kharkov," the diplomat announced as he snapped his fingers and directed Marshak to pick up an extension phone. "We don't have the capability to trace your call, but I've directed someone else to listen on another phone as a witness to this conversation."

"Listen all you want because you're going to tell me who killed Ivan and why. Was it because he uncovered your involvement with Tango Blue?"

"This has nothing to do with Tango Blue - which you could know about only because Ivan had penetrated those files and then passed the information to you. For all I know, you killed him."

"So he *was* killed; thanks for the confirmation. By the way, Kharkov, I'm in

Adelaide and there are people here who will testify to that. But I suppose you know where I am."

"I didn't, but judging by the fact that such people have been harboring an accused mass murderer, I doubt their testimony will be given much credibility."

"That remains to be seen, and believe me, what they have to say will be taken seriously."

"What do you want?"

"Ivan was an honest man - perhaps one of the few remaining ones around there - and he discovered your involvement with Tango Blue, which means you're involved with the Second Thirteen, which makes *you* the leading candidate for his murder."

"Who the *hell* do you think you are?" shouted the ambassador. "And what's this Second Thirteen?"

"Don't play games," replied Talanov. "They're Andropov's group of assassins and they're linked with Tango Blue. Ivan found your list of agents in the mainframe and now he's dead, just like Sergei. I know that Sergei was part of your operation and I know you brought him aboard. Or was it Fiona, the one who really buried that fireplace poker in his skull?"

"*Assassins?* You *are* mad!" shouted Kharkov. "And not only mad, but a psychopath. Fiona *saw* you kill her husband!"

"Fiona's lying and I have a witness to prove it. He was with me the night I went to confront Sergei about his involvement with the Second Thirteen. No, Mr Ambassador, Fiona killed her husband."

"I don't believe you."

"If I'm a madman, then why am I calling you?"

Ambassador Kharkov could give no answer.

"Well, let me tell you. At the bottom of this insanity is someone or something called Tango Blue and I want to know who or what it is!"

"This is absurd! Tango Blue is nothing more than-"

"Mr Ambassador, *stop!*" broke in Marshak. "Don't say anything! Talanov is trying to compromise your reputation by seeking information which he will twist to his own purposes."

"I'm doing nothing of the sort!" countered Talanov. "You know as well as I do that for *years* I've maintained unquestioned loyalty to Russia. I'm a known critic of our imperialist past - just like you - but now I'm being hunted by assassins who want to kill me for something they think I know or possess. Whatever the reason, it's connected to Tango Blue. It's my guess you've been told Tango Blue is one thing when it very well could be something else. But I need to know what or who it is. *Think*, Mr Ambassador: Ivan discovered something and now he's dead. *Dead!* So tell me the identity of Tango Blue, because whoever's behind it not only wants me killed, but they've *kidnapped my wife*."

"Kidnapped your *wife?*"

"Yes!" shouted Talanov. "Now, *talk*, damn you!"

Pacing the floor in the small office as far as the telephone cord would allow, Ambassador Kharkov brought a frantic hand to his forehead. To his great surprise, he found himself believing Talanov. True, Ivan appeared to be the one who had penetrated the Tango Blue files, which - of course - was no reason for him to have been *murdered*. Could Talanov be right? Was Tango Blue was something other than-

"Ow!" cried Kharkov as he jerked a hand to the sting in the side of his neck. He whirled around to see Marshak standing behind him holding a gold ball-point pen with a needle extending from its tip. With a smile, the major clicked the button on the top and the needle retracted into the pen. "What in God's name-?" Kharkov began.

A violent pain shot through the ambassador's chest and he dropped the phone, gasping for breath. Within seconds he had fallen to his knees, then toppled to the carpet and onto his back while his hands tore at the invisible coils now crushing the life from his body. Kharkov soon began to choke, his heart fibrillating wildly, his body jerking with powerful spasms. Fighting for air, with frightened eyes the ambassador pleaded with Marshak to help him. Instead, the major calmly replaced the pen in the pocket of his uniform and knelt beside him. "Yes, Mr Ambassador, I killed Ivan and I'm killing you," he said in a low voice. "The reason is simple: you're of no further use."

Kharkov's arms bolted straight, his torso and legs also stiffening, and with a final convulsion, he released a final breath. Slowly, as his body relaxed, his head rolled to one side, both eyes glassy and hollow.

Marshak leaned toward the telephone Kharkov had dropped. He heard Talanov's voice calling out. "Mr Ambassador, what's *wrong?*" Marshak suddenly shouted, angling his head toward the receiver. He then cupped a hand around his mouth. "Help, *help!*" he called out toward the closed door of the office as he loosened the ambassador's tie and with the heels of his hands began resuscitation measures.

Katcha raced through the door. "What's wrong?" she asked, her eyes widening in horror at the sight of the ambassador lying on the floor.

"Call an ambulance!" ordered Marshak as he continued to pump Kharkov's chest. "The ambassador was arguing with Talanov and suddenly collapsed. I think it's a *heart attack!*"

13 Chapter 34

While the wealthy dowagers of North Adelaide's old money discuss pedigrees over Devonshire tea, across the river on Gouger Street a patchwork of nationalities mingle for another day of business on the dirty asphalt of Central Market. For the coiffed dowagers, the tea must be English, the cream properly clotted to accompany the fresh scones and jam. In the Central Market, a rich spectrum of teas from Queensland to Sri Lanka compete with robust coffees from all over the world. The laughter is loud, the cry of hawkers even louder as visitors sip frothy cappuccinos at small tables while masses of shoppers surge slowly up and down the aisles searching for bargains.

The Kannellopoulos Brothers produce stand occupied one of the Market's prime locations on the main aisle bisecting this indoor mall of covered stalls and stands. Liz led the way into the large brick building past a meat counter advertizing a weekly special on sides of lamb.

Today was loud and boisterous, with baritone vendors shouting prices over the din of customers making purchases or inspecting produce. The fragrances of fresh flowers, roasted nuts, and ground coffee drifted over wooden counters piled high with fruits and vegetables. Further down the aisle, cheeses from around the world were displayed beside stacks of wood-oven bread, fresh pesto, olives, and numerous fermented meats.

A loud voice shouted a special price on watermelons. Liz grinned and looked in the direction of the voice to see Con Kanellopoulos holding a melon high above his head. Beside him a young female assistant offered samples to passing shoppers.

In his early sixties, Con had a broad grin, a physique similar to a Rottweiler, and a full head of silver hair. Above stocky calves covered with wiry black hair, Con wore denim shorts and a striped blue-and-yellow polo shirt.

But as the two women started toward the Greek, Liz suddenly took Gail by the arm and steered her behind a group of people standing near the escalator up to the parking garage.

"What's wrong?" asked Gail, surprised by the abrupt action of her friend.

"See those two men in jeans standing near the cheese stand?" she asked Gail, who looked and nodded that she did. "Well I know them and they're the police. Alex thought they might be watching." Liz stepped in front of Gail and looked directly into her eyes. "So in case they've got your description, I want you to go back and wait for me inside the Asian Kitchen Grocery. We walked by it on our way in. Once I've set up a meeting with Con, I'll come and get you."

But as Gail opened her mouth to protest, Liz held a warning finger advisedly in front of Gail's mouth. "Don't even try it, Gail. You're able to push that 'protective horseshit' routine on Alex because he's much too polite to push back. Sweetheart, I'm not Alex and I push back... hard, if I have to. So don't turn me into the bitch from hell. This time do what I tell you."

"Blimey, I think you mean it."

"I do... now go back and wait. I won't be long."

While Gail made her way back to the Asian grocery, Liz took a deep breath and stepped into the flow of pedestrians, making her way casually toward Con, who brightened when he saw her approaching. "Lizzy!" he bellowed, putting the watermelon back on the table and waving her over.

"Hello, Con," said Liz, walking up to the table as several people saw her familiar face and offered greetings.

Con gave her a kiss on the cheek. "What brings you down to the market?" he asked loudly. "Have you started a cooking show?"

Liz smiled sweetly and grabbed a red capsicum. "Very funny," she said in a low voice while examining the pepper. "You know how I loathe cooking. Now, when and where can we meet?"

"Six, did you say?" asked Con brightly and in the same loud voice, drawing a moment's scowl from Liz. He motioned for a plastic sack and one of his young female assistants handed him one. "Fifteen minutes... Kings Head Hotel," he replied quietly without looking at Liz while he picked out six of his finest capsicums and put them into the sack. He then looked at her and smiled. "That will be five dollars," he said.

"Five *dollars?*" Liz complained, glaring up at the grinning Greek before opening her wallet for the money. "You could have sold me *one*," she grumbled through clenched teeth as she slapped the correct amount into the Greek's hand. Con continued to grin broadly as she snatched the sack and nodded a disgruntled farewell.

While Liz browsed several more stalls on her way back to meet Gail, Con stepped behind the counter and started shifting boxes of bananas, the two policemen observing his movements. While his staff waited on customers, Con would kneel, then stand with a box, then kneel, then stand again with another box, which he invariably shifted to another location behind the counter. Before long, however, Con did not stand and the two policemen grew wary. Finally, one strolled over to the counter and pretended to look over the produce before peering inside. *Con was gone!*

With a look of alarm he ran back to his partner and the two of them began frantically looking over the mass of shoppers filling the aisles. The Greek was nowhere to be seen.

After having ducked out the other side of his stand, Con darted down the aisle and through several stalls to the end of the market, pulling on a long-sleeved gray shirt while he walked. He made his way outside, where he hurried along the sidewalk and into the Coles supermarket, crossing quickly to the other side of the store, then through the arcade and out onto Gouger Street. Con was crossing the street with a group of shoppers when his mobile phone sounded.

He switched it on, brought it to his ear, then began conversing in Greek as he proceeded down a small lane, pausing momentarily in the recessed doorway of a small brick office building to see if anyone was following. Seeing no one, he finished his conversation, then angled left across an asphalt parking lot, once more glancing back to make sure no one had seen him. Satisfied, he hurried down a paved alleyway to the end of the block, where he turned left and walked the short distance to the King's Head Hotel, a preserved bluestone Victorian building. A brown tram car full of passengers was trundling along King William Street just as he entered.

After greeting the barman and several of the regulars, Con walked out the other door, across a dimly-lit hall, and into a pub known as The King's Bar. Stained ceiling beams and rich paneling created an elegant frame for a bar of polished Tasmanian oak. Behind the counter was a balding man with a large moustache, and behind him was a mirrored wall displaying dozens of bottles. The barman nodded to Con then directed his eyes back to the cricket match being shown on a television set mounted near the ceiling. A strand of red and green Christmas lights was blinking above a handful of patrons chatting quietly on barstools, drinks in their hands. The low murmur of their voices was suddenly overpowered by a harsh sound of cheering from the television.

Looking to his immediate left, Con saw Liz and another woman seated in the corner booth. On the wall behind them was a chalk board advertising the prices of wine by the glass. Con grinned and approached the table.

"You rotten thief," Liz growled as Con pulled out one of the burgundy chairs and sat.

"Don't complain, you got a discount," he replied. He glanced under the table and saw there was no sack. "What did you do with the capsicums? I gave you six of my best."

"I dumped them in the first bin I came to," answered Liz as two short black coffees were brought to the table by the barman. After another glance at the television, the barman looked down at Con, who ordered a beer. Without a word, the barman returned to the bar to fill the order.

After introductions, Liz got to the point. "Have you found out anything?"

Con leaned up to the table. "It would be difficult for a group of assassins to access Adelaide directly by air although a few international flights arrive here from some of the Asian countries. However, immigration controls are tight, especially with the new computer links which make it difficult to use false documents. Therefore, it's my guess your killers arrived by ship. With that in mind, I called a few friends who know the waterfront like I know fruit. One of them just rang back to say that he did a little pushing on a Port Adelaide hustler named Mick. Mick claims he recently met three strangers who wanted to make sure no one knew they were in town. Based on the date Mick says he met them, I checked the roster to find that the only ship in port was a freighter out of Hong Kong named the *Coriander*. It's owned by a company called Spice Lines East and flies a Panamanian flag of convenience."

"Flag of convenience?" asked Liz.

"It means while the ship's registry is in Panama, it could be from anywhere and haul anything," replied Gail. "Aside from dubious ownership and a substandard safety rating, these rust buckets often hire tough crews whose only morality is cash. A team of assassins would fit right in."

Con looked at Gail with surprise. "How does a pretty bird like you know things like that?"

"This *bird* was six years in military reserve, that's how. Plus, I'm a pilot and a weapons-certified security guard with a decade of martial arts training."

"Holy shit."

"I'm also very impatient, so tell me about this ship."

The Greek waited for his beer to be served, then took a long drink and wiped his mouth. "The *Coriander* arrived in Outer Harbor several days ago, remained for twelve hours, then sailed to Melbourne and on to Sydney to off-and-on-load freight. It returned to Outer Harbor last night and will be sailing at six in the morning."

"That means we have to move fast," said Gail. She placed her elbows on the table and leaned forward over her cup. "Here's an outline of what we know: first, the assassins are connected to something or someone named Tango Blue, which is linked through a secret computer network to the Russian Ambassador. Alex is not sure how far the conspiracy has spread or what its purpose is, other than it's powerful and deadly. Yesterday, they ordered him to meet them here in Adelaide. Since they've been trying to kill him in Sydney, and since they're now holding his wife as a hostage and will be using her as bait to trap him, I figure they'd have to get here fast aboard something private and secure."

"Such as a diplomatic jet?" asked Con.

"That's my guess," answered Gail.

"Let's find out," said Con, pulling out his mobile phone along with an electronic diary. He typed a name into the diary and a number appeared on the screen, which he then punched into the phone. "I have a friend who works for the Federal Airports Corporation," Con said quietly while the number rang. Immediately a voice answered. "Greg? Con here. Fine, fine. Say, I need a favor. Can you tell me if any charters arrived within the last twenty-four hours under the diplomatic authority of the Russian Consulate? Illegal goods? I wouldn't think so, but I'll let you know if I discover anything. Yes, I promise." Con placed his hand over the mouthpiece. "Suspicious bastard. He's checking the computer now." Con removed his hand when Greg came back onto the line. "There was? This morning at Adelaide domestic, and they stepped into a waiting limo? Perfect! Thanks, Greg, you've been a big help. Regards to Heather."

"Found them!" said Gail. "Call Alex."

"Just a minute," said Con, punching another number into his mobile. It rang and a husky Irish voice answered. "Big Mike? Con here. Fine, fine, and you? Good. Say, what's the talk among the stevedores about the tub in Berth Six?" Con listened for several moments. "But no identities were listed for those in the limo? What was the code word they used?" There was a pause. "Tango *Blue?*" repeated Con for verification, his eyes on Gail. "Just a minute." To Gail: "Have you got a mobile?"

Gail shook her head. "Hate the damn things."

"Here, I've got one," said Liz, taking a small yellow one out of her purse.

"Get Alex on the phone," Con said to Liz, "and tell him a frantic woman was sighted earlier today on the deck of the *Coriander*. Inform him that a diplomatic limousine drove aboard using the name Tango Blue and there are rumors now being circulated about a delirious woman in one of the cabins with a contagious disease. All crewmen were warned to stay clear of her, no matter what she screams."

Liz quickly telephoned home. On the third ring, Talanov answered.

"Hang on, Alex, here's Gail," said Liz, handing over the phone.

"We've hit pay dirt!" said Gail. "Con says to tell you that a frantic woman was sighted on board a docked freighter earlier today by some of the stevedores. Furthermore, a diplomatic limousine was reported to have driven aboard that freighter using the codename Tango Blue, and there are now rumors circulating along the wharf about a delirious woman in one of the cabins with an infectious disease. The ship's crew were told to stay clear of her."

"*Andrea!*" exclaimed Talanov.

"So it seems," agreed Gail, "and they're doing their best to keep her isolated."

With Balashikha precision, Talanov took roughly ten seconds to calculate a plan, which was spoken to Gail, who passed it to Con, who relayed it to Big Mike. Several minutes of discussion then followed among the four individuals across two mobile phone connections as the idea was refined and confirmed. Alex then closed by telling Gail the news about Kharkov and Ivan. "I'm convinced now that Kharkov was being used," he said, "because he seemed to know nothing about the Second Thirteen, and when I pressed him on Tango Blue, he acted surprised and used the phrase, 'it is nothing more than-' before be was interrupted and warned by a second party not to tell me anything. He then suffered what must have been a drug-induced heart attack, for I heard him say 'Ow' - as though he had been pricked by a needle - and 'What in God's name' before he collapsed with an apparent heart attack, which to me indicates someone very near to him was the one working for the Second Thirteen."

"But I thought you said they're nothing but an illusion... that they no longer exist."

"I don't know what to think, Gail," replied Talanov. "They're definitely killers and they're after me. Still, I don't who they are or what they're doing. It's as if we're being led in a circle."

"Well maybe that circle's been broken," said Gail. "Talk to you soon."

Chapter 35

The cellular phone rang in Cheney's hand. "One here," Cheney said.

"Tango Blue," a familiar voice answered back. "How are things aboard ship?"

"Talanov's wife nearly escaped," Cheney replied. "Her anesthetic wore off, and while Four and I were gone, Three's urges got the best of him and she knocked him cold. Fiona popped another dart into her before she could jump into the harbor and she's now back in custody. But that's not all. Talanov's mobile phone seems to have a dead battery and we can't get through to set up a meeting."

"Fortune has smiled on us there," replied Blue. "I know how far Talanov has tracked us and what his next move will be. The unfortunate casualty of this discovery, however, is Ambassador Kharkov. Marshak found it necessary to kill him."

"*Kharkov?*"

"Talanov got through to him and he nearly started talking about the Tango Blue file, which was discovered by a young diplomat named Lazovic. He's also been eliminated and Marshak doesn't think the identity of the file has been penetrated."

"But there's nothing *to* penetrate," Cheney pointed out. "They were numbers, meaningless numbers."

"Which, if discovered, exposes the illusion. In any case, we're still intact and we've been alerted to how far he's tracked us."

"Still, it's a shame to lose Kharkov," remarked Cheney. "He's been a useful cover."

"He was to have been killed, anyway. Be that as it may, unless Talanov walks into your gun sights, I want you to abort the ambush and tell the others to stay low and sail with the ship. Ling Soo knows what to do with the woman once she's in Hong Kong. And for God's sake, tell Three to keep his pants zipped. I don't want her molested."

"Why not? You said we know what Talanov's next move will be."

"Because this isn't over yet and Talanov is still out there. You, of all people, should know how uncontrollably dangerous he could become should we force him into the position of having nothing left to lose. His wife is our only leverage."

Cheney ignored the reproof. "What are your instructions, then?"

"I want you and Fiona to fly to Vanuatu and meet Marshak. We've learned that someone - probably Talanov - telephoned Vanuatu for information on the corporation. This means he's discovered Sergei's bank book and knows about the circular blind. Since there's no traceable access to us apart from the lawyer who handled things, I want him eliminated before Talanov arrives there to question him. Once that's been accomplished, wait around for Talanov to show up. When he does, you know what to do."

Chapter 36

Still dressed in the yellow Carla Zampatti suit worn for the broadcast, Liz Langdon marched into news room where four cameramen in denim shirts and jeans sat chatting in front of one of the many television monitors positioned around the room.

Far from duplicating the set's tidy backdrop, the news room - where the stories were actually prepared - was a hectic arrangement of work stations divided by gray carpeted panels over which journalists could be seen working at computer terminals. Surrounding each reporter was an array of wires, schedules, and soft drink cans, and overlooking all this was "the bridge" - an elevated command center of more computers, control panels, police scanners, monitors, and telephones, all linked with various local, national, and international bureaus. On two of the walls were clocks displaying times in each of the three Australian time zones, while elsewhere were dozens of gray file cabinets and tall shelves crammed with supplies and video cassettes.

"You boys ready?" asked Liz as she removed a pair of clustered diamond earrings worth three months' salary.

"You're certain you want two cars?" one of the cameramen asked.

"It has to look authentic and urgent," Liz replied. "Two vehicles and a couple of beta-cams should create enough of a stir."

"But no link-backs to the station?"

"Correct," affirmed Liz. "Like I said, it's all an act."

"Mind telling us why?" another of the cameramen asked.

"I'm trying to save a woman's life," replied Liz. "Come on, let's go."

Within half an hour, the two four-wheel drive Mitsubishi news cars had parked within sight of Berth Six's high chain-link fence. To their immediate left was the marina of the Royal South Australian Yacht Squadron, its boats gently bobbing in the inky waters. Far out in the west, the lid of night was barely cracked open by a strip of Caribbean blue, a translucent remnant of the day which hovered over the cloudless horizon like a promise.

All eyes in the news cars followed two flat-bed semi-trailer trucks as they rumbled past and approached the lighted gate. The trucks were admitted onto the broad asphalt apron where hundreds of the ribbed-steel containers had been stacked and were now ready for transfer onto the decks of ships or the beds of trucks like these. Numerous straddle carriers moved containers about the yard beneath intense flood-lights which illuminated the yard like a stadium. Liz checked her watch. Five minutes to go.

"Car Two, come in," a voice suddenly crackled over the short wave radio.

The driver of Car Two pulled the microphone from its clip and brought it to his mouth. "Two here, what's up?"

"Have you and Five arrived yet for the stevedore strike?"

"Affirmative," the driver replied.

Liz grabbed the microphone away from the driver. "What the hell are you *doing?*" Liz yelled into the mike. "You *know* this frequency is monitored by the other stations."

"Tell me something new," came an annoyed reply from the station. "We always monitor one another's frequencies, so don't go ballistic. Besides, the stevedores make sure all the networks know there's a strike so they can get maximum exposure. That's standard operating procedure."

"Not this time, you ass!" shouted Liz, who clicked off the mike and cursed.

Suddenly, however, an alarming thought hit Liz and she closed her eyes and took a deep breath. She then brought the mike back to her mouth. "Brian, tell me you didn't send this out," she said, opening her eyes.

There was a long silence over the radio.

"*Tell me you didn't!*"

"I thought our affiliates in the other capital cities would want to know," Brian slowly replied. "A cruiser's on the way now for a link-back. The network's running it nationally."

"You bloody *idiot!*" screamed Liz as she slammed the radio back in its bracket and looked over at the driver. "Get over to the gate before this whole thing gets out of hand."

"I thought you said this was an act," the driver said as he started the vehicle.

"I did, which is why we've got to stop this. There is no strike - no real one, anyway - and suddenly we've got national coverage."

Floating in the darkness nearby, between two of the marina's yachts, was an inflatable black rubber boat. In the bow of the boat was Talanov, dressed in the blue overalls of a wharf hand, while in the stern were Gail and Con, who were dressed the same. Concealed by the night, the small craft sat immobile in the water, its motor quietly idling. Without exception, all three occupants had their eyes fixed on the illuminated hulk of the *Coriander* in the near distance. It was being loaded by the wharf's two giant gantry cranes.

Suddenly a ear-piercing horn blast occurred over a loud speaker in the yard and men began cheering and shouting. In less than a minute, all motorized equipment had ceased operating and workers began walking toward the front gate.

Another blast occurred over the yard's loud speaker just as the door into the ship's bridge flew open and in stepped a huge red-haired man with a wild beard and piercing blue eyes. The man, known as Big Mike, was followed by five stevedores wearing sweat-stained overalls and foul dispositions.

"What the hell's going on?" demanded the captain. "Why are things shutting down?"

"I'm calling a strike," Big Mike announced.

"You're bloody *what?*" roared the captain, himself a powerful man but several inches shorter than Big Mike.

"Wage dispute. And I've called a news conference down by the gate. Liz Langdon and her news crew will be arriving there any minute. I think you should be there, too."

The captain threw down his clipboard. "*News crew?* I'll break your bloody *neck* for this!"

The five stevedores moved forward like Abrams tanks. "You'd better think that over," Big Mike advised. "I'll expect an apology later."

"Apologize like *hell!*" growled the captain as he pushed through the stevedores and out the door of the bridge, descending a flight of stairs. As he reached the main deck, Cheney approached.

"What's going on?" Cheney asked.

"The stevedores are calling a strike," he replied, heading toward the gangway with Big Mike and his men close behind.

"What about our scheduled departure?" asked Cheney, grabbing the captain by the arm.

The burly captain shrugged off Cheney's hand. "I won't know anything until they spell out their demands. There's a news conference down at the gate."

Cheney grabbed the captain again. "We've got *cargo* aboard this ship."

The captain looked down at the hand, then back at Cheney. "I'm willing to forget you did that, you little piss ant. But if you don't take your bloody hand off me right now, I'll break every one of your fingers and stuff them up your ass."

After a quick glance at the stevedores, who had crowded around the captain in a sudden display of support, Cheney released the captain.

While the troupe clamored down the noisy metal gangway, Cheney paced angrily back and forth across the deck. Leaning on a section of iron railing nearby, Fiona and the two assassins watched the captain and the stevedores reach the concrete wharf below. In the distance they could see men gathering at the gate just as Liz Langdon and her cameramen scrambled out of their vehicles. Suddenly, far off to the right, more news vehicles from the other stations sped along the road toward the gate where the stevedores were gathering.

"Three, you and Four go find out what's happening," ordered Cheney. "Keep me informed on the mobile."

"Right," answered Three as he and Four ran down the gangway.

At the gate, Liz Langdon rushed through the crowd of workers toward Big Mike, who was approaching the flat-bed trailer-truck positioned there earlier for a stage. She pulled him to one side. "We've got to call this off, Mike," she panted just as the other news cars and cruisers skidded to stops nearby. Technical crews and journalists jumped out of the vehicles and began setting up lights and cameras, while inside the cruisers, operators in headsets switched on electronic control panels, bringing television monitors and communications equipment to life. Within moments, links had been established with networks all over Australia.

"It's a little late for that, don't you think?" asked Big Mike as he watched the television crews connecting black cables to their cruisers. He looked back down at Liz. "You and Con assured me this was going nowhere... that it was an act."

Liz ran a hand worriedly across her forehead. "It was but word leaked out. Now *all* the networks are involved and it's being run nationally."

The Irishman looked with amusement at the frightened expression on Liz Langdon's face. "I rather like watching you squirm," Big Mike said with a grin.

"What am I going to *do?*"

"Cooking shows, from the looks of it."

Liz closed her eyes. "Oh, God, not you, too."

Big Mike let out a hearty laugh and wrapped a burly arm around Liz. "What the hell, Liz, let's go ahead with it... on the level. Most of the lads thought it was a decent thing to do, and it's only for a couple of weeks. Call it a Christmas present, and when times are better, we'll balance the scales."

"I hate to think I owe you for this," said Liz, peering up at the red-haired stevedore.

"I'm single, available and willing."

"And I'm getting out of here while I can," said Liz after punching Mike in the side. The big Irishman only laughed.

While Liz hurried back to her crew, Big Mike climbed onto the flat-bed trailer and raised his hands. A silence swept over the crowd as brilliant halogen lights were switched on and camera operators edged nearer. In the background, reporters were making preliminary remarks before other cameras.

Big Mike stepped forward, his powerful arms hanging loose at his side. Several black foam-insulated boom microphones were hoisted above him as he looked into the collection of cameras now focused on his bearded face.

"This strike's about wages!" he announced in a booming voice.

A resounding cheer went up from the stevedores.

A male journalist holding a spiral note pad suddenly stepped forward. "With falling wool prices overseas and our farmers in terrible strife, how can the stevedores justify demanding a raise?"

In Canberra, the Prime Minister of Australia sat riveted to the live television broadcast while around him a number of high-ranking members of Parliament moaned in anticipation. Several of the men loosened their ties and poured stiff drinks while shaking gloomy faces at what looked to be a national disaster.

The emergency call to the Prime Minister from the parliamentary media officer had been frantic. A wire service announcement had just been received about a massive stevedore strike which would soon spread from Adelaide to every industrial port in Australia. The ramifications would be catastrophic, the ultimate severity dependent on whether or not the stevedores' demands could be met.

In the past, strikes had repeatedly crippled the Australian economy and fueled outcries for change in government. Because of relentless union greed, construction on bridges had been halted numerous times, requiring the partially-poured concrete pylons to be demolished and started again. Shopping centers had suffered the same fate, with overspending from strike settlements totaling in the millions.

And now, when so many Australian farmers were on the verge of bankruptcy, the stevedores were calling a strike. The nation's economy - not to mention the Prime Minister's reputation - would be in shambles by morning.

"The bastards didn't give us a moment's warning," the Prime Minister complained as he angrily watched the screen. "We had no time to formulate a reply or even *begin* counter-negotiations to try and head this off."

Big Mike's blue eyes glared at the journalist holding the note pad. "The stevedores are *not* demanding a raise," he thundered as all background murmuring disappeared instantly and the cameras zeroed in. "This symbolic one-hour strike has been called to announce the stevedores are *lowering* wage demands through Christmas in order to help our friends, the farmers. We say it's time to *restore* Aussie pride and *fight* for our place in the world with the same spirit Australians showed at Gallipoli."

"Bloody *hell!*" several members of Parliament exclaimed with the Prime Minister as an enormous cheer erupted from the stevedores surrounding Big Mike, who went on to expound the need for everyone to pull in their belts and sacrifice for the good of the nation.

"They'll use this to *double* their wages in six months," said one of the senators in an oak chair beside the Prime Minister as he drained the scotch from his glass.

"Who cares?" countered the grinning Prime Minister as he shook his head in amazement. He looked over at the senator. "In the eyes of the public, they're heroes. Which means, my friend, *we'll* be heroes. Get Big Mike on the phone. I want him addressing a televised session of Parliament as soon as possible."

While all activity on the wharf was at a standstill and the attention of those on the freighter had been focused on the gate, Con directed the black rubber boat quietly away from the marina and along the darkened shoreline to a narrow mooring pier near the stern of the ship. Moving silently, Talanov and Gail climbed up the ladder and crept along the narrow walkway to the unoccupied guard station near the ramp.

With their hands in the pockets of their overalls, Alex and Gail walked unobtrusively up the ramp and into the deserted, brightly-lit cathedral of the ship, which was filled with vehicles and containers of freight. Once inside, they started up the vehicle ramp toward the upper deck. Beneath their feet was a thick steel mesh which had been welded to the heavy metal plate of the ramp to give traction for cars and fork lifts.

They kept close to the hull while they climbed, scanning constantly for guards or stray crewmen. At the top was an enormous door which opened onto the main deck. It was large enough for a truck to be driven through, and visible outside were dozens of the ribbed steel containers which had been lowered into place by the gantry cranes.

Certain that the killers were holding his wife in a locked cabin somewhere in the ship's accommodation, Talanov paused at the top of the ramp, then nodded for Gail to follow as he started across the enclosed deck toward the stern of the ship. "We'll take the first set of stairs that we find," he whispered.

Thankfully, the deck was deserted. Yet that also added to the tension because without any competing noise, each of their steps echoed beneath the low ceiling of gray steel and pipes. To their left was a row of parked cars, and beyond these some steel rungs welded to the inner hull of the ship for emergency access to other decks. In less than a minute they came to an elevator.

"Up?" asked Gail, reaching for the call button.

Talanov shook his head. "Probably slow and noisy." He pointed to a nearby flight of stairs. "Let's use those." Alex led the way over to the stairs, and after pausing to listen for the sounds of footsteps, started up with Gail close behind.

They climbed the stairs to the deck above. Before stepping fully into the corridor, Alex stopped in the door and glanced up and down the passageway, one hand in his pocket on the handle of his pistol. Everything was deserted and quiet.

"Let's start there," Alex whispered, nodding for Gail to follow as he led the way to a door. He tried the handle. The door opened but the room was empty.

"Are we going to do this with every cabin?" asked Gail, her voice low as she continued to look nervously around.

"If I have to," replied Alex, walking to the next door and grasping the handle. He quickly opened the door - another vacant cabin - then closed it quietly. "Sooner or later we'll find someone home."

Alex pushed opened the next door and a resting Panamanian crewman looked up from his bunk. "Who are you?" he asked in accented English, sitting up.

Talanov walked over and stood over the man with a drilling intensity in his eyes. "This is an emergency, where's the woman?"

"The contagious one? No one goes near her!" the frightened crewman replied, his attention darting back and forth between Talanov and Gail, who was leaning beside the door, her arms folded, a menacing look in her eyes. "What do you want with her? Who *are* you?"

Talanov grabbed the man by his shirt and yanked him to his feet. "Listen to me! If you don't take Dr Warren and me to her *right now*, an epidemic will break out that will rot your flesh while you breathe. Do you remember that virus in Africa?"

The man's eyes grew wide with terror. "She's got *that?*"

"And we don't have enough vaccine!" Talanov said, releasing him and pushing him toward the door. "If I seem impatient, *I am*. Because unless *you* want to die in terrible agony, we must get her off of this ship."

"Holy *mother!*" the man exclaimed, making the sign of the cross on his chest. "But the men holding her say we are not to go near her."

"You don't have to. Just show me her room and keep quiet until we've gone. I don't want to cause a panic. Without a human host, any virus remaining in the room will die within twenty-four hours. Now, *move!*"

Although terrified, the crewman nodded and led the way down the corridor to Andrea's door. "That is the one," he said, pointing to it.

Talanov patted the man on the shoulder and gave him an affirming nod. "You just saved your life and the lives of the crew. Now hurry, get out of here. And remember: stay clear of this room for twenty-four hours."

The crewman ran back down the corridor and disappeared inside his cabin, slamming the door.

"That was quick thinking," said Gail.

"Tell me that once we get off this tub," he said, taking hold of the door handle, his gun poised. He tried it but it was locked. "We don't have time," he said, stepping back and kicking the door with all his strength.

It flew back and Talanov rushed through the opening gun first, scanning every corner of the room. His eyes then fell on Andrea, lying unconscious on the bed, her wrist anchored to the frame of the bed by a pair of chrome-plated handcuffs.

With his face frozen in horror, for a long moment Talanov stopped breathing. His wife's face was scratched and bruised from the beating she had taken and dried blood was caked on her nose. Her hair was tangled and her clothes were dirty from being dragged across the deck of the freighter.

Lowering his gun, Alex walked slowly to her side and dropped to his knees, letting go of his pistol. It clattered onto the floor. With his hands, he tenderly brushed the matted hair away from her face before leaning over and softly kissing her, then placing his face next to hers, his right arm drawing her near.

Gail looked on in silence while Talanov cradled his wife. Soon she could watch no longer and turned away, closing her eyes as she fought back the tears. The fantasy had ended.

But love was not something so easily extinguished, and Gail realized upon opening her eyes that while her love for Alex would live on, it must now and forever stay buried, never to find expression, at least not with Alex. A momentary sad smile formed on her lips while she watched Talanov's tender devotion. Gail was truly happy for Alex, although Henri, of course, had been right: her love would not be returned.

A door slammed somewhere in the ship and startled Gail out of her reflections. She glanced at her watch. Time was running out. "I hate to say it but we need to get moving," she said, scanning the corridor.

Talanov nodded and stood. "Is the coast clear?" he asked as he picked up his pistol, his eyes never leaving Andrea.

"It's clear," she affirmed, pulling her pistol from her pocket.

Taking a deep breath, Alex placed the barrel of his gun on the link fastening one cuff to the other, angling it away and down toward the floor. He then slid the pillow from beneath Andrea's head, placed it over the weapon and pulled the trigger. In spite of the pillow, the shot echoed through the ship.

Out on deck, Cheney put the mobile telephone to his ear and took the call from Three. "Yes?"

"The leader has been rambling on about Australian pride and lowering wages. Newscasters are already referring to him as the Berth Six Santa. He is now presenting his views on public education."

"Berth Six Santa... public education? How long will this go on?"

Number Three looked at his watch. "He stated earlier that this was a symbolic one-hour strike. That means there is approximately fifteen minutes remaining."

"This is so *pointless!*" fumed Cheney on the deck of the freighter, the accommodation's shiny white exterior rising behind him several stories into the darkened sky. "Get back here as soon as-"

But before the sentence was completed, the echo of a shot rang out. Cheney whirled away from the iron railing, the mobile telephone still to his ear, a look of alarm in his eyes. Who would be firing a gun from inside the ship?

Suddenly the thought hit him: no contact with Talanov because of a dead battery... a pointless and unexpected strike with all attention focused on the gate and away from the freighter - *Talanov!* "Get back here!" he yelled into the phone before switching it off. Then, after shoving the phone in his pocket, Cheney pulled out his own gun and ran into the ship.

With Talanov carrying his unconscious wife, Gail led the way to the flight of stairs up which they had come earlier. They hurried down them and emerged onto the enclosed deck above the cathedral. Off to their right was the same row of parked cars, and straight ahead the large door which opened out onto the main deck.

Already breathing heavily from the exertion of carrying his wife, Talanov paused to shift Andrea's weight, at the same time noticing that the switchback flight of stairs continued down, probably to the cathedral below. "Wait a minute, Gail," he said. "That gunshot made noise and I don't want to risk getting caught on the ramp. Anyone coming in through that big door from the main deck outside would see us, as well as anyone coming up from below. Let's use the stairs."

Gail nodded and led the way.

In less than a minute they had reached the cathedral. While Talanov waited on the bottom step holding Andrea, Gail cautiously peeked around the corner of the stairwell and saw, over several rows of new cars, the open stern of the ship. Looking the other way, toward the front of the ship, she took note of several large recessed hatches in the wall beneath the ramp. Signs above the hatches indicated that they led to the engine room. Further forward, beyond the rows of new cars and trucks, were dozens of ribbed steel containers stacked two-high and secured to mounting brackets in the heavy iron deck.

Lowering her pistol, with her other hand Gail pointed the way to the exit. Using the automobiles as cover, she would cross to the far side of the ship, and from there cover Alex. From that point they could then escape out the stern ramp and onto the wharf.

While Talanov leaned against the door to rest, Gail crouched and started between two rows of shiny new Holdens. Suddenly assassins Three and Four ran into the ship, their guns drawn. They stopped and looked around.

Gail ducked quickly back into the stairwell and with a finger over her mouth told Alex to remain quiet.

"Check your weapon," Three said to Four as they paused to inspect the quantity of ammunition in their pistols, the acoustics of the cathedral reverberating their voices and the metallic clicks of magazines being released. "You take the ramp and I'll take the stairs," Three then added as he and Four snapped the magazines back into the handles.

"They're coming this way!" Gail told Alex. "Quick, hide in one of those hatchways. I'll draw the killers up the stairs, and when I do, you drive out in one of those cars. I'll meet you back at Liz's."

"I can't leave you here!" said Talanov as he shifted Andrea's weight in an effort to ease his burning biceps.

"Con should still be waiting in the boat. I'll leave with him."

"He may have *gone* and you're outnumbered!" countered Talanov.

"This is no time to discuss it, Alex, or we'll be killed. Now, *move!*"

Gail kissed her finger and pressed it to Talanov's lips, then pushed him toward one of the alcoves.

Talanov hesitated then obeyed, and once he was safe, Gail stepped around the corner and uttered a brief cry as if surprised. Hearing her voice and then seeing her, Three yelled for Four just as Gail ran back around the corner and up the stairs, making as much noise as she could to draw them after her.

Accepting the gambit, Three and Four ran to the bottom of the stairwell, their guns poised. Upon hearing the sound of footsteps above, they raced up the stairs.

Once they were gone, Talanov ran awkwardly between the rows of new cars toward a dark blue sedan in the first row. He reached the car and peered in through the window; the keys were in the ignition.

Alex opened the rear door and laid Andrea in the back seat. He then pressed the door closed and climbed into the driver's seat, his hand on the key.

He could not do it! He could not leave Gail!

And yet if he did not drive out of here, Gail's sacrifice would be for nothing. Alex glanced over his shoulder at his unconscious wife, then back at the stern ramp out of the ship, knowing what he must do.

Two decks above, Gail paused on a landing, winded from her climb. Having remembered the emergency rungs welded to the inner hull of the ship, her plan had been to climb up several flights of stairs, fire a couple of shots back down the stairwell to delay her pursuers, then race across to the emergency access and climb down to where she left Talanov. She could then jump in a car and drive off the ship. The sound of screeching tires should be enough warning for Con.

Leaning over the stairs, Gail fired two rounds back down the stairwell. Shouts could be heard as the two killers ran for cover. Gail then stuck the pistol in her pocket and ran over to the emergency ladder and rapidly climbed down to the cathedral.

Her heart was pounding with excitement as she ran to the lead car and climbed in. She was going to make it! Gail reached for the ignition key but suddenly heard a moan from the back seat... *a woman's moan!* She turned and looked on the floorboard. There, beneath a covering of floor mats, *was Andrea!* "Oh, my God!" exclaimed Gail, climbing into the back seat and uncovering Andrea.

"Where am I?" asked Andrea in a groggy voice as she opened her eyes. "Who are you?"

"A friend of your husband," answered Gail, looking quickly around for the killers.

"My husband... Alex is here?"

"He is but we've got a problem."

Andrea winced and tried to sit up. "What is it... where has he gone?"

"That's our problem," replied Gail, pulling the pistol from her pocket. "I'm afraid he's gone after me."

Chapter 37

"Can you drive?" asked Gail.

"I'm still dizzy from the drugs," Andrea replied from the floorboard. She brushed a tangle of hair from her face.

Gail checked the pistol's ammunition. "I want you to keep this and stay out of sight," she said as she literally placed the gun in Andrea's hand. "I'm going after Alex."

"But you'll need it!"

"Hopefully, your husband won't require any help and we'll be back in the shake of a stick. If we're not, start this car and drive it to the front gate. There's a news conference there with the stevedores. Look for a woman in yellow. Her name's Liz Langdon and she's a friend."

Andrea looked at the beautiful, dark-haired woman dressed in overalls. "How did you become involved in this?" she asked.

"I'm one of those friends of a friend of Spiro. Besides, after listening to Alex talk about you, who could resist?"

A drowsy smile was Andrea's reply.

"Say, *you* don't have a twin brother, do you?"

"Pardon?" asked Andrea.

"Just being silly," said Gail. "Stay low, we'll be back soon."

Gail slowly raised her head out of the back seat and scanned the cathedral through the back window of the car. Seeing no one, but aware that a clear view of the interior was hindered because of the surrounding cars and containers, Gail carefully opened the door and slid into a crouching position on the dirty steel deck. After a smile and a brief wave, she pressed the door closed and ran quickly to the emergency ladder. Taking hold of a rung, she climbed up the side of the hull and through an opening to the deck above.

Once through the opening, Gail squatted behind one of the parked cars standing in a row with several others. She caught her breath for a few seconds, then laid flat on the deck and looked for feet stationed behind other cars. Seeing none, she stood and peered over the tops of the hoods in all directions. Again, no one was in sight.

Gail started forward between two of the vehicles but suddenly froze. What was that sound? She knelt down and with a concentrated expression, cocked her head and strained to hear what sounded like excited voices. She looked toward the stairs to her left, then in the direction of the loading door which opened out onto the main deck. The voices seemed to be coming in through that door.

Crouching as she ran, Gail sprinted silently to the edge of the opening and peered around the corner to see what was happening. To her horror she saw Alex being held between two of the ribbed steel containers, his arms pinned behind his back by a man who laughed heartily while another man smashed a fist across his jaw. Blood flew out of his mouth as his bruised face snapped to the side. Having already been severely beaten, Alex was nearly unconscious.

Gail clenched her fists but forced herself to take a deep breath. She then walked calmly through the door and approached the two killers. "Time to clear the deck," she said, trying to sound casual.

"Piss off," said Number Three.

"Sorry, mate, but the Maritime Worker's Union says the deck must be cleared until a strike is resolved."

Number Three pulled a pistol from his pocket. "I said, *piss off.*"

Gail shrugged and turned, then suddenly whipped her right leg in a powerful spinning arc to hammer the stunned assassin squarely in the mouth. Three's head flew back, the gun flying from his hand as he slammed dazed into the side of the steel container. Gail leaped forward, her knee a battering ram which she drove into the killer's solar plexus. Then, with a quick pivot, Gail took hold of his clothing and with a twisting motion flung him over her shoulder and into the other container, where he collapsed.

Momentarily stunned by the attack, Number Four abruptly dropped Talanov onto the deck as Gail turned her concentration on him. Baring his teeth in a curse, he plunged his hand into his pocket for the loaded automatic that he carried.

Gail recognized the movement and jumped over Talanov's body, her hands clawing at the killer's arm just as the weapon emerged from his pocket. Wrestling Four for possession of the gun, Gail planted her right leg behind the assassin and prepared to yank his arm down across her waist to throw him off balance.

But Four grabbed Gail by the hair and pulled her across his chest, ripping away her hands. As she fell, the killer swung the pistol toward her head, but not before Gail horse-kicked the assassin's ankles, knocking his feet from under him. The automatic discharged as he fell, the bullet deflecting off of the heavy iron of the deck and pinging its way out into the night.

Four hit the deck on his back and Gail leaped on top of him, one foot pinning his arm, her fingers rigid as hickory as she chopped them across his throat. Four let out a guttural yell just as Gail cracked a fist across his jaw. The killer's body went limp.

Panting, Gail climbed to her feet and ran over to Alex, kneeling beside him and gently rolling him onto his side. "Come on there, matey, we've got to get out of here," she said quietly as she reached around his back and pulled him into a sitting position. Talanov groaned and turned his swollen eyes toward Gail, his lips moving as he tried to speak. "Not now," said Gail, wanting to cry at the sight of the thickened blood oozing from his mouth and nose. "Just stiffen your legs, okay?"

Talanov nodded weakly.

Standing, Gail pulled Alex to his feet, then hoisted him over her shoulder like a sack of potatoes. After finding her balance, Gail hurried unsteadily across the deck of the freighter to the loading door, the towering white wall of the ship's accommodation rising above them in ghostly silence. She glanced up before they entered. Was that a shadow of movement? Had someone been watching her from a window? *Why hadn't she grabbed one of the killer's guns?*

Knowing it was too late now to go back, Gail entered the interior deck and paused near the top of the ramp, her legs burning from the added weight. Could she make it to the deck below? From where she stood, the ramp's angle looked horribly steep and the steel mesh was broken and uneven. One wrong step could result in a fall.

Shifting Talanov on her shoulder, Gail wondered what to do. To her left were the parked cars and the emergency ladder up which she had climbed earlier. Beyond the cars, however, were the doors of the elevator. She would take the lift!

Gail had already started forward when a small ding sounded and the doors of the elevator parted. Out walked Fiona with a gun.

Turning, Gail started to run down the ramp.

"I wouldn't if I were you," Fiona called out, easily overtaking Gail and stepping in front of her, the barrel of the pistol aimed straight for Gail's chest. "Now, who are you and how did you find us?"

"Just a wharfie earning a quid," replied Gail, trying her best to sound vaguely British. "This bloke's worth quite a few bob on the docks."

"I'll ask you one more time," stated Fiona, unimpressed. "Who are you and how did you find us?"

"Me name's Angie and I was told by a few of the lads down at the Lighthouse that I'd pocket a thousand dollars if I could get this bloke off the ship in one piece. I'm merely earnin' a living."

Fiona shrugged and shot Gail in the thigh.

The explosion was deafening and Gail cried out and crumpled to the deck holding her leg, Talanov falling beside her. Rolling onto her side, Gail tried frantically to stop the gushing of blood by clamping both hands over the wound. Beside her and barely conscious, Talanov could only groan.

"Okay, Angie, now the other," Fiona said, firing a bullet into Gail's other thigh.

A crippling tremor tore through Gail's body as she rolled onto her other side screaming. She desperately grabbed at one leg, then the other, panic tumbling over agony as she pressed hard against the wounds. But her fingers were like sieves, unable to stop the bleeding! *God, help me*, she pleaded instinctively as she tried to press harder. Crying yet knowing she must not surrender to the comfort of crying, Gail drew her knees toward her in an attempt to subdue the pain. But it only grew worse as every nerve fiber sent unbearable shrieks pulsating through her body.

"I want *answers!*" yelled Fiona. "Who are you and how did you find us?"

But all Gail could do was sob. She did not want to die - she wanted to *live* - yet her vitality was draining away with each accelerated heartbeat... with each salty teardrop which ran down her cheeks and into the oily grime on the deck. The legs of her overalls were now saturated with blood, and she tried again to put pressure on the wounds.

Why didn't her arms obey? Where was her strength? And what was that strange, cold emptiness digging its way up her spine? Why couldn't she stop it? Why didn't it leave her alone? Gail fought against the tears which flowed even more with the bitter realization that she had not been able to save Alex. She had lost... Alex had lost.

Fiona shrugged again. "All right, Angie, let's try your shoulder."

The deafening blast reverberated off the low gray ceiling. The pipes and conduits seemed to carry the sound deep into the ship's interior, echoing faintly again and again. Fiona flew forward, her face contorted, her arms flailing as the 9mm bullet from Andrea's gun sent her tumbling onto the deck.

Staggering unsteadily from between two of the cars, Andrea dropped her gun and hurried over to Gail, ripping the sleeves out of her blouse and kneeling to tie them around Gail's legs.

Gail groaned and looked up. "Hurry... get Alex out," she said weakly.

"Shhh," Andrea replied as she stroked Gail's face gently. "I'll stop this bleeding and then get some help."

"No time," insisted Gail. "Get Alex to safety."

"Not until I stop this bleeding. I need more cloth, have you got a knife?"

"Small one... front pocket."

Andrea pulled it out and cut the heavy sleeves out of Gail's overalls and tied them directly on top of the bullet holes, then tightening the sleeves already torn from her blouse on the region above the wounds. Blood quickly soaked the cloth but soon slowed to a trickle.

"Well, look what we have here," said Cheney as he came around the corner at the top of the ramp, his gun trained on Andrea. He glanced down at Fiona's contorted body lying motionless on the deck, the overhead lights casting shadows around her corpse. His cold eyes fell on Andrea. "Stand up and move away... over there by the cars."

Andrea started to rise, then knelt back down. "No," she replied firmly. "If you're going to shoot me, go ahead. But I won't leave my husband and this woman."

"*Do it!*" yelled Cheney, stepping forward angrily and jabbing the gun in her face.

Without flinching, Andrea looked up into his eyes. "Why... why all this senseless killing? What do you think Alex knows?"

Cheney stepped back and laughed. "More than he realizes," he said, the laugh disappearing as quickly as it had appeared. "Sorry, but I'm in no mood for questions. I'll give you one more chance to move."

Andrea scooted to the side of Alex and lifted his head into her lap. "I will never leave my husband. You think he's part of your system, but he's not... not anymore."

"Oh, he's part of it, all right, whether he likes it or not."

"But *how*, and *why?* Who are you... what do you want?"

Suddenly a low rumble sounded from below and Cheney stepped over and looked down the ramp. Pouring into the stern of the ship were the stevedores, led by Liz Langdon, Big Mike, and several cameramen, the pelting reverberations from their shoes and boots rising with the roar of their voices as they began marching up the ramp.

"*Help*, we're up *here!*" screamed Andrea when she heard the sound of voices.

Cheney whirled around with the pistol, pointing it first at Andrea, then at Talanov. *One shot and it will be over.*

But so would his own life - for murder!

"Put down that gun!" one of the stevedores said from the top of the ramp.

"Shut up!" yelled Cheney, whipping the gun toward them.

Suddenly, in through the huge loading door came the ship's captain, followed by several of his crewmen. "Get off of my ship!" he yelled at the stevedores. "You're not allowed on board unless I give the order. And I *don't.*"

"That bastard's got a *gun!*" several of the stevedores shouted, pointing at Cheney. "And there's a dead woman here on the deck!"

"Killed by her!" snarled Cheney, pointing at Andrea.

"The police can sort it out!" shouted the captain. "Now get out of here - all of you!"

"Don't leave us here! cried Andrea. "My husband and this woman need help."

"No!" yelled Cheney, stepping to the side of the captain. "Hold them for the police! That man is Talanov, the killer!"

"We must get them both to the hospital!" insisted Andrea.

"And I said, everyone *out!*" shouted the captain.

"Get a news vehicle up here!" Liz spoke into her mobile phone.

"*News vehicle?* Not on my ship, you don't!" countered the captain, stepping toward Liz to grab her phone.

"Get this ass on film," Liz told her cameramen, who switched on powerful lights and began filming. The captain held up his hands and tried to shield himself. Liz turned toward the stevedores. "Some of you men, carry these injured people out of here."

"Get back, all of you!" shouted Cheney, pointing the gun at them. The advancing stevedores stepped back.

Suddenly the lights of the camera were turned on Cheney and he quickly turned his head. "Get *out of here!*" he shouted.

"Captain, looks like we're at a standoff," Liz said while the cameras continued to roll. "So, either you allow us to remove these people to a hospital, or my film about you, your gunman, and your entire ship, goes straight to the authorities with a hundred eyewitness reports about how you're holding hostages at gunpoint. Sure, your trigger man can try something dumb. But unless he's a lot more stupid than he looks, I wouldn't think he'd want to anger a hundred stevedores. You and I both know the sharks wouldn't get a decent feed after they got through with him."

The captain looked angrily at Cheney, who had now jumped behind him to escape the cameras. "He's not my hired gun, but he *is* my passenger and, therefore, my responsibility." He looked down at the three people on the deck, then back at Liz. "All right, get them out of here, but the rest of this mob goes with you."

"No!" shouted Cheney.

"Shut your stupid mouth!" yelled the burly captain.

While the beta-cams rolled, Liz gave the stevedores the nod and several lifted Gail carefully into the arms of Big Mike, who started down the ramp, the workers parting to let him through. Another stevedore followed carrying Alex, while two more assisted Andrea, who was able to walk. Once the were gone, the stevedores closed ranks and slowly followed. Liz and the cameramen turned to leave.

"Hey, what about those cassettes?" asked the captain, pointing to the cameras.

Liz smiled coldly. "I'll hang on to them to make sure nothing happens to my friends. If it does, you can bet they'll reach the right hands."

"Get out, you rotten bitch," growled the captain.

"With pleasure," Liz replied before continuing down the ramp after the others.

While some of the ship's crew covered Fiona's body with a packing blanket, Cheney walked around to face the captain just as Liz and her cameramen disappeared out the stern of the ship. "What the hell do you think you're *doing* by letting them go?"

The captain looked at the assassin with controlled fury. "I didn't have much choice, now did I? Aside from video documentation and a hundred witnesses ready to tear us limb from limb, that news bitch would have called every government agency even remotely interested in your little schemes of murder, kidnapping, and God-knows-what-else."

"Ling Soo would have taken care of it."

"That worthless pig cares only that you're paying him," countered the captain. "Which is all anyone cares about."

"Well if that's the case, then you just let the most dangerous man in the world go free. Because if Talanov figures out what's going on, he can blow us out of the water, which means you won't get a single dollar. All you'll get is a slug and it'll be right between your eyes." With his index finger, Cheney reached over and tapped the captain just above the bridge of his nose.

The captain did not flinch. "And who will you get to do it for you - those two jokers out on deck? I'm not your problem, Cheney, and you know it. Your problem is Talanov. Sure, you pay good money for me to get you in and out of Australia. And while I don't know what it is you're up to - nor do I give a shit - I do know you're running scared."

"That's a nice little speech, Captain," replied Cheney. "Since you're so smart, how do *you* recommend we stop Talanov? Because if you want to be paid, we've got to stop him."

"How the hell should I know? You're supposed to be the brains."

"Well I'll tell you, since you seem to be lacking in brains: I need you to sail for Hong Kong as scheduled and take Three and Four with you. Once you've arrived, tell them to contact Ling Soo. New instructions will be waiting."

"Once *I've* arrived? Where will you be all this time?"

"Stopping the man you let go," Cheney replied. "I'm going to Vanuatu."

Outside, on the wharf, the two news cars from Liz's station screeched to a halt. The drivers jumped out and opened the back seat doors. "Put Gail here and Alex there," Liz instructed the stevedores carrying her friends.

Alex moaned as he was placed in the car. "Where am I?" he asked weakly.

Andrea climbed in the other door and eased her husband's head into her lap. "You're all right, I'm here," she said softly as she began stroking his forehead.

Talanov opened his eyes and looked up toward the sound of his wife's voice. "Andrea? Is that you?"

"I'm here, my love, and we're safe," she replied as tears filled her eyes.

Alex tried to sit up.

"Lie still," Andrea told him as he gasped in pain and collapsed back onto the seat, holding his ribs.

"No time," he replied, taking several breaths and then forcing himself to sit up. "We've got to stop them."

"You need medical help," said Andrea.

"I'm afraid we've got bigger problems," Liz announced as she hopped into the front seat and twisted to face Alex and Andrea. "The boys in Car Two intercepted a police dispatch. Apparently one of the other news teams phoned in a report about the shooting. Your name was mentioned, Alex, and I don't need to tell you they'll be searching every corner of the city to find you. If you're well enough to travel, Con can get you out of the state. But the only option for Gail is a hospital: she's lost a lot of blood. This means, of course, she'll be held in custody until things are resolved. I know your situation and why you've got to keep moving. But I don't mind saying she'll take the heat for all that's happened."

Alex winced as he shifted in the seat. "Then maybe it's time I turned myself in. Gail risked her life for me and I won't let her to face this alone."

Andrea took the hand of her husband. "She won't have to, Alex. You go and I'll stay with her."

"No!"

"Darling, listen to me-"

"*No!*" protested Talanov. "I just *found* you, how can I *leave* you?"

"You're thinking now with your heart," Andrea said with a smile as she looked into the swollen eyes of her husband. She raised his blood-splattered hand to her lips and kissed it. "And you need to think with your head... to be the expert you're trained to be."

Talanov shook his head. "I hate the man that I was and the way he drove you away. I love you... I won't go back."

"You have to."

"*No!*"

"But we'll never have any kind of a life together if those monsters are allowed to go free. We'll be killed, Alex - all of us - including Liz and Gail."

"I *can't!*"

"Listen to me," Andrea cut in, taking her husband's face tenderly in her hands. "Don't become that man, just use him... use his skills, make him your servant. We can't keep running forever, and if you don't stop them, they'll run us into the ground. Alone, you can fight them on your own terms. But with me along, the ground rules change. Besides, I'm the one who shot Fiona. The police need to hear my story and realize that I did it to save your lives. Gail will corroborate my story. Don't worry, I'll be safe, and I've got Liz and Con to help me."

"But-"

"No buts," interrupted Andrea. "Hurry, you must go."

Alex grabbed his wife and embraced her tightly, his joy at having found her now dashed by his having to run. But she was right - he had to get to Vanuatu and question Ferguson. Only then could he hope to stop the madness."

Talanov ran his hand softly through his wife's tangled hair, then kissed her on the neck, felt the warmth of her skin. Would life ever be normal again?

"I hate to break this up," interrupted Liz, "but she's right - you've got to get moving. I can already hear the police."

Talanov slowly released his wife as the faint wails of sirens grew louder.

Liz looked at Alex and hurriedly explained that she had arranged for one of the cameramen to drive him back to her house so he could pick up his belongings. The cameraman would then drive him to his flat, where Alex could shower and eat. After handing him a key, Liz turned to Andrea. "Sorry, but we need to leave. The police are just moments away."

Alex looked longingly at his wife. "I'll keep in touch," he said, his eyes desperately trying to record every detail of her face.

"My love goes with you," Andrea replied as she fought back the tears, her mouth drawn and quivering.

"And mine with you," Talanov replied, moisture welling up in his own eyes as Andrea, herself now starting to cry, kissed her first two fingers and touched them to his lips. She then jumped out of the car and ran back to the second news vehicle.

"Don't worry, she'll be safe," Liz said as she prepared to join Andrea, knowing the guarantees for Alex were not the same. "Take care of yourself, and good luck."

Not knowing what to say, Talanov merely nodded.

With a forced smile, Liz stepped away from the open door and hurried back to the second news car.

Once Liz was gone, a cameramen jumped into the driver's seat and started the engine. "Fasten your belt, we need to step on it," he said as the flashing lights of several police cars could be seen racing along the street beyond the fence.

But as he shifted into Drive, several loud banging noises on the passenger door sent his foot to the brakes. "Got room for another?" Con asked, getting into the front seat before anyone could answer. "Where's Andrea?"

Talanov motioned for the driver to go and then briefed Con about what had happened.

"I hate to say it but she's right," Con said. "Lizzie and I will take care of her." As flashing lights appeared up ahead, Con glanced briefly over his shoulder. "Police.

Better get down."

Loosening his safety belt, Alex quickly laid down in the back seat just as three police cars and an ambulance rushed by them from the opposite direction with their lights flashing.

After squealing out of the gate and around the corner, the news car accelerated away from the ship yard. The driver slowed to make two quick turns, then sped past the Royal South Australian Yacht Squadron on its way toward the city. By now Alex was sitting up again and Con had turned to face him.

"By the way, I picked this up." Con held out the gun used by Andrea to shoot Fiona.

"That's Gail's!" exclaimed Talanov, recognizing the weapon. "It must be the one that was used by my wife. Where did you get it?"

"In the excitement, I managed to walk on board with the stevedores. But instead of following them up the ramp, I climbed an emergency ladder welded to the inside of the hull. Once I reached the upper deck, I remained hidden behind a row of cars until everyone left. That's when I overheard the captain arguing with one of the killers. They were yelling at one another about your having been allowed to escape and the captain was warned that if you ever figured things out, you could blow them out of the water." Con paused and held eye contact with Talanov in the intermittent flashes of light from the streetlights along Victoria Road. "You're upsetting a lot of people, Alex, and not even the captain knows why. He's been hired merely to get the killers in and out of Australia."

"Interesting," remarked Talanov thoughtfully. "Were any names mentioned?"

"A man in Hong Kong named Ling Soo. From what I gathered, he's the captain's boss and will provide the other two killers with new instructions once they reach port."

"Ling Soo," repeated Alex. "Anyone else?"

"The captain addressed the killer as Cheney."

Talanov's eyes widened. "*Cheney?* My God, he's the one who murdered Andropov's banker back in eighty-three! Why would Cheney be trying to kill me?"

"He said one other thing," remarked Con.

"What's that?"

"That he's flying to Vanuatu to stop you."

"My God, he knows I'm on to them. Which means he'll either kill the one person who can identify them or use him to set a trap."

"Do you know who this person is?" asked Con.

"Yes, but I don't know how I can get to him before Cheney does. There's no way I can risk taking a commercial flight to the island."

"Leave that to me," Con said as the news car drove into Port Adelaide. "I'll get you to Vanuatu." As they neared the main intersection, strands of Christmas lights were visible on some of the wrought iron balconies of several downtown businesses.

After turning the corner, Alex leaned forward in his seat. "I can't begin to pay you for all you've done, Con, but I'll give you what money I've got - about four thousand dollars - and once things are over, I'll send you the rest."

"None of that is necessary, my friend. Like I said, I will get you to Vanuatu."

"But I want to reimburse you for all this is costing."

"I cannot accept it," answered Con.

"Why not?" asked Talanov. "We've got the money. It's just that I can't access it right now."

"Something I learned from Spiro. Back in the old country, when I was young and foolish, I committed a crime - a robbery, actually - and was caught by the police and sentenced to six months in prison. My father had died years before, and because I was the oldest son, I was responsible for the support of my family. To go to prison was not only a disgrace to my mother, but would place her and my brothers and sisters in terrible strife. That's when The Bull - Spiro - came into my life. Everyone knew him. He owned the local cafe and was the regional boxing champion. Spiro never turned down a fight, but never did I see him pick one. He would simply pound his challengers until they got tired of tasting their own blood.

"But while Spiro's fists were as hard as oak, his heart was generous and kind. I still remember the day, prior to my sentencing, when he came to my house and dragged me out the front door. I was petrified because I thought he was going to beat me. Spiro began yelling at me, demanding to know why I had done such a terrible thing to my mother by robbing a store. I told him we needed the money. That's when he *really* got mad. He wanted to know why I hadn't come to him for the money, saying that he would have given it to me. Naturally, I had no answer, so he marched me down to the magistrate and promised him that if I could be released into his custody, he would pay whatever fine the court ordered, adding that he would make me work off the debt - plus earn a living - as an employee in his restaurant. The magistrate agreed, and Spiro began teaching me about fruits and vegetables, which is what I still do today. I swore that I would repay him, but Spiro just smiled and said that he could not accept it, that someone else had once paid his debt and that he was merely passing it on. Instead, he told me to help someone else and I've been doing that ever since. So, rather than accepting your repayment, I invite you to pass it along."

While Alex sat speechless in the darkened back seat of the car, Con looked over at the driver. "Would you take my friend and I to the Central Market?"

"At this time of night? Liz told me to drive your friend to my place."

"The Central Market, please. I'll take full responsibility."

"I don't know. I prefer to follow orders in case I'm questioned by the police."

"Actually, this is for your benefit. In the event you *are* questioned, you can tell them where you dropped us and be clear of any further responsibility."

"They'll want to know where you went. Besides, I don't even know who you are... nor do I think I want to."

"As far as you're concerned, I'm just one of Liz's friends who needed a ride. However, if I provide you with an address, either you'll have to withhold it from the police - which puts you at risk for lying - or you'll tell it to them - which places you in even greater risk from me because I wouldn't think kindly of that."

"Hey, there's no need to threaten me!" the driver said defensively.

Con smiled and gave the young driver a friendly slap on the shoulder. "Think of it this way: a threat's less painful than a cricket bat."

The driver glanced over at the darkened figure beside him. "Cricket bat? So the bit about passing on kindness was nothing but rubbish?"

"I *am* passing it on," answered Con. "But if you keep pushing me, you're going to find out kindness isn't all I can pass on."

There was a short pause while Con's words were considered. "All right, to the Central Market."

Con smiled. "Good lad. With those kind of instincts, you'll be news director one day," he said as he punched a telephone number into his mobile phone. When the receiving party answered, Con spoke to them in Greek, the conversation taking just under two minutes before the call was disconnected.

"Speaking of the police," remarked the driver, "how do you know I didn't understand every word you just said?"

"Because if you did, you wouldn't be asking me that question," replied Con. "At least not without a very worried look on your face."

13 Chapter 38

One of Bob's three cellular phones sounded discreetly in his hotel room in Washington, DC. Having already risen and showered, Bob had just taken a sip of his morning coffee and was watching World Network News.

Bob recognized the shrill warble and knew just which phone it was. He walked quickly to a table by the window and opened the briefcase he had placed there last night. Inside was an electronic scrambler with a power cord plugged into the wall socket. He pushed a switch on the electronic console, connected three wires into the cellular phone, then picked up the microphone. "Tango Blue," he said, "this line is secure."

"One here," Cheney said from aboard the *Coriander*. "Three and Four were badly beaten a few hours ago but are now bandaged and on their feet. The captain will take them to Hong Kong, where they will go to Ling Soo for instructions. My advice is to kill them."

"Who did it?" asked Bob.

"A friend of Talanov's... a woman. Three and Four were working Talanov over when she surprised them. They tried using their guns but say she overpowered them with martial arts."

Bob's face grew twisted with anger and he jabbed the air with his finger as he spoke. "Both Three and Four were carrying weapons but an unarmed woman beats them up? I've seen more competence from the *Three Stooges!* What the hell were they doing? I presume this means Talanov escaped."

"Him and his wife."

"What?"

"There was an uprising with the stevedores and we didn't have much of a choice. The captain had to let them be carried off the ship."

"Three and Four will be eliminated."

"But that's not all," said Cheney. "Fiona's dead. She was killed by Talanov's wife."

Bob was stunned. Fiona *dead?* It could not be!

The news screamed through his mind, and with his teeth clenched in anguish, Bob closed his eyes and stood there, one hand clutching his hair. *Fiona was dead.*

"By every power there is I will kill Talanov and his wife by the slowest, most painful way possible," Bob vowed. "I set everything up, planned this for *years.* I even arranged for Sergei to marry Fiona. Kharkov always had a soft spot for her and it was not difficult for us to persuade him to transfer Sergei to the consulate in Sydney. Sure, Fiona and I had our disagreements, and she knew I didn't approve of the way she threw herself on that young man in the credit bureau. Still, his assistance in tracking Talanov through their credit cards was invaluable, and the freezing of their funds even now might still lead to their capture. But... Fiona *dead?"*

Cheney did not speak - dared not - for Fiona was Bob's only sister.

"How did it happen?" asked Bob, opening his eyes, now hardened with hate.

"Apparently Fiona captured the woman who took out Three and Four. She was attempting to carry Talanov off the ship when Fiona shot her. Talanov's wife must have crawled up one of the ship's emergency ladders and ambushed Fiona from behind. I was coming up the ramp when the shots rang out. I crept up on them only to have an army of stevedores and television crews surround us and demand Talanov's release. The captain tried controlling them but we were no match, especially when they started filming."

"All right, listen to me: get to Vanuatu as planned. Marshak will meet you there. Kill Ferguson and let Marshak pose in his place. When Talanov shows up, *kill him.* The fact that he's got this far means he's close to blowing our cover."

"He's a survivor," said Cheney. "I know him... know his training."

"So do I," said Bob. "And I also know he's surviving because things have been bungled by those idiots of yours. Talanov *must not* get beyond the circular blind, and Ferguson's his only hope of doing that."

"Are you sure? I know we fire-bombed Talanov's house, but isn't it possible the document escaped?"

"I don't know that he ever had it. If he did, then I'm certain he would have taken some kind of action. Which reinforces the importance of killing Ferguson."

"I'll take care of it," promised Cheney.

"You'd better. Our future is riding on it. Tango Blue out."

Bob replaced the microphone, clicked off the scrambler, then disconnected the cellular telephone and shut the briefcase. He went back to his coffee, which was now cold. He poured it down the drain, then refilled his cup from the thermal pot sitting on a room service tray. Fresh croissants and fruit had been served earlier, along with the morning paper and a rose in a slender crystal vase. Outside, a sheet of anvil-gray cloud cover had spread across the December sky like an oil slick.

Bob's attention was suddenly drawn to the television. Taking a sip of fresh coffee, Bob lowered himself onto the burgundy velour sofa, his interest focused on Marnie, the familiar blonde announcer for World Network News.

"The world community has been shocked and saddened by the sudden heart-attack death of Andrei Kharkov, Russian Ambassador to Australia. Known all across America for his popular university lecture series on marketplace economics,

Ambassador Kharkov was also a member of the prestigious International Development Council - an organization dedicated to helping underdeveloped countries achieve economic independence. He will be replaced on the council by a man from the American business sector whom Ambassador Kharkov had nominated for membership just last year. Bob Hoskings is one of America's top financial consultants and his confirmation will take place in Washington tomorrow."

With a smile, Bob Hoskings picked up the remote control and switched off the set just as a full-screen picture of himself was shown.

Chapter 39

The twin-engine Cessna Conquest descended through the layer of scattered cumulus clouds toward Vanuatu, a chain of more than eighty volcanic islands on the southwestern rim of the Pacific Ring of Fire. Talanov was asleep in one of the passenger seats, his head on a pillow stuffed against the window. A small pocket of turbulence awakened him and he slowly opened his eyes.

"Not long now," said the pilot, noticing Talanov's movement. "That large island at two o'clock is where we're headed."

"Ef-ate?" asked Talanov, looking out on the shimmering blue waters below.

"*Ef-aw' tay,*" corrected the pilot. "It's the third-largest island in the chain. We'll be landing at Port Vila - known simply as Vila - which is the nation's capital near that large bite out of the lower-left-hand-side."

"I see it," said Alex. "What's it like?"

"Like most South Pacific islands, poverty cohabits with wealth. It's a real contrast - idyllic resorts, streets in disrepair, exotic colorful drinks, local shacks of corrugated iron. Yet the aristocratic parts of Vila have French Colonial charm rubbing shoulders with new Chinese money. I can't say that I like the casinos, though; they ruin more lives then they help. But the people are friendly, the food superb, and the beaches don't get any better. Give the coconut crab a try: it's nothing short of excellent."

"You sound hooked," said Alex, looking at the muscular, dark-haired man in command of the plane. On his bare forearms were several tattoos. He looked to be in his early thirties and had been introduced simply as Joe.

"I've been in and out of here a number of times handling business for Con."

"Is there anywhere Con's *not* in business?" quipped Talanov.

"Thar's gold in them thar islands," Joe said in his best Kentucky accent. "At least for Con."

"I'm surprised you're not loaded down with blue jeans and whisky."

"Who says I'm not?" asked the grinning pilot with a quick glance over his shoulder. "Truth is, I don't come here without a few cases of scotch for the lads at the airport. Makes getting in and out a whole lot easier, if you know what I mean."

"I get your drift. By the way, is Joe your real name?"

"Sorry, Mr KGB, but you don't know me and I don't know you. I'm merely a pilot making a business trip for my boss."

"Mr KGB? It appears you know who I am."

"One slip. It won't happen again."

"Look, Joe, I'm not prying - just curious - and I appreciate your help. Con emphasized that you were good at your job... that I could trust you regardless of what happened in your past."

"My past?" asked Joe with a frown of suspicion. "What exactly did he tell you?"

"That the accusations don't matter."

"They're not true, I can guarantee you that. So, he told you that I did time!"

"Which took its toll on your military career."

"It bloody-well ruined it. And not just military - *SAS*. Hey, look, I didn't kill her. I was drunk and, yes, we spent the night together, which was why they found my DNA in a number of places, if you know what I mean. She was definitely hot - Chinese, long dark hair, body like a gymnast. But she must have had an unsavory history: maybe a pimp or a jealous boyfriend - who knows? Anyway, we fell asleep together in her flat, and when I woke up, she was dead on the floor and I had a lump on my head. I served time although they finally had to release me because the evidence was circumstantial and they could never pin me with motive. Still, it was enough to ruin my career. But I swear I didn't do it."

"I believe you, Joe. Otherwise, you wouldn't be working for Con."

A long moment of thought passed. Finally, Joe glanced back over his shoulder. "Did Con really tell you all that?"

Alex smiled and shook his head. "No, you did."

Joe chuckled to himself as he checked his gauges. "And I fell for it, hook, line, and sinker. How'd you know?"

"I'm trained in surveillance. Your tats - they're military, as is your bearing - and your vocabulary is intelligent, with American overtones, which means you're educated and well-travelled. Plus, you're a capable pilot. But you're making what amounts to rum runs for Con - in your statement you said he's the one making the gold, not you - which to me indicates a likelihood that your career took an abrupt, involuntary change some time back and that Con's helping you get back on your feet, which means he trusts you. To test my theory, I made a vague opening statement which you filled in."

"Son of a gun," said Joe, shaking his head. "Who said you older fellas aren't sharp?"

"Older fellas?" repeated Talanov with a raised eyebrow.

Joe laughed. "No offense, Mr K. And I wouldn't even begin to think about matching my new Holden against a vintage Shelby Cobra."

"Thanks... I think."

Joe grinned and glanced over his shoulder again as he took the plane lower. "Speaking of which, I've got a Shelby on a freighter bound for Adelaide. She'll fetch a small fortune if I don't decide to keep her for myself. Bright red... mint condition. A real beauty."

"Looks like you're prospecting for gold of your own," said Alex.

"Yep, and you sure got it right when you said Con's helping me out a bit. He says I'll be flying a bird of my own one day."

"You've got the Lindbergh touch, all right. There's a lot of water between here and Australia. Thanks for getting us here."

"No worries," Joe replied as a voice crackled over the radio. He reached for the microphone. "Like I said, Con's helped me and I'm merely passing it on."

Another one passing it along, thought Talanov as he gazed out the window while Joe communicated with the Tower at Efate's Bauerfield Airport. When finished, Joe replaced the microphone in its bracket. "We're cleared for landing."

"Good," replied Talanov. "But I need to tell you there could be trouble waiting for me in Vila. Sure, we don't know one another. But that doesn't change the fact that others might not appreciate what you've done by bringing me here. Therefore, I'd like you to find a nice restaurant and get stuck into some of that coconut crab. I don't want you taking a bullet."

"The SAS didn't train me to wait in restaurants, Mr K, so whether I take the point or guard your six, consider me part of the team. I don't bail when the going gets rough."

"These aren't just thugs, they're trained assassins."

Joe glanced around briefly, the humor gone from his eyes. "I don't like speaking to you this way, Mr K, you being a lot older and all. So pardon me for saying that I doubt you're capable of tackling this by yourself. You're pretty beat up, which means you'll be fragile and slow. Yes, I know you're KGB, but the way I see it, you're going to need some help." He looked back out the window at the approaching runway.

"*Former* KGB, Mr Know-it-all. And what makes you think I'd want your help, not that I'm for a moment admitting there's any truth to what you just said?"

Joe grinned to himself. "Lucky guess... I guess."

Irritated, Talanov touched the swelling around his eyes and mouth, then winced as he shifted in his seat, his bruised ribs sending an unmistakable message of caution about sudden movements. "Say, for sake of argument, that I *would* accept your help. Have you got any weapons?"

"I'm surprised you'd ask such a question," said Joe, glancing over his shoulder. "Guns are strictly forbidden on Vanuatu."

"Wonderful. Now, what exactly does that mean?"

"That I have some, of course," said Joe with another grin. "Small calibre, fits nicely in the pocket."

"What about the airport authorities?" asked Talanov as he touched Sergei's bank book in his shirt pocket just to make sure it was there. "There's a danger that I could be recognized."

"All eyes will be on Johnny Walker," said Joe. "Fasten your safety belt."

With all eyes indeed on the liquor, the presentation of a false passport at the counter was unnecessary and Talanov was waved past the desk. Nodding for Alex to wait outside, Joe lingered to exchange jokes with the guards before casually inquiring whether any of them knew a solicitor named Maxwell Ferguson. They did, with one of them describing a sixty year-old man with a pear-shaped belly and a fondness for good Scotch whisky. He possessed a flushed - probably pickled - complexion and a pleasant personality, both of which which tended to disarm one into thinking the old guzzler's gray matter had long ago turned to mush. In actuality, he was an encyclopedia of statutory facts. Plus, he was as shrewd as an outhouse rat when it came to creating tax-free shelters. Ferguson had been a resident on Efate for more than two decades and maintained a small office in town which was closed more than it was open. These days, he was more likely to be found at home, especially for afternoon cocktails, which usually commenced after lunch.

After being directed to the most reliable taxi on the island, Joe thanked them before departing to find Alex, who was outside pretending to have trouble with an obstinate shoelace. Joe quickly filled him in on what he had learned as he led the way to the taxi, which was parked in a "no standing" zone.

Joe leaned his head in the open window of the old white Toyota. "*Yu toktok Engglis?*" he asked the black driver in the native pidgin language of Bislama.

"*Lelebet*," the man answered.

Joe looked at Talanov. "Do you want to find a room first? If we do, we should go back to the plane and get our things."

"I reckon our belongings are safe where they are. Ask him if he knows where Ferguson lives."

"Do you know the house of Maxwell Ferguson?" asked Joe.

"*Ostrelyans?*" asked the middle-aged islander with a bright smile upon hearing the two men's accents. "I work once in *Ostrelya*... Queensland! Gudday, Mete!"

Joe smiled. "Yeah, G'day. Can you take us to Ferguson's house?"

"Yes, yes!" he said eagerly. "I know it. Please, get in."

Maxwell Ferguson's residence was a T-shaped house on a large property twenty minutes from Vila. It overlooked a wide stretch of beach with tall coconut palms lining the sand. Between the sand and house were more palm trees and shrubs dotting a gentle slope which climbed up to a spacious lawn. A thatch of tangled bougainvillea covered a wide porch full of wicker furniture from which Ferguson and his guests consumed many a bottle.

The afternoon was getting late when the taxi pulled into the driveway. While Alex remained out of sight in the back seat, Joe walked to the front door, ostensibly to seek directions to the home of the Beaumonts, whose house the driver told him was but a kilometer down the road. If someone fitting Ferguson's description answered the door, he should, of course, know the way to the Beaumont house, whereupon Joe could verify Ferguson's identity and signal Talanov. If the person answering the door was not able to give accurate directions, however, then Joe would thank the person and leave. Then, once they were out of sight, the driver could discharge them beside the road, and he and Talanov would return on foot to take up surveillance positions within sight of the house. After nightfall, they would move in to conduct a thorough questioning.

Joe knocked and waited. Soon the silhouette of an approaching man could be seen through the frosted glass window. "Yes?" the man said with a pleasant smile after opening the door. In his late thirties, he stood nearly six feet tall and was definitely not the sixty year-old pear-shaped man the guards had described at the airport.

"*Plis,*" Joe began, gesturing with his hands and pointing back up the driveway, "*Beaumont haos... hem i wea?*"

"I beg your pardon?" the man asked in aristocratic English, his eyebrows slightly arched.

"Sorry," apologized Joe while he mentally noted the man's description. "I'm looking for the Beaumont house. Do you know where it is?" *Slight non-English accent, military posture, doesn't know Bislama. The man's not Ferguson and not a local.*

"I'm afraid I don't," the man replied. "I'm merely visiting and the owner's not in."

A visitor - but on the level? Joe scratched his scalp and looked around as if he were lost. "They gave us directions but I got them all wrong." He looked back at the man. "Do you know when your friend will return?"

"Not for a while, I'm afraid."

"I guess I can try one of the neighbors."

"Forgive me for asking," said the man, his eyes revealing more suspicion than the casual tone of his voice indicated, "but how is it that you speak the native language and yet do not know your way around?"

Joe smiled. "Because I'm from the big island - Santo. And to make matters worse, my driver says he's never heard of the Beaumonts. Damn rotten luck."

"Yes, a pity."

"By the way, that's an interesting accent you've got."

"Accent?" repeated the man, concealing his surprise.

"Yeah. You said you were visiting, but I can't quite place from where."

"You've a good ear," the man said, eyeing Joe carefully.

Joe laughed good-heartedly. "I watch a lot of television, and I was in Europe once. You from Europe?"

"No," the man replied, glancing at his watch then back at Joe. "Do forgive me, but I must get back to my work. Sorry I can't be of help."

"That's all right. My apologies for having troubled you."

The man smiled. "No bother at all."

"Thanks," Joe said, waving as he returned to the taxi and climbed in. In less than a minute they were driving away from the house, with Alex still out of sight in the back seat. Once they reached the main road and were out of sight of the house, Alex was told he could sit up.

After the driver had gone a short distance, Alex asked him to pull over so that he and Joe could relieve their bladders. Once they had stopped, Talanov led the way into the dense undergrowth where Joe quietly recounted what happened.

"That doesn't sound like a description of Ferguson," said Alex, "but I've no idea who it was. Did you see anyone else in the house?"

"No. The airport guards said Ferguson occasionally visits his office but that he's usually home and sauced by now."

Alex glanced back toward the waiting taxi. "Since Con overheard one of the killers telling the captain that he was coming to Vanuatu to stop me, it means they know I'll be coming to question Ferguson. If one assumes Ferguson was merely a hired solicitor, then he becomes the weak link in their chain since he can identify who hired him and the nature of their activities."

"But if he's involved at a deeper level," said Joe, "then Ferguson could be as dangerous as the rest of their mob."

"That's certainly possible. But to me, the fact that a visitor answered his door starts tipping the scales away from his being part of their team. Any other time and circumstance and I wouldn't have thought twice about a stranger answering his door. But not now and not here. Add to that his age, long residency on the island, drinking habits and reputation, I see the profile of a man who seems unlikely to be part of a group of assassins. Clever - yes - particularly when it comes to creating tax free shelters and circular blinds. But Second Thirteen material? I seriously doubt it."

"What's this Second Thirteen?"

Talanov told him.

Joe shook his head. "That means Ferguson could be dead, bound and gagged, or somewhere in Argentina. You're into some heavy stuff, Mr K."

"Not by choice, I can tell you," said Talanov as he zipped his trousers. "As to Ferguson's whereabouts, a lot depends on whether or not my inquiry into the Reishi Pacific Banking Group set off an alarm. If it did, then Ferguson would have had plenty of time to escape. Aside from then having to deal with the issue of where he went, we'd have to identify the man you just met and find out the reason he's here. I reckon he's one of their killers."

The two men walked back to the waiting taxi where Joe opened the front door and paused with his hand on top of the window. "But isn't this still speculation? We don't know if Ferguson is dead or alive, on or off the island, running for his life, or helping them out."

"What we need is information on Ferguson's whereabouts from one of the locals."

"You want information on Ferguson?" the taxi driver asked, drawing the two men's attention. They both looked in through their open doors. The driver motioned them into the vehicle. "I take you to someone who know him."

"Will this person talk to us?" asked Talanov as he climbed in.

"Of course!" the driver said with a broad smile. "She is my wife, and she cleans his house! I think she saw Ferguson last week!"

"Then let's go!" said Talanov.

Chapter 40

It was dark when the taxi stopped in front of a dirt path leading to a corrugated iron hut surrounded by tree ferns and palms. Its curtained windows were lit and smoke curled lazily from a stove-pipe chimney. The night was warm and peaceful, and the air was filled with a chorus of insects and wild birds which contrasted with the distant beat of rock music blaring from a neighbor's radio. Behind the hut, a small diesel generator droned a steady stream of power to the lights inside.

After telling Alex and Joe to wait in the taxi until he had arranged matters with his wife, the driver grabbed his mobile telephone, climbed out, and sauntered up the path to the front door. A brief burst of light flashed into the night between the opening and closing of the door.

Several minutes passed.

"I don't like this," whispered Alex, growing nervous with each passing minute.

"He's only been gone a short while," replied Joe, scanning their surroundings but seeing nothing.

"Listen," said Alex.

Joe leaned his head out the window. "I don't hear anything but music."

"Neither do I," replied Talanov, looking toward the shack. "No insects, no birds... nothing. Things have suddenly gone quiet."

"As when predators are on the prowl?"

"Particularly the human kind." Talanov leaned toward Joe in the front seat. "Put your pistol inside your sock and don't go for it unless I utter the words, 'lamb stew'," he said quietly, then leaning back and doing the same.

"Expecting trouble?" asked Joe.

"Call it 'being prepared,' " replied Talanov as he and Joe turned toward another momentary flash of light from the front door. Both men watched as the driver strolled casually down the path toward them.

"My wife, she say it okay," the driver said. "Please, you follow me. She know where Ferguson is."

Alex and Joe got out of the taxi and followed the driver up the darkened path toward the house. Suddenly, from the deep shadows of the surrounding foliage, half a dozen men sprang forward and grabbed Talanov and Joe just as the driver whirled around with a large knife, which he flashed in the face of each man. With a nod, Talanov and Joe were searched and all belongings removed from their pockets. They were then propelled up to the house and through the front door, where they were pushed to the center of the room.

The inside of the hut was as shabby as the outside, with a bare wooden floor and a naked light bulb dangling from one of the log rafters beneath a corrugated iron roof. Along the far wall was an old double bed, and next to this were a table and four chairs which had been hastily pushed into a jumbled arrangement. Beneath the window was a sink, and nearby stood a stove made out of an oil drum, in which was an open fire. On top of the drum were two saucepans being attended by a large dark-skinned woman.

"If you're wanting to rob us-" Talanov began.

"If robbery were my motive," interrupted the driver in articulate English, "you would not be standing here now. What I want to know is why you are looking for Maxwell Ferguson." He handed the knife to one of the men and motioned for the wallets and passports which had been taken from Alex and Joe.

Alex looked at the man. He no longer spoke like the poorly educated taxi driver they had been led to believe that he was. "That was quite an act you put on for us," Talanov remarked.

"I find it advantageous to let visitors assume we island folk are simple and ignorant. I have an economics degree from Berkeley. Now, please answer my question." He began examining Joe's passport.

Talanov glanced casually at the men standing in a broad semi-circle behind the driver. All were young and wiry, and each had moved invisibly in the darkness outside. Talanov had never witnessed such lightning-quick movements, and even now Alex was not sure he would have time to reach his pistol. The intensity in their eyes told Alex that his and Joe's every move would be constantly watched. Talanov looked back at the driver. "It's our belief someone may be trying to kill Ferguson."

"And why is that?" asked the driver without looking up.

"I'll take that up with Ferguson," replied Talanov.

"You will take it up with us," the driver told Alex without the slightest inflection in his voice, "or you will not leave this room." He closed Joe's passport and raised his eyes to meet Talanov's.

Alex glanced at the men flanking the driver. Each had stiffened in anticipation of trouble. "It concerns the Reishi Pacific Banking Group," he answered.

"What business is that of yours?" asked the taxi driver as opened the false passport Talanov had been carrying.

How much should he tell this man? Alex wondered, knowing that he could not reveal too much, for to do so posed the risk of their being turned over to the police.

"Say, are you getting hungry?" Joe unexpectedly asked Alex, drawing everybody's attention.

"Hungry?" repeated Talanov quizzically.

"You know, for lamb stew or something like that?"

"What is this talk of lamb stew?" the driver asked Joe, approaching him with an angry look in his eyes. "Some kind of code?"

Joe held up his hands. "Hey, I don't mean no harm."

"You will talk only when addressed and not before."

"Sorry, I was just asking 'cause something's cooking on your stove and it's making me hungry." He slowly looked down then over at Alex, who casually looked at the other men, who had all stepped closer. There was no way they could get to their guns.

The driver moved over and stood before Talanov and held up his German passport. "Now, I will ask you again - Wolfgang Hauser - what business is this of yours?" He then held up Sergei's bank book. "And what is this?"

The single bulb hanging above threw a harsh wash of light across each man's face. The driver's dark eyes were impatient, his brown lips taut as he scrutinized Talanov. Several small insects flew in erratic patterns around their heads.

"Ferguson knows about a circular blind set up with the Reishi Pacific Banking Group," explained Talanov. "I've no idea what all that means, but it's somehow linked to a group of assassins who want to kill him to make sure he stays silent. Whatever it is that he knows will also unlock the reason those assassins are trying to kill me. So you ask what business is this of mine? I guess you can call it survival."

"You tell me *nothing!*" the driver yelled, raising his hands above him angrily.

"That's because I *know* nothing!" Alex yelled back, "other than Ferguson's name and the name of the Reishi Pacific Banking Group. For God's sake, call him and ask. But also tell him this - that whether he agrees to talk with me or not, the killers who ordered the creation of that circular blind will eventually find him, and his only hope of *ever* having a normal life again is to help me stop them."

The driver leaned toward Talanov aggressively and jabbed his finger an inch from his eye. "Perhaps it is *you* who wants to kill Ferguson. Maybe we should get rid of *you* and he will be safe."

Talanov did not flinch. "I told you once and I'll tell you again: I don't care whether I see Ferguson or not. All I need is information which I can get over the phone. But what about the stranger in Ferguson's house? How many times do I have to repeat myself? Ferguson knows too much, and as long as he's alive, he's a threat to their plans."

The driver whirled around, his fists clenched as he paced to the sink, unsure what to do.

"We're not your problem," Alex said. "But what about that stranger?"

The driver looked at Talanov from across the room. "He is from the International Development Council."

"The *IDC?*" asked Talanov, trying to conceal his alarm at what amounted to a confirmed link between the stranger and the Second Thirteen. "Who is he, when did he get here?"

"That is not your concern."

"Maybe not, but why is he in Ferguson's house?"

"He is here looking for someone."

"Does Ferguson know this man?"

The driver hesitated. "No. But he is aware of the man's purpose."

Talanov glanced over at Joe. The killer, of course, was looking for him as well as Ferguson, which meant they must make contact with Ferguson before his own identity as Aleksandr Talanov was discovered.

And before Ferguson could be murdered.

"Is Ferguson safe?" pressed Alex.

The driver looked hard at Talanov. "Why is this a concern to you?"

"Because I need information and others are wanting to kill him before he gives it to me. Now, is he safe?"

"Yes, but I will not tell you where he is. I am not even sure myself."

"I told you I don't need to meet with Ferguson personally. You've got a mobile phone. Dial his number and let me talk with him."

"Why?" asked the driver.

"For God's sake, man! I want to find out about the Reishi Pacific Banking Group and warn him about the killers!"

"Ferguson is aware of the danger," replied the driver. "He does not need you to tell him that."

"Then let me ask him about the Reishi Pacific Banking Group. What's its purpose... and who directed him to create a circular blind with the Pekoe Trading Company of the Cayman Islands? My life - and his - are on the line."

The driver looked intently at Talanov, impressed with the fact that he was not attempting to locate Ferguson. A long moment passed. "All you want is some information?" he asked. "You don't need to meet with him personally?"

"No. Tell him to remain where he's safe."

After another long moment, the driver nodded. "I will see what he says."

But as he reached for his mobile telephone, it rang.

Surprised, the driver picked it up and answered it, his eyes suddenly narrowing as he listened. He then turned away from Alex and Joe and conversed quietly in rapid Bislama for roughly ten seconds. After switching it off, he whirled around. "Grab them!" he yelled to his men, who sprang forward like spiders.

Alex jumped quickly to his left, avoiding the first attacker. The shoulder of the second one, however, caught Alex squarely in the ribs, sending an explosion of pain through his body. Alex let out an agonizing cry and tried to twist free from the man's grasp. Suddenly a third attacker hit him at the knees. Talanov raised an elbow to hammer it against the man's head, but could not keep his balance as he was pulled to the floor.

Not saddled with injury like Alex, Joe leaped to his right and drove a single punch into the jaw of the first attacker. The young man's head snapped to the side and he fell to the floor. Attackers two and three flew at Joe, one high, one low, their flailing arms and screams splitting Joe's concentration. In his moment of hesitation, one set of arms locked around Joe's waist while the others went for his face. Joe ducked to one side and with an upward block, deflected the attacker away from his face and down onto the back of the other. A savage chop to the neck then dislodged the other attacker arms. Joe kicked them away and with one smooth bending motion, pulled the pistol out of his sock.

"Let him go... *now!*" screamed Joe as he pointed the small automatic at the driver, then at the attackers who had pinned Talanov on the floor.

"Drop de gun, sonny boy," came a female voice from behind him. " 'Less you wanna be scraped off de flo' like jam."

Joe slowly looked around to see the large islander woman aiming a twelve gauge shotgun at him, the white of her eye clearly visible along the top of the barrel. With a bitter sigh of defeat, Joe dropped his gun.

The driver walked over and kicked away the automatic while one of the injured islanders, blood trickling from his mouth, limped toward Joe with a knife.

"No!" the driver commanded. "We will hold them for the authorities."

Cursing, the young islander watched Joe while two others again searched Talanov again, this time discovering the small gun in his sock. After removing it, they pushed Alex over with Joe.

"What's this all about?" demanded Talanov, holding his ribs. "All I wanted was information."

"That call was from one of the guards who searched your plane," the driver replied with a sneer. "In your belongings he discovered another passport. It seems your name is *not* Wolfgang Hauser but *Aleksandr Talanov* - the Russian killer who is wanted for murder! We were told you to expect you."

"Who told you that?" asked Talanov, still holding his side.

"It does not matter. What matters is that you will not succeed with your plans to kill Maxwell Ferguson."

13 Chapter 41

Bob's call from Number Three seemed catastrophic. Over the adamant protests of the captain, the South Australian police had boarded the *Coriander* and ordered it to remain in port. To make matters worse, the ship would probably be delayed even longer because no murder weapon had been found. The ship was still being searched and witnesses to the killing were now being sought.

By her own confession, the shooting had been committed by Talanov's wife, supposedly to defend the life of her husband and a female security guard. She was, of course, taken into custody, with the story making headline news. But no trace could be found of Talanov, who presumably had escaped the country.

Excusing himself from morning cocktails at a special IDC reception in his honor, Bob sought immediate privacy for the remainder of the call and had been shown across the carpeted hallway into the mansion's East Room, with its pastel yellow walls and polished hardwood floor. With his mobile phone to his ear, Bob crossed a plush Persian rug and sat on one of two Queen Anne sofas positioned on either side of a rectangular coffee table once used by Robert E. Lee. Even on cold wintry days like today, the cheerful room, with its view of the Potomac River, was awash in light from three tall windows lightly veiled with embroidered voile. Nearby, in an ornate marble and cherry wood fireplace, several chunks of oak burned lazily on a bed of embers.

And yet after listening to the entire report, Bob found himself surprisingly calm. Things may not be so bad after all.

Without question he wanted revenge for Fiona's death, and now, strangely, this unexpected turn of events was handing him the means to accomplish it.

Bob walked over to the window and looked down the gently sloping lawn toward the river. Outside, some vines of Virginia creeper dangled leafless over the window. "Now listen carefully," he said. "I want you to arrange for a member of the crew to file a deposition which supports the testimony of Mrs Talanov."

"*What?*" asked Three, surprised.

"You heard me. I want him to state that he saw the whole thing and that Mrs Talanov killed Fiona in defense of her husband and the female security guard. Pay him whatever he wants. Just get him to swear unconditionally."

"But *why?*"

"Because I want her released, that's why."

Three began to smile. "I see what you mean. After we take her, what do we do?"

Bob smiled coldly. "We use her to kill her husband."

Chapter
42

Earlier, the taxi driver had walked out the open front door of the hut and made a quick call to Ferguson to advise him of Talanov's capture. He was understandably relieved. Now, in the far distance through the trees, the driver could see the flashing lights of a police car as it sped along the dirt road. Inside, his two prisoners had been ordered to sit back-to-back in the center of the floor. Each had once again been thoroughly searched and no longer would their capabilities be underestimated. With their own guns, they were now being guarded.

Ferguson had been right: Talanov was in Vila to kill him, and he had even managed to slip by the airport authorities using a false passport. As luck would have it, his real identity had been discovered by a guard searching his plane for drugs.

Thankfully, the guard was familiar with Talanov's name, not only because it had been in the news, but because of an International Development Council warning sent to all the island authorities advising them about Talanov's intent to kill Ferguson. All points of entry were to be placed on alert, and when captured, Talanov was to be held for a Major Pyotr Marshak, special envoy from the IDC, who would transport him back to Australia for trial.

The driver lowered himself onto an old wooden chair and listened to the sounds of the night, thankful that Talanov had been captured.

Maxwell Ferguson had been his friend for nearly twenty years now. Originally from some intolerably cold part of America - Newark, or was it New York? - the old fox had settled in the islands in an attempt to retire with a hundred grand acquired by questionable means. Which meant, of course, that Ferguson was on the run with some other crook's loot. In fact, Maxwell Ferguson was probably not his real name, not that it mattered now. Unless, of course, the crooks were still on his trail.

He remembered the day he gave Ferguson a ride. Emerging from the airport with a trolley loaded with one suitcase and six cartons of scotch, the lawyer had carefully placed each of the boxes in his taxi with the care shown by a mother when she tucks in her baby. After a gentle ride to Ferguson's new house, the two men then spent the rest of the afternoon sampling the goods.

The simple life of the islands agreed with Ferguson, and he took quickly to the mangos and crab. Still, it came as no surprise to the driver when, several years later, Ferguson sank into a depression. The reason: his money was gone. Carefree spending - including a house and no telling how many hundreds of cases of whisky - had indeed depleted his funds to the point that he was presented with the terrifying necessity of having to go back to work. And that's when he began creating tax-free shelters.

Gradually, Ferguson's activities brought foreign investment to Vila. Which meant increased revenues for schools, streets, and public facilities. Then, as Ferguson's business increased, so did his popularity, including the pressure to run for parliament, which he adamantly refused. His preference was to quietly pursue those endeavors which allowed him to sleep late and drink early. Public office, he insisted, required one to act responsibly - something he was not prepared to do. All he really wanted was enough cash for some good food and whisky.

Except for now. Now he was hiding in fear of his life.

While the chorus of crickets and frogs rose to a piercing crescendo over the thumping beat of the rock music, the driver tilted his chair back against the wall of the hut and watched the flashing lights of the police car draw nearer. It would not be long until Talanov was in custody.

With Ferguson safe - or nearly so, anyway - why, then, was he still unsettled? If he were honest, he knew the reason. For as much as he wanted to believe that Talanov's capture signalled the end of Ferguson's problems, in truth he was not so sure. Who *were* the people who had paid Ferguson to create the circular blind? Talanov had called them assassins.

He remembered Ferguson telling him about the request. According to Maxwell, a voice on the telephone had expressed interest in an investment account capable of receiving and transmitting funds untraceable beyond the account. Ferguson had suggested a circular blind and the anonymous client agreed. Ferguson then explained what was required for the transaction, including his fee.

Creating such a legal entity would be as simple as peeling a banana. At least that's how Ferguson had described it one afternoon as he was pouring them drinks on his porch. The names chosen by the anonymous client had seemed odd - one based on a tea, the other a mushroom - but people these days entertained all sorts of fetishes and he was not one to judge.

But neither was Ferguson naive, for he realized that circular blinds were desired by people with things to hide. No surprise there. And the fact that everything had been handled by telephone also came as no surprise, nor was the payment of his fee in cash. What began to raise those bushy eyebrows of his were the client's corporate details. In the first place, the two boards of directors were obvious fabrications, being nothing more than a collection of the most common and untraceable surnames in existence, with the addresses of each listed in care of the other corporation. The client was likewise insistent that the corporate addresses on both Vanuatu and the Cayman Islands be those of empty lots rather than Ferguson's post office box, with no telephone listings whatsoever.

In fact, it was the extreme care these clients had taken to remain anonymous which caused Ferguson to implement a number of safety procedures to alert him in case people should started asking questions. He then made copies of all documents before sending the originals to a post office in Sydney. A little detective work, however, revealed the box had been rented by a Russian diplomat named Sergei Zinyakin. The question then became: why would people in the Russian Consulate need a circular blind unless they were planning something subversive?

The taxi driver thought back to the day Ferguson told him about the diplomat's murder, which had been in the news. The blood drained even more from Ferguson's face when the authorities called to inform him that the IDC had just telephoned to say that Zinyakin's assassin - a man named Talanov - was coming to Vanuatu to kill him. He had no choice but to run until Talanov was captured.

The Port Vila police car came to a stop in front of the corrugated iron hut and switched off its lights. The driver pushed himself out of his chair just as he heard two car doors slam in the darkness. As the sound of footsteps grew closer, the driver was aware of his own uneasiness. Why was he not convinced that Ferguson's problems were over?

For one thing, it seemed odd that the prestigious International Development Council would be sending a special envoy for Talanov. Was this not the domain of the police? If indeed Talanov had come to Vila to assassinate Ferguson, why did he not push for a meeting? Instead, he sought nothing more than information about the Reishi Pacific Banking Group, insisting that those who ordered Ferguson to create it were really the killers. And who was the man with Talanov who spoke Bislama? He was not from the islands but looked vaguely familiar.

"We came as fast as we could," the local constable told the taxi driver as he and another man approached. "This gentleman is from the IDC."

"I am Major Marshak," Pyotr said, "and I've shown appropriate identification to your constable. Where is the prisoner?"

The driver looked at the man from the IDC. In the faint light from the window he could see the man was tall and stern, with short brown hair and a broad, square jaw. "He's inside," the driver said.

"Show me to him. I want him locked up for the night."

With his back to Joe's, Talanov had been sitting on the dirty wooden floor, his head resting against his drawn-up knees. Although his eyes were closed, he was not asleep for through his mind kept flashing images of his wife. A lifetime of memories had been compressed into those few moments in Adelaide... memories which now fueled his fears. *Would he ever see her again?*

Fear was something Talanov the agent had never experienced. But fear was something Talanov the husband was now facing for the first time.

Could he overcome it?

He had successfully bridled his anger against Sergei, Fiona, and all the Second Thirteen killers who had beaten his wife, killed his friends, and turned the rest of his life into tatters. Yes, he had bridled his anger and used it to harden his resolve.

But fear was something else. Creature of the night, fear had a way of knowing one's weakest moments, then finding the soul's tiniest of fractures and seeping in like toxic gas. Where anger might stir one to action, fear crippled and bled one of strength.

Alex thought back to the child he had rescued at Chang's. With cold precision he had out-maneuvered the man with the knife, defeating him mentally, then physically.

But what if the child had been his? The loss of a child would be terrible; the loss of *his* child - unbearable.

Was it any different now with his wife?

Alex recalled telling Gail how he must act with the dispassionate skill of a surgeon. Alex wondered if it were possible, for the sight of his drugged and beaten wife on board the freighter was almost more than he could bear. But nothing could have prepared him for the agony of that moment when he watched her run from the news vehicle, his joy at having found her dashed when he had to run. Alex imagined Andrea sitting alone in a concrete cell while he was here, an ocean away, surrounded by more than half a dozen men - some of them armed - with the authorities now on their way. That grim truth was made even worse by the realization that once the authorities had him in custody, the Second Thirteen would be able to kill him. His only hope was avoiding capture. And yet how could they fight so many?

Andrea's words suddenly came back to him: *Don't become the agent, but use him... use his skills... make him your servant.* With his eyes closed, Alex reflected on those words and set about visualizing the room, assessing the odds. Even with Joe's SAS capabilities, the odds did not look good.

For one thing, a simple deep breath reminded Alex of his own injuries. Which meant his speed and stamina were handicaps, not strengths. Overpowering his opponents - even outrunning them, for that matter - were simply not viable options.

Alex then thought about the axiom he had discussed with Spiro - the "Goliath" principle - and how ones opponents can sometimes become careless when armed or with a feeling of unquestioned advantage. That principle could well apply here. Plus, although they were outnumbered, the men were for the most part young and inexperienced, and as such, might easily be diverted or driven to panic. However, when spooked, such people could react as a mob, a particularly lethal trait when mixed with guns. Nevertheless, it was this potential instability which gave Alex hope. All he needed was the right opportunity.

A roach ran up the inside of Talanov's trouser leg and he jerked, causing the insect to tumble back to the floor and scurry away. At that moment the front door of the hut flew open and the taxi driver entered, followed by two men, one of them a uniformed policeman.

Joe recognized Marshak at once. "You!" he said.

"At home with your friends, the Beaumonts?" inquired Marshak with a smirk as he pulled handcuffs from a leather case and looked at Alex. "Aleksandr Talanov, I hereby arrest you on behalf of the Commonwealth of Australia. Stand up and place your hands behind your back."

Joe leaped to his feet. "On whose authority?"

The constable with Marshak pulled out his pistol and stepped forward. "On the authority of the International Development Council."

"Sorry, pal, but the IDC has about as much jurisdiction as Coca Cola."

"I have seen his papers!" the constable said, exerting his authority even more by pointing the gun at Joe's face.

"I don't care if you've seen his little pink undies! He has no jurisdiction!"

"Do you mind if I see a warrant?" asked the taxi driver.

With a disapproving frown, Marshak looked at the driver, then pulled three sheets of folded paper out of his shirt pocket and held them out.

The driver accepted the papers and read them. "Are you Russian?" he finally asked, raising his eyes to meet Marshak's.

"I am and I work in an official capacity for the Russian Consulate. Why do you ask?"

The driver smiled. "Just curious." He folded the papers and handed them back.

Marshak accepted the documents and stuffed them back into his pocket. "Then, if you're satisfied, I will secure the prisoner." He readied his handcuffs.

"Before you do that, Major," the driver said, stepping between Marshak and Talanov, "I'd like to repeat the prisoner's question: by what authority is the IDC allowed to extradite prisoners? It occurs to me that if this or any prisoner is transported illegally, it could well constitute an infringement of his rights, which could then lead to his release on technical grounds. Surely we don't want that."

"I just showed you documents which authorize my actions," stated Marshak icily.

"And they were quite impressive," the driver agreed, "on official IDC letterhead, complete with signatures and stamps. However, having the IDC grant permission to the IDC doesn't constitute sanctioned approval. What about something from Interpol, or the Australian Federal Police?"

"I didn't realize it was necessary for the IDC to have the approval of taxi drivers," stated Marshak, hardening his stare. "Your constable here knows the law, but so that I can get on with my job without any further interference, I will explain it to you. As an IDC officer with the rank of Major, I am in Vanuatu under the authority of the London Scheme for the Rendition of Fugitive Offenders of 1966, in which both Vanuatu and Australia are participating as Commonwealth nations and members of the International Development Council. Therefore, as an officer with the IDC, I am within my jurisdiction to require you to render assistance so that I may place Talanov in custody for extradition back to Australia."

"And I didn't realize it was necessary for taxi drivers to give jack shit to the IDC," the driver replied, drawing laughter from the young men seated around the room. "Who do you think you are, coming into this house and giving orders about what we must do? You are in *our* country now."

After glancing at the circle of islanders watching him carefully, Marshak looked back at the driver, then at the policeman. "Constable! I commission you to place the prisoner under arrest."

"On your feet," the policeman told Alex.

"You can't let him *do* this!" Joe whispered to Talanov as he helped him get to his feet, Talanov still holding his ribs.

Opportunities will present themselves. Alex straightened and with difficulty tried finding his balance, both Joe and the taxi driver assisting him. In truth, Alex exaggerated his unsteadiness in order to test the response of the driver. By offering assistance, the driver may well have indicated a change in allegiance. What Alex needed was a way to tip the scales while exposing Marshak.

Talanov turned to the driver. "Whatever you do, don't say a word about Ferguson's whereabouts."

Marshak pushed by Talanov and approached the driver. "Do you know Maxwell Ferguson?"

"Most of the locals know him."

"Where is he?"

"You've been in his house, don't you know?" asked Joe.

Marshak glanced angrily at Joe.

"Well?" asked the taxi driver.

"Yes, I am staying in his house, but I don't know where he is. However, I fear something terrible may have happened to him."

"I'm touched," said Joe.

"And I'm growing weary of your mouth," replied Marshak. He then turned back to the driver. "I need Ferguson to sign an affidavit."

"No!" Alex cut in. "Don't tell him a thing."

"You, shut up!" Marshak told Alex. To the driver: "Where is Ferguson?"

The constable stepped forward. "Tell him!"

"Don't do it!" countered Talanov.

Marshak looked at the constable. "Constable, we've paid you *five thousand dollars* for your help. I demand to see Ferguson!"

The policeman swung his gun toward the driver. "Tell him where Ferguson is!"

The taxi driver narrowed his eyes. "You've taken *money* from this man?"

"Talanov is a wanted *killer!*"

"But Ferguson is not. And you come at me now with a *gun?*"

The policeman lowered his weapon. "Then tell him. All he needs is a statement."

The driver stepped away from the constable. What a fool he had been! Ferguson was in danger, not from Talanov, but this man from the *IDC*. Why hadn't he seen it earlier? Sergei Zinyakin - a Russian diplomat - had been the one to whom the circular blind documents had been sent. And now, another Russian official was the one trying to locate Ferguson, supposedly as part of an IDC effort to bring Talanov to justice. Was Talanov even guilty of the things for which he'd been accused?

The taxi driver looked back at the constable. "You would turn against Ferguson, our friend? Look what he's done for Efate."

"Five thousand dollars is more important to me than revenues which the government spends. I see none of that."

Marshak looked at the young men seated around the room. Two of them had guns and all were slowly getting to their feet. "One thousand dollars to every one of you if you will help me find Ferguson," he shouted. *"One thousand dollars each* for

Ferguson's statement!"

The young men suddenly began looking at one another, interested but not knowing what to do. They were, of course, loyal to their friend, the driver. But one thousand dollars *each*. After all, the man from the IDC wanted only a statement.

Alarmed, the driver whirled around, glancing at Talanov and Joe, then at the others. He recognized what was happening.

Looking up, the driver hoped his gesture revealed what he was about to do. Suddenly, with his fist, he swung at the room's single light bulb hanging above his head. It shattered, slicing his hand but throwing the hut into total darkness.

Talanov and Joe were ready, and with a twisting cartwheel motion, Joe flung himself at the constable and major, his horizontal body catching each of the men in the chest. All three hit the floor, the constable's gun discharging as he fell. A scream sounded from across the room just as Joe pounded his fist into the constable's face, the gun clattering noisily over the floorboards.

Marshak rolled quickly to the side and to his feet just as Talanov rammed him with his shoulder. Marshak flew headlong into the wall of the hut, tripping over a chair and crashing to the floor.

The discharging of the constable's gun caused an outcry of angry shouts and confusion as the circle of young islanders began running into one another and pushing in all directions. That chaos was what Talanov wanted as he and Joe ran to the door and pulled it open.

Barely able to see one another in the darkness, the two men sprinted down the path and along the dirt road , Talanov limping and soon growing winded. "I can't go on," he said a few moments later in a hushed voice.

"Quick, in here," said Joe, leading the way through some tall grass to a large stand of banana trees, the surrounding forest of ferns and mango trees making an impenetrable wall of black.

Talanov followed and knelt behind the trees. "We've got to make them outrun us," he said, holding his ribs and catching his breath.

"Interpretation, please," said Joe nervously as he looked back toward the app-roaching clamor of voices. The money-crazed mob was on its way.

"Find three or four rocks the size of your fist and throw them across the road and into the trees at increasing distances. With luck, they'll follow the noise."

Joe located some rocks, and as the shouts of the posse grew nearer, he hurled them as Talanov said, the throng of young men running down the road in the direction of the noise, followed by Marshak and the constable in the police car. Once they were gone, Joe picked up two more rocks and hurled them even farther, the shouts of the young men growing more even excited with the crackle of branches. Two shots then rang out and the voices grew hysterical."

"Come on... back to the hut," said Talanov as he got to his feet and led the way out of the trees.

"You sure about that, Mr K?"

"That taxi driver helped us, and what we need is a ride out of here. Sooner or later that mob will return."

Talanov and Joe hurried back to the hut, and upon entering, found the driver - in the wash of his flashlight - kneeling on the floor beside the woman, who was covered with blood. Hearing footsteps, he swung the flashlight their way.

"They must not find you!" he said frantically but in a lowered voice. "Get out of here!"

"She needs a doctor," Talanov replied as he crossed the floor. "Come on, let's get her to the car."

"Don't waste time, I've stopped the bleeding."

Alex glanced at Joe, remembering Spiro and Con and all the people who had helped him. "Steady her head," he said as he and Joe bent down and slid their hands under her back. "Ready... now, lift."

Working as one, the three men lifted the groaning woman and carried her out of the hut and down the footpath to the taxi. "Put her in the back seat," the driver said, opening the door.

"Your wife?" asked Joe as they slid her carefully into the car.

"The wife of a friend. Once we heard you were coming, they said we could use their hut for a trap because it was well out of town. Little did we know we were trapping the wrong man."

"What changed your mind?" asked Talanov.

"A lot of things didn't add up, not the least of which was the fact that you were concerned about Ferguson's safety. Sure, you may have wanted to keep him alive only to get information about the Reishi Pacific Banking Group. But the fact is, you wanted him safe... and you didn't push for a meeting. That's not the behavior of an assassin."

"I still need that information," Alex said as he closed the door.

The driver walked to the rear of the car and, aided by his flashlight, inserted his key in a lock. With a twist, the trunk lid sprang open. "Then you'd better climb in," he said.

"In the boot?" asked Talanov.

"It's the only way you'll get out of here. And I wouldn't debate this too long."

They didn't, and soon they were pulling away from the hut only to be stopped by the excited mob wanting to know where he was going and had he seen the escaped criminals. The driver paused only long enough to point out the obvious: he had a wounded woman in the back seat who needed to get to the hospital. The mob waved him past and soon the taxi was bouncing along the road toward town.

At the hospital, the driver did not like leaving Talanov and Joe in the trunk for as long as he did. But the paperwork took longer than expected, and with his own hand needing medical attention, it was nearly an hour before he returned and started the engine. Once they were clear of Vila's lights, the driver pulled over and opened the trunk.

"I was about to wet my pants," said Joe as he jumped out and ran into the grass.

Talanov climbed out and stretched, inhaling the refreshing onshore winds as he looked up into the darkened sky. Extending to the limits of sight was a vast galactic colloid - distant solar systems suspended in black, the immensity of space reducing the light from these systems into familiar patterns of dots.

"Man, was that ever close," Joe said as he returned to the car.

"Close calls seem a way of life these days," replied Talanov as he turned toward his friend.

"Some you can fight, and some you can't," commented Joe.

"Considering our quarters, I'm glad you fought that one."

Alex then approached the driver, who was standing near the door of his taxi looking out toward the sea. "I haven't had a chance to thank you," he said.

"You thank me for rescuing you from a trap which I made?" asked the driver, glancing at the darkened form beside him. "It is I who should thank you."

"At least you saw through them in time."

The driver faced Talanov fully. "Why are you here, Mr Talanov? If you're indeed a clever liar, then I guess I've been taken in. You could easily kill me and run."

"I'm no killer and I'm no liar," replied Alex, who then briefed the driver on what had transpired, beginning with the massacre in his home. "Which is why I need information from Ferguson. If I'm to have any chance of stopping these killers, I need to know who they are. Like I've told you, my only hope of doing that is through the circular blind. But what I said earlier still holds true: Ferguson's life is in danger. He's the only one who can expose them."

"Was that why you pulled that stunt?"

"What stunt?" asked Talanov.

"Telling me not to say anything about Ferguson's whereabouts. You knew Major Marshak would react."

"Yes, I did. But I didn't know how else to force his hand."

"Pretty damn smart," said the driver.

"Pretty desperate," replied Talanov. "My only hope of stopping them is to stay both alive and out of jail."

"Then let's see what Ferguson knows."

"I meant it when I said I don't need to meet him," Alex told the driver. "A simple phone call will do."

"It will have to. Even though I believe your story, you could still be a liar. Bottom line: I won't take that chance. Besides, I doubt he would meet with you, anyway. When the IDC called the island police with the news that you were coming to kill him, he went into hiding. He's on a remote part of the island and the only way I can reach him is by phone."

"Is he carrying a mobile?"

"No, he's at a... oh, *no!*"

"What's wrong?" asked Talanov.

"My mobile phone - I left it in the hut!"

Talanov grabbed the driver by the arm. "What was the last number you entered?"

"Ferguson's," stated the driver. "After your capture, I stepped outside and called him to let him know what had happened. He was relieved."

Alex yanked open the rear door to the taxi and jumped in. "Then get in and get us to a phone!"

"But why... what's the problem?" asked the driver as he climbed in and started the engine.

"The *recall button!*" exclaimed Talanov just as Joe hopped into the passenger seat. "If someone pushes that button, his number will appear on the display and they can use it to trace his address!"

"My God, what have I *done?*" screamed the driver, shifting into Drive. He rammed the accelerator pedal to the floor and the taxi spewed a plume of crushed coral out behind them as they raced away into the night.

Chapter
43

The telephone rang and rang. "Dammit, no one's *there!*" the taxi driver exclaimed as he slammed the receiver back in its cradle. He ran out of the resort lobby and jumped into his car, where Talanov and Joe were waiting. "No answer," he announced as he started the engine. "I just hope we can make it in time."

"I thought you didn't know where he was," remarked Talanov.

"So I'm the liar," stated the driver. "Back then, I wasn't about to tell you; now I don't have a choice."

"I hope he's not registered in a hotel."

"We're not that stupid," growled the driver as he sped away from the resort.

"Stupid as in leaving your mobile phone in the hands of killers?" asked Joe without taking his eyes off of the darkened road.

The driver threw Joe an angry glance but did not reply as he directed the taxi onto the main road east out of Vila, the lights of the city soon vanishing behind them. After crossing a river, the taxi followed the main road as it angled south. Near Narpow Point, they again veered east and began following the coast.

To their left was Efate's mountainous interior which was dominated by an extinct volcanic cone, Mount MacDonald, some twenty-five kilometers to the north. Sporadic penetrations into the island's dense jungle had been made over the last century both by cattlemen and farmers clearing the land for their respective pursuits. At various points along the island's perimeter, large plantations of coconut palms had been planted in symmetrical rows. For most of the year they swooned peacefully in the intoxicating South Pacific breezes, only to cower and sometimes fall in the violent storms which hurled fury like invading conquerors.

As the taxi sped along, a ribbon of white breakers showed dimly far off to the right, the sound of their rhythmic pounding carried along by the balmy night winds. Ahead, the twin circles of the Toyota's headlights illuminated the main road's gravel of crushed white coral.

Within forty-five minutes they were approaching Eton, a rustic beach-side village on Efate's southeastern coast. Eton was little more than a store and church surrounded by numerous huts of thatched roofs over walls of corrugated iron. Near the church, however, was a solar-powered communications tower which linked Eton with the rest of the world. Technology had indeed arrived in a village without public electricity.

"How much further?" asked Talanov as they continued out of Eton.

"We're getting close," answered the driver as they began to decelerate. "In the trees up ahead on the left is a walled villa owned by Madame Li. Ferguson helped her with a few tax shelters some years back and occasionally he retreats here when he wants to slip free of the phones. Madame Li's away frequently on business and Ferguson passes the time sipping his scotch on her balcony. Her two-story residence, furnished with Chinese flair and Western affluence, is tucked in among the palms and mangos."

"Sounds like a place of seclusion," said Talanov.

"It is," agreed the driver as he began applying the brakes.

Joe glanced over his shoulder. "You thinkin' what I'm thinkin,' Mr K?"

"More than likely," answered Talanov. To the driver: "Is that her lane?"

"That's it, on the left."

"Pull over and switch off your lights."

The driver did so, the tires crunching on the pulverized coral as they coasted to a stop. Across from them, a narrow side road cut inland into the jungle.

Before opening his door, Talanov looked over at the darkened form of the driver visible in the dim wash of light from the dashboard. "Joe and I will get out here. If Ferguson's in the house, beep your horn two times, then five. If we hear that signal, we'll join you. If he's not, or if there's trouble, play ignorant and get out fast. If anyone asks, you haven't seen us."

"Understood," responded the driver, whereupon Talanov and Joe got out of the car and quietly pushed closed their doors.

Once the driver had turned down the lane, Alex and Joe crossed the road. "I presume this means you're going to rest your middle-age bones under some tree while I scale the wall?"

"You're getting to be quite a smart-ass," replied Talanov as he led the way into the trees which bordered the lane.

Joe grinned. "Just keepin' a step ahead of you, Mr K."

"Well, Tarzan, before you go climbing walls and setting off alarms, you may want to check the gate. It could be open."

"I knew that."

"Of course you did. Now get going. When you come back, be sure to whistle like a bird. That way I'll know not to kill you."

"You're all comfort."

"Be careful."

"Careful's my middle name," replied Joe before sprinting noiselessly down the lane.

Moving forward slowly in the darkness, Talanov squinted but could see little more than indistinct shades on shadows. Soon, however, his vision had fully adjusted from the dashboard lights of the taxi and he could discern the silhouettes of trees against the starlit depths of the sky. The gentle rustling of leaves provided further information about density, nearness, and height, adding dimension to the monotones of black. Talanov soon chose a tree set back between two others on the inside curve of the lane.

But he had not been hidden for more than five minutes when another car - a police car - sped up the lane toward the villa. In less than a minute, another one followed.

A chill swept over Talanov. Who had summoned the police? Had Joe triggered a silent alarm? Had Ferguson called for help? Reminding himself of his injuries, Talanov resisted the urge to investigate and remained concealed in the foliage. Yet his mind was racing to deduce what might have happened.

Had an alarm indeed been set off? Based on what Joe had told him earlier about the island, the police were headquartered in Vila, which meant the two squad cars would have had to leave town at about the same time as they had in order to be arriving here now. Hence, it was unlikely they were responding to Joe or the taxi driver, although a previous intruder might have tripped an alarm. However, if such a break-in were still in progress, Joe or the driver would have raised a cry. And since there had been no cries or shots, it was probable the intruder was gone - if indeed there had been one at all.

It was, of course, conceivable that Ferguson himself had called for help, the worst-case scenario being that Marshak or Cheney had broken into the house and murdered him. But this was simply a guess and not one he wished to consider, at least not now. Thus, with there being little else to do, Talanov knelt down and patiently waited.

The minutes passed agonizingly slow. What was going on? There still had been no word from Joe. Nor had there been any signal from the taxi driver. Was he being questioned by the police? Had Joe been captured?

A twig snapped off to his right. Talanov picked up a rock and slowly stood. Suddenly he heard a whistle.

Alex whistled in return.

"Mr K! Where are you?"

"Over here," Talanov replied in a lowered voice as he stepped away from the tree.

"Bad news, I'm afraid," said Joe, once he found Alex.

"Ferguson?"

"Dead," Joe replied. "At least that's what the cops are saying. There's a broken back door and blood all over the place. Apparently his body was dragged outside through the trees to a waiting car. It seems there's a wide path along the back of the property which connects to a little-used road. That road just happens to cut through the interior of the island and back to Vila. The cops are scouting the area now. Our friend, the taxi driver, is being questioned, and you'll never guess who showed up with the police."

"Marshak?"

"Yep. And I don't mind sayin' I think he's in on it. Plus, from what I hear, the constable's now gone missing. It's my guess Marshak paid the bastard to race over here and kill Ferguson, then haul his body away."

"But why waste time removing the body?"

"Because as friendly as these islanders are," replied Joe, "they take murder very seriously. I figure the constable planned to do away with him quickly and clean up the place. But because Ferguson put up a fight, the job took too long and he got scared."

"Either that or he's still alive."

"Ferguson? I don't see how. There's one helluva lot of blood."

Alex wandered off several steps, his fist pressed thoughtfully against his mouth. Had the constable indeed been the one who killed Ferguson? The lure of Marshak's reward money had certainly turned his hand earlier, and to lose Ferguson now was to lose his one chance of identifying the killers. But was he dead? If he was, why would someone go to all the trouble of dragging the corpse through the trees only to leave a blood-soaked house behind? According to what Joe overheard, the police were saying that a fight had ensued and the killer fled with the body to avoid getting caught. Was that what happened?

"I know what you're thinking, Mr K," said Joe, coming to Talanov's side. "I don't want to believe it, either - for your sake. But we've got to look at the facts and Fact One is this: Ferguson is missing. Fact Two: there's a lot of blood and overturned furniture which points toward a fight and serious injury - if not murder altogether. Granted, it's possible he's still alive, and perhaps he's being held as a hostage, although for what reason I can't imagine."

"Perhaps to set a trap to catch me," offered Talanov.

"No need, Mr K. Without Ferguson, you're dead in the water. Fact Three: the same constable who was willing to accept Marshak's reward money is now conveniently missing. Fact Four: Marshak shows up with the police. Conclusion: it doesn't look good for Ferguson, and the Second Thirteen achieves their goal of stopping you."

"Hang on, Joe. We laid in the boot of that taxi for - what - over an hour? That's plenty of time for the constable to get over here, shoot Ferguson, and clean up his mess. But if Ferguson were still alive and being held for questioning, we have a compelling reason for the constable to remove him to the car and drive away. To go back for a clean-up means Ferguson might escape."

"I repeat - why would they need him for questioning? Wouldn't it be easier to deep-six the guy and put an end to their problems?"

"I don't know. Maybe they wanted to make sure he didn't hide copies of his documents or something. All I'm saying is that it's possible."

Joe understood Talanov's need to keep hope alive, and although he did not share that hope, he would not argue the point. "Well if that's the case, we need to follow Marshak when he leaves. If Ferguson's alive, he'll lead us to him."

But in the darkness of a mango tree, a blinding realization hit Talanov like lightning. "My God, we may have been duped."

"Duped? What do you mean?"

"By pushing the recall button on the taxi driver's mobile, they trace the number to this address and send the constable to investigate. He discovers it's Ferguson and either kills him or seriously wounds him. But in order to trap me, they figure we'll try and find Ferguson either by following Marshak or the taxi driver. Remember, we disappeared immediately after our escape from the hut, so I reckon they will have assumed we circled back and talked the taxi driver into taking us to meet Ferguson. Don't forget, it was the driver who smashed the light which set us free. Still, because they couldn't be sure, Marshak accompanied the police to this address to complete the diversion."

"But why go to the trouble of diverting us, especially if they've already killed or captured Ferguson?"

"Either to make sure that we *think* he's dead, or to keep us safely away from where they're questioning him - say, in his house. They could well have taken him back there to search for any incriminating files he may have stashed."

"But if Marshak is here, who's questioning Ferguson? Surely you don't think they'd entrust it to that idiot, the constable."

"I'm afraid not," answered Talanov. "Remember Cheney, the killer I mentioned earlier? It's my guess he'll be tightening some thumb screws on Ferguson."

Suddenly, the glare of headlights scattered through the trees, causing Talanov and Joe to drop to the grassy earth. Within seconds one of the police cars roared past.

"One down, one to go," whispered Joe.

The two men had just started to rise when a second pair of headlights cut through the darkness. Their same reactions were simultaneous and immediate.

But instead of roaring past, this car skidded to a stop near the tree where Alex had been hiding. "Where are you?" the driver called out in a hushed but anxious voice.

Joe leaped to his feet, ran over to the car, and looked inside. "All clear," he called out to Talanov.

"What the hell was *that* for?" the driver said. "Do you think I'd turn on you now?"

"Just making sure," Joe replied as Alex trotted over to the car. "Marshak could have had a gun to your head."

"My God, I hadn't thought of that."

"Well, I did," answered Joe as he rounded the car and hopped into the front seat while Alex climbed slowly into the back.

Once they were on the main road back to Vila, the driver recounted the horror he felt at having seen Madame Li's house in such bloody chaos. "Naturally, the police wanted to know what I was doing there and did I know who might have killed Ferguson. I was in shock but managed to tell them that I was merely one of Ferguson's friends who had stopped by for a visit after taking a friend to the hospital. One of the investigators even telephoned the hospital to verify my story. When that checked out, I was told how the police station had received a call from Ferguson earlier tonight begging them for help, that someone was trying to break in. Smashing glass was then heard, followed by frantic shouts, after which the phone went dead. At that point, the police asked me if I knew where you or the constable were, that both of you had gone missing. Thankfully, I had the presence of mind to say No. Marshak was standing to one side during the questioning but seemed distracted. It looked to me like he was along only for the ride."

"He probably was," replied Talanov. "What else?"

"The police think you did it," the driver said to Alex, glancing in his mirror but seeing only a silhouette. "I heard them talking, and they think you dragged the body through the trees to a waiting car for disposal elsewhere. When I asked if they had any evidence that it was you, they said they did not, but that you were a known killer who had come to Efate to kill Ferguson. The theory is that you planned to kill Ferguson quietly and clean up the house, but that he put up a fight and you got scared. An all-points bulletin has been issued for your arrest."

"I'm not surprised," answered Talanov without inflection.

The driver glanced at the darkened figure sitting in the back seat of his car. "You told me not to say that I'd seen you," he said hesitantly. "And now you're their primary suspect. I could have easily cleared your name."

"I'm glad you didn't," replied Alex, "not with Marshak there. However, in a day or two I'd like you to verify to the police that Joe and I were with you in the boot of your car. Ask the wounded woman to corroborate your story. Even if we've disappeared by then, I want you to file a statement."

"What do you mean, 'disappear'?"

"We may get killed or we might have to run. Either way, I'd like you to file that statement. Will you do that for me? It's important."

"Whatever you say. Where to now?"

"I need sleep and need it badly," Talanov replied, unable to suppress a yawn. "Then, after a few hours, we'll go and search Ferguson's house."

"Want me to go, Mr K?" asked Joe, looking over his shoulder.

Talanov shook his head. "Weariness causes mistakes, Joe, and you've been up much longer than I. Anyway, Marshak is staying there and could return at any time. Tomorrow's a better shot. We'll have to think of a way of diverting him, though, so that we can make a search of the house to see if Ferguson left something behind."

"Such as paperwork relating to the *Reishi Pacific Banking Group?*" asked the driver.

"Anything which gives us a clue."

"We may find more than a clue," said the driver. "Ferguson once told me he made copies of the circular blind documents."

Alex bolted forward in his seat. "*What?*"

"That's right. He suspected something wasn't quite right and said he made duplicates of everything he filed. He then sent the originals to a post office box in Sydney. A little snooping, however, revealed that it had been rented by a Russian diplomat named Sergei Zinyakin."

The news swept away Talanov's weariness like a blast of cold air, and for the next fifteen minutes, the driver recalled everything he could remember from those many afternoons spent with Ferguson on his front porch. Because he had been educated at Berkeley, the taxi driver told how he had quickly earned Ferguson's respect, and because the lawyer tended to talk freely when he was drinking - and since he drank most of the time - he had been the unique recipient of many of Ferguson's confessions.

Talanov sat forward with intense interest, his elbows resting on the top of the seat, both rear windows rolled down to help keep him awake. When the driver finished,

Alex sat back and reflected on what he had learned, which actually wasn't much aside from the startling news that Ferguson had made copies of the circular blind documents. But would they really be of much help since everything had been handled over the phone, with Ferguson's fee arriving in cash? In other words, it appeared Ferguson had no idea why the circular blind had been created nor who was behind it. Beyond that, the driver repeated pretty much what Ivan had told him. What he needed was to examine those documents. The question was: where had Ferguson hidden them? And closely related: had Marshak found them?

The Toyota hit a small pothole and Alex jumped, opening his eyes. How long had he been asleep? He slapped himself lightly in the face and tried to focus. But his surroundings were dark and he once more fell asleep, his head bobbing, then jerking again. "I've got to have rest," said Alex, his eyes already shut.

"You can sleep at my house," offered the driver.

"It's likely to be watched," stated Alex, barely opening his eyes. "Pick a place the police won't suspect."

"At this time of night, about the only other place I can think of is the hut where we tried to trap you."

"And nearly did," said Joe.

"Again, I'm truly sorry," apologized the driver. "But Ferguson was told by the police - who were told by the IDC - that you were coming to kill him. We didn't know that it was a lie. Anyway, the hut will be empty. The wounded woman is, of course, in the hospital and her husband will stay with her through the night. Also, I stacked your belongings on the kitchen counter. They should still be there."

"What about the boys from your posse?" asked Joe. "Two of them still have our guns."

"Most of them are from the village of Malapoa, on the other side of Vila. They will be home and in bed by now."

"I certainly hope so," said Talanov. "There's nothing more embarrassing than getting killed with your own gun."

"Killed with your own gun," repeated Joe. "How embarrassing!"

And Talanov and Joe laughed outright for the first time since coming to the island.

Chapter 44

Talanov opened his blurred eyes to see that he was the only one in the shaded room. The dawn had long ago given way to a bright sunny morning although the forest - especially the large mango trees - shielded the hut from the sun. The sound of trickling water caught Talanov's attention and he slowly sat up, allowing the sleep to clear from what was one of the most disoriented sleeps within memory. He recalled the previous night and how he finally collapsed into bed, not bothering to remove his clothes.

Although the stove was now cold and dark, the room looked much the same as it had when they were here last night as prisoners. The only other exception were some mangos on the counter beside their belongings. After running a hand over his stubbled face - how long had it been since he'd shaved? - Alex stood, his body aching. He walked to the window and heard the sound of trickling water more clearly. Then he heard quiet singing. Joe was taking a shower.

Alex picked up his Wolfgang Hauser passport and stuck it in his pocket. He then picked up his wallet and the loose change he had been carrying. But where was Sergei's bank book? He looked beneath Joe's passport and on the floor. It was nowhere to be found.

With the floorboards squeaking beneath his steps, Alex walked over to the front door and opened it. He stepped outside and frightened away several birds, who flew high into the branches overhead, scolding the intruder for disturbing their day. Aside from the chatter of the birds, the day was peaceful and quiet.

Talanov's thoughts, however, were not so tranquil when he noticed the taxi was gone. *Where was the driver? Didn't he know they needed to get over to Ferguson's house? Why hadn't someone awakened him earlier?*

Alex hurried around the side of the hut and saw a corrugated iron booth attached to the iron siding. A shower head was spraying water unevenly down over Joe as he vigorously lathered his hair. He looked over and noticed Talanov. "Morning, Mr K. There's no hot water, but it doesn't matter, not in this weather. I'll be finished in five and you can have a turn."

"There's no time!" Talanov snapped back. "Why didn't you wake me? And where's the driver? Doesn't he know-"

"Whoa, Mr K - hang on," Joe cut in. "We tried to wake you but you wouldn't budge. So I told Maurice - that's the driver's name - to go grab our things from the Cessna. He should be back here any moment."

Annoyed, Talanov walked back around to the front of the hut and in through the door. He stopped as he entered and looked around the primitive residence, not knowing what to do but wanting to do something... anything to keep himself busy. But with Joe singing in the shower, there was little to do but eat, and admittedly he was quite hungry.

Crossing to the pile of fruit, Alex picked up a ripe mango and, using a kitchen knife, sliced it in half and removed the pit. He then cut a crisscross pattern through the meat, pushed upward on the skin, then ate the protruding cubes of sweet yellow flesh. By the time he finished six more, his face and arms were covered with juice.

"I bet you're deadly with chocolate icing," said Joe with a grin as he strolled into the room. He walked to the counter and noticed the lone mango that remained. "Thanks for saving me one," he grumbled.

Talanov finished licking his fingers, then rinsed his mouth and arms under the tap. "Where in the hell is Maurice?" he asked, his frustration evident in his voice. "We've got to get over to Ferguson's to look for those documents."

"I'm sure you know the odds of finding something aren't good," said Joe. "Marshak has been staying in the house and he's certain to have torn it apart."

"We've got to try."

"We'll give it a go, but don't get your hopes up too high."

"I'm afraid hope's about all that I've got," answered Talanov. "Now where is *Maurice?*"

Outside, a car ground softly to a stop.

Chapter 45

The cellular phone sounded in Cheney's hand as he sat in one of the lounge chairs at Bauerfield airport. "One here," he said into the instrument.

"Tango Blue," a familiar voice announced. "What's the status on Talanov?"

"Dead within the hour," was Cheney's reply as he laid down his newspaper on the empty seat beside him.

"Excellent!" Bob replied with an icy smile of satisfaction. "We can finally proceed." He looked at his watch. "It's evening here in Washington and I've another reception tonight with some senators. Tomorrow I have meetings through dinner but I'll be on the red-eye to London out of Dulles. I'll meet you in Switzerland the following morning."

"Where will we be staying?"

"The Parkhotel, in Zug. They've got a conference center with computer access which we'll use to set up a link with Hong Kong. But call first and reserve us some rooms. Use my name."

"What about Talanov's wife? So long as she's alive, she poses a problem."

Bob smiled again. "I'll get rid of her... problem solved. Tango Blue out."

Chapter 46

Number Three was grinning when he clicked off his mobile phone. "Eliminate immediately," he told Four, who was sitting in the passenger seat of the rented gray Ford.

"I have been waiting for this moment!" replied Four.

The two assassins had arrived before daybreak and parked down the street from Liz Langdon's house. It had been relatively easy to wait for Andrea to be released and then simply follow her. Tango Blue had been right: the crewman's sworn affadavit had assured Mrs Talanov's release.

Four climbed into the back seat of the Ford and opened his black canvas bag. He withdrew an automatic pistol, then a silencer which he screwed onto the end of the barrel. "What is our strategy?" he asked as he pushed a clip of ammunition into the handle and slid back the cocking mechanism. He then brought out an adhesive moustache, which he pressed into place beneath his nose, followed by a wig of closely-cropped hair. A pair of wire-rimmed glasses completed the disguise.

"We will wait here, away from their view," answered Three. "Sooner or later they must leave the house, and when they do, we will shoot them when they pass."

"What if they turn the other way?"

"Then we follow them until you can get a clear shot. Once we are finished, we will abandon the car and take a cab to the airport. Hand me my moustache and wig."

"But now for the fun part," said Four as he rolled down each of the rear windows and placed the pistol in his lap.

The wait was not long, for in less than half an hour, Liz Langdon's car backed out of her carport and paused. Three started the engine just as Andrea came running out the front door of the house and jumped into the car.

"There she is!" said Four, sitting forward just the sedan backed out of the drive and turned the other way. Three immediately started after the sedan.

Liz sped to the corner and made a quick right turn onto Unley Road. Three followed her to the corner but had to wait for a string of cars to pass by before he could bolt across, all the while cursing the fact that Australians drove on the opposite side of the road from Europeans. Pushing the accelerator to the floor, he raced after the two women, speeding through the Cross Road intersection just as the light changed yellow.

"Keep your speed down," Four said from the back seat. "We don't want to be stopped by the police."

"Do your job and I'll do mine," Three snapped back as he changed lanes and passed several cars waiting to make right-hand turns across the oncoming traffic. Whipping by them, he then pulled back into the center lane to avoid a number of parked cars on the left. He was gaining!

Suddenly there were brake lights... *they were slowing down!* "Get ready," Three said.

However, after passing a line of small shops which fronted the road, Liz made a quick left turn into a lane between some buildings which led into a drive-through liquor store. Three slowed and watched her angle right into the service area. Guessing they must exit onto the side street just ahead, he raced to the corner and turned, then quickly pulled over to the curb to wait. Up ahead, a car driven by an old man was emerging from the liquor store exit. Three inched forward and stopped, motioning for the old man to pull out. The man waved his thanks and turned back toward the intersection. Another car then followed, which paused before turning the other way.

With his foot on the brake, Three kept the car in gear and watched as the nose of Liz Langdon's car pulled forward and stopped. An attendant rounded the front of the car and asked what they wanted.

Although he did not have a full view of the two women, Three could see the attendant fetch a bottle of wine from a shelf and take it to the car, accepting some money as he handed over the bottle. Three waited for the car to drive forward.

But the two women were just sitting there! What was going on? Three nervously looked in his rear view mirror, wondering if this was some kind of a trap. Suddenly the attendant reappeared and handed the driver her change. She waved and directed the car forward.

"Slide over to the right side," Three told Four. "If they turn this way, shoot the driver. Then jump out and take care of the bitch."

Four slid across and readied his pistol.

Liz Langdon's car paused before entering the street, then quickly turned left, away from the killers.

"*Shit!*" exclaimed Three as sped after her.

At the corner, Three made a hard right turn and followed the two women back to the main road, where they made a fast right turn, barely pausing to stop.

"She drives like a *maniac!*" Three shouted as he had to wait for several cars to pass before he could turn after her. "She was even talking on her *mobile phone!* I thought that was illegal."

"You're getting stressed," warned Four. "Slow down and drive normal."

"I want to finish this job!"

"So do I. But we won't if we get pulled over."

"I can catch her!" Three said as he sped around a line of cars held up by someone wanting to make a right-hand turn. He could see the heads of the two women, the driver finally finishing her call but continuing to gesture with her hands as she talked.

With his gun in his lap, Four slid across the seat to the left window and nervously watched while they gained on the sedan, then fell behind as their lane of traffic slowed. He mentally cursed the traffic, for not only was it hampering their ability to catch the two women, but it created the problem of witnesses. A few seconds was all he required for the kill, but even a few seconds became dangerous in front of so many people. The disguises, of course, would help, but the glut of cars at this hour seriously threatened their chances of escape.

"I do not like this traffic," said Four. "I think we should go back to the house and wait. When they return, I will take them out."

"And what if she now is changing locations?" countered Three. "We cannot be assured of a second chance." There was a pause. "Look: they are turning into that small shopping center," he said, pointing to their flashing yellow indicator light.

"Luck is with us!" said Four, a smile reappearing on his face. "I will get to see the terrified look in her eyes when she realizes she has been caught."

Three nodded in agreement, his expression then hardening. "I want to see it, too. I still hurt from what she and the karate bitch did to me on board the ship."

"Do you want to handle this assignment?"

"Of course!" said Three.

"Then it is yours."

Smiling, Three clicked on his indicator light and made a left turn into the Unley Shopping Center parking lot, keeping his eye on Liz Langdon's sedan, which pulled into a vacant space near the two-story brick arch that was the main entrance into the small covered mall. A large red plastic WELCOME sign was mounted between the pillars and a few customers were already circulating in and out of the doors.

Three backed the Ford into a parking space beneath a spanning eucalyptus tree near the sidewalk. With the motor idling, the two assassins watched as Liz Langdon opened her car door and stood, her bright copper hair and enormous earrings as loud as the laugh she let out. After slinging her purse over her shoulder, she retorted with a wisecrack, then waved and walked toward the entrance.

"Talanov's wife is still in the car!" exclaimed Three. "Leave the car running, I will not be long."

"Terror," said Four: "don't shoot until you see it in her eyes."

Three nodded as he accepted the pistol and stuck it under his shirt. And with a grin he climbed out of the car.

To mentally plan their escape, Three quickly surveyed their surroundings. There were two exits from the parking lot that he could see: the drive where they came in, and another which opened onto a side street. That exit led either to a stop light back at Unley Road or into an unfamiliar residential area. Too many unknown variables in that direction, thought Three. They would leave by the way they came in.

After a momentary glance at Four, he started toward the sedan, his hand on the grip of his pistol. He could see the back of the Talanov woman's head as she waited for her friend. Approaching the car, Three looked again toward the entrance into the mall. The other woman was nowhere to be seen.

Just a few more steps.

Three did not hear the clicks of the camera. Crouched on the upstairs balcony of the two-story cream-colored building across the street, a South Australian police officer snapped photo after photo through a telephoto lens. Oblivious to what was taking place, more than a dozen people sat with newspapers and coffee in the sidewalk cafe below.

Beside the photographer was Captain Ian Trevillian. He squinted at what was taking place across the street and brought a walkie-talkie to his mouth. "Cat is closing on mouse. Spring the trap."

From the back seat, Four was watching Three and did not see or hear the two plain-clothes officers who quietly made their approach from the rear. He became aware of their presence only when the cold steel of a gun barrel was pressed against his temple through the open window. "Place your hands on top of the seat in front of you," the officer said in a low voice.

The stunned assassin obeyed.

Number Three's eyes were riveted to the back of Andrea Talanov's head. Removing the pistol from under his shirt, he stepped to the side of the car window and pointed the gun at her face, expecting to see a look of startled terror in her eyes.

A mannequin! They pulled a switch in the liquor store!

Whirling around, three saw more than a dozen Star Force police officers, each dressed in black and wearing a bullet-proof vest, appear behind various parked cars, their rifles trained on him. Three looked in all directions. He was completely surrounded.

Glancing toward his rented Ford, Three saw Four being handcuffed by several other policemen.

"Drop your weapon," a voice called out.

Three looked at the officer and dropped his gun.

"Come into the clear and lie down on your stomach, your arms extended," the officer said.

The assassin obeyed, was immediately surrounded, and soon had cuffs on his hands.

"We'll be out by the end of the day," Three said with a chuckle.

Con Kanellopoulos walked over to Three and knelt down, bending his face to the assassin's ear. "I hope you are," he said. "Because once you set foot on these streets, I guarantee you'll disappear into one of my warehouses where you'll discover the versatility of piano wire. And when I'm done, I'll feed your wriggling remains to the ants."

"That's enough, Con," the deep voice of Captain Trevillian told the Greek. He nodded and two officers stood the sobered killer on his feet.

"By the way," said Con, "you clowns are sure lousy at tailing the one person we knew you'd be following. You've been as easy to track as a barium enema. And your smell is about the same."

Three heard a noise behind him and looked around to see a powerful man in a wheelchair. Behind him were two women. The assassin's mouth dropped open when he recognized Spiro, Spiro's wife, and Andrea Talanov.

"Recognize this man?" Trevillian asked the trio.

"He's the man who tried to kill me," Spiro said, looking at Three.

"And that man kidnapped Andrea," added Demetria, pointing at Four as he was brought to the side of his accomplice.

"Yes, Captain, these are the men," agreed Andrea.

Trevillian nodded and smiled. "Lock these bastards away."

Chapter 47

Cheney stood on the upstairs observation deck of the large rectangular metal shed that was the Bauerfield terminal and watched a local flight take off for another island. With the mid-morning sun gentle on his face, he leaned his elbows on the metal railing and followed the craft as it pushed its way up into the bright blue sky and bank slowly to the left, the sound of its twin propellers soon dwindling away in the distance.

His relaxed gaze then wandered over to several tall coconut palms undulating in the last of this year's easterly trade winds. He liked Vanuatu with its unhurried elegance and rustic charm. Perhaps he would return here one day to retire now that this business with Talanov was finished.

It had been uncanny how the bastard had managed to slip away from them time and again. But not this time.

Life had certainly taken its peculiar turns since that night in eighty-three. It is doubtful Andropov realized what he set in motion with the creation of the Second Thirteen. To be sure, had his restructuring plans been allowed to succeed, the Russia of today would not be in such turmoil and decay. The rusting deterioration of their once-formidable military was indicative of a disintegrated empire now groveling for the barest of necessities. While the West climbed to new heights of wealth, Russia sat huddled on the global street corner begging for bread. To make matters worse, crime lords now sold Russia's discarded nuclear arsenal to petty dictators who one day would use it against them.

And yet Andropov seemed to sense that his own plans for *Peristroika* would not succeed. Otherwise, he would not have betrayed them. Cheney clenched his fist at the memory: what had gone wrong? Andropov's instructions had been meticulously followed, with new identities created and concealed even from members of the restructuring committee. No detail had been overlooked.

Why, then, had Andropov double-crossed them? Had the Soviet President somehow perceived the double-cross they had been planning? Did he suspect something when his trusted aide, Talanov, had been manipulated out of the conference? Months later, when it became apparent what Andropov had done, Cheney began to follow the incomplete, often obliterated, threads of evidence which ultimately led him to realize that Andropov had entrusted the future of the Second Thirteen into Talanov's hands. Even more amazing, however, was the fact that Talanov had never been told. Thus began Tango Blue - the new strategy between him and the man known today as Bob Hoskings.

Bob Hoskings! If Talanov only knew.

At first Bob thought Talanov may have the one document in his possession which could destroy their plans. Hence, the fire-bombing of his house. Hence, also, the killing of General Timoshkin, whom Bob thought might be able to warn Talanov about the existence of the document. Instead, the general died warning Talanov about the Second Thirteen, which actually furthered their plans.

But the real goal had always been Talanov's death... Talanov's *certifiable* death, which they now had, or would have shortly. Finally they could proceed.

With his eyes closed, Cheney again leaned on the railing and turned his face toward the sun. Yes, perhaps he would return here one day. Vanuatu offered everything a man in his position could want: sun, seclusion, and a banking system unrivaled for secrecy. What more did one need, except a few of those waitresses with the caramel complexions.

Cheney heard a noise and opened his eyes to see a man standing beside him.

Resting his elbows on the railing, Marshak gazed out at the palm trees Cheney had been watching earlier. "It's a beautiful day, is it not?" he remarked.

"You tell me," was Cheney's reply as he turned to face him.

Marshak looked over at Cheney with a smile. "It is, indeed. I found Ferguson's copy of the circular blind documents concealed inside a frame on his bedroom wall."

"Excellent!"

"I also found Sergei's bank book in a pile of Talanov's belongings. Without it, we can't be traced."

Cheney's approval was evident in his expression. "And Talanov?"

"The police have his body now. They're calling it a brutal murder. He was blown away with a shotgun."

"Is it official?" asked Cheney.

Marshak nodded. "I have his death certificate in my pocket."

Chapter

13

48

Less than thirty minutes after having been handed the signed confessions of the two assassins, Captain Ian Trevillian knocked on the front door of Liz Langdon's house. It should have been joyful news he was bringing, for the two statements effectively cleared Talanov of all charges against him. But on the same day that his name had been cleared, news arrived from the Vanuatu police that Alex had been murdered. And Trevillian was not sure how to break the news to Talanov's wife.

The front door was opened by Con, who looked twice at the grave expression on Trevillian's face. Con stepped outside and closed the door. "What is it, Ian?"

"Talanov's dead," he said, removing his cap as a gesture of respect, his eyes then looking up and away as he sighed wearily at yet another senseless death and the heartache it would produce. In spite of all the violence he had seen in his years on the force, he had never grown used to the tragedy of untimely death, whether in a traffic accident, through domestic abuse, or by the cold brutality of murder.

"How did it happen?" Con asked quietly.

"Shotgun. Tore him apart. The Vanuatu authorities suspect one of their constables of having done it. They're searching the islands for him now."

"Holy shit," whispered Con as he leaned back against the faded red brick of the house. He ran a hand through his thick silver hair and shook his head. "Telling his wife isn't going to be easy."

"Want me to handle it?" asked Trevillian.

Con shook his head. "I'll do it... I'm just not sure how."

"I've had to do it - a number of times, in fact - and I can tell you there *is* no right way to inform the victim's family. Be direct, be gentle, let her cry. It's the crying that really helps."

Trevillian was reaching for the door handle of his white patrol car when he heard the thickened shriek. He paused and looked back at the house, the screams then rising into uncontrollable wails which rose and fell with each rending of the heart. With an instinct he did not understand, Trevillian looked up, hoping whoever was up there would somehow help her through this.

13 Chapter 49

Andrea was finally given a sedative but was asleep only because she had no strength left for crying. Numbed and speechless, Spiro and Demetria sat at the antique dining room table with Liz, their eyes red and swollen, Spiro's large hands covering his face. At the other end of the table, Liz rested her forehead against one fist, while in a stuffed chair in the attached family room, Con stared up at the ceiling.

Demetria wiped her eyes with a tissue, wishing she could turn back the clock and slide a bowl of lamb stew in front of Alex. Like a persistent child, he considered his blatant hints somehow discreet. The man had been a bottomless pit when it came to her cooking and Demetria loved him for it. The joy of the kitchen would never be the same.

Sitting next to his wife, Spiro found it easy to recall the good times with Alex although, in truth, they were not all so good. Even so, Spiro could not remember specifically which issue had divided them although his refusal to compromise on the matter had infuriated Alex. The memory of that night still lacerated him with remorse and he could vividly recall the anger in Talanov's eyes as he stormed out of the restaurant, never to return until the night of Helena's wedding. Interestingly, it was that same uncompromising nature which Talanov ultimately trusted.

Spiro recalled the look in Talanov's eyes and how it confirmed his convictions, in spite of all that was being said in the media. He simply would not accept the notion that Alex was guilty, and like brothers they had fought to prove it. But then, just when his name had been cleared, some monster had gunned him down. And the bitterness of the irony was almost unbearable.

For Con it was likewise the bitterest of ironies. Trevillian and his team had worked hard and fast to break the assassins, using the tiniest differences in the two testimonies to create a schism of fear and suspicion, the cracks then masterminded into a gulf as one was played expertly against the other. Finally, in an effort to be the first to negotiate a reduced charge in exchange for the truth, Number Four confessed how Three had directed the murders in Talanov's home. He went on to explain how Three had also been the one who killed the policeman the night the house was burned, and how Fiona Zinyakin had been the one who bludgeoned her husband to death. When asked why Talanov's death was so important, Four admitted it was for money and that Tango Blue had promised them lots. When questioned about the identity of Tango Blue, Four stated that he did not know. No names - only numbers - were used. The only other information gleaned from the assassin was that he and Three were to meet the others in Zug, Switzerland.

Four's confession was, of course, relayed to Three, and fearing that he would be saddled with the blame, Three responded with a similar confession which detailed Four's involvement. In the end, Trevillian felt that he had enough evidence to justify an interdepartmental recommendation to clear Talanov of the charges against him. The New South Wales police concurred and Talanov was immediately cleared.

Then he was murdered.

Con shook his head. Sometimes, life wasn't fair.

"Does anybody want coffee?" Liz asked awkwardly as she walked to the electric kettle and pushed a button on its handle.

No one answered.

"I will," stated Andrea as she entered the room.

Everyone looked over at her with surprise.

Although the skin around Andrea's eyes was still swollen from crying, the eyes themselves were no longer red. Her hair was pulled back in a ponytail and she wore a loose denim work shirt hanging down over a pair of black tights. "I've decided to go after them," she announced to the sound of water beginning to boil. She walked over to the sink for a mug and for a moment stood looking out the kitchen window. "Those bastards made the biggest mistake of their lives when they killed the one person who gave meaning to my life. Whatever it takes, I'll make them pay." She turned and glanced quickly at Spiro. "And no bullshit about love and forgiveness," she said, handing her mug to Liz. "I can't - I'll *never* - forgive them."

Spiro did not reply.

"What will you do?" asked Demetria worriedly. "Those men are trained *assassins*."

Andrea looked over at Con. "Did I hear you mention Switzerland?"

"I knew you weren't really asleep," Con replied. "Trevillian said one of the assassins made a statement about Zug. It's a town between Zurich and Lucerne."

"Well that's where I'll be going," said Andrea.

Demetria turned to Spiro. "*Say* something. Those men will kill her!"

Andrea walked over to the table and sat across from Spiro and Demetria. "I'm sorry I yelled at you, Spiro, but please don't try and stop me. This is something I've got to do." She took their hands in hers. "And, yes, you're right: I'm not trained for this sort of thing and I'm liable to get myself killed. But they just murdered half of my soul and what's left is bitter and angry. I know you love people - that's your gift - and if I come out of this alive, I'll be back because I'll need lots of love. In the meantime, these bastards are mine. Aside from that, I want you to know that Alex loved you. He was never very good at telling people - me included - but I know without doubt that he felt it." Andrea squeezed their hands affectionately and Demetria started to cry.

"Are you sure you can do this?" asked Liz, joining them at the table with two mugs of coffee. She placed one in front of Andrea. "I don't doubt you have the motivation, but Demetria raised a good point. Those men are trained assassins."

"When I was a prisoner on board that ship, my anger helped me survive. Anger, coupled with the influence of my husband, gave me the ability to fight, and it amazed me how easily I began forming strategies, calculating weaknesses, controlling my emotions in order to beat them. Qualities that I used to despise in Alex had somehow become my backbone, and only now am I beginning to understand the burden he carried. So you ask me if I can do this? The same rage that allowed me to pull the trigger once will enable me to carry this through."

"You're one tough bird," said Liz with a shake of her head.

"Not tough, just mad as hell," Andrea replied. "And it's the anger that's giving me strength." She looked over at Spiro. "I don't mean to offend you, but that's the way I feel."

Spiro smiled sadly at Andrea. "I think you misunderstand me. I, too, feel anger because Alexi was someone I loved. And like you, I want them stopped."

"Then how can you be so calm?" she demanded.

"Don't be so hasty to judge me," Spiro replied. "Your anger burns bright, but mine runs deep. Unfortunately, I am in no condition to go with you."

"I'll go, you know that," said Con as he approached the table. "Just say the word." He drew back a chair and sat.

Andrea smiled at Con appreciatively, then looked at Spiro. "I'm sorry... I had no right."

"Are there family members who should be informed?" asked Spiro.

"My parents, of course, in Perth, and Alex has a brother in Europe. I'll call my mother. She has his number and can make the call."

"Tell her we will help in any way possible. Give her Con's number, plus Lizzie's and mine. Naturally, I will cover any expenses to bring Alexi's body home."

Suddenly feeling guilty, Andrea lowered her head.

Spiro reached over and placed his calloused hand on top of Andrea's. Looking up, Andrea saw an understanding smile on Spiro's tired face. Yet in spite of his many weathered lines, there was also a deep strength which soared above his wearied condition. Andrea recalled the man who had strode into the center of the room the night of Helena's wedding. His presence was commanding, and yet it was neither his physique nor his personality that had drawn Alex back. It was something far greater.

"So what would you do?" Andrea asked.

Spiro's smile faded. "The defeat of evil comes at a price," he replied. "Our last world war testifies to that, and the blood has continued to flow, not only on the battlefield, but in bedrooms, on street corners, and in cities around the world. Alexi knew better than any of us about the effects of violence. Even when there is no alternative, it still leaves us with scars. Your husband was not a violent man, but he was trained in its ways. And the knowledge of those ways both protected him and haunted him. So to answer your question: what would I do?" Spiro paused, then spoke slowly in a voice deep with conviction: "I, too, would pursue them. Once again, though, I urge you not to misunderstand: I take no pleasure in the defeat of an enemy, but sometimes their defeat is required."

"But *how* do I defeat them?" she asked.

"Ask Alexi," said Spiro gently. "He lives in your heart, in your mind. Allow his strength and wisdom to teach you. Just remember - justice is one thing, vengeance another, so take care that you don't become like them. If you do, then their evil lives on."

Andrea buried her face in her hands. *Oh, Alex, what should I do? How can I go this alone?*

Chapter
50

Maurice gunned his taxi after making a sliding U-turn and shot a spray of crushed coral out behind. The Toyota skidded back and forth several times before gaining traction on the main road back to town.

Hearing the news on the radio had stunned him. Talanov... *dead?* Maurice could not believe it and so raced back to Vila as fast as his vehicle would take him. Once there, he rushed into police headquarters only to be told that the body had indeed been identified as one Aleksandr Talanov, with a death certificate having been issued.

Maurice stared at the young white officer. "Are you sure?" he asked.

An affirmative nod was his reply. "We had a positive I-D."

Numbed by the news, Maurice turned to go, then approached the officer again to ask how a death certificate could be issued so quickly.

"That is not my department," the officer replied. "You will need to inquire in Home Affairs."

So it was true, Maurice thought as he walked out of the building: *Alex was dead*. Sickened by the news, he made his way over to the office of Home Affairs in the Civil Status Building, where a tall black woman again confirmed Talanov's death, informing him that although the victim's face had been obliterated by a shotgun blast, Major Pyotr Marshak of the International Development Council was able to make a positive identification based on the victim's passport, clothing, and body size.

Marshak, thought Maurice bitterly, knowing he must be chuckling with delight in some bar.

With his sickened feeling now giving way to anger, Maurice again thought about the death certificate and asked the woman how one could have been issued so quickly. She replied that since the major had been the one who identified the body, and since he held a ranking position with the IDC, it was the least she could do for the gentleman since he said he needed it before boarding this morning's flight. After mumbling his thanks, Maurice left the building.

So Marshak was leaving Vila now that Talanov was dead. Maurice shook his head and climbed into his taxi, slumping down in the seat, discouraged. The sickened feeling was returning, along with a growing sense of guilt. *Perhaps if he had not left Alex and Joe alone-*

Maurice suddenly lurched forward. My God, what about *Joe?* he thought as he started the engine. Within minutes he was speeding out of town.

For Maurice, time and distance were like drunken distortions, and in what seemed like seconds and yet an eternity, he was bringing the taxi to a halt in front of the corrugated iron hut. He turned off the ignition and sat listening to the unnerving silence around him. Reluctant to go inside for fear of what he might find, Maurice remained seated in his vehicle, his forehead resting against the worn black steering wheel, his eyes focused on nothing in particular as he squinted instead at some unanswered questions.

The first question was easy: had Marshak been the one who killed Alex? The second was not: had Joe been involved? Earlier that morning, Joe had asked him to go back to the Cessna to pick up their things. Had that been part of some premeditated plan, or had Joe anticipated trouble and used the request to send him to safety? If so, was Joe dead, too? If not, was he with Marshak?

The fact that Marshak was leaving confirmed the achievement of his objective. The question was - *was Marshak the killer?* For in the wake of hearing that he was indeed leaving, Maurice wondered how he could have murdered Alex way out here, transported the body back to town for identification, then requested and received a death certificate - all in the space of one hour, or the time it had taken Maurice to drive to Bauerfield Airport, town, and back. Which brought up the question of Joe's involvement.

"Hey, whatcha doing?" a voice asked.

Maurice leaped with fright and, with an ashen face, turned to see Joe grinning in at him, then pulling back quizzically.

"You look like you've seen a ghost," said Joe.

"My God, it's *you!*" exclaimed Maurice, wishing now he had locked the door.

"Of course, it's me," replied Joe. "But I'd better warn you, Alex is pissed. He wants to get over to Ferguson's. Like *now*."

"You mean, he's not *dead?*" asked Maurice, grabbing the handle and opening the door.

Joe chuckled and stepped back to let Maurice out. "Thirty seconds ago he wasn't. Are you sure you're all right?"

Ten minutes later, a frantic Maurice had explained everything to Alex and Joe.

"So Marshak is *gone?*" asked Talanov.

"That's what they told me in Home Affairs," answered Maurice. "The clerk said he was catching a flight."

"Son of a gun, they've called off the hunt!" exclaimed Joe.

"So it appears," replied Alex thoughtfully. "The trouble is: *why?* If I were dead, I could see the logic. But I'm not, so why is he leaving?"

"Isn't it possible he mistook the corpse for you?" asked Maurice. "I was told Marshak was the one who made the identification."

"But you said a minute ago that Marshak made that identification based on body size and clothing," replied Alex, "and that my passport was found on the victim. If I remember correctly, my passport was seized by one of the customs officials while searching our plane for drugs. For it to then end up on a dead body which Marshak identifies to be me means he must have acquired it from that official and then planted it. Which to me indicates he knew very well what he was doing, although for what reason I couldn't tell you. It makes no sense for them to devote all this time and energy into trying to kill me only to be satisfied with a body they know is not mine."

"But if Ferguson's the dead man, then maybe they figure they don't need to kill you," said Joe. "Maybe he was the remaining weak link, and now that he's out of the way, they know they're home free. That would fit with what happened last night at Madame Li's: Cheney broke in, murdered Ferguson, then dragged his body away for disposal."

"It makes sense," agreed Maurice, "and explains why Marshak is leaving."

Talanov walked to a window. "If it was a simple matter of killing Ferguson, why go to the trouble of planting my passport on the body just so Marshak can make a false identification? They've got to know the whole scenario will fall apart once I come forward." He turned at looked at the others. "Why not simply put a bullet in Ferguson - or whoever it was they killed - then leave the body and let Marshak saddle me with the blame? They were sure as hell blaming me last night. Why not this morning?"

"I didn't know we needed to burrow so deep on this," said Joe. "Hell, if they're satisfied enough to give up on trying to kill you, why knock the gift horse in the mouth?"

"Because so long as they're allowed to continue toward their goal - whatever it is - then I'm still a potential threat. Sure, for now they may consider me marginalized enough to let go. But who's to say they won't come back? Or go after my wife? Or go after you? Maybe this is just a ruse in order to bring me out into the open."

"Damn, I never thought of all that," said Joe.

"Well, I have to," stated Talanov as he walked away from the window. "I have to keep well ahead of them."

"So what are you going to do?" asked Maurice.

"Go and search Ferguson's house," replied Alex. "Marshak has probably ripped it apart, but there could well be something he missed."

"Let's hope so," said Joe.

Chapter 51

Ferguson's house looked the same, at least on the outside, and a pleasant on-shore breeze was orchestrating the movements of the palm trees in a slow rhythmic dance. Although Marshak was supposed to be gone, Talanov and Joe concealed themselves in some shrubbery near the main road while Maurice drove down to the house and knocked on the front door. When there was no answer, Maurice located Ferguson's spare key concealed in the thorns of the bougainvillea and used it to unlock the door. A quick glance inside sent Maurice running to signal the others.

Within minutes the three men were standing speechless in Ferguson's living room. Hundreds of books had been pulled from their shelves and all chairs and tables had been turned over. In some cases, pieces of furniture had been slashed open or dismantled, and in the kitchen, the refrigerator had been cleared and overturned, with all canisters emptied of their contents. Drawers had been removed, as had all pans from beneath the counter.

Ferguson's bedroom, however, was different. Nothing had been touched with the exception of a framed photo of Ferguson holding a large fish. The picture had been disassembled, then dropped on the floor.

"We're too late," said Talanov, kneeling down and examining the remains. "Ferguson must have hidden the documents here."

"And Marshak found them," added Joe.

Talanov nodded and stood. "Which is why it was unnecessary for him to tear apart the rest of the room."

"What now?" asked Joe.

"There's nothing we *can* do," Alex replied. "I don't have Sergei's bank book, so I can't trace that number, and we don't have Ferguson's documents. Sure, the bad guys are letting me live, but they've disappeared without a trail. All my wife and I can do now is go into hiding and hope they never find us."

"Where will you go... what will you do?" asked Maurice.

"I can't go back to Australia. Our only option is to take what remaining money we have and make a start elsewhere with new identities."

Discouraged, the three men walked silently out of Ferguson's house and paused on the front porch while Maurice locked Ferguson's house. Down on the beach, ribbons of froth washed up on the sand while some seagulls darted above in erratic movements. After replacing the key in the bougainvillea, Maurice joined Alex and Joe, who had been absently watching the birds, neither man knowing what to say, any joy about the departure of the killers dashed by the grim fact that they could reappear at any time. Having to look over one's shoulder for the remainder of one's life was not a burden Alex wanted to carry.

Shoving his hands in his pockets, Alex followed Maurice and Joe to the taxi.

"Where to?" asked Maurice as they reached the car.

"Find me a phone, I'll call Andrea," Alex said with a weary sigh as he opened his door and climbed in. The other two did the same.

Starting the engine, Maurice pulled away from Ferguson's house, the tires crunching on the coral gravel as they drove up the lane and turned onto the main road back to town. "Here, use my mobile," he said, picking up his phone and glancing at Alex in the mirror. "That way no one will recognize you standing at a box." He held it back over his shoulder.

"I'll reverse the charges," said Talanov, reaching for it.

"Don't worry about it," said Maurice. "Just switch it on and dial."

But at the moment Alex accepted the instrument, it sounded. Surprised, Talanov handed it back and Maurice switched it on, placing it to his ear. "Maurice here," he answered, after which he screamed and swerved over onto the shoulder of the road, nearly hitting a tree before he stopped. "What did you say?" he shouted into the phone.

"Yes, Maurice, this is Maxwell Ferguson," the familiar voice said again. "Am I catching you at a bad time?"

Chapter 52

Although her eyes were closed, Andrea could not sleep as she again shifted in the airplane seat and rearranged the gray woollen blanket around her. The mask and earplugs helped seal out flashes and sounds of the movie, but the real culprit was her mind, which was far too active.

She had refused the quick slumber a few vodkas offered, not wanting the mental sluggishness that came with them. Admittedly, she was frightened at what lay ahead. But while that was indeed the case, she felt a growing confidence because of her rage. That rage was her strength, and she did not want it distorted by alcohol.

It had been an emotional farewell back in Adelaide. Spiro was still in his wheelchair and her kneeling down to kiss him goodbye had brought tears to them all. Andrea then hugged Demetria and Liz for what each of them knew could be the last time. She then joined Con in the car and the two of them drove away, Andrea waving a final time as they turned the corner.

There had been a lot to do and their first stop was the Central Market, where two muscular young men ran out of a wide delivery entrance and climbed into the back seat of the sedan. Con spoke quickly to them in Greek and all three laughed as he pulled away from the curb.

"What did you tell them?" asked Andrea.

"I told them they will soon have to look ugly and mean," he replied.

"Why did that make them laugh?"

"Because they are both studying to be youth workers. But I want them with us because they lift weights, and where we're going, we may need some muscle."

The next stop was at a beauty salon where Andrea's long brown hair was cut into a shag, then dyed a strawberry blonde, then moused into place. A pair of blue-framed glasses were then added and in forty-five minutes they were back in the car.

For their final stop, Con turned left onto Hindley Street, the tawdry neon district of Adelaide known for its tattoo parlors and easy sex. City officials had long wanted to improve the look of the strip, but in spite of a number of upgrades, it retained an image of sleaze. Loud video arcades and dark cafes lined the narrow street and offered their respective enticements. Extending west from Rundle Mall - a pedestrian thoroughfare of trendy boutiques and department stores - the fast-food grime of Hindley Street was a direct contrast to Rundle Mall's fashionable appeal. And yet while their differences outdistanced any similarities, the two districts lived in relative harmony with one another, the one more active during the day, the other well into the night.

Con pulled into a parking space near a small Lebanese cafe. A pair of police officers strolled past them on the sidewalk, conversing casually while keeping a watchful eye on a boisterous group of teenagers across the street.

With the two muscular Greeks walking behind with frowns on their faces, Con led Andrea down the block toward a tattoo parlor. After a quick word from Con, the two Greeks entered the shop first and parted a company of motorcycle gang members standing in the doorway. Inside, they were met by a short muscular man with thinning brown hair pulled back into a ponytail. He wore a snug white t-shirt and stretch blue jeans which emphasized his broad shoulders and narrow waist. He glanced at the two Greeks, then at Con, giving Andrea but a passing glance.

"What can I do for ya?" he asked, his eyes on Con. "Tattoo for the little lady?"

"We're here to see Phil," Con replied, glancing around the store.

"Do you have an appointment?"

With a cautious eye on two gang members who were browsing nearby, Con looked back at the muscular attendant. "My name's Con and Phil's expecting us."

The attendant walked over behind the counter and picked up a concealed telephone. Within moments he was conversing into it quietly.

Inching nearer to Con, Andrea looked nervously around her. On the wall of the narrow shop were hundreds of tattoo designs, all in blue ink, some accented with red or green. Next to several styles of roses were a variety of demonic figures, skulls, and mythical creatures, while nearby were the more familiar emblems of motorcycles and cars. Looking toward the front of the shop, Andrea noticed an array of articles in the front window. In the center of the window were two mannequins. One was dressed in leather lingerie, while the other wore revealing black silk. Scattered around them were leather masks, straps, handcuffs, various flavored massage creams, all of which were designed to heighten or create sexual fantasy.

"Phil says you can go right up," the muscular attendant told Con, replacing the phone and pushing a button which activated an electronic lock. "Through that door and up the stairs."

Con nodded his thanks and led the way to a panel in the wall which had sprung open slightly. Pulling it open fully, he started up a narrow flight of stairs, a single bulb on the landing above casting forty watts of anemic light down upon them.

The dirty wooden stairs looked like they should squeak and they did, and soon the four visitors were standing before an enameled red door. Con knocked once and then opened it without waiting for a reply.

"Well look what the cat dragged in!" said a buxomed woman with teased hair the color of creamed wheat. She was dressed in leopard tights and took a final puff on her cigarette before crushing it out in an ashtray piled high with other butts encircled with bright red lipstick. She had been seated behind a large mahogany desk scattered with papers. Nearby were two mobile telephones. "Nice to see you, Con," Phil said as she stood and stepped forward for Con to kiss her on the cheek. "Am I finally going to get you together with one of my girls?"

"I'm married, Phil, you know that," replied Con. "So why offer me burger when I've got steak at home?"

"I could have killed Paul Newman for that remark," Phil replied with an annoyed scowl. She then turned her eyes onto the two young Greeks. "But what about these pretty boys of yours?" she asked, flashing a flirtatious smile their way. "Want to lend them to me for the night?"

The two young men looked nervously at one another, then at Con. Seeing their reaction, Phil let out a raspy laugh, then pushed by them and spread herself out in a stuffed green velvet chair next to a fully-stocked liquor cart. "Any of you want a drink?" she asked, pouring herself a tumbler full of bourbon.

Con declined and ushered Andrea to a matching green velvet couch across from Phil, then sitting beside her. The two young Greeks took up standing positions behind them.

"You said on the phone you needed my help," Phil said after taking a large swallow of the bourbon. "I presume this means the bird is in some kind of trouble?" Phil asked, glancing at Andrea, then looking back at Con.

"She needs a passport," Con explained.

"One-way or return? Returns take time and money, and Aussie immigration is a lot tougher these days. Damn computers."

"It doesn't need to get her back in," answered Con. "For now, just get her out."

"One-way, then," said Phil. "Any country? I've got a Nigerian I can let you have cheap."

"Come on, Phil. You can do better than that."

"Don't tell me you want American?"

"I wouldn't say no."

"Bloody hell, Con. And I suppose you want this yesterday?"

Con smiled. "So she can leave on this evening's flight. I'd be most appreciative."

"How appreciative?"

"Probably not as much as you'd like."

Huddled in her airline seat beneath a gray blanket, Andrea smiled at the memory. Phil certainly knew how to forge passports. Or, more precisely, a pair of graphic artists two blocks away knew how to forge them as they traded jokes while performing intricate surgery with photos and paper. The result was a United States passport which enabled Andrea to now be on board a flight to London as Natalie Cox.

Andrea thought back to the words spoken by Alex the night of Helena's wedding: *If we're to live, we need to vanish... vanish from the face of the planet.*

On that occasion, Spiro had talked them into staying.

But not this time. This time Alex was right. She needed to vanish... to go deep, become invisible. Therefore, in both name and appearance, she was no longer Andrea Talanov. Now she was Natalie Cox, and as such, she would travel to Switzerland and find the murderers of her husband.

And once she found them, she would kill them.

Chapter 53

"Maxwell, where the hell *are* you?" Maurice shouted into his phone.

"Easy there, Mate," Ferguson replied. "I'm at thirty-something-thousand feet with a single-malt in one hand and this damn airplane phone in the other. Destination unknown, at least as far as you're concerned."

"But... but we thought you were *dead*."

"Nearly was, thanks to that APB from the IDC about Talanov coming to kill me. The next day, some tall military bastard - Talanov, I presume - got off the plane and started asking questions. One of the guards at the airport called me about him, and I knew then my circular blind activities had landed me in deep shit. That's when I went out to Madame Li's to finalize my plan."

"Plan? What plan?" asked Maurice. Over the phone, he could hear the clinking of ice in a glass.

"Sorry to have kept it from you, old boy," Ferguson said after taking a swallow of his scotch, "but I really couldn't have you involved, not that I didn't want to. You're about the best mate a man could have. But I couldn't allow Talanov to place you in his sights, so I faked my own murder. Some poor rooster was the sacrificial victim. I hated to deprive his hen house, but I needed blood and lots of it. And certainly not my own."

"But Talanov wasn't the danger. It was a group of assassins connected to the IDC. In fact, Talanov's with me right now. He's being hunted by the same lot wanting to kill you. We were just in your home looking for those copies of the circular blind documents you told me you made. They were Talanov's last hope of tracking down the killers. Unfortunately, Major Marshak - he's the military guy you mentioned - turned your home inside-out and found them behind that photo of you and the fish."

"Damn good eating, that fish," said Ferguson as he finished his drink.

"*Maxwell*... what are you going to *do?*" asked Maurice.

"Order me another double. Hang on a sec."

"He's ordering another *drink*," Maurice explained with exasperation while shaking his head in disbelief. "Do you know what this means? It means Ferguson's *not dead!*"

"I gathered that," replied Talanov. "May I talk with him?"

Maurice stared at Alex and held his gaze while he considered the request. His protective instincts said No. But Ferguson was well beyond danger now and a telephone conversation was all that Talanov had wanted, anyway. Still, he hesitated for fear that Ferguson might inadvertently reveal his whereabouts and again place himself in danger.

"Mo... you there?" asked Ferguson.

"I'm here," answered Maurice guardedly.

"You say Talanov's with you right now?"

"That's correct. But-"

"Put him on," Ferguson cut in. "I may have something that will help him."

Maurice looked slowly over at Alex and held out the phone. "He says he wants to talk with you."

Talanov put the phone to his ear. "Mr Ferguson, this is Alex Talanov."

"Max will do," said Ferguson. "I understand you were trying to locate my copy of the circular blind documents."

"I was hoping those documents could shed some light on why a group of assassins wanted you to create a circular blind. Unfortunately, one of them has already taken your copy and disappeared."

"First of all, I hid those documents in a place where I knew they'd find them."

"Where they would *find them?*" asked Talanov with incredulity.

"That's right. I figured they would assume I'd made myself a copy, so I needed to let them find that copy in order to relieve the pressure to kill me. Then I faked my own death in order to make *damn* sure they'd leave me alone, which is why I'm alive and on this flight. Second, I just happened to have made myself another copy."

Alex was stunned. "A *second copy?*"

"Yes, and they're here in front of me. Literally, I might add, for I just took them out of my briefcase." Ferguson paused and thanked the flight attendant for bringing him another drink. "Now, to answer your question about the purpose of the circular blind. It is - quite simply - to prevent a traceable flow of funds. The blanks you need to fill in are why these assassins would want me to do that, and whose money they would be laundering."

"Launder, as in illegal drugs?"

"Possibly, but not necessarily. The source of the funds could be completely legal."

"Do you know the identities of any of the people who hired you?"

"No, everything was handled anonymously by phone and I was paid in cash."

"For a while I was in possession of a small bank book which belonged to Sergei Zinyakin, a Russian diplomat - now deceased - who was associated with the killers. It was for an account with the *Reishi Pacific Banking Group*, but had only one hundred dollars in it. Do your documents reveal anything about that account and what its purpose might be?"

"I'm afraid not," said Ferguson. "My documents merely created a financial structure which prevents funds being traced beyond the circular blind. Even in this day of electronic transfers, the circular blind obliterates the transaction trail from source to destination, and vice versa. You, for example, obtained Mr Zinyakin's account number - a destination - and traced it back to the circular blind. But that is where your journey ends. There is no way you can travel beyond the circular blind to the source."

"Then I'm dead in the water," said Talanov.

Ferguson took a long drink of his scotch and, with a smile, savored its flavor. "Well, not exactly," he said, dabbing his mouth with a starched linen napkin. "I happen to know the source."

Talanov sat forward. "You *do?*"

"Yes, although what I'm about to tell you may create more problems than it solves. In fact, it's downright absurd." Ferguson took another swallow and lowered his voice. "The source is an account with the banking giant, Credit Suisse, in the town of Zug. And not just any account, but a numbered, double-alpha account. The type which holds *very* large sums of money. As in multiplied millions."

Millions! At the mention of the word, Talanov again saw himself standing in a secret conference with Yuri Andropov. Across the table, a Russian banker - that's right, his name was Georgi Vaskin! - had just announced a deposit of seven million dollars. He then thought about what Sergei had shouted shortly before Fiona killed him - that he had worked too long and hard to allow Andropov's double-cross to succeed - the implication being that he, Alex, was Andropov's double-cross or somehow associated with it! Coupled with what Ferguson had just told him about a secret account in Switzerland, was it possible Andropov transferred the seven million dollars into his name? Had the Second Thirteen been trying to kill him merely to access those funds? Is *money* what this is about? If so, does a transfer document exist, and was the destruction of such a document the reason assassins had fire-bombed his house?

"Mr Talanov, are you there?" Ferguson asked.

"Sorry, I was merely trying to extract some meaning from all of this madness," replied Talanov, again focusing on the present. He then relayed to Ferguson what he had been thinking, including a brief history of events since the night of the massacre. "But what I can't understand is why they put so much time and energy into trying to kill me, only to suddenly call the whole thing off. As crazy as it sounds, it looks like Marshak planted my passport on a faceless corpse which he then identified to be me. It doesn't fit."

"I'm afraid that part of the puzzle does fit," said Ferguson.

"What do you mean?"

"More important than your death was *verification* of your death."

"But why, when it's a lie?"

"That doesn't matter," answered Ferguson. "Verification was what they wanted. Oh, sure, they tried killing you at first, but from what you just told me, you kept slipping away even though they managed to freeze your funds and kidnap your wife. However, in Vanuatu opportunity knocks. Assuming me to be dead and thinking themselves to be in possession of my only copy of the circular blind documents, they blast the face off of some poor bugger, identify that person to be you, then ask for and get a certificate of your death."

"Which - to repeat - doesn't make sense. Why go to all that trouble only to settle for a piece of paper they know is a lie and which can easily be disproved once I come forward."

"Because they're figuring you won't come forward, at least not anytime soon since you're still wanted by the police. For their purposes, they're quite content to settle for that piece of paper - which, although false, *is still official*."

"But what's the point?"

"The point is this: an official certificate of death satisfies the requirements of Swiss law, which can then allow funds originally placed under your guardianship to be transferred to someone else. Swiss law, which is based on Roman rather than Anglo-Saxon law, dictates that the guardianship of an account is fixed unless surrendered by the guardian or upon verification of the guardian's death. In your case, Andropov must have nominated you as guardian of the account by means of a power of attorney. Hence, although the assassins could not manage to kill you, they happened upon a situation which satisfied their needs."

"My *God*, it *does* fit together," stated Talanov. "They killed General Timoshkin - a dying man - probably because they thought he knew about the power of attorney and could warn me in the event they missed killing me and I started asking questions. He didn't know anything about it, though, and used his dying breath to warn me about that which he *did* know but what was actually no longer in existence - the Second Thirteen. Thus, he inadvertently presented them with a diversion which kept attention off of their real purpose of stealing that money. I've been such a *fool!*"

"Go easy on yourself, Mr Talanov," said Ferguson. "No fool could have done what you've done."

"I've got to stop them, which I can do by presenting myself to the officials at Credit Suisse. That account is my way of stopping them!"

"Are you sure you want to do that?" asked Ferguson. "It's preposterous to risk your life for what's in that account."

"Seven million dollars is hardly preposterous," replied Talanov. "People have been killed for a pair of Nike shoes, so it's not unreasonable to regard this much money as sufficient motivation."

"That's true," said Ferguson, speaking softly but very clearly. "Unfortunately, there's no money in that account. I know that for a fact because I recently telephoned Credit Suisse, and after quoting the alpha-numeric sequence to the accounts manager, made a request for verification of funds."

"Are you saying there's no money *at all?*"

"That's exactly what I'm saying. That account, Mr Talanov, has a zero balance... it's completely empty. So you may want to think twice about going to Zug. Because when those killers find out they've been chasing a mirage, they may come looking for you again."

Chapter 54

Nothing, *nothing*, made sense, thought Alex as he sat on the old wooden chair in front of the corrugated iron hut. So much killing for an empty account... an empty account which might well revive the assassins' determination to kill him once they discovered the truth. His only alternative was to run.

At least that's what Ferguson had told him and his suggested plan was simple: while the killers were en route to Zug, he should bring Andrea to Vila. The two of them could then call on an old friend of Ferguson's who would be able to forge some new passports. The cost, of course, would be considerable. But the final product would enable them to make a new start in some other country.

Ferguson's logic made sense, for even if the seven million dollars were still in Switzerland, it was not worth the loss of their lives.

So why couldn't he accept the package? Perhaps it was because of that poor bastard lying in the morgue with his face blown off. Perhaps it was because he and Andrea would still have to live the remainder of their lives always wondering if they had been tracked. Perhaps it was because of Ivan, Spiro, and Gail, and all of the others who had been victimized by these killers. Alex knew that he had to fight. He could not simply disappear.

In going after them, Alex knew his biggest advantage was the element of surprise. Thinking Ferguson to be dead, there was no reason for the assassins not to think they had isolated themselves behind the protection of their circular blind. *But if killers have a potential weakness, it is in the blind spot created by their weapons. One can easily become careless when heavily armed or with a feeling of unquestioned advantage.*

Alex thought about what he had learned so long ago at Balashikha. A feeling of unquestioned advantage had certainly caused them to become careless this time, and in doing so, they had allowed him to live, not considering him a danger to their plans.

But Alex was very much alive and knew their account number, the name of their bank, and its location.

What he had not yet figured out, though, was *why*. Why were they going to all this trouble for an account with a zero balance? Surely the killers knew the status of the account, for if Ferguson could telephone Credit Suisse and obtain that information, so could they. What, then, was their objective, and why had they directed Ferguson to link an empty account to a circular blind? Was it for some purpose other than the money? Were they engaged in *Peristroika* activities and had long ago spent the seven million? If not, where had it gone?

Alex had decided to go after the killers only because he knew Andrea was safe in Adelaide. Knowledge of her safety was paramount to his being able to concentrate on his task. If he were to have any kind of hope of stopping them, he needed to function without distraction. Which meant without emotion and worry.

The first step, then, was to call Andrea and tell her about his plans. She would not like it, but she would accept it.

Standing, Alex dialed Liz Langdon's number and placed the mobile phone to his ear. In six seconds Liz was answering. In nine seconds Liz was screaming.

From that point the conversation turned even more frantic, with each of them shouting and interrupting one another: you're *dead*... I'm *alive*... she's gone... she's *what?*

Talanov could not believe what he was hearing! "*Andrea's gone?*"

"After the killers," replied Liz. "She thought - we all thought - you were *dead*."

More anguished shouts followed, after which Joe - who was now standing beside Talanov - took the phone from Alex and ushered him back into the old wooden chair. Joe calmly finished the conversation with Liz, who repeated what she had told Alex: yes, his name has been cleared and, yes, it's gone out over the wires. Yes, all their bank funds have been released, and - yes - Andrea's gone after the killers. No, there's no way anybody can reach her. She's gone deep, new look, new passport. She's traveling as Natalie Cox.

Joe thanked Liz and terminated the call, then walked over to Alex and placed a gentle hand on his shoulder. Alex was seated quietly, his shoulders hunched, his head drooped.

"It's not all bad," said Joe.

"Bad enough," Talanov said, not bothering to look up. "They'll kill her, those bastards will kill her. And there's no way we can reach her."

"But she's traveling under a new identity - as Natalie Cox - and she's apparently got a new look. I doubt they'll be able to recognize her."

Talanov looked up with reddened eyes. "And what will happen once she finds them? She's trained as a caterer, not a killer. Sure, she may hate Cheney enough to pull the trigger, assuming he doesn't pull one first, assuming even further that she can manage to get a gun from someone who won't first slit her throat. And let's not forget about Marshak and the others she doesn't know but who will gun her down the moment she tries something. That world is inhuman, Joe, and you know that as well as I do."

"Yes, I guess I do," Joe replied, removing his hand and squatting beside Alex. "But I also know that without hope, we won't survive, regardless of what we're attempting. You won't, I won't, your wife won't. Now, we can paint this window completely black with despair or we can crack it open and let in some light."

"Hope?" repeated Alex bitterly. "What's the use if it's just an illusion?"

"Because despair cripples, but hope motivates. As odd as it sounds, your wife has hope or she wouldn't be thinking she could finish what you started. She's got heart, she's angry, and she's determined. But kamikaze she's not. And she just happens to be the soul-mate of one hell of a spook. So I reckon you and I need to get motivated and get over there fast as we can."

With a deep breath, Alex leaned back and closed his eyes for a moment, then opened them and looked at Joe. "You say my name's been cleared and verification of that has gone out?"

"That's what Liz told me," Joe replied, standing. He stepped back to the side of Maurice, who had been observing them silently.

"All right, first move: Maurice, I'd like you to telephone police headquarters and confirm that my name has been cleared. If it has, then go get my passport. I'll need it to prove my identity."

"You got it!" said Maurice with a grin as he ran for his phone.

"Want me to call the boys at the airport and have them tank up the Cessna?" asked Joe. "She can be ready by the time we get there."

Talanov shook his head. "No, I'd like you to phone a travel agent instead and book us on a fast flight to Zurich."

"What's our plan once we get there? Your wife could be anywhere."

"True, but her focal point is Cheney, and Cheney's is Credit Suisse. We begin there."

Chapter 55

Zug, Switzerland is a picturesque town beside a beautiful Alpine lake. Zug also happens to be a magnet for investment within a country that's a magnet for investment. Low taxes and tight lips were what drew investors to Switzerland and Zug has the lowest and tightest.

Ferguson had provided Talanov with this simple overview and he reflected on it as he and Joe sped along the Swiss autobahn in their rented Audi. Was it more than a passing coincidence that the double-alpha account resided in one of the most lucrative tax havens in the world? Mysteries aside, one thing was certain: they needed to get to Zug - safely, anonymously, quickly. And to help guarantee this, Alex had used his Wolfgang Hauser passport on all flights, thereby eliminating the likelihood of delays should the name of Talanov still be flagged.

Several hours prior to their arrival, Alex had unclipped an airplane telephone from the back of the seat in front of him and called Directory Assistance in Zurich, who in turn connected him to a man he had not seen since their days in the KGB. No mention of the past was made, with both men conversing lightheartedly in German. During the course of this conversation, Talanov asked how many grandchildren the man now had.

There was a brief pause. "Grandchildren? Now you make me feel old," the man said with a quiet laugh. "I have three, my friend. And you?"

Talanov also laughed. "Still waiting. Four would be my preference - two girls and two quiet boys."

The conversation then drifted onto other unimportant matters, after which the call was ended. To anyone eavesdropping, their talk had been dull and meaningless. In actuality, a number of important code words had been used which carried a great deal of meaning: grandchildren - we need guns; four - the quantity needed; two girls - two pistols small enough to conceal; two quiet boys - two larger pistols with silencers.

The result was a briefcase which was transferred to Alex in the terminal by a white-haired man in a brown tweed coat. He wore a forest-green Alpine hat and sported a short Vandyke beard, also white. Alex and Joe had paused in front of a kiosk to purchase a map when the white-haired man came up beside them, setting the briefcase down in order to buy a newspaper. The man selected his paper, paid for it, then thanked the attendant in German before walking away.

After paying for the map, Talanov casually picked up the briefcase and led Joe toward the car rental counter.

"You can open that briefcase now," Alex told Joe as they drove along the autobahn in the early morning drizzle. Scattered patches of snow were still visible on each side of the pavement.

Joe reached into the back seat and brought the briefcase into the front. He snapped the latches and opened the lid. "Well, Merry Christmas to us!" he exclaimed with a smile. Inside the case were four pistols: two with silencers and two small enough to conceal inside a pocket or sock. Also included were two boxes of ammunition and an envelope. "Was Mr Tweed back there an old mate o' yours?" inquired Joe as he inspected one of the weapons.

"Many years ago, Balashikha imported him from the DDR," said Talanov, squinting into the gray mists ahead. "He taught me German and conversational cipher. He was later reassigned to Munich and operated our Residency there. When the Wall came down, he flushed his card and retired across the border in Switzerland. He's been here ever since."

"Handy little network you've got," said Joe. "What's his name?"

"Wolfgang Hauser."

Joe snapped his head toward Alex. "Are you serious?"

"Completely."

"But he has to be twenty years older than you! You're taking an enormous risk using the passport of a man who's still living."

Alex did not take his eyes off the highway. "Actually, I've got the passport number of his son, who died of measles when he was six. Those were hard days after the War and there weren't enough doctors or medicine. Anyway, no certificate of death was ever filed and we'd be roughly the same age now. Before leaving Balashikha, Wolfgang presented me with his son's passport number in case I ever needed it for a cover. He knows I'm using it now."

The two men fell silent to the rhythmic swishing of the wiper blades. Joe finally replaced the pistol in the briefcase and picked up the envelope. "What's in here?" he asked.

"Some shortcuts, if we're lucky," Talanov replied. "I mentioned to Wolfgang that some businessmen I know once went to Zug and loved their hotel. By not mentioning the hotel's name, Wolfgang will realize I need a prioritized list of the hotels where businessmen might stay. It's my guess Marshak and Cheney would choose efficiency rather than quaintness. I also asked him for any bits of news that he's heard." Alex then glanced over at Joe. "Go ahead and open it. Wolfgang speaks fluent English but usually writes in German."

Joe tore open the envelope and pulled out a sheet of paper. "Yep, it's in German," he said. "But this I can understand - *Parkhotel* - and this: *Bob Hoskings, vom IDC.*"

"The *IDC?*" said Talanov, grabbing the note and scanning it while keeping an eye on the highway. A Porsche suddenly flew past them and splattered water across the windshield.

"Who's Bob Hoskings?" asked Joe as the wipers dutifully swept away the water. Talanov handed back the letter. "Never heard of him. But the IDC we've heard of and it's no coincidence one of their people happens to be in Zug at this time. *Damn!* My wife's out there and their big guns are coming to Zug. Why couldn't she let things go?"

"Probably because she's married to you and you're both alike," Joe replied, drawing a sharp glance from Talanov. Joe gave Alex a reassuring slap on the shoulder. "Don't give up," he said. "We've got hope... remember?"

With a frustrated sigh, Talanov nodded.

"Could Bob Hoskings be Tango Blue?" asked Joe. "This is twice the IDC has popped up - first with Ambassador Kharkov and now with this guy, Hoskings."

"It's possible. I just wish I knew his background... who he is beneath that position with the IDC."

"How do we find out?" asked Joe.

"First things first," said Alex, again glancing at the letter. "Wolfgang says the hotels are full, so he's arranged rooms with a farmer named Dieterich."

"Another one of your network?"

"This one is Wolfgang's network, not mine. I've never met the man. Wolfgang says the farm's on the Zugerberg road and they're expecting us to call for directions once we reach town. Wolfgang says he'll meet us there."

In the distance off to their right a lone string of Christmas lights floated by in the gray mists. "My God, is it really Christmas?" asked Joe as the lights faded away in the fog. "Hunting assassins on the birthday of Christ." He shook his head at the contradiction and looked over at Alex. "After finding the farm, what next?"

"Get Wolfgang to make some quiet inquiries as to whether a Natalie Cox is registered in town. While he works on that, we'll stop by the bank, then scout the hotel."

"That's a fair bit of work in the open."

"We don't have much of a choice."

"Maybe we do," countered Joe. "Your wife may have hit on something with that disguise of hers. I realize Marshak and Cheney won't be expecting us, but I'd just as soon sweeten our prospects of survival. The less recognizable we are, the better."

"Not a bad idea," said Talanov, "but I may have to stick to my sunglasses-and-hat routine. I'll need to look like my passport photo if I'm to convince the officials at Credit Suisse that I'm who I say I am."

"Good point. But I needn't remind you that, if you're seen, Marshak and Cheney won't be letting you slip away from them again."

Alex glanced sideways at Joe. "Thanks for not reminding me."

Joe grinned. "What are friends for? Anyway, while you go check out the bank, I'll find a secluded little salon and have some sunshine washed into my hair. When this mess is over and you're back in the arms of your wife, I'll tell you whether or not blonds have more fun."

Back into the arms of my wife, thought Alex. I hope to God you're right, Joe.

The drizzle had stopped when Talanov veered off of the autobahn toward Zug. Within minutes they were on the outskirts of town and had stopped at a public phone, where Alex placed a call. A man with a deep voice answered.

Talanov introduced himself as the friend of Wolfgang Hauser.

"*Ein moment, mein English... nicht gut,*" the man replied.

Over the phone, in the background, Talanov could hear shouts. The seconds stretched into nearly a full minute. Finally a winded woman spoke into the phone.

"Yes, I am Maria Dieterich," she said in English after catching her breath. "May I help you, please?"

"I'm the friend of Wolfgang Hauser," said Talanov again. "He told me to call you for directions. Is he there?"

"No, not yet, but he did telephone us and said he will be here soon. Arrangements have been made and your rooms are waiting."

"You're very kind to help us. We'll pay you once we change money at the bank."

"There is no need," Maria replied. "Everything has been settled."

"You mean Wolfgang's already *paid?*"

"Everything has been settled. Now, to get to our farm-"

Talanov memorized Maria's directions and was soon steering the Audi along a winding country road which climbed upward through the sullen gray mists hugging the contours of the mountain. The single lane of pavement would level out, then switch back and climb higher, an occasional roadside cherry orchard coming into momentary view, its black trunks and wet branches now barren of foliage.

Before long, the road dipped down through a thick stand of conifers clinging stubbornly to the side of the mountain. To the right, a canyon fell away through the trees like a dark tunnel of gloom. A metal guard rail could hold back cars but not the nervousness of drivers as Talanov glanced down the steep precipice and cautiously steered the Audi through that section of forest and out onto another stretch of rolling highland, where the road turned left and again climbed higher. Soon the clouds began to thin and shreds of blue could be seen above.

"I'll tell you what I've been thinking," said Talanov as the road crested a hill. "According to Ferguson, there's no money in the Credit Suisse account. He said it's a numbered account but with a zero balance."

"I wasn't in on that conversation but I'll take your word for it," said Joe.

"Well, what if the Credit Suisse account has been linked to a blinded account somewhere else? That would explain why the killers are still devoting so much effort into gaining control of it. That would also explain why the account number hasn't been scrubbed. Think about it: for an account with a zero balance, most banks would simply close the books. But not in this case. In this case, the account's still open even though there's nothing in it."

"And you think this hypothetical other account has been blinded?"

"Yes, which is why Ferguson wasn't told about it."

"Okay, Sherlock - if it's blinded, what good does that do us? We can't access it, either."

"But we can make a withdrawal and see what happens," said Talanov, looking at Joe.

A slow smile of realization spread across Joe's face. "And if it's successful, then we - you - will receive a copy of the transaction record!"

"Which will identify the other account number, which we can then trace."

"So what do you plan to do - just rock up to the bank and verify you're not dead, hoping this enables you to retain jurisdiction so that you can submit a withdrawal request?"

"Right."

"And all of this in broad daylight? I needn't remind you-"

Talanov held up a hand. "You've *already* not reminded me."

"Just doing my job, Mr K."

"Well do it a little more quietly."

Joe chuckled. "Say, are we getting close?"

Alex glanced down at the odometer, then focused on a small cluster of buildings up ahead. "That must be it," he said.

It was and Talanov had soon directed the Audi down a short gravel drive and parked in the shadow of a huge barn. The walls of the ground story were white plastered concrete, the upper stories of dark brown wood. A massive roof rose to a high central ridge, while beneath the broad eaves was enough split firewood to last several winters, all evenly sawn and neatly stacked. A small shed stood nearby, and beyond a fence of barbed wire was a small orchard of dormant fruit trees, mostly cherries and pears. Above, the sky was clearing.

As the two men opened their car doors and stood, a shout drew Talanov's attention. He turned to see Wolfgang standing on the balcony of a small chalet. Alex waved and motioned for Joe to follow as he closed his door and started toward the house.

The chalet was cubical in shape and similar in construction to the barn. Smoke curled from the chimney and scattered patches of snow dotted the lawn. Rolling fields lay beyond with another farm visible in the distance. Far off to the right was more forest, and beyond this the wooded Zugerberg summit.

Wolfgang met Talanov at the front door and the two men embraced, then pulled back to look at one another.

"You look well," Wolfgang told Alex with an approving nod.

"As do you, old friend," replied Talanov with a smile. Alex then introduced Joe, who shook hands with the white-haired German, who was still in his tweed coat and hat.

"Come in, come in!" Wolfgang said, ushering the two men into the house and closing the door behind them. They were shown into a comfortable living room with two sofas and two chairs centered around an iron stove in which was a roaring fire. Several throw rugs covered parts of the wooden floor, while overhead were thick beams on which were hung dozens of ceramic beer mugs. Two of the room's walls contained numerous windows, all double paned, with various plants positioned to take full advantage of the sun. Through these windows, far to the south, could be seen the snow-covered peaks of the Alps.

While Alex and Wolfgang chatted, Joe's eyes roamed over the clutter. Tables were laden with books and magazines, and most wall space was occupied by an assortment of old wooden utensils, cow bells, hand tools, and farm implements. Near the door into the kitchen, a carved Dutch speculaas cookie board hung on a wooden peg next to an old saw, while baskets and bookcases were positioned tightly around the room. Near the bathroom door was a wooden staircase which led to the upstairs bedrooms.

Suddenly Joe heard other voices and turned to see a man and woman, both in boots and blue overalls. They were standing beside Wolfgang and Talanov, having come into the house through the kitchen.

The man, whose name was Johann Dieterich, was in his mid-thirties and had the rugged look of a farmer. He had wild brown hair, large calloused hands, broad shoulders, and ruddy cheeks. Yet in spite of this toughened appearance, he possessed a reticent politeness. Maria Dieterich, who was standing beside Johann, appeared to be slightly younger. She, too, had the seasoned look of the outdoors, with tanned skin, medium-length brown hair, and a vitality in her eyes which crackled with a love of the highlands.

Joe stepped toward the couple, his hand extended. "A person could sit through quite a few blizzards in here," he said with an approving nod toward the room. "My name's Joe, and you've got quite a house."

"I am glad you like it," Maria replied with an amused smile at the visitor's forward manner. "My name is Maria," she said, shaking Joe's hand.

"Johann," the man stated simply, also shaking Joe's hand.

"*Junge*, may I present my old friend, Alex," Wolfgang announced, placing a hand on Talanov's shoulder. "An old pupil, in fact, and one of my best."

"Flattery will get you everywhere," Talanov said with a laugh as he shook the hands of Johann and Maria. "But I'm afraid the credit is yours, Wolfgang. Without your help, I'd have learned little more than what's in the books."

"Ahh, now you flatter *me!*" Wolfgang laughed. "I could tell from your call on the plane that you remembered your conversational cipher. Very good, Alex, very good. Come, let's talk by the fire." Wolfgang's offer was a polite opportunity for Johann and Maria to leave.

"I'm afraid the reason for our being here is both serious and urgent," Alex said once the others had left. "We're tracking some assassins, but so is my wife. Thinking me dead, she's decided to go after them by herself. Unfortunately, she's gone deep and dark."

"Dark?" asked Wolfgang with a concerned frown. "A new identity?"

"Natalie Cox," answered Talanov. "And she's an amateur. So, if possible, I'd like you to find out if she's registered in any of the hotels in Zug."

"Of course," said Wolfgang, writing the name on a slip of paper. "I'm afraid I must write everything down these days," he added with a smile. "My memory is not what it was."

"Neither is mine," agreed Alex, after which he began telling Wolfgang all that had happened.

Having heard the story, Joe got up and walked into the kitchen to where Maria was kneading pastry dough on a floured section of the table. "How do you know Wolfgang?" he asked, trying to make light conversation.

"I'm sure he will tell you," Maria replied, now wearing an apron. "Would you mind peeling and slicing some apples? They're in a barrel down in the basement." She pointed toward a narrow flight of stairs obscured by a small railing and two large stone crocks, one filled with onions, the other potatoes. "Six will do."

Joe disappeared and soon returned with six apples.

"Have you and your husband lived here long?" Joe inquired as he began peeling the apples with a knife.

Maria smiled. "The farm has been in my family for well over a hundred years. To buy such a property today is nearly impossible, for they are passed from one generation to the next and almost never come up for sale. Our farm was handed down in such a manner, which is why we can make a living from twenty-two milk cows and some chickens."

While Joe carefully removed the skins in long spirals, Maria finished kneading the dough. She then opened a cupboard door and removed a low round cake pan, which she buttered. Next she began pressing the dough into a thin layer along the bottom of the pan.

Once he was finished with the peeling, Joe sat quietly staring at Maria's unadorned beauty. With admiration he watched how delicately she spread the dough up the sides of the pan, knowing she could probably mend fences, fix tractors, and deliver calves. Johann was a lucky man.

"Are you going to stand there all day?" Maria asked while concentrating on the spreading of the dough in the pan. She glanced over at him with another amused smile and then returned to her work.

"Sorry," Joe replied. "I was impressed with how quickly you do that."

"Which won't save me any time if those apples aren't sliced."

"Right. What are you making?"

"Apple cake."

"Apple cake? That's odd," Joe remarked as he tossed the peelings into a small bucket on the floor filled with other scraps.

"Why do you say that?" asked Maria. "It is a cake made with apples."

Joe sliced his knife through the center of an apple and shrugged. "Here in Switzerland, I thought it would have an authentic name like *apfelkraut* or something."

After a momentary look of surprise, Maria broke out laughing.

In the other room, Wolfgang added more wood to the fire, then closed the stove's iron door and latched it. Standing, he shook his head. "I will, of course, do as you ask, but today is the twenty-fourth and the banks will be closing at noon for the Christmas holiday."

Talanov looked anxiously at his watch. "*Noon?* It's now eleven-fifteen. When will they open again?"

"Not until Friday, the twenty-seventh."

"*Friday?* I've got to get in there today!"

Wolfgang again shook his head. "I'm afraid you're too late."

"Too much can go wrong before Friday," said Talanov, shouting for Joe and grabbing his coat. "Come on, we've got to try."

Chapter 56

Like most European cities, Zug was an blend of the old and the new. Located on the shores of a lake, Zug's Medieval fortifications shared space with sleek buildings of stainless steel and glass. Expensive cars sped along over worn cobblestone streets while computer codes, not stone walls, protected the city's wealth in banks linked electronically with financial centers around the world.

Because they had errands of their own, Wolfgang and Joe got out on Baarerstrasse, one of Zug's main downtown streets. Alex then drove the rental car several more blocks to a small parking lot near the post office. With his collar pulled up against the cold and wearing one of Wolfgang's hats, Talanov hurried across the cobblestones toward the conservative gray concrete building that was Credit Suisse. It was a modern four-story building which stood quietly in line with other buildings positioned modestly along the street.

His fingers curled in front of his mouth for warmth, Talanov paused in front of a shop window across the street, ostensibly to look at their display. Because many shops were already closed, it was easy for Alex to scan the sidewalk and check the few faces that he saw. Neither Cheney nor Marshak were anywhere to be seen. Satisfied, he crossed the pavement and entered the bank.

The interior of Credit Suisse was as contemporary and colorless as the exterior, with a stainless steel acoustic ceiling spanning a floor composed of large squares of coarse gray granite. Straight ahead were the tellers and to his right was a reception counter occupied by a man and woman, both of whom were laughing quietly at something the man had said. To one side of the counter was an elevator, and on the other side, an ascending flight of stairs.

"*Darf ich Ihnen helfen?*" the man asked after glancing at his watch. It was eleven-fifty - ten minutes before closing.

"I must speak with someone about a numbered account," replied Talanov in English. "I need to verify jurisdiction and then submit a withdrawal request."

"I'm afraid that is not possible," the man replied in fluent English. "We are closing in just a few minutes. You may return and conduct business on Friday."

"But you're still open," replied Talanov.

"Yes, but you must return on Friday. We are closing soon for the Christmas holiday."

Talanov leaned over the counter slightly. "It's my understanding that until you're actually closed, you're still open. Your front door is unlocked and your tellers are manning their stations. Now, must I take my request to some higher authority?"

The man's eyes turned cold although he managed to keep a smile firmly in place. The woman beside him - she was a very bleached blond - stood silently by, her eyes lowered, her expression non-committal. Without responding to what was now a demand, the man picked up a phone and punched several buttons. Within moments he was talking quietly to one of the cashiers upstairs.

"Some jackass down here insists on seeing Frau Hunziker," he said in German.

"We are closing in five minutes!" scolded the cashier.

"I told him as much but he insists. He has a numbered account."

The cashier responded with an exasperated sigh. "What's his name?"

The receptionist looked at Talanov, his smile still in place. "Your name, please?"

Talanov smiled back and replied in perfect German: "the name of this jackass is Aleksandr Talanov. What, may I ask, is yours?"

The man's smile melted into a look of horror. He quickly looked down and away as he spoke into the phone. "The gentleman's name is Herr Talanov and I beg Frau Hunziker's generous assistance."

"All right, bring him up," the cashier said in an annoyed tone.

The man replaced the phone in its cradle, not able to look Talanov in the eyes, his hand clinging to the receiver. After swallowing, he finally looked up. "Frau Hunziker will see you."

"Shall I escort Herr Talanov to the first floor?" the blonde woman asked. The man looked over and nodded. "This way, please," she said pleasantly as she led the way to the elevator.

Upstairs, Talanov was shown into a small conference room directly above the reception counter. An oval table of natural wood was positioned in the center of the room and was surrounded by six chrome-and-black-leather chairs. The high narrow windows which overlooked the street were covered by sheer curtains, while on a small desk near the window was a computer monitor. Several watercolor prints hung on the walls.

Alex removed his hat and sat in one of the chairs.

The door soon opened and an attractive woman in a dark blue business suit entered briskly with a small notepad in her hand. Her smooth, almost black hair was pulled back tightly into a bun. She looked disapprovingly at Talanov and sat across from him.

"I am Mrs Hunziker," the woman said in English. "How may I help you?"

"I need to verify the jurisdiction of a numbered account," Alex replied.

"Your name?" asked the woman, her pencil poised.

"Aleksandr Talanov," he replied, spelling it for her.

"The account is in your name?" she asked after writing his name on the pad.

"I'm not sure," replied Talanov.

Frau Hunziker raised one eyebrow reprovingly.

"It is my belief that I was given jurisdiction over a numbered account," Talanov explained. "I'm not sure how it's listed but I have the number." Alex gestured for the notepad and Frau Hunziker slid it over to him. He wrote the sequence of alpha-numeric characters beneath his name and slid it back.

She glanced at what he had written, her eyes widening. "This is a double-alpha account."

"What's the significance of that?"

"Double-alpha accounts are very exclusive and highly restricted."

"Well, I have reason to believe someone possessing a falsified death certificate may be trying to obtain control of the account." Talanov reached into his pocket and withdrew his passport, which he laid on the table. "Therefore, I need you to verify my identity and tell me whether there has been any activity."

"Until we have established your legal right to make such an inquiry, all records are confidential," answered Frau Hunziker, inspecting Talanov's passport and comparing it several times to the man sitting across from her.

"Then can you tell me whether or not I hold jurisdiction?"

No reply was Frau Hunziker's reply as she continued to inspect the passport.

"If so, I'd like to withdraw some funds," added Alex.

Frau Hunziker handed Talanov his passport. "I can verify who you are, Mr Talanov, but I'm afraid nothing else can be done today. Our bank is officially closed, so I can only record your details which we can then process on Friday."

"But this request was initiated while you were open!" countered Talanov. "It is imperative that I prevent this account from being fraudulently invaded."

"My sympathies are with you, Mr Talanov, but no activity - yours or anyone else's - will take place today. Many of our personnel are now off duty and we require advance notification for cash withdrawals from accounts such as these. Come back on Friday."

"At least investigate whether or not the account has been compromised, which you can do when you process my request. One hundred francs, that's all I ask."

"*One hundred francs?* From a double-alpha account? If you are in such a desperate need of pocket money, Mr Talanov, then I advise you to seek it elsewhere."

"Make it a thousand... a *million*, if that makes you happier. The amount is irrelevant, Frau Hunziker. What I need is a recorded transaction."

"And what I need is for you to come back on Friday. No transaction will take place today."

"I don't need the money right now, but *please* submit the request. I'll come back for it on Friday." Talanov's eyes were pleading with the woman.

The woman folded her arms and glared at Alex. "You will not receive the time of day if there is even the slightest irregularity with your claim."

"That's fair and it's all that I ask."

"One hundred francs," said Frau Hunziker, writing it down.

"Thank you!"

Frau Hunziker stood and walked to the door, brusquely opening it. "Good day, Mr Talanov, our meeting has ended."

Chapter 57

Talanov heard the door being locked behind him as he left Credit Suisse. He only hoped Frau Hunziker would not wait until Friday to process his request. If she did, then by tomorrow the killers would be gone, either with Andrea following them or lying dead in their wake.

It was logical to assume the killers had already filed for a transfer of jurisdiction using his death certificate. If that were the case, the account - assuming there was one - could be emptied and closed, especially if the funds were then transferred to a third account.

But if Frau Hunziker *did* enter his request - and assuming further that the assassins wanted cash and, therefore, this nuisance of closing early for Christmas had also hampered them - then not only would they have to remain in Zug until Friday, but the two concurrent requests would probably freeze all activity until the matter of jurisdiction was settled.

Which meant there was still time to find Cheney and, therefore, Andrea.

Alex entered a covered walkway created by the overhang of an upstairs department store. It led through to the next street and Talanov paused midway to pull out his map. It showed a schematic diagram of Zug with an inserted enlargement of the Old City. Wolfgang had pointed out the general vicinity of the Parkhotel earlier and Alex compared his present location with the lot where he had parked the car. He then located the hotel on the map's legend and set off on foot to find it.

Because Zug was a compact city, it was but a five-minute walk before Alex saw the Parkhotel, a four-story modern structure of concrete and glass with several tall banners on flagpoles positioned near the street. Wolfgang was in the hotel at this very moment talking with one of the owners - an old friend named Jules - would be able to discreetly telephone the other hotels in town to find out if a Natalie Cox was registered with any of them. While privacy was sacrosanct in Switzerland, in certain rare and justified instances, hotel managers assisted one another with the location of important people. This, Wolfgang would assure him, was such a rare and justified instance.

Across the street from the hotel was more contemporary architecture in the form of a conference center and bank mall, which in turn were connected to an even more extensive shopping complex known as Metalli. An advertisement on his map alerted Talanov to the fact that the hotel owned the conference center. Because hotels which owned conference centers catered primarily to business clients, they usually provided efficient service and computer facilities with advanced communications links. This, coupled with the fact that Bob Hoskings of the IDC was staying at the hotel, indicated a likelihood that Cheney would be found, too. The Parkhotel, then, was where Alex would start looking for his wife.

From a diagonal corner, Alex surveyed the hotel and the small hill behind it. Most of the trees were now barren although the conifers were a rich dark green. Several Mercedes sedans were parked near the entrance and a group of businessmen, all in dark suits, were getting into one of the cars.

With his hat angled over his forehead, Alex walked a short distance down the block, crossing the street in front of a clothing boutique before turning toward the Metalli shopping center. He continued down the sidewalk and paused at the glass doors leading into a long covered arcade lined with shops. Last-minute shoppers were hurrying in and out of stores with bags laden with Christmas purchases. Alex checked his watch. It was time to get back to the car.

Quiet laughter and murmured conversations greeted Marshak as he entered the paneled elegance of the Exchange Bar, located in a front section of the Parkhotel to one side of the front entrance. Dressed in a dark gray suit, he paused at the door to look for a table. Suddenly, he was bumped from behind.

"I'm terribly sorry," a woman in a tight red skirt and white blouse said as she adjusted her high-heeled shoe. "My ankle twisted, I hope you're not hurt." She then knelt to pick up her purse.

Marshak smiled, his hand reaching the purse at the same time as hers. "Hardly," he said, noticing the woman's cleavage as she leaned forward. "And you?"

The two of them stood, Marshak releasing the purse as they did.

The woman was chewing gum and smiled an embarrassed smile. "I feel rather foolish, that's all."

"May I buy you a drink?" he asked. "The bar is quite full, so it would be wise if we shared a table."

"Now that's a line if I've heard one," the woman replied with what looked to be an interested smile.

"I confess I'm being rather obvious. Major Pyotr Marshak, at your service." He stiffened momentarily and snapped his head in a slight bow.

"Wow, a real major!" she said, her accent obviously American. "I'm impressed!"

"Is that a 'yes,' then?" asked Marshak with a thin smile as he began thinking of ways to maneuver this beauty from the bar to his bedroom.

"Sure," she said. "I've never met a major before."

Marshak nodded his approval and led the way toward a vacant table, where he withdrew one of the chairs and seated the woman, then sitting across from her. "And with whom do I have the pleasure of this occasion?" he asked, leaning up to the table.

"Natalie Cox," the woman said, putting her gum in the ashtray.

Chapter
58

Alex parked the rental car in a vacant spot on Baarerstrasse and waited. In less than a minute the front and rear passenger doors opened and Wolfgang and Joe climbed in. Alex glanced casually at Joe in the rear view mirror, then swivelled in his seat with surprise. No longer did Joe have wavy black hair, but short blond spikes and rose-colored glasses.

"What happened to *you?*" asked Talanov.

"Alex, meet Charles," said Wolfgang, clipping it into *Chahls*. "He's going to be one of the waiters at tonight's reception."

"What reception?"

"Drive on and I'll tell you," said Wolfgang.

On their way back to the farm, Wolfgang told Alex his news. The first bit was not encouraging: a few preliminary calls to several hotels had not turned up a Natalie Cox. Jules said that he would continue searching and phone later with the results. A photo, of course, would be useful, to which a discouraged Talanov shook his head that none were available.

Wolfgang then brightened because the next item was interesting indeed. "Upon hearing that Bob Hoskings of the International Development Council was coming to Zug, the Trade and Service Association set about organizing a formal reception - which is tonight - at the Montana Institute, a wilderness training school high on the Zugerberg mountain. The view from the restaurant is spectacular and dignitaries from government, industry, and banking will be in attendance and by invitation only. Security will be tight and the single road to the institute will be closed."

"How will the guests arrive?"

"By the cog railway, which leaves from the neighboring village of Oberwil. It travels directly up the mountain to the restaurant."

"Can you get me an invitation?"

"Unfortunately not," answered Wolfgang. "It appears each name on the guest list had to be approved personally by Hoskings and his security staff. However, if you wish to conduct surveillance, I've got field glasses and can arrange for Maria to take you there after dark. She knows the paths through the forest, and in this way you can bypass the police roadblock and slip onto the grounds unnoticed."

Alex steered the Audi up the mountain and past a cherry orchard. "I need to do more than watch through binoculars," he said. "Those killers have got to be stopped and Hoskings could well be their leader. I want to attend."

"What would that accomplish?" asked Wolfgang pointedly. "You can't just walk in and start shooting. Not only is that illegal, but to my knowledge these people have committed no crimes here in Switzerland. And not only that, you would also jeopardize the lives of others attending the reception."

"I couldn't agree more," said Talanov. "Which is precisely why I must be there. My problem is this, and you see it, too - in spite of all the killing they've done, no one knows them to be killers. Nor can I prove it... at least not yet. So I've got to make them come commit the first move. In fact, I'm counting on the presence of all those guests to keep *me* from getting shot."

Wolfgang chuckled and shook his head. "I should have expected such a strategy from you. How do you plan to execute?"

"Yeah, how do you plan to execute?" echoed Joe. "Because I have the funny feeling you'll be using yourself as bait for a trap."

"You're perceptive," remarked Talanov with a quick glance at Joe in the mirror. "It's my intention to confront Hoskings in front of his guests and tell him what I know and what I'm planning. I'll mention Kharkov's murder and how I'll be having the account thoroughly investigated in order to expose any fraudulent attempts to gain control of it. The shock of my being there should cause a reaction of some kind, especially once I leave. When one of them follows me and tries using a gun, I'll be justified in how I respond."

"And what if your wife is there?" asked Joe, removing his rose-colored glasses. "How will that affect your ability to carry this off? If you take her with you, she slows you down, not to mention becoming a target. And if you leave her behind... well, I know you're not that stupid."

"No, I'm not, but you raise a good point. Wolfgang, do you think Jules can find out whether or not Natalie Cox is on the guest list?"

"I'll phone him from the house."

"If she's not, we're in the clear. If she is, then would you get her out, Joe?"

"Glad to, Mr K."

"One other thing: I'm concerned about Maria being the one who guides me through the forest. I'd much rather have Johann. He much stronger than his wife, and if I need back-up support, he's got the muscle."

"Wife?" laughed Wolfgang. "Johann and Maria are brother and sister."

Joe put his glasses back on and leaned forward in the back seat. "You mean they're not married?"

"Of course not," said Wolfgang. "But make no mistake: while Johann has the strength of an ox, he also makes noise like an ox. Maria, on the other hand, moves like a deer and knows the trails. And she is an excellent shot with a rifle. I should know: they are my niece and nephew."

"Bloody hell," said Joe. "And she cooks as well?"

"It appears our young friend has been smitten," Wolfgang said to Alex, then looking back at Joe with his blond spikes and glasses. "Many men have come calling, my young friend, and most have gone packing, although a few still linger in hope. Yes, the same Maria who cooks a heavenly pork roast and rosti can shoot the eye out of a rabbit at a hundred meters. She and Johann are both in the reserves."

"What's she lookin' for in a guy?" asked Joe.

Wolfgang laughed again, his pale blue eyes sparkling beneath bushy white eyebrows. "You seek the solution to a riddle that has stumped more suitors than I can count."

"Does that mean you don't know, or that you know but aren't telling?" asked Joe.

Wolfgang's eyes seemed to crackle with glee. "I'm afraid the answer to that question will elude you even more."

With a grumbling frown, Joe slumped back in the seat.

"You may have lost ground with that hairstyle," said Talanov with a grin.

"Ahh, but our friend's hairstyle does bring up an important issue," Wolfgang said, "especially since it appears you are planning to drop in on tonight's occasion. As I mentioned to you before, I've arranged for Joe - I mean, *Charles* - to be one of the waiters. The Parkhotel will be catering the reception and Jules was only too pleased to have him as one of the servers. I assured him Charles would meet the Parkhotel's usual high standards, but that the real reason he needed to be there was to provide undercover security of the most sensitive and confidential nature. When Jules asked if it had anything to do with the Natalie Cox about whom I had been inquiring, I replied that I was not at liberty to say. It was, in fact, because of your wife that I thought Joe's presence might be useful."

"Thanks, Wolfgang, and I really mean that," said Alex.

The old German smiled. "It is my pleasure. By the way, I think your plan is an excellent one. It is vital that we force them into acting first but away from the others."

"We?" asked Talanov.

"I thought it prudent to have my name added to the list of managing personnel attending tonight's function. In fact, I've always felt drawn to positions where I supervise the labor of others."

"Then why are you requiring me to tramp through the forest at night in sub-freezing temperatures?" asked Talanov as he steered the Audi around yet another curve. "It seems to me one more manager wouldn't have been difficult to arrange."

"Perhaps not," replied Wolfgang, looking over at Alex. "But Mr Hoskings' security agents - Marshak and Cheney - won't recognize me."

Talanov locked eyes with Wolfgang for a moment before he nodded with resignation and returned his attention to the road. "This does, of course, raise the question about why Hoskings would want tight security in the first place. I could understand it if he were a movie celebrity or politician. But he's merely an IDC committee member, which is hardly a controversial position. Why, then, is he going to such lengths?"

"Perhaps he thinks you're on his trail?" asked Wolfgang.

Talanov shook his head. "As far as he knows, I'm still in Port Vila. What I hadn't thought of until now is that he may have discovered that *Andrea's* on his trail. Perhaps the security's for her."

"But how?" asked Joe. "She's got a new look, new name, new passport."

"I don't know," said Alex, his brow now furrowed with worry. "Leaks can sometimes occur, even in the best of covers."

"Indeed they can," agreed Wolfgang. "So you may wish to reconsider the possibility that Hoskings is expecting you. Perhaps he knows you've tracked them to Zug."

"I don't see how," replied Alex. "I used my Wolfgang Hauser passport all the way and there's no way anyone could know about that. Your giving it to me dates back to our days at Balashikha."

"But as you have already said: leaks occur in the best of covers."

Talanov looked over at Wolfgang. "Then we'd both better hope I'm wrong."

13 ✶ Chapter 59

The fog had finally lifted from the city and Bob Hoskings was drinking a cup of bitter black coffee on his balcony above the entrance to the Parkhotel. Cheney sat across from him, his eyes closed, his feet stretched out on a neighboring chair, his face raised toward the sun. Suddenly the familiar warble of one of Bob's three cellular telephones sounded from his briefcase on the bed.

Bob went inside and answered it. "Tango Blue, this line is secure," he said, informing the caller that the telephone was connected to the scrambler unit.

"This is Ling Soo," a Chinese voice replied. "Our bank in Hong Kong received the Credit Suisse confirmation of Talanov's death. As soon as Credit Suisse opens again on the twenty-seventh, the transfer can be completed. The money will then be ours."

"Excellent!" exclaimed Bob. "What's our balance?"

"Wu Chee Ming begs your indulgence, for he has been investigating some additional investment opportunities in Japan. He thinks their economy will soon collapse and create opportunities beyond belief."

"He's doing *what?* The little prick *knows* we filed a notification of intent to liquidate. He should have calculated a balance by now."

"Please understand, Wu Chee Ming wants to maximize profits, which is how his share - and mine - will be calculated. I implore your patience and trust, Tango Blue, for you yourself know that I have never misled you, even from the beginning. Yes, it was unfortunate that President Andropov transferred jurisdiction of the account to Talanov. This, of course, mattered little when the balance was but seven million dollars. But Wu Chee Ming has turned the seven million into a fortune, investing and selling Hong Kong real estate in order to take advantage of the cycles of crisis and prosperity. Wu Chee Ming listens to the voice of the cricket, the farmer, the general, and the student."

"Crickets? Don't be ridiculous!" exclaimed Bob.

"Do not be skeptical, Tango Blue. He purchased valuable properties early in eighty-four, when prices were low. And by listening to the voices you now scorn, he knew to sell at the high point in eighty-nine, just prior to the Tienamen crisis. By then your seven million dollars had become nearly one hundred and fifty million. The cricket, the farmer, the general, and the student, Tango Blue: each has a story to tell. After repayment of the loan, a balance remained of eighty-seven million. Then, in the slump following that crisis, and while others grieved, Wu Chee Ming borrowed seven hundred million and made aggressive and strategic purchases, which boomed and which he sold at peak prices just months ago. However, he is convinced a financial catastrophe is coming which will affect the entire Far East."

"What was the balance when he sold?"

"Over 1.48 billion. Of course, there is still a loan of seven hundred million which must be repaid. That leaves a profit of close to eight-hundred-million."

"Why didn't you tell me that figure when I asked?" asked Bob impatiently.

"Because, as I said, Wu Chee Ming is investigating opportunities in Japan. In addition, he has been buying and selling foreign currencies to create additional profits."

"Tell Wu Chee Ming I want the funds back in the Hong Kong account by the time we finalize matters here on Friday. Jurisdiction will then be mine and I'm going to liquidate the account."

"As you wish," answered Ling Soo. "Please call me when you are finished at Credit Suisse."

"You'll hear from me. Tango Blue out."

After terminating the call, Bob joined Cheney on the balcony.

"What was that about?" asked Cheney.

"Wu Chee Ming's still playing with the money. Ling Soo tells me he's buying and selling foreign currencies."

"Using what amount of capital?" asked Cheney.

"Nearly one-and-a-half billion, American."

Cheney lurched forward in his chair and looked at Bob, his mouth hanging open in shock. "One and a half *billion?* I knew we were in this for money, but this is unbelievable!"

"Apparently there's an outstanding loan of seven hundred million, which leaves us with eight-hundred million."

"I think we can live on that," said Cheney with a smile as he leaned back in his chair. "Let's see... eight hundred million, divided among-" But Cheney stopped short as he remembered Fiona. He looked over at Bob, whose eyes had now turned angry. "Sorry, I didn't mean-"

"Forget it," Bob cut in as he walked back into the hotel room. "Talanov's responsible, not you."

"What did you find out from the airlines?" asked Cheney as he followed Bob into the room.

"I had the IDC officially contact all airlines serving Vanuatu, both large and small. They located the name I gave them on one of the passenger lists."

"What name was that?"

"Wolfgang Hauser."

"How do you know it was Talanov?" asked Cheney.

"Talanov made some close friends at Balashikha and Hauser was among them. I knew Hauser and knew the old man's young son died shortly after the War. He later presented Talanov with his son's passport number."

"How can you remember such details? That was a long time ago."

"Not that long," answered Bob. "Remember: I, too, was in that loop, and the recollection of such details can mean life or death. In this case - Talanov's death. Furthermore, I found out that Hauser has relatives on a farm near Zug. Talanov's probably with them right now."

"Marshak and I can take care of him. We'll leave at once."

Bob shook his head. "They'd see you coming a mile away, and Talanov is sure to be armed. Hauser would see to that. We'll let him come to us."

"Surely you don't think Talanov will crash the reception?"

"I'm not taking any chances, which is why I told the Swiss police that some protesters have threatened to cause trouble. They've agreed to assist with security, both at the cog railway station and out on the service road. They won't allow anyone to pass who's not on the guest list and in possession of an invitation. In addition, they'll have patrols in the forest."

"Three and four would have been useful for this," remarked Cheney.

"Where are those two idiots? They should have been here by now."

"I've tried calling their mobile but it's switched off," Cheney said. "They're probably on their way."

Suddenly, for the second time, one of Bob's mobile telephones sounded. Bob walked to the bed and picked it up. "Bob Hoskings," he said, knowing this to be the phone number normally called by the public.

"Herr Hoskings, this is Esther Hunziker, with Credit Suisse."

"Yes, Frau Hunziker, how are you? You're still coming to the reception, I hope."

"Yes, of course. It is an honor to be included."

"It's my pleasure," Bob replied. "How may I help you?"

Frau Hunziker lowered her voice. "I thought you would want to know that a man named Talanov came into my office today inquiring about the numbered account you and I spoke of earlier. He verified his identity with an Australian passport and claimed jurisdiction over the account. He made several requests for information and funds, which I said could not be processed until Friday, when we again open for business. As you know, if there is a dispute over jurisdiction, the bank will insist it be cleared before transferring control to you."

"But the death certificate has already been filed."

"Yes, of course. But now we have a man claiming to be the deceased walking into my office insisting he is very much alive. You understand the predicament this presents."

"Naturally," Bob replied, clenching his hand into an angry fist. "I was afraid some imposter might try this. Therefore, I suggest we all meet together on Friday and settle the matter. If he shows up - and imposters frequently do not - then we'll let the police decide who he is and whose passport he's forged."

"I knew I was right to call you," Frau Hunziker said with relief. "Thank you so very much."

"No need to thank me, Frau Hunziker. I want this handled properly the same as you."

"Well, then, until tonight."

"Yes, until tonight," Bob replied, switching off the phone. He then whirled angrily toward Cheney. "Get Marshak! I want Talanov killed *tonight!*"

Chapter 60

Andrea crossed her legs, exposing more of one thigh as her short red skirt slid up higher. Marshak was finishing his third vodka and caught sight of her leg. A tingle of arousal crept through him and fueled his determination to get her in bed.

Having arrived in Zug earlier that day by train, Andrea figured Cheney would choose efficiency and service in a hotel, and so asked a businessman on the street about the best ones. There were but two choices, the man had said; was this for business or pleasure? Business, Andrea told him. The Parkhotel, the man then replied.

Thankfully, there was an open dining area inside the hotel and within sight of the front counter. Andrea took a table near a large picture window overlooking a patio outside. The potted plants enclosing the dining area did not obstruct her view of the lobby, and it was on her third cup of coffee that she saw Cheney. He came out of the elevator with two men: one tall and straight, the other with the impatient authority of a politician. Andrea made mental pictures of the men, knowing that she would kill one if not all of them in order to fulfill her vow. But first she had to join them.

"Well, Miss Natalie Cox - actress - of Los Angeles: what are you doing this evening?"

"What did you have in mind?" Andrea asked with a playful smile as she sipped her wine.

Marshak appeared to grimace at the rising level of noise. The Exchange Bar was now full and people were laughing and talking. He took the opportunity to scoot his chair nearer to hers, placing an arm around her shoulder and leaning his mouth close to her ear. "I work with an organization called the International Development Council. Perhaps you've heard of it?"

"Can't say that I have."

Marshak smiled. "I'm afraid we don't have much of a presence in Hollywood. Anyway, one of the ranking committee members is in town for a reception being held tonight in his honor. It's at some mountain restaurant outside of town, and since I'm part of his security staff, I'll be attending. The 'who's who' of Zug will be there, and I'd like you to come as my guest."

"Really?" asked Andrea excitedly.

"Really," whispered Marshak in her ear, again glancing down at her cleavage.

"How can I say 'no'?" Andrea said, smiling as she turned to look into his eyes.

"Great!"

"But I'll need to go back to my hotel in Zurich to change clothes. Any girl on the arm of this major should look absolutely stunning."

"Then I have a proposal," said Marshak, opening his wallet and taking five thousand francs out of it. "Buy what you need in Zug and meet me back here at six. The clothing stores should be open. When you return, you can change in my room."

"I can't accept that money. Major, I hardly *know* you."

Marshak placed the cash in her hand and closed her fingers around it. "Yes you can. Choose something black and sexy."

She laid the money back on the table. "You're very sweet, but I really should get back to my hotel. Besides, I'll need lingerie and shoes. I'll take the train."

"I insist," Marshak answered, picking up the money and adding another two thousand francs to it as he placed it back in her hand. *Having her body will sure be worth it*, he thought. He watched her eyes widen, then handed her an extra thousand. "This is for just-in-case."

Andrea looked at the money with a stunned expression. "But-"

"Please, do not protest," Marshak said in a gentlemanly tone. "It would be an honor and a privilege." *So long as you give me what I want.* "Now - please - enjoy yourself."

"Well, if this isn't cozy," Cheney called out as he politely apologized to several people between whom he had to squeeze. He sat down at the table just as Andrea was closing her purse. She looked over and managed to keep her expression neutral toward the man who had imprisoned her on a freighter in Adelaide. *And she hoped he would not recognize her.*

"Have we met?" asked Cheney with an inquisitive expression.

"Don't think so," replied Andrea in her broadest American accent. "Ever work in LA?"

The assassin laughed lightly. "No, I haven't," he replied.

"May I present Miss Natalie Cox, from Los Angeles," said Marshak. "Natalie is an actress."

"An actress?" asked Cheney with raised eyebrows. *More likely a high-priced hooker.*

"I was in a lipstick commercial recently," explained Andrea with a quick glance at the polish on her fingernails. "Got me an agent now. He thinks I'll get a speaking role next time, maybe for dog food or a toilet bowl cleanser."

"How interesting," Cheney said, then turning to Marshak. "We're needed upstairs for a meeting. There's been a new development."

Marshak suddenly leaned forward. "Is he here?" he asked, his alarm then abruptly softening as he returned his attention to Andrea. "I'm afraid you must excuse us, my dear; we have some dreary security business to discuss." He rose and offered his hand. "See you at six?" he asked as Andrea took his hand and stood. He then gave her a light kiss on each cheek.

Andrea smiled. "At six," she replied, then giving Cheney a parting smile.

Marshak escorted her through the crowd to the door. "I'm in 401," he said. "Just ask for the key at the desk."

"Are you sure you want to do this?" Andrea asked, still holding his hand. "This is costing a lot of money."

Marshak squeezed her hand. "Money's only good for one thing, and soon there will be a lot more... an insurance settlement. Maybe you can help me decide how to spend it."

With an excited smile, Andrea gave Marshak a lingering kiss, then left the hotel. Marshak watched her proceed happily toward the street.

"I swear I've seen her before," Cheney said from beside him. "I don't know where, but I've seen her."

The smile faded on Marshak's face. "She'll be good for a few nights of fun. Now, what's this new development?"

Cheney nodded for Marshak to follow and they left the crowded bar, crossing the lobby. "Talanov's in Zug," said Cheney as they stepped inside the elevator.

"But that's impossible!"

"I'm afraid it's not," answered Cheney. "He's already been to Credit Suisse and advised them that he's alive and claiming jurisdiction over the account. If he's not dead by Friday, we lose everything."

"Has this been confirmed?"

"By Credit Suisse. Hoskings got a call from one of their people. Thankfully, Talanov's staying on a farm up in the hills. Tonight you'll visit that farm. He mustn't leave there alive."

Outside, Andrea crossed the street at the carefree pace of an infatuated woman. But once she was out of sight, she nearly collapsed against the side of a building, wanting to vomit. She looked down at her trembling hands. *Now what?* she asked herself as she leaned her head against the wall of the building and took a deep breath. She had, of course, achieved her first goal of penetrating the group. But could she go through with Phase Two? Could she go to bed with a man she would kill... with a man she truly despised?

She had bypassed the problem of a gun when she realized there were quieter methods of accomplishing her goal. All she needed to do was gain their trust.

Their very intimate trust.

Andrea then thought back to Spiro's words about the contagious nature of revenge. Was revenge infecting her now? Was she becoming the monster she'd set out to kill?

She was.

And yet what other choice was there? How could she hope to trap these human infections if she didn't enter their world... think like them... be like them? Forcing Spiro and his words out of her mind, Andrea hardened her resolve. Steadying herself, she continued along the sidewalk, reflecting on Marshak's comment to Cheney: "*Is he here?*" Without question, he was alarmed, and in an odd sort of way she had felt the presence of Alex at that instant.

But Alex was dead and she had but one single purpose: to avenge his death.

Which meant she would go through with Phase Two. Yes, she would sleep with Marshak in order to kill him.

And then she would kill Cheney as well.

Chapter 61

The darkness swept in like a cold front and inside the chalet Maria added another chunk of spruce to the fire. Jules had called earlier to inform Wolfgang that no one named Natalie Cox had been located in any of the hotels in Zug, nor was she on tonight's guest list. Wolfgang thanked Jules, then inquired about tuxedos they had discussed. As promised, they would be waiting at the hotel. Wolfgang then informed Jules there had been a slight change in plans and could an extra one be delivered to the farm? Jules agreed to arrange it immediately.

Wolfgang and Joe had been gone for nearly an hour now and the pressed tuxedo was hanging on the door.

A section of wood settle in the stove and sent a brief flurry of sparks swirling in the iron box. Maria walked over and knelt beside Alex. "I must tell you something," she said.

"What is it?"

"My uncle is dying. He did not want me to tell you, but I think you should know."

"*Wolfgang?*" asked Talanov, sitting forward.

"Cancer. He's known for some time."

"For God's sake, why didn't he say something? I never would have involved him if I'd known."

"I am certain that is precisely the reason he did not tell you. Your arrival here has given him purpose... a reason to live. He will not rest until you are back with your wife."

Talanov leaned back and looked again into the flames. "Then he's told you all that's happened and why we're in Zug." A statement more than a question.

"Yes, and he knows the danger."

Alex looked over at Maria. "That danger is very real, Maria, and not just for Wolfgang, but all of you. That's why I must insist you leave the institute once you've taken me there. I won't risk something happening to you."

Maria smiled and stood. "My uncle has issued similar instructions."

"Good," said Alex, relieved.

As Talanov turned and again stared into the fire, Maria watched the orange reflect-ions flicker over his face. "You were his favorite, you know," she said. "He said his son would have been like you."

A sad smile formed on Talanov's face. "I suppose you know whose passport I carry?"

"I know," answered Maria. And without another word, she walked back to the kitchen.

A few minutes later, the echo of a slamming door drew Talanov's attention. He turned to see Johann standing in the kitchen, his cheeks flushed from the cold. Johann removed his thick coat and woollen cap and hung them on top of the other coats hanging on wooden pegs. Above the coat rack was a shelf holding jars of brandied cherries.

Johann walked to the side of Maria and began warming his hands in front of the oven while the smell of fresh bread wafted through the house. A hushed conversation in German ensued and Alex looked back at the fire. Even though he was trying to talk softly, Johann's deep voice resonated like a tuba. Talanov could hear his anxiety and glanced back at Johann gesturing emphatically with his hands.

Alex did not blame Johann for his worry; he, too, wished Maria would stay home. But without her, Alex knew he could not make his way safely through the forest to the institute.

The sound of pans being moved across the stove drowned out Maria's reply, although the look on Johann's face showed his displeasure at what had been said. Maria had obviously stood her ground. Talanov then smiled to himself: he was certain Maria stood her ground in most situations.

Just like Andrea.

And Talanov's smile faded.

The meal was eaten in virtual silence. At first, Maria tried making light conversation, but eventually fell silent like the two men. Johann finished first and rose from the table, taking his plate and glass to the kitchen. He then grabbed his coat and cap and told Maria he was returning to the barn. Maria nodded and Johann walked out the door.

Maria tried apologizing for her brother.

"That's not necessary," Alex replied. "He's worried and I'd be the same. I trust you reassured him that you were merely taking me to the institute and then leaving?"

"I told him, but he worries just the same. Johann is very protective."

When finished, Talanov helped clear the table. Then, while Maria washed dishes, he stepped into one of the bedrooms and put on the tuxedo. After tucking the larger pistol with the silencer inside his belt, he put on the black formal jacket, making sure that it covered his weapon. The smaller pistol he then placed in the front pocket of his trousers.

Alex walked back into the living room and over to a table on which was a small rectangular walnut cabinet with a hinged top. The top was open, and inside was a record turntable. Across the glass panel on front of the Bernina Radio-Gramma-Phone were the various radio frequencies of wartime Europe, while next to the cabinet was a stack of records, each in its original paper sheath.

"*Kannst du vergessen, wie schön es einst war?*" Maria asked, quoting the title of the record on the turntable while drying her hands on a dish towel. She was looking at Alex from the kitchen doorway. "Uncle Wolfgang loves that old waltz. It is slow and sentimental and reminds him of the past."

Alex smiled reflectively as he looked at the record. "Can you forget, how beautiful it once was?" he translated in English. "I just hope I can say it one day for myself."

"Don't give up... you will," said Maria. She hung the towel on a peg near the oven.

Not wanting to carry anything which could be stolen or lost, Alex laid his wallet and passport next to the stack of records where Wolfgang and Joe had placed theirs. He then picked up the slip of paper on which Wolfgang had written the name of Natalie Cox. His cursive was uneven and crooked, as if written with difficulty, perhaps even pain. Alex replaced the note and wondered how much pain Wolfgang was really feeling.

"Here, put these on," Maria said, handing Talanov a pair of Johann's insulated blue overalls.

Alex took the garment and stepped into one leg. "Where are yours?" he asked.

"In the kitchen," she answered as she returned to the coat rack by the door. She pulled hers from the peg and put them on, then hurried downstairs to the basement, returning in just over a minute. "It will be cold, here is a cap," she said, coming back into the living room. "We will ride Johann's motorcycle most of the way, then walk a short distance."

"Don't get us too close," said Talanov as he zipped closed his overalls. "I want to be sure you get safely away."

"No one will know we are there," stated Maria as she tucked her hair up under her cap before pulling it down over her ears.

Chapter 62

The hissing torrent of the shower competed with the brash sound of Andrea's voice as she sang the chorus of *Oklahoma!* for the fifteenth time. Steam had long since fogged up the mirrors, especially after Marshak pulled closed the door, as much to insulate his ears from the obnoxious song as to keep Andrea from seeing him open her purse. He had been careful to observe its exact placement on the bed before opening the clasp and lifting out her passport and wallet. It seemed strange that she carried no credit cards, nor even a driver's license. The passport, however, was American - as expected - and was in order - again, as expected.

To be safe, Marshak wrote down Natalie's passport details on a piece of hotel stationery, then replaced things as he had found them. He folded the paper and stuck it into his pocket before removing a bottle of chilled Bollinger champagne from an ice bucket near the television.

"Champagne for *mademoiselle?*" he asked moments later as he opened the bathroom door and placed a full glass on the counter.

Seconds later, the shower stopped. "Is this for me?" Andrea called out.

"Is what for you?" Marshak called back with a grin as he was pouring his own. "Perhaps I should come and see what you mean."

"Well aren't we feeling cheeky?" she replied, then making herself giggle loudly as a vacuous female would do. *Give him no cause for alarm.*

"I'm afraid there's been a slight change in plans," Marshak said as he took a sip.

"What do you mean?" Andrea asked, emerging from the bathroom with a large white towel wrapped about her, the overlapping ends of which were twisted and tucked together. She took a drink from her glass before placing it on the dresser.

Marshak noticed the swell of her breasts and walked over to her. He then saw what looked like discolorations on her face. "Are those bruises?" he asked, gently touching the spots.

Andrea drew in a short breath and stepped away. Her injuries from the freighter... *and she had washed off the makeup!* She smiled and touched the spots. "Remnants of a bicycle accident," she said, forcing a slight laugh.

"Were you hurt badly?"

"No, but you should have seen my bike. Had to put the old girl down."

Marshak chuckled and came close again, his hand again touching the spots, his eyes then moving down once more to her breasts. His hand then followed his eyes and he untwisted the towel. It fell free. He pulled Andrea to him and kissed her, his arousal turning quickly to passion.

Controlling her desire to scream, Andrea ran her hand slowly down over the sudden swelling in his trousers, then pulled back and slipped deftly from his arms. *She would kill this bastard.* "The night is still young," she said with a coy smile as she strolled naked over to her champagne and took a tantalizingly slow drink, then picked up her towel and walked to the closet.

"You toy with me!" Marshak said, his eyes fired with lust.

"Call it an appetizer," Andrea said with a playful grin as she opened the closet door and pulled out an elegant black gown. It was on a hanger and draped in clear plastic. "So what's this change in plans?" she asked as she casually returned to the bathroom.

"I won't be escorting you to the reception."

Andrea rushed back into the bedroom. "*What?*"

Marshak chuckled lightly. "Don't worry, I'll meet you there. I have some business to complete. Cheney will escort you up the mountain."

"Cheney?" asked Andrea, suddenly worried but managing a smile. "But I want to go with you."

"I'm afraid that will not be possible," Marshak replied, pleased at her response. He took another drink of his champagne.

"But... but why?"

Marshak was enjoying what obviously was her strong preference for him over Cheney. "A security matter, but I shouldn't be long. Then the night will be ours."

But Andrea was already concerned at having to spend time in close contact with Cheney. How observant had he been of her mannerisms in Adelaide? Would he notice her bruises beneath the makeup? Would her disguise continue to fool him?

"Unfortunately, I must go," said Marshak, downing the remainder of his drink. "But I'll stop by and tell Cheney that you're expecting him." He set his empty glass on the dresser and glanced at his watch. "In fact, my dear, you should hurry. He'll be here in half an hour."

Chapter 63

Talanov did not know he could be so near to the pavement and still not touch it. With a quick down shift, Maria had banked the motorcycle around the last corner and Alex swore his knee should have scraped. But it did not, and with an accelerating scream, the bike straightened, Maria then shifting into high gear before giving the throttle grip another firm twist which sent them hurtling forward through the night like a bullet. With his arms wrapped around Maria's waist, Alex placed his face against her hunched back for protection against the fierce wind whipping by them. Ahead, the motorcycle's single headlight stabbed the darkness with a pencil of light.

His ears were ringing from the roar of the engine when Maria began to decelerate. Alex sat up just as they turned off the highway and onto a bumpy dirt track which sent them bouncing. Maria shifted to a lower gear and did her best to steer them around the numerous ruts and holes defacing the trail, the heavy motorcycle jerking them back and forth. Finally they crested a small rise and turned left, following a fence. Alex glanced up at the stars while the clear winter sky scrubbed his face with invigorating cold.

They soon entered a forest, the crisp night air quickly turning damp. The path became a soft blanket of mulching leaves and pine needles as it wound downward through the trees, Maria then angling the big machine to the left and up a narrow trail toward the top of a hill. Near the summit she stopped, the idling engine of the motorcycle pumping like the heart of a race horse.

Maria switched off the ignition. "Now we walk," she said. "The institute is not far."

Alex climbed off slowly and stretched from side to side, breathing deeply several times as much to relax himself from the harrowing ride as to prepare himself for his task.

"About your friend, Joe-" Maria began as she leaned the motorcycle against a large tree.

"Yes?" said Talanov.

"Is he a capable man?"

"He is. Joe flew me across the South Pacific in a twin-engine Cessna and found a chain of volcanic islands - small dots, actually - in the middle of all that water. Threaded the needle and made it look easy. He's stuck by me through some pretty rough times, and - I hear - he can peel an apple with the same skill that he flies."

Maria smiled in the darkness. "Yes, but he tends toward distraction."

"Considering the distraction, I can understand why," stated Talanov.

Maria then blushed but Alex could not see it.

"Joe's first class, all the way," said Alex. "I think you've impressed him."

"I like him, too," Maria said with an affirmative nod. "But his hair, and those awful glasses-"

Talanov chuckled. "Purely for show. One of the killers has already met Joe once and Joe doesn't want to be recognized by him again. With luck, he won't be."

"Will luck be enough?"

"It will have to be," answered Talanov.

But Maria was not so sure.

"What's the terrain like ahead?" asked Talanov.

"The Montana Institute is situated near the rim of the mountain, with its cliff-side restaurant served by the Zugerbergbahn cog railway, or the ZBB, as we call it. There is some fairly dense forest on the upper side of the slope near the institute, but open paddocks on the other, where the terrain is fairly level. The entrance to the institute cuts across the open paddocks from the main road, and will be controlled by the police."

"How close can we get in the trees?"

"Very close," answered Maria. "They encompass some of the buildings."

"Then I want you to steer me away from those trees and buildings. I'll make my approach from the open."

"But why? There is no protection for you out there."

"Precisely, and I'm hoping the killers are thinking that, too. If they are, then they won't suspect me of trying to make an approach from an open field."

"Do you think they suspect you at all?" asked Maria.

"I don't know," answered Talanov. "But Joe and I both know that if we under-estimate them even for a moment, it could be our final mistake."

Chapter 64

Under the dirty glare of a single bulb, Johann tossed the pitchfork down out of the loft and into the hay he just finished stacking. He then descended an old wooden ladder to the concrete floor of the barn. In the workshop, an accordion was playing a German polka over the radio while several cows, having smelled the dusty fragrance of the hay, lowed restlessly in expectation. Johann's deep soothing voice answered their calls with a promise to feed them early the next morning.

His conversation with Maria before dinner had been pointless and frustrating, for she was determined to accompany Talanov to the institute. They had been gone for well over an hour now, and with the restless energy that conversation had generated, he had already raked the stalls, cleaned the storeroom, and repaired a broken feed trough. Knowing he needed to keep busy, Johann then stacked tomorrow's hay although the continued activity did little to relieve his worries. Why had Wolfgang brought them this danger? And why had Maria been so stubborn about assisting?

The barn where Johann was working was several stories high but really had only two floors: the ground floor of concrete - where the workshop was located and where the cows were housed and milked - and the loft.

Reached by any one of several wooden ladders and rising like an immense cavern, the loft was constructed over the ground floor rooms on a platform of heavy planks. Massive log pillars shouldered horizontal joists, which in turn supported a network of even higher beams and struts which bore the weight of the rafters and roof. Smaller lofts occupied remote positions high in the upper reaches and served to store feed and supplies. Decades of dust clung to cloaks of spider webs which were suspended like drapes from the rafters. A virtual mountain of hay filled the cavity, having been blown up and into the huge room by means of a blower and shoot.

Johann removed the pitchfork from the small stack of hay and hung it on a nail by the barn's main double-door. The storeroom was to one side of this, while straight ahead was the main feeding room of individual stalls where the milking was done. Parallel to the main feeding room was a wide aisle with windows through which hay and other feed could be distributed to the stalls, and at the far end was an exit to the barnyard. On the other side of the aisle were more stalls and an indoor corral.

At the far end of the barn, down a short corridor, was the workshop. It was a large room which occupied a full one-fourth of the ground floor. In it lumber could be milled, engines hoisted, and horseshoes smithed over coals. A wood stove still glowed with embers, while nearby, the radio was playing another polka.

Johann flipped a switch and entered the main feeding room. This long room, plus the corral, was where the cows spent much of the winter, particularly when snow covered the highlands. Calling each cow by name, he patted them on their backs, speaking gently to them as he walked.

Up at the chalet, Marshak had slipped in the back door, his pistol with silencer poised near his ear. The faint smell of bread still drifted in the darkened kitchen as he quietly closed the door.

Earlier, he had driven several kilometers past the farm before turning around and driving back, stopping well before the farm came into view. With the engine idling, he extinguished his headlights and sat motionless until his eyes became accustomed to the dark. Then, with his lights still off, he drove slowly down the road toward the farm.

When the chalet's lighted windows came into view, Marshak parked the sedan and switched off the engine. After climbing out, he stood beside the car and studied the house from a distance. The rear of the building was dark, so he would investigate the possibility of entering there. After all, Talanov might well be expecting them to employ the usual method of knocking on the door and shooting the one who opens it.

Minutes later, Marshak was standing in the darkened kitchen, listening carefully. No one appeared to be home! Walking on the balls of his feet, he crept toward the living room. The lights were on, but the room was empty. He would, of course, search every room in the house to make sure. And if indeed the chalet was empty, he would wait until Talanov returned.

Lowering his gun, Marshak stepped into the living room and paused. A recently-tended fire was burning in the stove. Raising his pistol again, he started quietly across the floor, his eyes catching sight of some passports. He walked over and picked one up. It was Australian. He opened it, his eyes suddenly widening. The passport belonged to *Talanov!*

So Talanov was here! But where? Marshak laid the passport back down and reached for another. But his eyes then noticed a small slip of paper. On it was written a name.

Natalie Cox.

The stunned Marshak picked it up. Why would Natalie's name be written on a piece of paper next to Talanov's passport? And in the home of Wolfgang Hauser?

Cheney's words came back to him: "*I'm certain I've seen her before.*"

Where would Cheney have seen Natalie? Certainly not in Los Angeles. But where? Australia? When introduced, Natalie had given no indication that she had ever seen Cheney. Was that because she had never met him, or because she had met him but did not want it known? Natalie's protest over having to go to the reception with Cheney now began to raise doubts. She had insisted it was because she preferred his - Marshak's - company. But maybe that was not really the case. Maybe it was because she wanted to avoid contact with Cheney.

But why... what was she hiding? Her identity?

Marshak knew Natalie's passport had been in good order. Nevertheless, as a precaution, he had given her details to Cheney, who would check them with Bob.

After glancing at the other passports, Marshak tossed them back down and conducted a search of the rest of the house. Finding no one, he returned to the kitchen.

Standing in the dark, Marshak found himself growing impatient, even angry. *Who was Natalie Cox?* Was he being played for a sucker? Had that meeting in the bar not been an accident?

Assuming Cheney *had* met her before, what woman did Cheney know that Talanov also knew? If he were honest, there was only one woman who fitted that description - Talanov's wife. Yet this should be immaterial, because Three and Four would have killed her by now.

Unless Three and Four had again failed in their assignment just as they'd failed in the others.

Marshak's mind began to race. Even if Talanov's wife were alive, why would she be in Zug? How could she possibly know to come here? There was little doubt she would have been notified about her husband's death by now, even though it had been the constable, not Talanov, who had been killed.

But what if Three and Four had indeed failed in their assignment to kill her, being captured instead by the police? And what if one of them had talked? And what if Talanov's wife - thinking her husband to be dead - was now in Zug gunning for revenge... as Natalie Cox?

With a curse Marshak crumpled the paper in his fist. Natalie Cox must be Talanov's *wife!*

Some movement caught Marshak's eye. He glanced around quickly, then peered out through the kitchen window to see a silhouette pass across a lighted window in the distance. *Someone was in the barn.*

Tightening his grip on his gun, Marshak slipped out the back door and hurried down the footpath. He quietly approached the lighted window and peeked through the dirty pane into a large workshop filled with machinery, hoists, and wooden benches surrounded by hand tools hanging on nails. He could hear a polka being played on the radio but saw no one.

Marshak lowered his head and moved to the other side of the window to get a different view. Again, he could see no one.

He ducked under the window again and walked to the door, taking hold of the handle and giving it a gentle twist. The door opened and Marshak entered.

High up in one of the smaller lofts, Johann placed a sack of feed on the wooden slide and released it. Propelled by gravity and making a mild scraping sound, the sack slid down the long incline, making two switchback drop-turns before reaching the feeding room near the cows. Johann then switched off the light and prepared to climb down just as a figure raced to the feeding room door far below. In the reflected light from the workshop, Johann could see the person was a man and that he was carrying something in his hand. The man paused and peered through the door, the instrument in his hand now visible in the dim wash of light. *It was a pistol with silencer!*

Johann jumped off the ladder and back onto the wooden platform, his heavy boots scuffing the planks as he did. Marshak spun toward the noise and fired.

Short, muffled bursts were all that was heard as the dry timber of the platform splintered once, twice, then three times in rapid succession. Johann cried out and fell back as fragments of wood flew into his face.

Suddenly the light came on. Marshak had found the switch! His eyes fixed on the high corner of the barn, Marshak started up the ladder.

Knowing he would be killed if the man with the gun reached him, Johann picked up an ax and swung it at the insulated wiring running out of the top of the switch box to the overhead lights. Sparks flew as the wire was severed. The loft went dark.

Marshak stopped halfway up the ladder, unable to see up into the cavernous heights of the barn. If he continued, and with the workshop light illuminating the floor behind him, he knew he would be an easy mark for a pitchfork. An option would be to riddle the loft with bullets, but his ammunition was limited and at best would be hit-and-miss. No, he needed a sure means of killing his opponent without endangering his own safety. Climbing back down to the concrete floor, Marshak noticed the fresh pile of hay standing on the floor beside him. He then looked up at the mountain of hay rising above him. A thin smile appeared on his face and he took out some matches.

The dried grass ignited immediately, with thick white smoke unfurling and twisting upward in ominous narrow spirals. At the smell of smoke, the cattle in the feeding room became nervous. Ignoring the sounds of the animals, Marshak instead fixed his attention high up in the loft where reflections of orange were skipping about. Sooner or later his target must climb down.

But while the growing fire was indeed giving off light, the dense smoke it produced was obscuring it. Marshak was soon dodging from side to side, trying to see up through the swirling cloud. Suddenly, he saw movement. Marshak fired - a *scream!* He then fired again, then again.

By now, the small pile of hay was a full blaze which was taking hold of the loft's wooden floor. Other flames had already crawled across the platform and were bursting up the side of the mountain.

Barely able to breathe, Marshak was having to shield his face from the intense heat and knew he could not stay inside. While the panic-stricken livestock kicked at the sides of their stalls and bawled, Marshak ran outside to catch his breath, then quickly began circling the barn to look for other doors where his target might escape. Flashes of orange and yellow could be seen in the barn's high windows as Marshak ran along the back of the structure.

Marshak came around the corner and stopped. The workshop door was open! He ran over and looked inside - the room was empty - then out at the darkened countryside. Had his target escaped? Marshak suddenly jumped back against the side of the building, for high above came the sound of exploding glass as smoke and flames burst through some of the windows and began leaping into the night sky with demonic frenzy. Glass fragments rained down around him while he looked anxiously for his target. *Where had he gone?*

What was that? From the other side of the barn came the clamor of terrified cows stampeding into the night. Marshak raced back around the corner and saw what he had heard - stampeding animals, although they were being waved to safety by a large man in overalls. The scream from the loft had been a trick... the open workshop door a diversion! Marshak cursed and took aim, the man diving back into the barn just as he fired three quick shots. The bullets missed.

Not remembering how many cartridges had been used, Marshak unclipped the magazine and it popped free from the handle. He then inserted a full clip and snapped the cocking mechanism which slid a loaded cartridge into the chamber. He then ran after the farmer.

Marshak approached the open door, his gun aimed at the opening. Suddenly two more cows came charging out. He stumbled back, firing twice and hitting a cow, which squalled and fell.

He tried aiming at the large dark figure lunging toward him. But the barrel was knocked away just as he pulled the trigger, the bullet penetrating the side of the barn instead. Johann grabbed the gun with both hands, wrenching it up, then twisting down. He yanked the pistol free just as Marshak hammered his fist into Johann's stomach. But to Marshak's horror, his fist bounced off.

Johann threw the gun aside and turned on Marshak with a roar. But Marshak ducked under a wild swing and ran for the pistol. Johann turned and charged again, catching Marshak in the back with his shoulder just as he grabbed for the weapon. Both men hit the frigid ground and rolled, Marshak's fingers missing the weapon.

Rolling and wrestling, the two men fought one another, Marshak using his fists and knees - all to no avail - while Johann, who was much slower than his adversary, tried in vain to grasp Marshak firmly enough to deliver a blow.

Within minutes, both men were winded from their tumbling fight as Marshak pounded his fist against another attempt by the big farmer to encircle his waist. Johann's arms loosened and Marshak scurried to his feet. But as Marshak started to run, Johann managed to clamp both hands around one of his ankles. Thrown off balance, Marshak hit the frozen ground like a downed tree, the blow knocking the air from his lungs.

Scrambling to pin his adversary, Johann lumbered forward on his hands and knees. But Marshak twisted, his knees and feet kicking away Johann's hands.

Marshak jumped up... *where was the gun?*

That moment of hesitation was what Johann needed, and leaping up, he encircled Marshak's ribs from behind and began squeezing with all of his strength. Marshak wrenched to the side and began pounding his fists against the powerful arms now crushing the breath out of him. Gasping for air, Marshak hurled himself to the earth, twisting and clawing, then in desperation smashed his head back into Johann's face. The thick cranial bone caught Johann on the nose, temporarily blinding him with pain. Again the arms loosened... Marshak was free!

Crawling and stumbling, the winded Marshak clambered to his feet. Although he was trained in hand-to-hand combat, one could not fight a bear with fists. He must find his gun!

The back of the huge barn was now a sheet of yellow which was engulfing the broad eaves and filling the darkened sky with cinders and fire. And in the dancing glow from the flames, Marshak saw a reflection.

His fingers extended, his eyes riveted on the hardened steel, Marshak ran toward the gun. But as he flew toward the weapon, just as suddenly he saw two other hands appear in the periphery of his vision. Both men reached the pistol at the same time and tumbled to the ground, wrestling each other for possession of the deadly automatic. Marshak smashed a fist into Johann's face. But the heavy jaw of the Swiss was like a fence post and he merely responded with an angry roar. In his fury, Johann ripped the gun from Marshak's hand and flung it away, then reared up and prepared to pound his fists into Marshak's stomach. But while Johann's arms were extended, Marshak kicked upward at Johann's face, catching him in the nose. The big Swiss screamed and fell back.

Blood was pouring from Johann's nose as he slowly climbed to his feet. After finding his balance, he tried wiping his eyes but they would not clear. He lowered his hands and squinted around him but could see nothing other than clouded distortions of yellow from the burning barn.

The pistol... where had he thrown it? If only he could *see.*

But he could not see - not clearly, anyway - and there was no time to search for it now. His only chance was to run.

Johann, however, knew that he could not run far without sight, and even then he could not outrun bullets. He moved like an ox, not a deer.

Not like Maria.

An excited shout sounded in the darkness behind him. The killer must have located his gun. Johann's thoughts turned again to his sister, his protective instincts exploding within him.

And with the bellow of a wounded bull, Johann ran into the burning barn.

After grabbing his pistol, Marshak spun and prepared to shoot just as Johann rushed into the inferno. Keeping a safe distance, he circled back toward the door only to see Johann's clothing catch fire. Like a surrealistic character from a horror movie, Johann writhed, then stumbled forward just as a ceiling of burning boards collapsed upon him.

Stunned by the scene, Marshak lowered his gun without having fired. He wiped his forehead with his other arm, then looked toward what sounded like a siren. In the distance he could see the flashing lights of a fire truck speeding up the road. He had to run... no one must see him!

Marshak sprinted around the corner of the barn and ran toward the house. Suddenly, he heard a shout in German. He paused to see a man and woman hurrying down the lane toward him, pointing excitedly at the barn and waving their hands. Marshak smiled coldly and raised his gun, firing two quick shots which dropped each of them dead on the gravel.

And without looking back, he ran past the chalet and into the darkness.

Chapter 65

With a furrow of concern on his forehead, Bob Hoskings was adjusting his bow tie although his eyes were on the slip of paper in Cheney's hand. "This note says that Natalie Cox's passport - which is obviously one of the old ones - was issued by the regional center in New Orleans," said Bob.

"I guess so," replied Cheney. "Marshak copied the information and he's usually precise."

Bob looked at Cheney. "Why would someone living in Los Angeles, which has its own center, get a passport from New Orleans? Nowadays, all of them are issued from the national center in Philadelphia, but back then things were handled regionally."

Cheney shrugged. "Maybe she used to live in New Orleans."

"Maybe," Bob remarked as he looked again in the mirror. Satisfied, he picked up his tuxedo jacket and put it on, then straightened his cuffs. "It's a minor - perhaps inconsequential - detail," he continued as he stepped over to the bedside table and picked up his wallet and one mobile phone, "but with everything that's at stake, I want irregularities - no matter how small - to be thoroughly investigated. Ask her a few questions, such as how she's financing this trip. If she's not carrying any credit cards, then she's either left them back in her room - which no intelligent traveler would do - or she's toting a lot of cash, which apparently was not in her wallet."

"Marshak's interest is not in her brains. She may well have left them in her room."

"Try and find out. Marshak can pick up whom he wishes, but until our transaction with Credit Suisse has been finalized, we've got to be careful, especially with Talanov on the loose." He glanced at his watch. "I'm late, I'll see you on the mountain."

Chapter 66

Talanov followed Maria silently through the trees to the edge of the open paddocks bordering the Montana Institute. Far off to their right, the lights of the institute were but a cluster of bright dots on a black canvas. The tree line tore across the top of this canvas in a jagged edge, exposing the luminous depths of the sky. Suddenly, Talanov dropped to the ground, tugging Maria down with him. "Be still," he said in a hushed voice.

"What is it?" she whispered.

"Voices, off to the right."

Gradually, the sound of two men talking and laughing became audible. They were walking casually along the edge of the forest, making unconcerned noise as they tramped over the crunchy grass. Obviously, they were expecting no trouble, at least not out here. One stopped to light a cigarette, the momentary flash of light illuminating a young face of perhaps twenty-five.

Inexperienced youngsters, thought Talanov as he and Maria remained motionless in the black of the forest. In less than a minute the two men has passed by, Talanov allowing several additional minutes to elapse before he stood.

"This is where I leave you," Alex whispered as Maria joined him. "Be careful on your way back. There may be others."

"I will," replied Maria. "Good luck."

Talanov ran silently across the open field, aware that he needed to keep low and out of the line of sight of the guards so that his silhouette did not eclipse their view of the institute lights, even for an instant. The two young guards may have been careless but certainly were not stupid. If they saw even a darting movement across the yellow dots in the distance, they would radio for others to investigate.

As discussed earlier with Wolfgang and Joe, Talanov's plan was to walk into the reception and confront the killers in public, perhaps even taunting them by having a glass of champagne. During this time, he also hoped he would be able to meet the mysterious Bob Hoskings, about whom he would imply a connection with Andropov's group of assassins. After the confrontation, he would vow publicly to involve the police in order to settle matters with Credit Suisse. Then he would leave.

The entire strategy was based on the assumption that the killers would do nothing in front of so many guests. He was, in fact, counting on that to motivate Cheney to follow him away from the reception in order to kill him. Joe, of course, would be armed and would follow Cheney. Wolfgang would remain behind and listen to what Hoskings said.

Because of all the brutality committed by the assassins, Talanov wished he could just gun them down. But he could not. To be sure, he would do everything in his power to bring them to justice, and he had no hesitation in defending himself.

But he would not commit cold-blooded murder for the sake of revenge. He had sold his soul to such ethics while at Balashikha and the effects nearly ruined his life. Never again. His wife and his own sanity were much too valuable, and the poison of such actions too deadly.

He just hoped his plan would work.

Chapter 67

The restaurant was filling with guests. The men wore dark suits or tuxedos, the women conservative but elegant gowns draped with expensive furs. In one corner, surrounded by several displays of fresh flowers, a young woman in a flowing white gown plucked a undulating melody on the strings of a harp, the subdued music an accompaniment to the subdued conversation and laughter. Executives and their wives chatted with executives and their husbands, exchanging compliments when warranted or unavoidable.

While Cheney went outside to monitor security, Andrea watched a smiling Bob Hoskings work the crowd like a politician. After an exaggerated introduction by Jules - who knew everyone of importance in Zug - Bob would graciously understate his new role with the IDC, as well as his fund-raising successes throughout Europe and America, the more spectacular of these somehow always being mentioned. Obligatory nods and polite exclamations were then rewarded with a return salvo of effusive compliments about Swiss ingenuity and Zug's importance in the world of finance. And with the next group, the process was repeated.

Andrea accepted a glass of white wine off a silver tray from a waiter in rose-colored glasses. *What dreadful hair,* she thought about his blond spikes as he moved on to serve other guests. Other members of the hotel staff circulated through the crowded room with platters of hors d'oeuvres, and Andrea the caterer found herself drawn to regional delicacy of air-dried shavings of beef and ham. The Swedish meatballs and crabmeat spring rolls were likewise superior, but the barbequed chicken wings were dull and ordinary.

Earlier in the evening, while they were leaving the hotel, Andrea realized her fears about recognition had been for nothing. All the way down in the elevator Cheney did not show the slightest suspicion. In fact, it pleased Andrea that Cheney had difficulty keeping his eyes off her revealing gown. She had dressed in such a gown for that very reason - distraction - but wore extra makeup to help guarantee that her facial bruises would not be noticed.

Her plan was to kill Marshak later that night after engaging him in enough sex to completely exhaust him. Later, while he slept, she would crush his skull with a bottle of wine... perhaps with one of his Bollingers! Then, wearing the black silk negligee she had purchased with Marshak's money, she would knock on Cheney's door with the pretense of being unable to sleep. Wanting company to help her drink the bottle of champagne she would be carrying, she would manipulate Cheney into bed, exhausting him as she had exhausted Marshak. That plan was her single focus when she climbed in the waiting limousine with Cheney for the ride to the cog railway station.

On the way over, Andrea crossed her legs and leaned toward Cheney, revealing more of her cleavage. She smiled while Cheney kept his gaze fixed straight ahead, occasionally making eye contact, but not often. He talked about travel - had she ever been to New Orleans? - and how Andrea seemed to travel so light. Didn't she worry about theft?

A test, go with your instincts, she seemed to hear Alex say. Yes, she had been to New Orleans, but - no - she did not worry about theft; she always placed her valuables in the hotel safe.

While Cheney rambled on, Andrea suddenly found herself focusing on Alex. She saw herself sitting beside him the night of Helena's wedding, with Spiro across the table.

Spiro! Andrea forced his image away, not wanting the conviction of his words to detract her from her purpose. Whatever it took - and whatever the cost - she would avenge what these killers had done. They had destroyed *everything*. And in her unyielding resolve to get even, it was frightening to see how she, too, was becoming a killer, a whore, a robot - a person incapable of feeling. Even hatred no longer had place, for hatred involved emotion. Once again, Andrea realized how such detachment had protected Alex, and she relished that protection now. In fact, it did not bother her that she felt no guilt about any of her motives or actions. Aside from the occasional longing she felt for Alex, Andrea felt nothing. Soon, for the sake of survival, she knew she would drive his entire memory from her heart.

Cheney watched Andrea accept another glass of wine from the blond waiter. "She seems to be on the level," he told Bob in a lowered voice as another waiter poured them two glasses of mineral water at a long table set up as a bar. "She stores her valuables in the hotel safe and admits to having spent time in New Orleans."

"Good job," said Bob as he accepted the drinks and handed one to Cheney. Bob took a swallow and surveyed the crowd, then took Cheney aside, their backs to the guests. "I've got to play to good ol' boy and placate these boring snobs. So keep an eye on security, especially in the forested area. The fact that Hauser's here is a concern although he didn't remember me. Nevertheless, I want you to remove him."

"How removed?" asked Cheney.

"Out of commission, but alive. We may need him in case Talanov shows."

"Do you think Talanov will try something tonight?"

"We've got to assume it's possible until Marshak actually returns and tells me he's dead. Now, introduce me to Miss Natalie Cox."

"More wine for the lady?" asked Joe, holding out the tray.

"Thank you, but I think I've had enough," Andrea answered, handing Joe her empty glass. He accepted the glass and turned.

"Natalie, allow me to introduce you to Mr Hoskings," Cheney said, walking up and taking her gently by the elbow.

At the mention of Natalie's name, Joe whirled around just as the others directed their attention to the compact man in a tuxedo walking briskly toward them.

"Miss Cox, I'm Bob Hoskings," Bob said, extending his hand to reveal a diamond Rolex watch near turquoise cuff links. "I'm so pleased you could join us. But I'm afraid Major Marshak's rather dazzling description of you has failed miserably. Your beauty exceeds vocabulary."

"Thank you, Mr Hoskings," Andrea replied, shaking his hand. "I'm afraid your flattery exceeds vocabulary."

Bob laughed. "And sharp as a tack! I like that in a woman. Please, call me Bob. I'm just a country boy."

"Which country? I detect an accent."

The remark gave the former Russian an unexpected moment of alarm. A broad smile then spread over his face. "You almost fooled me with that one," he said, regaining his easy composure. He laughed again and Cheney did the same. "Which country... that's a good one! I'm from the South, my dear."

Andrea smiled. "Of course, I should have known."

Bob then grew serious. "Natalie, I'm afraid the blame is all mine for Major Marshak's absence tonight. We had a security matter which demanded his expertise. He should be joining us soon."

"No apology required. Mr Cheney is excellent company."

"Good," said Bob, then nodding to Jules, who was waving that he was ready for another round of introductions. "I beg your forgiveness, but duty calls. We'll have more time later to talk."

"I look forward to it," answered Andrea.

All smiles, but surface only, thought Andrea as she watched Bob leave. *And he's definitely not from the South*.

"Let's circulate," said Cheney, his eyes on the elderly Wolfgang greeting some friends. "I must leave from time to time, but until Major Marshak arrives, I'll do my best to stay by your side."

Andrea looked up at Cheney and smiled. "Thanks, I enjoy your company." *Prepare him for later*.

They wandered through the crowd, pausing to chat briefly with different guests. As part of Bob's staff, Cheney elaborated on the IDC's goal of fostering economic independence for needy nations. Andrea just smiled and kept silent.

Soon, however, Andrea became aware that she was being watched. Even when Cheney excused himself, she felt the presence of someone's attention. Looking casually around, Andrea finally identified the person: the waiter in rose-colored glasses! He had served her several glasses of wine during the course of the evening and seemed never to be far away. Yet his look was not one of physical interest. A woman can tell when lust fills a man's eyes, and this man did not have that look.

Why, then, was he watching her? Did he know who she was? Smiling and nodding to the strong opinions of the woman in the fox stole and short black hair, Andrea asked herself how a waiter in Zug could possibly know her identity. *He could not*, she told herself. Then who was he and what did he want?

Cheney was suddenly at her side again, entering the conversation as though he had never left it. Yes, the IDC provides necessary financial assistance and food, but even more crucial is teaching impoverished nations to care for themselves. "Give a man a fish and you save him today," Cheney said. "Teach him to fish and save him forever." The listeners heartily agreed.

A short distance away, Joe looked again through the crowd for Wolfgang. He must tell him about finding Talanov's wife. He had tried not to be obvious with his surveillance, but several times she had turned and noticed him watching her and he was now certain she was aware of his presence. He only hoped she would not report it.

Ideally, she would step aside and personally question him, at which time he could inform her about Alex. But with so many people around, and with her escort or Hoskings nearby, he must not initiate contact, at least not yet. To do so prematurely meant risking his cover as a waiter, which would endanger his ability to help Alex.

So where was Wolfgang? Setting his tray on the table, Joe walked outside on the balcony where several guests stood smoking. Far below, the lights of the city stopped in an abrupt line at the edge of the lake, now a massive black void surrounded by clusters of tiny white dots. Joe walked along the balcony to the ZBB station. The cog railway car was standing empty beneath an overhead light. Rubbing his hands together for warmth, Joe looked around but saw no one. *Where was Wolfgang?*

On the other side of the restaurant, Talanov stood in the shadowed protection of an ornate wooden house called Chalet Suisse and removed his overalls, tossing them next to the building after using them to wipe off his shoes. He then adjusted his bow tie and jacket and started toward the lights of the restaurant.

But a car suddenly came roaring down the lane toward the institute, Talanov stepping quickly back out of sight. The car skidded to a stop and a man jumped out and ran toward the restaurant, leaving the door to the vehicle wide open.

An emergency of some kind, thought Alex as he stepped away from the darkened chalet once the man had disappeared. He strolled over to the car and peered inside. There, in the glare of the interior light, Alex saw the silencer of a pistol protruding from beneath the seat. Alex knew the Swiss police did not carry pistols with silencers. No, *this* was the weapon of an assassin.

After looking around to make sure no one was watching, Alex reached into his pocket and took out a handkerchief, and with it removed the pistol, being careful to preserve any fingerprints. He smelled the barrel. The gun had been recently fired. An alarming thought then came to Alex. Johann, Maria... *the farm!*

Hastening back over to the chalet, Alex picked up his overalls and carried them to a more protected spot near the rear of the house. After wrapping the pistol loosely in the overalls, he tucked them beneath the branches of a bush. He then hurried toward the restaurant which was resounding with music and laughter. *Things will not stay happy for long,* he told himself as he checked his weapons, the larger one inside his jacket being within easy reach.

Alex descended a gentle slope and walked through a breeze way with a regional map of Zug mounted on the wall. He turned left and made his way past several groups of people talking, wine glasses in their hands, smiles of glazed unconcern on their faces.

Walking along the balcony toward the entrance, Talanov looked in through a wall of windows built to give daytime customers a view of the valley. Now the situation was reversed, with the darkness outside making the crowded restaurant the focus. Ahead, several couples stepped out through the door and paused to light cigarettes. Draped in furs and jewelry, the women held their wine glasses with their fingertips, the men as though grasping a baseball. All were chatting merrily as they strolled toward the railing.

Talanov's eyes scanned the faces in the room. Where was Cheney?

Suddenly, his attention became fixed on a woman in a revealing black gown. The hair color was different and so was the cut, but behind the glasses was a face he knew.

Andrea!

A compact man in a tuxedo approached the group and said something, the people then laughing at what had been said. After another humorous comment, Bob Hoskings then offered apologies for himself and Miss Cox before taking Andrea by the elbow and escorting her away through the crowd.

Talanov could not move. He *knew* that man... a man he had not seen since 1983 *when he was murdered by Cheney!*

How could this be possible? How could Georgi Vaskin be alive?

Alive and in the company of his wife!

Chapter 68

His eyes blinded by pain, Johann had known he could not run or fight. A man of the land since his youth, he had always worked with his hands, an instinct which would now cost him his life.

Two times he could have used the attacker's gun against him, and two times he had thrown it away, preferring the strength of his hands. But this time his hands weren't enough.

And there certainly would not be a next time.

Johann did not fear death. He knew there was a God and he believed in that God. But then he thought of Maria. Would the attacker go after her? Losing his own life did not matter, but he would not - *could* not - allow harm to come to his sister.

Yet what could he do? True - his eyes were clearing and the pain subsiding. But enough to outrun bullets?

Then an idea hit him: the feeding room for the cows! On the other side of that room were two doors, and between them a limestone water trough which, if he reached it, just might save his life. Without doubt the barn was a death-trap, but also his one chance to live. Perhaps he would perish while trying, but at this point he had nothing to lose.

Rushing into the flames, Johann felt his overalls ignite, the pain of cauterized skin and hair causing him to nearly collapse on the spot. But he could not quit - not now - and so forced himself forward. Suddenly the ceiling behind him collapsed, the stench of charred flesh - *his* flesh - propelling him in agony toward the water.

His foot struck something hard... he twisted and fell, the cold water in the trough extinguishing his clothing and soothing his back. Swallowing a gulp, then another, Johann coughed and climbed out just as the timber ceiling above him cracked. Through the gap a jet of orange flames billowed down, the burning boards groaning under their own weight just as Johann reached the storeroom door and pushed it open. He stumbled through it seconds before the remainder of the ceiling crashed down.

The barn was a roaring furnace, and drenched with perspiration, Johann spun away from the door and tried wrapping an arm across his face to shield him from the heat. Disoriented and unable to see because of dense smoke, he groped along the wall of the darkened storage room for the outside door. Moving clumsily forward, he hit a metal shelf and it fell over, spilling cans and boxes onto the floor. Now dizzy from inhaling so much smoke, he tripped on the shelf and fell.

Gasping for air, Johann crawled over the shelf and tumbled onto his side. His parched lungs could only wheeze as they heaved in vain. He rolled onto his back. *Got to get up*, he told himself, rising to his knees. But his mind was spinning... he was losing consciousness.

Johann fell, his outstretched hands grabbing the metal latch as he did. The door pushed open and Johann's face landed in the cool dirt outside.

The jolt tore open his eyes and in the distance he heard voices... a man and a woman... then suddenly, silence.

With fresh air filling his lungs, Johann pushed himself up onto his hands and knees, choking and coughing, his seared back and blackened arms screaming with pain. One knee inched forward, then the other.

Johann slowly reached the path leading up to the chalet. Behind him, the burning barn began to sag, parts of the massive roof then caving in and sending an explosion of sparks and debris into the air. Falling onto his side, Johann watched other parts of the roof collapse just as a fire truck turned into the driveway. Men in protective gear jumped out and rushed toward the barn while two young female paramedics ran over to him with a small oxygen cylinder and medical kit. Johann tried to get up but could not.

"Please, lie still," one of the paramedics told him in German while the other one turned a valve on the cylinder and placed the mask over Johann's mouth. "We will treat your burns and get you to the hospital."

"*Nein!*" protested Johann hoarsely, pushing the mask away. But his attempt to speak only caused deep coughing which doubled him over.

"You must be quiet and *lie still!*" the paramedic emphasized, nodding for the other one to secure the mask. "Your lungs have been weakened by the smoke."

The other paramedic again secured the oxygen mask over Johann's nose and mouth, then ran over to the bodies nearby. Within moments she had returned. "The others are dead," she said. "Poor Johann is lucky to be alive with those burns."

"Do you know this man?" the first paramedic asked as she removed some sterile bandages from the kit.

"Of course, and also his sister. She and Johann work the farm together."

The first paramedic paused momentarily and stared at her friend, then glanced at the raging barn as more of it collapsed. "Sister?" she asked with alarm.

"Oh, my *God!*"

"What's her name?" asked the first paramedic.

"Maria," the other one answered.

"Then where is Maria... and who is responsible for killing those other people?"

In the distance, the tail lights of Marshak's car were but two small red dots as he sped back toward the Montana Institute.

Chapter 69

Talanov had just started toward the restaurant when a gun barrel was pressed hard into his back. "Well, look who we have here," Cheney said in a low voice as he quickly frisked Talanov's body. He located and removed both weapons and stuck them beneath his jacket.

"You and Vaskin... you planned this from the beginning! You *faked* Vaskin's death so that you could steal the seven million for yourselves."

"So you finally figured it out! Yes, Colonel, once we learned Andropov was creating an investment account from which he would fund *Peristroika*, we decided to put that money to much better use. It did not take a crystal ball to see the system was doomed to collapse."

"But he suspected something and transferred the account to me."

"How he found out, I'll never know," replied Cheney, his gun still in Talanov's back. "But - yes - he transferred jurisdiction of the account to you. We planned to go after the money back in eighty-four, but found out - much to our dismay - that his investment banker in Hong Kong had already moved the funds and purchased some speculative properties. Figuring it was lost, we forgot about it until we learned the pot had grown."

"Grown? What do you mean?" asked Talanov.

Cheney smiled. "Your account now contains one-and-a-half billion dollars."

"One-and-a-half *billion?*" asked Talanov, spinning around, only to be met by Cheney's pistol thrust under his chin.

"Not on your life!" growled Cheney, grabbing Talanov by the arm and turning him back the other way. "Inside, let's go. But remember: cause any trouble and you're a dead terrorist I had to shoot. I'm sure your fingerprints on these two guns - one of which would end up back in your hands as the one I'd swear you pulled on me - would be more than enough to satisfy the police, who know me as Hoskings' chief of security."

"Bob Hoskings," said Talanov softly, shaking his head. "So Vaskin changed his name."

"Question-and-Answer time is over," said Cheney as he pushed Talanov toward the door, his gun now concealed in his jacket pocket.

Inside, the restaurant was filled with a convivial crowd and Talanov was steered through them by Cheney's hand on his shoulder. Alex knew that he had to act quickly, for he would be killed once they were in more secluded surroundings. The reason was obvious: the only way anyone could gain control over the account now was by getting rid of him before Friday.

His one advantage, at least for the moment, was the hesitation Cheney would feel about pulling the trigger in the midst of so many people. Even if the police knew him to be Hoskings' chief of security, a certain propriety must still be maintained, particularly in front of witnesses. Were they alone in the forest, Cheney would simply gun him down. But here in the restaurant, things were different. Cheney would not risk losing a fortune by landing himself in prison on a charge of murder.

"Don't even think about it, Colonel," Cheney said quietly in Talanov's ear. "I know every detail of your training - as I'm sure you recall when I recited it from memory that night when we first met - and at this moment I know you are assessing your options. I repeat: if you try *anything*, after killing you I will make *sure* you end up with a gun in your hand. I will be exonerated completely for my actions and - yes - I will collect my reward on Friday, if you know what I mean. Now keep walking, into the kitchen."

"*Meine dame und herren*," Jules suddenly called out from a position near the harpist, one hand raised to draw the attention of the guests, who quickly grew quiet. Cheney halted Talanov while all eyes turned toward the owner of the Parkhotel, who continued speaking in German. "Our distinguished host, Mr Bob Hoskings, has been called into an international telephone conference over an incident which requires his immediate attention. Therefore, I'm afraid it is my sad duty to conclude tonight's festivities although Mr Hoskings has invited all of you to brunch tomorrow morning as his guests. The venue will be the hotel's *le Boulevard restaurant*, with cocktails to be served at eleven and a full buffet to follow. Mr Hoskings begs your forgiveness, thanks you for coming, and hopes to see you tomorrow. Limousines are waiting for those of you who do not wish to ride down the mountain in the ZBB."

Surprised, then disappointed, then pleased to be included in tomorrow's buffet, the guests began finishing their champagne.

"Well done," Marshak told Jules as he surveyed the crowd. "The police have been dismissed, so do a quick clean up and leave. I'll handle the rest."

"Do you want me to leave Miss Cox's security man here to assist you?"

Marshak, still in dirty clothing, looked down at Jules. "Which security man?"

"I thought you knew," said Jules. "It's most discreet, of course. Charles - the waiter with the blond hair and rose-colored glasses - is here tonight for the expressed purpose of protecting Miss Cox." Joe was busy accepting empty glasses on his tray when Jules pointed him out to Marshak.

"Who ordered this protection?" asked Marshak, watching Joe.

"I am not certain," replied Jules, not wishing to reveal Wolfgang's name, then suddenly conscious that he had not seen Wolfgang all night. "It is a very private matter."

"Naturally," said Marshak, aware that the owner of the hotel was not about to tell him anything further. He looked at Jules with a smile. "Yes, allow him to remain and complete his assignment. I have no objection and I'm grateful for the help. We professionals must work together. But say nothing to him. It is a great embarrassment to have ones cover exposed."

Jules was relieved. "My lips are sealed, *mein Herr!* And my staff and I shall be gone with the last of the guests."

Downstairs, Georgi Vaskin - Bob Hoskings - unlocked a door, switched on the light, and ushered Andrea into a storage room lined with metal shelves full of boxes and cans. Once they were both inside, he shut the door.

Andrea turned and looked at Bob with concern. "What are we doing in here?"

"Just a few questions... Natalie," he said. "It *is* Natalie, isn't it?"

Andrea tried not to show her alarm. "What kind of question is that? You know my name... you've been using it all night."

"Yes, I guess I have."

"Then what are you talking about?" she asked.

Bob walked casually away from the door, his hands behind his back. "Because I need you to tell me why your name was found written on a piece of paper in the home of Wolfgang Hauser."

"I don't know any Wolfgang Hauser."

"Are you sure you don't know him? He's a retired instructor with the KGB."

KGB? Andrea was careful to communicate her displeasure, both with an annoyed expression and by the tone of her voice. "I *told* you I don't know any Wolfgang Hauser." She tried to step around Bob but he grabbed her by the arm. "Let *go* of me!" she said, trying to wrench free.

"Not until you tell me why Wolfgang Hauser would be looking for you," repeated Bob, tightening his grip.

"How many times must I tell you that I don't *know* any Wolfgang Hauser?" answered Andrea. "Now *let me go.*"

Bob jerked Andrea toward the door. "Then perhaps we'll see if he knows you. He happens to be in the next room."

"Go ahead and ask, because I told you I don't know him and I don't."

"Perhaps not. But you may know one of his friends."

"And who is that?" demanded Andrea, pulling away from Bob. She ran to the other side of the room.

"Aleksandr Talanov," said Bob.

Chapter
70

Cheney guided Alex toward the kitchen door and Alex knew what that meant: somewhere beyond, a bullet was waiting. His moment of advantage had almost vanished.

Off to his right, Alex caught sight of a woman in a cluster of people. Dressed in a jacket of Russian fox over a long black gown, Frau Hunziker wore a single strand of pearls around her neck and was actually laughing. Her dark hair was still pulled back in a bun, around which was a smaller strand of pearls.

Talanov veered quickly to his right, catching Cheney completely off guard.

"Frau Hunziker!" exclaimed Alex with a broad smile, his hands extended as he approached her. "How wonderful to see you!"

"Mr Talanov?" said a startled Esther Hunziker.

"You remembered!" said Talanov enthusiastically just as Cheney grabbed him by the shoulder. He turned and drew Cheney into the group. "May I present an old associate? Mr Cheney works for Bob Hoskings."

Impressed to meet one of Bob Hoskings' staff, people in the group began to warmly greet Cheney, who restrained his anger while bowing politely.

"I'm afraid you must excuse Mr Talanov and I-" Cheney began, taking Talanov by the elbow.

"Oh, nonsense!" interrupted Alex, pulling away. "Frau Hunziker and I met earlier for business and it's a pleasure to see her socially. Is this your husband?" he then asked, turning to the man beside her and extending his hand.

"Gustav Hunziker," the man said in a deep voice, shaking Talanov's hand and then introducing the others in the group. With a broad smile, Talanov began shaking hands with each of them in turn.

Cheney realized Talanov was using the group both as a shield and as a delay. He also knew that to pull a gun right now would cause a panic. And that would bring the police. Hence, by whatever means possible, he must get Talanov away from these people.

"The restaurant is closing," Cheney told Talanov, again taking him by the elbow, "and we must allow these good people to get on with their evening."

Alex, however, ignored him and again pulled away. "Waiter!" he called out, raising a hand toward Joe. "Waiter, may we get more wine?"

"Of course, sir!" answered Joe, recognizing Alex. He grabbed two bottles and some glasses and hurried toward the group.

"Mr Talanov, the restaurant is closing," Frau Hunziker said quietly, becoming embarrassed as other members of her group exchanged looks of apprehension. "Did you not hear the announcement?"

"Oh, but we must toast the success of your verification!" said Talanov as Joe arrived and began filling glasses. "You see," Alex continued, now addressing the others in the group, "someone is trying to convince Frau Hunziker that I'm *dead*."

Cheney grabbed Talanov firmly by the arm.

But Talanov twisted his arm free and accepted a glass of wine from Joe. "Now, Mr Cheney works for Bob Hoskings and he's carrying a *gun*."

Frau Hunziker looked up at her husband with alarm just as Talanov turned and held out his glass. "Waiter, please hold this while I take off my jacket," he said, hoping Joe would follow his lead. For once Joe had taken the glass, Alex planned to hand him his jacket so that Joe could slip a pistol into one of the pockets.

Joe accepted the wine glass.

But before Talanov could remove his jacket, he heard his name being called. He looked across the room to see Marshak, still soiled and scuffed, hurrying toward him with a piece of folded paper. "Mr Talanov, I have an urgent message from Wolfgang Hauser. He says it's very important."

Talanov stared at Marshak as he approached.

"My apologies for my appearance," Marshak said pleasantly to the group. "Car trouble, I'm afraid." He then looked at Talanov and held out the paper. "From your dear friend, Mr Hauser."

Joe stood by watching, as did Frau Hunziker and her friends. The restaurant was now virtually empty. Talanov slowly unfolded the paper and read the message, which was printed in pencil: *I've been detained.*

Alex looked coldly at Marshak, well aware of the statement's meaning: *the killers had captured Wolfgang.*

And if he continued his diversion, Wolfgang would die.

"He said you'd know what it meant," Marshak said with a friendly expression.

"Where is he?" asked Talanov, crumpling the paper.

"He said you'd know that, too," replied Marshak with a smile.

"Yes, I suppose I do," answered Talanov, looking over at Cheney. "Come on, let's go," he said as he started toward the kitchen door.

Suppressing a smile, Cheney followed.

Chapter
71

The name had been a thunderbolt out of heaven: *Aleksandr Talanov* - her husband - was *alive!*

Yet it had also been a thunderbolt out of hell. For if it were true, then she had become a whore for nothing, and the thought of that filled her with rage.

Andrea fell back against the metal shelf, her hands covering her ears as if to keep out the words. How could Alex be alive and she not know it? And if he *was* alive, *how could he not have told her?* As if bent over in pain, Andrea sank to the floor and let out an agonizing cry. Chuckling, Bob Hoskings strolled over and prepared to pull her back up to her feet. *So Marshak's suspicions had been accurate: Natalie Cox was Talanov's wife.*

Andrea's rage detonated like a warhead. Catching Bob by surprise, she exploded from her crouching position, her fingers extended like daggers, her nails gouging and clawing. With a scream, Bob stumbled back, dropping the keys as his hands flew up to his face. Andrea smashed her knee into his groin, and with a guttural cry, Bob collapsed to the floor. Grabbing the keys, Andrea left Bob writhing in agony and ran to the door, pulling it open, her one obsession to locate her husband.

She started up the stairs, then stopped as she glanced at the other door. *Wolfgang Hauser... one of his friends.*

If this man were indeed one of Alex's friends, she could not leave him locked in that room. Andrea jumped back down and tried the door handle. It was locked. She attempted to use one of the keys but it did not fit. Hurrying to select another, she fumbled and dropped the whole ring of keys onto the floor. Snatching them up, she tried inserting another one, which did not fit, then another. On the third attempt, the key twisted and she pushed open the door.

Inside the darkened room, Andrea saw a frail old man with white hair gagged and tied on the floor. She turned on the light and ran over to him, untying his mouth and hands.

"You must be Natalie," Wolfgang said with a smile. "I'm so glad we get to meet. Alex has been trying to find you."

"Is he here?" asked Andrea while working rapidly on the knots which held his feet.

"Yes, but we haven't much time. Get upstairs, I'll take care of my feet. If they've captured him, divert everyone back into the restaurant. It's imperative you be in the restaurant."

"For God's sake, why?" asked Andrea.

"No time to explain, just do it. Now, *run!*"

Andrea jumped to her feet and ran up the stairs while Wolfgang untied the remaining ropes. As he started to stand, a pain tore through his stomach and he collapsed back to the floor, gasping for air. *Not now!* he told himself, and gritting his teeth, he forced himself onto one knee, where he paused to catch his breath. Hearing a noise, he looked up to see Bob Hoskings limp out of the other storage room and start climbing the stairs. With a grimace, Wolfgang forced himself to stand, grabbing one of the shelves to steady himself, the pain still intense. He then staggered out of the room.

Upstairs, in the empty restaurant, Cheney and Talanov reached the kitchen door just as Andrea came bursting through it.

"You *bastard!*" Andrea screamed at Alex without losing a stride. Knowing she had to control the next few moments - including their position in the restaurant - she began pounding her husband on the chest. The clamor drew the startled attention of Jules and his staff, who were ready to leave. "Do you know what you've done... what you've made me *become?*" she shouted.

"What I made you become? Andrea... I don't understand!"

"That's because it happened to *me*, not you!" She pushed him, driven both by Wolfgang's words but also her growing anger. The whole despicable Natalie Cox contrivance had been for *him*... to avenge his death.

But Alex was not dead, he was *alive*.

Stunned by the sudden argument, then amused, Cheney stepped aside to watch. *The great Talanov was getting whipped by his bitch.*

"I've become a *whore* because of you... because I thought these bastards had *killed* you! I was actually going to go to *bed* with that asshole-" she pointed at Marshak "- in order to *kill* him. I'm like *you*... I've become a *killer!*"

Andrea's voice had risen to screams as she slapped at Talanov's face, her strategy to drive Alex back into the restaurant now fueled by her rage and guilt. She had never once considered being unfaithful to Alex. And yet thinking him to be dead, she had willingly thrown aside these morals for the sake of revenge, with her hatred soon giving way to a hardness which choked out all feeling. What was disturbing - what was *loathsome*, in fact - was how easily it had occurred. How powerful had been her determination to get even, and how close she had come to succeeding.

"But I called Liz and she said you had left," Alex hastened to explain while ducking from side to side to avoid her blows. "No one knew how to *find* you!"

"I don't *care*," shrieked Andrea. "You made me a *whore*... a bloody *whore!*" She then dropped to her knees and began weeping.

Alex knelt beside her. "Don't give in... fight it... come back to me."

Andrea suddenly lashed out with her hands, slapping and clawing. "Don't give *in?* You don't know what it's *like* to give in to everything you despise!"

"Yes, I do!" replied Alex, grabbing her hands and pulling her close.

"No you don't, you *can't!*" she cried, her face now wet with tears. "You're too cold... you're nothing but ice."

"Not anymore," said Alex, his eyes pressed closed with grief.

Joe had been watching the exchange quietly, waiting for Talanov to give him a sign. Suddenly, he felt a rod of steel against his ribs. He glanced sideways to see Marshak standing beside him. "I would hate to blow your guts all over the floor and ruin this show."

"But *suh*, I don't understand," said Joe in his best British accent.

"Cut the English crap," Marshak replied, pressing the pistol more firmly into Joe's back. "Vanuatu... that night in the shack. Now, *gently* hand me your guns."

Using his thumb and forefinger, Joe pulled the pistol with silencer from beneath his waiter's jacket and handed it over. After taking the weapon, Marshak knelt down and felt Joe's socks. He felt a small lump in one of them and withdrew the small automatic Joe had been carrying there. He then stood and stuck it in his belt.

"Dang, I forgot about that one," said Joe as Marshak shoved him toward Talanov and Andrea, then motioning for Jules and his staff to join him.

"I hate to break up domestic entertainment," said Marshak, "but now you've become rather boring." He looked pointedly at Andrea, a cruel anger visible in his eyes. "My, my, what an act."

Andrea looked up with reddened eyes.

"What are you going to do?" Jules asked nervously. "Surely you don't think we're a part of this."

"Not in the least," said Cheney as he walked to the side of Marshak.

Jules bowed humbly in appreciation. "Thank you... when may we go?"

"Oh, but I'm afraid leaving is out of the question," said Cheney.

"But *why?*" pleaded Jules as he began wringing his hands together.

Suddenly the kitchen door slammed open and Bob Hoskings staggered into the room, bent over in pain. He paused by a table to catch his breath. "You little *bitch!*" he said, pointing at Andrea. Close behind him was Wolfgang.

My God, we've been set up, Andrea thought, seeing Wolfgang standing near Bob. *We've been herded into a trap.*

But Wolfgang walked around Bob, who was still bent over, and looked him in the face. "Let them go," he said. "You gain nothing by harming these people."

Bob managed a momentary laugh, then grimaced again as he tried to straighten. "Place this old fool with the others."

Cheney reached over and grabbed Wolfgang by the arm and pushed him roughly across the floor. He then handed his pistol to Marshak.

"A vicious and terrible tragedy will occur tonight," said Cheney, walking toward them and pulling out the pistols he had taken earlier from Alex. "These fine people will be killed by Talanov the terrorist. At least that's what we will say and what Swiss ballistics will support from these guns which, of course, will end up in your hands.

Regretfully, you will be killed while trying to escape. And as for your *whore* there-"
Cheney smiled at his use of the word "-well, we wouldn't want her to die unfulfilled,
now would we?"

"*No!*" roared Talanov, leaping furiously to his feet.

"Alex!" said Wolfgang, stepping in front of his friend. "Remember your plan!"

"My *plan?* We've failed, can't you *see* that?"

Wolfgang held eye contact with Alex for a long moment before turning and
stiffening his posture, his gentle white eyebrows narrowed with determination. "If I
must die, I die with dignity," he declared. "Give me a drink."

"Are you *mad?*" asked Jules. "We're about to be killed and you want a *drink?*"

"I don't expect you to understand," Wolfgang told Jules, glancing at him. "No
one can understand who has not been through Balashikha. We drink to life - that a
man lives to reach a hundred - but when that does not happen, we face death with a
final drink."

Wolfgang started toward the table.

"Stay where you are!" ordered Marshak, raising his gun.

"Let him go," said Cheney.

"A final drink?" asked Marshak. "I've never heard of such rubbish."

"And you were never at Balashikha," answered Cheney, motioning Wolfgang to
the table with his gun.

Everyone watched Wolfgang reach the linen-draped table and pick up an empty
glass, then fill it with white wine from an opened bottle. He replaced the bottle on
the table and brought his full glass back to the center of the room, where he lifted it
in a toast. "To life, and to death," he said solemnly, whereupon he hurled it into the
face of Cheney. And with a rousing cry, he then turned and ran toward the door.

For Alex, the next few seconds unfolded like scenes in a nightmare.

Alex saw his hands reach out in desperation to stop Wolfgang, his mouth
forming words but without time to utter them. Suddenly, off to his right, he saw the
twisted face of Cheney dripping with wine. He saw him curse and raise the pistol,
his finger curling around the trigger, pulling it once, twice, then again. He saw the
gun jerk with each round, the empty brass casings tumbling in a wide arc through
the air. He saw Wolfgang's arms fly out, the force of the bullets hurling him against
the large glass panel already splattered with his blood. He then watched
helplessly as Wolfgang crashed through the glass and fell lifeless onto the
balcony.

Cheney then turned the gun toward Alex.

Using an infrared scope pulled from one of her baggy pockets, Maria had located
the police patrol on the far edge of the forest, still ambling along. She then scanned
the grounds of the institute but saw no one.

Crouching as she ran, Maria followed the approximate path Talanov had taken
across the open paddock, at the top of the lane turning left until she had circled to a
concealed position on an embankment from which she could view the restaurant.
The facility's large windows afforded her a clear view of most, but not all, of the
dining area.

In her own mind, she was fulfilling her pledge to Alex to remain clear of the reception while at the same time fulfilling the pledge made to her uncle about keeping watch in case there was trouble. She only hoped Wolfgang was right when he assured her that if any trouble did occur, it would be in the dining area and not involve him. As instructed, she had not told Alex.

Reaching into another of the long pockets sewn down the leg of her overalls, Maria took out the disassembled components of the high-powered rifle retrieved earlier from the basement. She had earned several awards for marksmanship in the reserves and kept a number of weapons in the house. Working expertly in the dark, Maria fitted the pieces together, then clicked on a normal scope since the interior of the restaurant was well lighted. She then screwed a silencer onto the tip of the barrel.

Lifting the overalls from around her ankle, Maria took six cartridges out of the leather loops sewed to the side of one boot. A half dozen more were mounted to the other boot although six should be enough - if any were needed at all. Placing them on the ground beside her, Maria loaded one into the chamber.

From her vantage point, it was a boring evening. Zug's social elite were inside drinking and laughing while she laid in the cold with her hands tucked under her arms. Her breath came out in small white puffs as she observed what looked like fish in a giant aquarium. Some were colorful, some were plain, some were assertive, some were shy. She smiled at the sight and soon began giving them names. At least it helped pass the time.

Eventually, Maria realized that she had not seen her uncle all night. Logic told her not to worry, for the restaurant was filled to capacity, making it difficult to view what was happening on the other side. Plus, she did not have a clear view of the whole interior. Nevertheless, she should have seen him at least once or twice, and her failure to do so made her uneasy.

These thoughts were interrupted when a string of limousines drove into the parking lot and people began leaving. Maria checked her watch. It was still early. She watched while people streamed out of the restaurant, chatting and laughing. Since nothing appeared to be wrong, Maria decided to maintain her position. At least the monotony of the night had been broken and soon she would be able to go home. But not until Uncle Wolfgang had stepped onto the balcony and given a whistle. That was to be her sign.

More minutes passed and the restaurant was now almost empty.

But wait. There was Alex talking to a some guests. He was certainly acting strangely... and who was that man who kept trying to interrupt? She smiled: there was Joe! He looked so funny with that hair and those glasses.

Suddenly, a man in soiled clothing walked up to the group and handed Alex a piece of paper. Alex read it, then turned and walked out of view. The people to whom he had been talking left quickly, looking relieved.

A few moments later, Maria was startled to see Alex stumble back into the center of the room followed by a woman screaming and hitting him. Standing, Maria watched the argument taking place. What was going *on?* Why was that woman so furious?

A shiver of alarm swept over Maria when she saw Joe being shoved into the center of the room *by a man holding a gun!* She grabbed her rifle and watched as the hotel staff were ordered to join them. Suddenly another man stepped to the side of the man with the pistol. Were they going to rob everyone? Robbery was certainly a crime, but not one which justified the use of her rifle.

Maria then watched in shock as her uncle was pushed into the center of the room by one of the robbers, that man then pulling *two guns out of his jacket!* The man then said something which caused Alex to jump angrily to his feet. Uncle Wolfgang then stepped in front of Alex and tried to calm him down.

What was her uncle *doing?* He was actually walking over to the table and pouring himself a glass of wine! He brought it back toward the group... he was lifting it in a toast-

Wolfgang suddenly threw the wine into the face of one of the robbers! Now he was *running away!*

In horror, Maria watched Cheney raise his gun.

"*No!*" she screamed as she hoisted the rifle to her shoulder, the cross hairs of the scope moving to the forehead of the man as he fired once, twice, then a third time. Maria was completely stunned: *Uncle Wolfgang* had just been *murdered!* Maria was then jolted back into reality when she saw the killer turn his gun toward Alex.

The penetration of the bullet through the window was but a tinkle as Cheney's eyes went hollow, the pistol in his hand swaying, then swiveling downward on his rigid finger as a large red dot appeared between his eyes. Marshak first noticed the disbelief in Talanov's eyes, his own gaze then following their trajectory to Cheney as he fell to the floor. Immobilized with shock, Marshak could only stare at Cheney's corpse just as Talanov leaped toward his gun.

Starting to both shake and cry from the horror of seeing her uncle gunned down, Maria lifted the bolt and slid it back, ejecting the empty casing, then placing a loaded cartridge in the chamber. She rammed the bolt forward and looked up just as Marshak lifted his pistol. She shouldered the rifle and tried sighting, but could not through the tears now flooding her eyes.

Two blasts resounded through the dining room of the restaurant just as Talanov's hand reached his gun. He hit the floor, his face smashing against the hard surface.

With a groan, Alex looked up just as Marshak tumbled backwards over the table, scattering wine glasses and bottles in all directions as he landed on the floor with two bullet holes in his chest. Alex glanced quickly around, then rolled over and trained his pistol on Bob Hoskings - Georgi Vaskin - who stood holding a small revolver.

"Drop it!" commanded Talanov.

Bob dropped the pistol and held out his hands.

Alex climbed slowly to his feet, being careful to keep Bob covered.

"I'm as shocked about this as you are," Bob declared. "I had no idea these men were such *criminals.*"

"You rotten bastard," growled Talanov. "You and Cheney were in this together!"

"Not *this*," countered Bob. "The two of them handled my security - I don't deny that - but I had no idea they had planned something so vicious. When I saw what they were attempting, I acted as soon as I could."

"Bullshit! You killed Marshak to keep him from *talking*. Now it's just my word against yours about who you really are and what you've been doing. All the killing... *you're responsible!*"

"That is pure speculation," countered Bob. "I don't blame you for being angry over tonight's misunderstanding, but there is no need for wild accusations."

Andrea rushed up to Bob. "*Misunderstanding?* What about that little session downstairs in the storeroom? What about your holding Wolfgang bound and gagged as a *prisoner?*"

Bob smiled. "My dear, I have no idea what you're talking about."

Talanov ran over and jammed his pistol up under Bob's chin. "I should blow your rotten head off!"

"Alex, don't," Andrea cut in, gently moving the gun barrel away from Bob's chin and looking her husband in the eyes. "We have no proof and this scum isn't worth it. Let's not go back - neither one of us - to the perversions of that violent world."

Encouraged by a smile from his wife, Alex lowered the pistol while Bob turned away, a thin line of a smirk on his face.

A moment later, Alex and the others heard the sound of heavy boots running along the balcony and turned to see Maria. When she approached the body of her uncle, she let out a wail of anguish and fell down beside him. With tears in her eyes, she tenderly brought his limp body up next to her chest and cradled it.

And rocking back and forth, she began to sob.

Chapter
72

Christmas came and went, with Alex and Andrea spending a quiet day in the chalet beside the fire while Joe accompanied Maria to the hospital. Johann would recover but require skin grafts to much of his back.

Wolfgang was to be buried in the family cemetery beside his wife. Ursula - who had long ago left the family farm on the Zugerberg to marry the dashing young teacher - had come home to her final rest place more than a decade ago. Her beloved Wolfgang would now be joining her.

There was so much Alex had wanted to explain but Andrea simply placed a finger to his lips. "Don't talk, just hold me," she said as she curled her feet up on the couch and snuggled close to his chest, her eyes on the flames in the blackened stove. "And please don't ask about Natalie Cox. She's dead and I want her to stay there."

Talanov understood, and while the fire crackled peacefully, he began stroking her hair. They were back together at last.

On Friday, Talanov rose early to the smell of baking bread, and after a hot shower, made his way quietly downstairs to the kitchen. Maria had awakened before dawn and had his coffee poured when he came into the room. Joe was already seated at the table.

"You're up early," Talanov said to Joe. He then greeted Maria and thanked her for the mug of hot coffee.

"Got a lot to do," replied Joe. "Since Johann's out of commission, I've offered to help build the new barn. I'm handy at most things - as you know - and figure we'd start right away. I reckon it may take a while."

"I'm sure you'll see that it does," said Alex with a grin. "But are you certain Maria can put up with that hair?"

"Got an appointment for a color this morning," said Joe. "And you can forget that nonsense about blonds having more fun."

"Thanks for the tip," said Alex. "I've been breathless with anticipation."

"Hey, you're back in the arms of your wife, aren't you?"

"Is Andrea still asleep?" asked Maria, opening a drawer and grabbing a knife.

Talanov took a large swallow and nodded. "Exhausted, emotionally and physically."

Maria placed the knife in front of Joe, then set a bowl and ten apples before him. "Time to be useful again," she said, jostling his hair. She then glanced over at Talanov as she returned to the stove and laid some bratwurst in a large blackened skillet. "We have eggs. How do you like them?"

"Will that be scrambled, coddled, poached, basted, or sunny-side-up?" asked Joe in an exaggerated Southern drawl as he started peeling the first apple.

"Over easy," said Talanov.

"Smart ass," grumbled Joe.

A long moment of silence passed while the bratwurst sizzled in the hot skillet, Maria tending it while taking half a dozen eggs out of a wire basket on the counter next to some canisters. Through the kitchen window, Talanov could see the morning was overcast and windy.

Suddenly frustrated, Joe slapped the knife down on the table, drawing the attention of Alex and Maria. "Why did he do that?" he asked. "Why did Wolfgang make them shoot him?"

"Because he knew Maria would not fire unless they fired first," answered Alex, coming to the table and sitting. "He tried to let me know when he told me to remember my plan. Plus, because he had cancer, it was a way he could die with dignity. He gave his life that we might live."

Joe thought about Talanov's words and picked up the knife again. "I guess it beats wasting away in a hospital," he said. After peeling half of an apple, he paused and looked at Alex. "But didn't I hear him laugh?"

Talanov chuckled and nodded. "He died as he lived, on his own terms."

At the stove, Maria turned the sausage in the skillet. She was smiling but had tears in her eyes.

An hour and a half later, Talanov had parked the rental car near the post office. He buttoned his coat against the windy gray skies and crossed the gray cobblestone street toward Credit Suisse. In less than a minute he had pushed open the door and was walking across gray granite. Frau Hunziker was at the reception counter and, thankfully, was wearing red. She greeted Talanov in English and then continued conversing in German with the male receptionist, who picked up the phone. Frau Hunziker showed Alex to the elevator.

Upstairs, Alex was shown into the same conference room where they had met previously, sitting in the same chrome-and-black-leather chair. On the large oval table were two glasses and a pitcher of water.

"May I get you a coffee?" asked Frau Hunziker.

"Nothing, thank you," replied Alex.

Having not yet seated herself, Frau Hunziker poured herself a glass of water.

Suddenly, there was a knock and Frau Hunziker went to the door and opened it. Two uniformed police officers entered, their hats under their arms, their holstered side arms visible. Frau Hunziker closed the door behind them and each of the officers showed his identification to Alex.

"What's this all about?" asked Talanov, looking at the two officers and then at Frau Hunziker.

Frau Hunziker returned to her chair but still did not sit. "In light of everything that has occurred, I thought it prudent for these officers to assist with a proper verification of your identity."

"May I see your passport, please?" the first officer asked politely in English.

Talanov took out his Australian passport and handed it to the officer, who took it with him out of the room while the other officer remained stationed by the door.

"Are you sure I can't get you a coffee?" asked Frau Hunziker again.

"You can tell me what will occur once my passport has been authenticated," replied Talanov, his hands folded on the table.

Frau Hunziker remained standing: it was her gesture of not-yet-acceptance. "Assuming there to be no irregularities," she said, "and once your jurisdiction over the account has been established, then I can then proceed with the processing of your request for a withdrawal of funds."

"Did you initiate any of this on Wednesday as I asked?" asked Talanov pointedly.

After clearing her throat, Frau Hunziker glanced briefly at the officer, then back at Talanov, her expression softening. "No, I did not. But after seeing you at the reception, I was quite disturbed by the way those men treated you and felt compelled to reconsider your request. It was, after all, reasonable and completely within the established guidelines of the bank. Therefore, I came into the bank yesterday-"

"On Christmas Day?" Talanov broke in.

"Yes - on Christmas Day - and entered your request into the system."

"Isn't that highly *irregular?*" asked Talanov, enunciating the last word for emphasis.

Remembering her threat to Alex on Wednesday about irregularities, Frau Hunziker nodded humbly in agreement. "Yes, it was. Nonetheless, I felt it was my duty."

"And?"

Frau Hunziker straightened again to a formal posture. "Once your identity has been verified, we can access the results of your request on that terminal by the window. Until then, I can tell you nothing more."

With a sigh, Talanov relaxed in his chair and waited while Frau Hunziker remained standing, her eyes directed out the window. The guard stood watching Talanov.

Five minutes later, the other guard knocked and was admitted by his companion. He entered, closed the door, and handed Talanov back his passport. He thanked Alex, after which he addressed Frau Hunziker, speaking in German. "The Australian Consulate matched the number with the name and confirmed there to be no restrictions against either the owner or the passport itself."

"Thank you," Frau Hunziker said to the guards. "You may go."

The two guards put on their hats and nodded both to Frau Hunziker and Talanov before leaving.

Once they were gone, Frau Hunziker pulled out a chair and sat down. "There were no irregularities," she said. "Would you care for that coffee now?"

"Would it make you feel better if I did?" asked Talanov.

"It would make me feel better if we both did," was her reply. "Sometimes the responsibilities of my position are most unpleasant."

"Just doing your job, as they say," remarked Alex.

"Yes, I think that expresses it correctly."

"Then order us coffee," said Alex. "And while we're waiting, click on that computer."

13 Chapter 73

Frau Hunziker stood. "Please remain seated until I have your particular details on the screen," she said, walking over to the computer keyboard and entering a series of commands. The wait was not long. "Here it is: a double-alpha account opened in 1983 with a deposit of seven million US dollars, with jurisdiction seniority granted to Aleksandr Talanov by means of a power of attorney."

"Jurisdiction seniority?" asked Talanov as he rose from his chair and rounded the end of the table. "Does that mean there are other names listed besides mine?"

"That information is confidential," answered Frau Hunziker, switching off the screen and turning to face Alex at he sat in a nearby chair.

"You mean the type of confidentiality which almost resulted in the account being handed over to the wrong person?"

Frau Hunziker gave Talanov a stern look. "We had no way of knowing Mr Hoskings' evidence was misleading."

"Yes you did, because I came into your bank on Wednesday and presented you with documentation which proved my identity. I then asked you to investigate the matter with a withdrawal request because I suspected someone was trying to gain control of the account."

"Your claim was highly irregular and - well - it seemed farfetched, at least in light of the information we had already received from a highly-respectable source."

Talanov leaned forward for emphasis. "Just so I understand your meaning, Frau Hunziker: are you telling me that because my claim seemed farfetched, you felt justified in your decision not to investigate the matter on Wednesday before closing, bearing in mind that by doing so you would have ascertained who legitimately held jurisdiction over the account? 'Irregularity,' then, was your excuse for nearly allowing the fraudulent invasion of a double-alpha account to the tune of one and a half *billion* dollars?"

Frau Hunziker looked at Talanov angrily, then turned away. Finally, she dropped her head. "What do you want, Mr Talanov? My dismissal... our bank to be discredited?"

"Not at all," he said. "But I do want your reasonable cooperation without all these door-slamming excuses. I hold legal jurisdiction over one of your accounts and what I need is information pertinent to that account."

There was a long pause. "What do you wish to know?" she asked, straightening her posture and switching on the screen.

"Are there any alternate names?"

"There are several," said Frau Hunziker, scrolling to the appropriate section, "although none are empowered to debit the account except upon presentation of certifiable evidence of the death of the senior nominee."

"And I'm the senior nominee?"

"That is correct."

"Who's next on the list?" asked Talanov.

"Georgi Vaskin."

"So Vaskin could have accessed the account had I not turned up and presented you with documentation which proved I wasn't dead?"

"Like I said, we had no way of knowing his evidence was misleading."

"That doesn't answer my question," stated Talanov.

Frau Hunziker sighed. "Yes, he could have accessed the account."

"And withdrawn all the money?"

"Every dollar," answered Frau Hunziker quietly.

"Were you aware that Bob Hoskings was - or is - Georgi Vaskin?" asked Talanov.

"Yes, although he told me he had to adopt another name for political reasons. Many celebrities do it, and to us it was not an issue so long as he could provide evidence which proved Bob Hoskings and Georgi Vaskin were one and the same man. He supplied us with a notarized fictitious-name certificate."

"Did you confirm the certificate's authenticity?" asked Talanov.

"It is not our position to confirm the authenticity of every document. If it appears authentic and we have no reason to suspect otherwise, we accept it."

"Except in instances like mine."

Frau Hunziker snapped her head toward Talanov.

Alex met her glare with a resolute expression of his own and she turned back to the screen.

"So, where's the money?" he continued.

"What do you mean?" she asked.

"I learned by way of a recent verification-of-funds request that the account has a zero balance. If it's not in your bank, where is it?"

"That is really a separate matter and quite distinct from the actual resident account here at Credit Suisse."

"Do you want me to call in the bank examiners?" asked Talanov. "Or perhaps the Press?"

Frau Hunziker glared at Talanov again, then looked back at the monitor while drumming her fingernails on the desk. She had no choice but to cooperate. "It is in Hong Kong," she finally answered, opening her eyes but not consenting to look at him. "The original deposit instructions authorized Credit Suisse to organize an investment broker to manage the account, and since the Far East was seen at that time to be a promising environment for investment - especially in real estate - that is where the money was sent. Technically, the funds are still under the jurisdiction of Credit Suisse, with final jurisdiction being yours."

"What's to keep the broker from running off with the profits?"

Frau Hunziker gave Talanov a look of reprimand. "Credit Suisse deals *only* with highly reputable firms."

"And you scrutinize their books on an ongoing basis?"

"I am not at liberty to divulge such procedures. I should think the rather substantial results achieved with your deposit should be enough."

"What's the balance, in round numbers?" asked Talanov.

Frau Hunziker scrolled down to the spread sheet. "One billion, four hundred and eighty-nine million dollars," she said.

"Minus one hundred francs," added Alex.

Unable to suppress a laugh, Frau Hunziker looked over at Alex. "Minus one hundred francs," she said with a reluctant but genuine smile. "Which you haven't collected."

"Deposit it back in the account."

An exasperated sigh was Frau Hunziker's response just as a tiny beep sounded from the monitor, drawing her attention. Her eyes widened and she began hurriedly entering commands.

"What's wrong?" inquired Alex as he observed the flurry of typing.

Without answering, Frau Hunziker suddenly punched a button on the monitor and jumped from her chair and ran out the conference room, leaving Alex bewildered. He glanced at the screen, but there was only a dark background.

Alex sat waiting for a full fifteen minutes, and when Frau Hunziker returned, her face was ashen, her eyes darting and nervous.

"What is it?" asked Alex, rising quickly and walking toward her.

"Please, sit down," she replied as she pulled out one of the chrome-and-black-leather chairs and sat. She awkwardly refilled her water glass.

Alex sat, never once taking his eyes off her worried face.

Frau Hunziker took a drink. Then, after rubbing her hands together nervously, she looked solemnly at Alex. "When Mr Hoskings - Mr Vaskin - filed his request for a transfer of jurisdiction, we forwarded authorization for the transfer to Hong Kong, telling the broker there to initiate proceedings and that we would be back on-line to complete the transaction once we opened for business this morning. Then you came in contesting the request although I did not immediately process your claim, for reasons I've already stated. But like I told you, after seeing you at the reception, I came in yesterday and forwarded your data on to Hong Kong. There was, then, a brief window of time when jurisdiction had been transferred out of your name, although the error has now been corrected."

"And control of the account went to Vaskin?"

"It went to no one because we had not completed the process of transferral. We merely sent verification - or what we considered to be verification - of your death, which released the account from your exclusive control."

"Has jurisdiction has been restored to my name?" asked Talanov.

"Yes, it has."

"Then what's the problem?"

There was a long pause. "The money has disappeared."

Talanov leaped out of his chair. "*Disappeared? You mean gone?*"

Frau Hunziker nodded gravely.

"But who? *Vaskin?*"

"No... someone in Hong Kong-"

"Such as your highly reputable broker?"

Frau Hunziker swallowed nervously. "It may or may not be the broker, but someone in Hong Kong - we do not know who - has drained the entire account. We are trying to trace it now."

"Assassins have destroyed virtually everything I own, killed God-knows-how-many people while trying to kill me and my wife, and you're telling me the money's just *disappeared?*"

Tears were forming in Frau Hunziker's eyes as she looked helplessly at Alex.

Talanov planted his hands on the table angrily. "Could Vaskin have coordinated this from Zug - from *anywhere* - by computer?"

"I don't know... nobody knows. It's simply gone."

13 Chapter 74

Talanov stormed over to the Parkhotel and marched through the door. Jules had seen him coming and met him as he entered.

"Where's Hoskings... where's *Vaskin?*" demanded Talanov.

"Alex, please come with me," Jules said, pointing toward an unoccupied table in the dining area where they could talk quietly over coffee.

"I don't want coffee!" protested Talanov, continuing toward the counter. "I want Vaskin."

"That is precisely what we must discuss," countered the Swiss. "Please, there isn't much time."

Noting the urgency in Jules' voice and the strain on his face, Talanov followed him into the dining area. Jules quickly ordered two coffees before ushering Talanov to a seat near the window.

With his elbows on the table and his hands folded protectively in front of his mouth, Jules leaned his head toward Talanov and broke the news. Georgi Vaskin - Bob Hoskings - had filed a statement with the police early this morning which essentially cleared him of all involvement with the actions of his two security guards. In addition, the shooting death of Major Marshak was ruled to have been committed in self defense. His statement was eagerly supported by a number of business leaders, who somehow knew to come forward - probably by request - as well as several hotel employees who worked as waiters and witnessed everything. Statements are still being taken although Mr Hoskings has been given clearance to leave Zug in light of his assurance that he will be in Geneva for a week of IDC discussions, during which time he can be contacted should any questions arise.

"They're letting him *go?*" asked Talanov, whose hands were now fists as two small white porcelain cups of coffee were served by a young woman.

"They have no choice," Jules replied, stirring milk and sugar into his cup. "As you so accurately stated last night, it is his word against yours about his alleged involvement. Our departed friend, Wolfgang, of course, cannot contradict his testimony, and now that a number of witnesses have corroborated it, at least in part, the weight of evidence is strongly in his favor. The front counter made a train reservation for Mr Hoskings a short while ago. He leaves for Geneva this morning."

Closing his eyes, Talanov rested his forehead against one fist. "The rotten bastard goes free," he said. "He didn't win, but he sure didn't lose."

"Even our police captain, Gustav Hunziker, whom you met last night with his wife, said there was no way Mr Hoskings could be detained."

Talanov looked up. "Gustav Hunziker works for the police?"

Chapter 75

Standing under the spanning steel girders of the station, the uniformed conductor looked both ways for any late passengers before waving to the engineer. He then stepped onto the last car as the train began slowly moving. Before long, it had left the buildings of downtown Zug, picking up speed as it passed through the residential outskirts before curving away into the hills. Soon it entered a tunnel.

Bob Hoskings had the first class compartment to himself and was casually flipping through an English magazine he had purchased at a kiosk in Zug. The rhythmic clacking of the steel wheels on the tracks was soothing and Bob relaxed in his padded seat. Soon the train emerged from the tunnel and the rural Swiss countryside began passing by in a colorful panorama of forest and farms.

A discreet warble sounded from the briefcase next to Bob. He snapped open the locks and lifted the lid just as the cellular phone sounded again. "Yes?" Hoskings said into the instrument.

"I presume you have heard what happened?" Ling Soo asked.

"Talanov took control. There was nothing I could do."

"Then you haven't heard," said Ling Soo.

"Heard what?" asked Bob.

"The money has disappeared."

"*What?*" asked a startled Bob Hoskings, throwing aside the magazine and sitting forward. "When... how?"

"That I cannot tell you. The bank received an initial authorization from Credit Suisse for a transfer of jurisdiction, then a rescission the next day listing 'erroneous documentation regarding the death of the senior nominee' as the reason. An order was issued to reinstate Mr Talanov as the senior nominee."

"So what happened?"

"It looks as though someone took advantage of the window and accessed the funds. Apparently, Credit Suisse did not complete the transaction when they filed it, but only initiated the change, which left open the opportunity for someone to invade the account."

"Was it Wu Chee Ming?" asked Bob.

"No. And Wu Chee Ming is most upset that all of his work has been for nothing. He demands payment, of course, but is in no position to pursue anything in the courts."

"Serves the little bastard right," growled Bob. "Are there any clues?"

"No," replied Ling Soo. "Plus, there is an outstanding loan of more than seven-hundred-million dollars. That is because the entire account of nearly 1.49 billion was taken before the loan had been repaid. I fear there may be terrible reprisals."

"What do you mean?" asked Bob.

"The source of the loan was from a questionable source."

"You mean organized crime?" asked Bob.

"Yes," replied Ling Soo. "Wu Chee Ming now fears for his life. He had no choice when they came to him demanding that he borrow investment capital from them instead of a bank. Hearing of his previous success, they wanted a 'piece of the action,' as the Americans say."

"Are you certain someone in the crime syndicate didn't take it?" asked Bob as the train rocked from side to side.

"None of them would have dared steal it for reasons you can imagine. My source with them says the leaders are demanding the culprit's blood. This means, of course, that regardless of Wu Chee Ming's innocence in the matter, he will become the first of many casualties in order to satisfy their demands for retribution. I fear his future and the future of many others will be most unpleasant."

"Like I said, it serves the little bastard right. He should have repaid the loan. What about you... are you in danger?"

"I do not think so, for I was but an intermediary for you and my name is on none of the paperwork. Nevertheless, I am taking precautions and I will be leaving Hong Kong immediately."

"What about your position with Spice Lines East? You're a senior vice-president!"

"Titles mean nothing in the grave," Ling Soo replied. "Perhaps I will come to America. Perhaps you may find my talents to be of use in Washington."

"I'm afraid I don't have anything going right now, but give me a call."

"You are most kind," replied Ling Soo.

"In the meantime, keep on the alert. I'd like to know who did it."

"I shall with the time that I have."

Bob clicked off his phone and tossed it back in his briefcase. So Talanov didn't get the money. Too bad, for he would have enjoyed killing him to get it back. Still, if Talanov didn't take it, who did? Someone in the syndicate? Wu Chee Ming? *Ling Soo?* One thing was certain: whoever it was would one day feel a knife across his throat. One and a half billion dollars was worth the pursuit. In the meantime, he would continue milking the IDC for all it could provide him. Integrity was essential in fund-raising, and his new position would guarantee him access to the budgets of hundreds of charities. Which would make him a wealthy man.

The train was gliding along beside a lake when the compartment door slid open. Bob looked up just as Talanov stepped in.

Bob hardly reacted. "Well, if it isn't the good Colonel Talanov," he stated, motioning Alex to a seat. "I've been wondering when I would see you."

"I'm sure you have," Alex said as he turned to close the door. When he turned back around, Bob had a small automatic pointed at him.

"Still have the urge to kill?" asked Talanov as he opened his jacket. "I'm unarmed, as you can see. All I want is information."

"Such as?"

"Such as who took the money," said Alex as he sat near the door.

Bob chuckled. "I'm afraid no one wins this time," he said as he draped a magazine over the pistol while keeping it trained on Alex. "It vanished overseas. But mark my word: I'll find out who took it. And when I do..."

"You'll what?" interrupted Alex. "Start killing again?"

A confident smile was Bob's reply.

"You're nothing but a greedy parasite," said Talanov. "So mark *my* word: I'll see you in prison."

The smile on Bob's face disappeared. "My, how you do exaggerate. I'm afraid no one will pay you the slightest mind, Colonel, not after your ungrounded outburst in the restaurant. I made sure witnesses confirmed that little episode in writing and included it in their statements to the police. Those statements, incidentally, cleared me of any guilt. So threaten me all you want. You'll not prove a thing."

"There's no need to threaten anyone now that the head of the serpent is dead," replied Talanov.

Bob's eyes narrowed. "What do you mean?"

"Cheney... the brains... Tango Blue. I finally figured it out."

"Don't be preposterous!" laughed Bob.

"Sure, you were the rookie banker, but I recall Andropov telling us that Cheney had been chosen to direct *Peristroika*. He concocted the whole illusion."

Bob glared at Talanov for a moment, then turned his gaze out the window. A few boats dotted the lake and there were low peaks in the distance.

Talanov continued. "Even his name in Russian - *Ceeneey* - means 'blue.' He boasted to me about it in Adelaide while he was standing over me with a gun on the freighter. Amazing how careless one can become when armed or with a feeling of advantage. You, Marshak, Sergei, Fiona: all of you took orders from Cheney. Even Kharkov was a triumph of Cheney's ingenuity. The Russian Ambassador!"

"Cheney's a liar and you're a fool!" retorted Bob angrily. "It was *me*, not Cheney, who was in charge. *I* was Tango Blue and it was *I* who set Kharkov up as our cover and got him to nominate me for membership on the IDC. That way, after his death - which I'd planned from the very beginning - I'd have the international connections needed to turn our fortune into a *mega*fortune. We had investments lined up in Indonesia and Malaysia, where the ruling families hold monopolies in shipping and real estate. Through those monopolies, we would have become rich beyond imagination." Bob's face then galvanized into a bitter sneer. "So don't sit there and tell me about Cheney. He was *nothing.*"

"Not the way I read it. No one but Cheney could have fire-bombed my house, kidnaped my wife, and killed my friends. He was *there!*"

"He was there, but I was the brains, even back in eighty-three when we faked my death. I planned it, Colonel, and the money will be mine once I find out who took it. The difference this time is that I won't need to share it with anyone. Cheney's dead and so is Marshak."

"Ah, yes, Marshak. I bet he would have had plenty to tell, such as how you knew about my friendship with Wolfgang and sent him to the farm to kill us. The police have his fingerprints on a murder weapon, not to mention his attempt to kill Wolfgang's nephew. You shot Marshak to keep him from talking."

"True, but you'll never prove it, just as no one will prove I killed you."

Talanov folded his arms. "Because I know too much? Come now, that's hardly original."

Bob nodded. "You leave me no choice, although I'm surprised you're taking it so well. Most people become sniveling fools."

"I must say I'm impressed. Back in Zug, you fooled everyone into thinking you were innocent."

"And I'll do it again," said Bob. "People will lick your boots if you have the right status. It was not difficult to rally the support I needed thanks to my position with the IDC. Can you believe it? After exonerating me, the Swiss police actually apologized for the inconvenience. What a bunch of fools."

"Perhaps not as foolish as you think," replied Alex. "What you may or may not realize is how advanced the Swiss are in surveillance technology, which - as you know - is an interest of mine. More specifically, the tiny microphone concealed in my pocket has not only allowed this entire conversation to be recorded, but a live broadcast to be patched through to the IDC headquarters in Geneva, where the council will now convene hearings to consider your impeachment."

"*What?*" yelled Bob, jumping up. He reached over and ripped the tiny transmission unit out of Talanov's pocket, throwing it to the floor and stomping it into fragments. He then backed up and aimed the gun at Alex's chest.

Suddenly two heavily-armed Swiss policemen appeared on each side of the glass window separating the compartment from the corridor. They had pistols pointing at Bob. "Drop your weapon!" one of them shouted.

"You *traitor!*" screamed Bob at Talanov, his eyes darting back and forth between the two policemen.

"It's over, Vaskin... drop it," commanded Talanov.

"You've ruined everything... *everything!*" screamed Bob, his face red with fury.

"Drop your *weapon,*" the Swiss officer shouted again. "*Now!*"

Talanov's eyes suddenly widened at the movement of Bob's finger as it curled around the trigger. The pistol jerked once, then twice as it discharged, whereupon Bob threw down the gun and raised his hands as he turned to face the two officers, begging them not to shoot.

The concussion of the bullets smashed Alex against the seat, his elbows lifting, his arms flying out like ropes cut loose in the wind. Their impact exploded against his sternum, snapping his head forward, then back, his chin hitting his chest, then the back of the seat. A slow gasp was the only sound he made as he collapsed to the side just as the two officers rushed into the compartment, their guns trained on Bob.

"It was a mistake... a *mistake!*" Bob cried out as his hands were yanked behind him and cuffed by one of the officers. "I was startled... the two of you *startled me.*"

While Bob was led quickly down the corridor to a secure compartment, Gustav Hunziker ran into the compartment with a medic. "Give him oxygen while I take off his vest," Gustav told the medic in German.

While the mask was being placed over Talanov's mouth, Gustav tore open Talanov's shirt and unfastened the thin bullet-proof vest from around his chest. Two flattened wads of lead were embedded in the fabric.

Talanov began to slowly move.

"Lie still," urged the medic in English. "You are badly bruised, and may have suffered injury."

"Did... you get it... on tape?" whispered Alex, his eyes barely open.

"It came through with great clarity," Gustav replied with a nod. "The criminal activities of Mr Hoskings are finished."

Chapter
76

Maria and Joe drove Andrea to the hospital as fast as the rental car would take them, Joe repeatedly reassuring Andrea that Alex was safe. No bones had been broken although something he couldn't pronounce had been badly bruised. What Alex needed was plenty of rest.

Convincing Gustav Hunziker to set up the sting had not been easy, although the officer's own suspicions - coupled with an adamant phone call from his wife - had finally persuaded the policeman to cooperate. A cellular telephone connection with the IDC in Geneva had been organized, which was then linked to the micro-transmitter's amplified receiver and tape deck in a neighboring compartment on the train. It was Swiss efficiency at its best.

After Bob Hoskings - Georgi Vaskin - had been taken into custody, various law enforcement agencies in the Russian, Australian, and American governments were advised of his confessions and capture. All three said they would be pressing to have Hoskings extradited to face numerous charges, such requests to be considered as soon as his activities in Switzerland had been duly prosecuted. The unquestionable verdict: in some quarter of the world, Georgi Vaskin would be buried in prison.

The next morning was sunny and mild - unusual for late December on the Zugerberg - and Alex sat with Andrea on the balcony of the chalet watching Joe help Maria demolish the charred remnants of the barn. Even the ground floor's walls of concrete would be torn down as the intense heat had cracked and disintegrated much of it. The livestock would be housed by neighbors.

Although the air was crisp, the sun felt warm on Talanov's face as he leaned his head back against the small wooden shingles coating the southern wall of the chalet like scales. Above him, the broad eaves of the roof sloped down toward the branches of a cherry tree.

"So my brother is staying with Con?" Talanov asked his wife.

"He flew to Adelaide as soon as Mum called him from Perth. He arrived fully expecting to give a eulogy." Andrea looked at her husband and wrapped her arm through his. "He's a fine young man, Alex. You two should get reacquainted."

Talanov nodded with a chuckle. "I will now that he isn't having to speak at my funeral. Did he ever graduate from school?"

"Last year. He's now a doctor on the outskirts of London although he's considering a move to Australia. Like you, he loves the sun. Gail nearly fell out of her hospital bed when she met him. Apparently you told her you had a kid brother in school, so she had images of a gangly teenager, not the tall dark-haired younger version of you she now wants as her personal physician. I don't know Gail very well, but I suspect she's interested in a lot more than an occasional prescription."

Talanov laughed. "You're not wrong there. Gail's as rough as bags, but I couldn't have made it without her. Or Spiro, Con, Ivan, Liz, or Joe." He paused, then added sadly, "Or Wolfgang." With a sigh, Alex gazed away at the snow-covered Alps far off to the south, reflecting on Wolfgang and the others who had been killed. Several minutes passed. "I couldn't have made it without you, either," he finally said, his eyes still on the mountains. "And I nearly had to lose you before I discovered how much you mean to me." With a sad smile, he looked over at Andrea, his attention lingering on those details he'd so often ignored: her freckles... the tiny scar under her chin where a dog had once bitten her... her eyes and the way they whispered how happy she was.

Details. They were putty in the gaps of memory.

Andrea leaned over and kissed her husband, then snuggled in close. "What about the money?" she asked. "Do you think you can let it go?"

"We lost everything because of that money, so to have it vanish like that is a little difficult for me to accept. A lot of people could have used a slice of it, like Maria for a new barn. It makes me angry that even now there's still so much treachery going on to acquire it."

"It's only money," said Andrea. "Quite a lot, I grant you, but still only money. All one can do is spend it, and most of the time it buys only misery, at least when there's that much involved. I say let it go."

"To tell you the truth, I'm glad to be rid of it," replied Alex as he watched Joe signal Maria on the tractor. The tractor crept forward, several ropes growing taut as the skeletal remains of a blackened wall wobbled under the strain, then gave way and crashed to the earth. Alex looked back at his wife. "All I want to do now is rebuild our lives."

"Then let's start now," she said, snuggling up to him affectionately. "Joe and Maria will be busy until lunch."

"Start now? What do you mean?" asked Alex.

Andrea pulled back with a mischievous smile. "You're not this slow at everything, are you?"

Chapter 77

The shades of Hong Kong tonight were, as always, mirrored banners of vivid color in the waters of Victoria Harbor. High above the neon lights and chaotic noise, Wu Chee Ming entered his final instructions into the Internet computer of Spice Lines East, which in turn sent them to dozens of destinations around the world.

"Are you not finished yet?" asked Ling Soo, glancing at his watch as he entered his office on the twenty-fourth floor of one of the ubiquitous high-rise office buildings that is both a blight and a blessing to the island. He paused to view himself in a framed mirror on the paneled office wall, straightening his tie and carefully smoothing a lock of oily black hair into place. He then hurried over to his own walnut desk where Wu Chee Ming was working. "The women are waiting!" he said. "They will have eaten and gone if we do not hurry, finding other men for the night."

Wu Chee Ming adjusted his glasses and kept watching the monitor.

Annoyed, Ling Soo rushed into the next office and picked up the phone on his secretary's desk, impatiently punching the buttons and looking at his watch several more times before someone at the restaurant answered. Ling Soo identified himself and gave instructions that the four women waiting at his usual table were to be brought another round of drinks and a platter of hors d'oeuvres. "Tell them Ling Soo begs their indulgence and that he and his associate would be there shortly."

After hanging up, Ling Soo came back to the side of Wu Chee Ming, whose black eyebrows were now wrinkled in thought.

"What is it... is there a problem?" asked Ling Soo, noticing his expression. He positioned himself behind Wu Chee Ming's shoulder and looked at the monitor.

"More of a curiosity," the investment specialist replied without taking his gaze off the screen. "Talanov made a withdrawal of one hundred Swiss francs."

"I think we can afford that!" said Ling Soo with a laugh.

"But why such a ridiculous amount?"

"Because he did not have the confidence to withdraw the entire amount. Such cowardice has cost him a fortune." Ling Soo straightened, then noticed Wu Chee Ming's hands. "Are those surgical gloves you're wearing?"

"I must wear them all the time," replied Wu Chee Ming, again typing. "The pustules on my hands can infect door handles, faucets, computer keyboards-"

"Never mind! What of the transactions?"

"They are finally complete. You realize, of course, that the syndicate will not willingly accept the loss of seven hundred million dollars."

"Why do we not simply pay them?" asked Ling Soo. "We can manage well on eight hundred million and not have to live in constant fear."

Wu Chee Ming glanced over his shoulder at Ling Soo. "One does not walk away from the syndicate. One either cooperates or one is dead, and I was involved only for the short term, and certainly not by choice. Once my usefulness for profit was over, my life was to end." Wu Chee Ming smiled. "Therefore, I will be using their money to help me live quite comfortably in the land of the living."

"Have you covered our trail?"

"And the trail of the money."

"But how? One and a half billion dollars is not easily disguised," said Ling Soo.

"It is not as difficult as you think," Wu Chee Ming replied. "We are not transporting it in a tangible form like bullion or paper. The money exists, of course, but moves about only as numbers in an electronic dimension. It can be sent to any account in any country, and merely with the push of a button. That does not mean the actual dollars are shipped to those locations, but only an electronic notice."

"But such transactions still leave a record," Ling Soo pointed out.

"Except when that record is blinded. One does not seek what one does not see."

"You speak in riddles. The money exists and the syndicate knows it exists. Which is why we must run for our lives."

"Do you know the location of the money?" asked Wu Chee Ming.

"Of course not. You have been handling the transactions."

"Precisely. In other words, it could be in your bank account at this very moment, but if I disguised its presence, you would not know it was there."

"But officials in my bank would know."

"Again, not if I deleted the indications of its existence," answered Wu Chee Ming with a smile of confidence. "You may compare it to the creation of a blind file in your computer. It is there but you have made it invisible to the uninformed, to be accessed only by someone with the proper code. I repeat: one does not seek what one does not see."

"Are you certain no one can trace it? Our very lives are at stake."

"I am certain."

Ling Soo nodded approvingly. "Then you have done well."

Wu Chee Ming stood and bowed. "You are most kind," he said, then gesturing to the chair. "As I am finished, all that remains is for you to properly exit the system."

"With pleasure!" said Ling Soo, sitting in the chair and entering the proper commands.

The feeling of pain was but a light prick, and reacting as though he had been stung by an insect, Ling Soo smacked the spot on his neck just above the hairline. Indeed, the needle was so tiny it could pass for the bite of an insect.

But it was not.

Suddenly, a constricting spasm shot through Ling Soo's chest, causing his heart to begin pounding rapidly, then erratically as he gasped for breath. He grabbed his tie, attempting to rip it off, then turning toward Wu Chee Ming as he clutched at his chest, his eyes desperately pleading for help. Wu Chee Ming stepped back as Ling Soo fell to the floor, his face red, his mouth moving wordlessly as bubbles of saliva dribbled onto the carpet. Within a matter of seconds he was dead.

Wu Chee Ming left the body as it had fallen and walked toward the door. "No telltale fingerprints," he said with a smile. "That's why I wear gloves. You, an unfortunate heart attack victim, will be identified as the thief of the stolen millions because of the transactions traced to your computer. The confusing trail will crisscross the world, again and again leading nowhere yet everywhere." Wu Chee Ming chuckled and reached for the handle, pausing one last time to look at the body. "Everywhere except to the money!"

And Wu Chee Ming walked out of the door.